A Place

in

Time

A Place

in

Time

by

Carole Lehr Johnson

INK MAP PRESS

A Place in Time

© 2021 by Carole Lehr Johnson

Published in Pollock, Louisiana, by Ink Map Press
www.inkmappress.com

Cover Design by Victoria Davies (vikncharlie on Fiverr.com)
Interior Design by Morgan Tarpley Smith (morgantarpleysmith.com)
Map by Artist Monica Bruenjes (artistmonica.com)
Editor (historical accuracy) by Barbara Henderson at the History Quill
Cover Photos courtesy of Ingleby Manor

Scripture quotations are from the King James Version of the Bible.

ISBN 978-1-952928-10-9
ISBN 978-1-952928-11-6 (ebook)

Publisher's Cataloging-in-Publication Data

Names: Johnson, Carole Lehr, author.
Title: A place in time : a time travel novel / Carole Lehr Johnson.
Description: Pollock, LA: Ink Map Press, 2021. | Illus. ; 1 map, 33 b&w photos.|
    Summary: Can three women in a time not their own survive seventeenth-
    century England and fulfill the purpose God has for them?
Identifiers: LCCN 2021903486 | ISBN 9781952928109 (paperback) | ISBN
    9781952928116 (ebook)
Subjects: LCSH: Faith—Fiction. | Female friendship—Fiction. | Man-woman
    relationships—Fiction. | Time travel—Fiction. | Wiltshire (England)—17th
    century—Fiction. | BISAC: FICTION / Christian / Historical. | FICTION /
    Christian / Romance / Historical. | FICTION / Romance / Time Travel.
Classification: LCC PS3610 O36 P5 2021 | DDC 813 J64--dc22
LC record available at https://lccn.loc.gov/2021903486

Printed in the United States of America
2021—First Edition

10 9 8 7 6 5 4 3 2

To my mother, aunts, and grandmother,
who instilled in me a love of reading

For, lo, the winter is past, the rain is over and gone; the flowers appear on the earth; the time of the singing of birds is come.

Song of Solomon 2:11-12 (KJV)

Other Books by
Carole Lehr Johnson

Permelia Cottage

Their Scottish Destiny
(co-authored with Tammy Kirby)

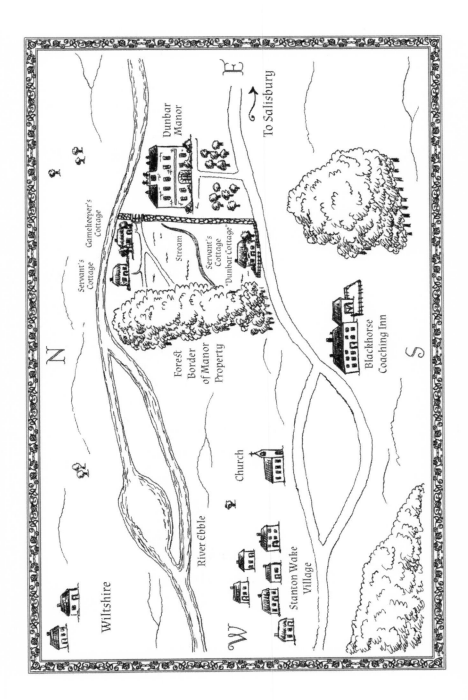

Chapter One

Stanton Wake, England
March 2021

Adela Jenks rummaged through a dusty crate, from time-to-time glancing across the room at her friends, Kellie Welles and Leanne Harcourt.

The pungent scent of incense nearly choked her, a thread of smoke drifting from the counter next to the cash register. Ever the optimist, she searched for what she hoped would be a memorable keepsake of this trip with her two closest friends.

The shopkeeper had told her the charity shop began as a meat market five hundred years before, developing into many businesses through the centuries, and was reborn in the late twentieth century as Charity's Charity Shop. Not a clever name, to be sure, but one you wouldn't forget along with its history.

Everything was so much older, more historic in England—one reason Adela had longed to come.

She heard robust laughter and looked up to see Leanne plowing through a rack of vintage garments.

Leanne met her eyes. "Kellie, what's Adela doing in the corner? She sounds like a humongous pack rat."

Kellie held a long flowing silk robe up against her tall, curvaceous figure. "I have no idea . . . how does this look on me?" She twirled and tilted her head from side to side. "Hmm?"

"The two of you do *know* this is not a large shop," Adela said matter-of-factly. "I can hear everything you say about me. But—" She paused to sneeze.

"All you're doing is stirring up dust and aggravating your allergies," Leanne quipped.

"I'm determined to—" Adela sneezed again. "—find a keepsake that won't take up half of my carry-on."

Another sneeze. The potent incense had to be the cause. With a moment of reprieve, she looked at Kellie. "That silk thingy is beautiful. Don't you think so, Leanne?"

Leanne turned to Kellie. "Yes, the emerald complements your blonde hair, and the size of the print suits your height. You should get it."

"Really? I do like it, and it will please Adela since it doesn't take up much room in my bag." Kellie grinned and flung the garment over her shoulder.

Adela stood, dusting off her hands, and approached them.

"I heard that." But she grinned and held up a small item in triumph. "I found the perfect keepsake."

Kellie and Leanne exchanged questioning looks, probably thinking of her penchant for *unusual* purchases.

"Don't give me *the* look," Adela admonished them. "It's something truly unique."

"What is it? A seventeenth-century fork for your cookbook project?" Leanne teased. "Whatcha gonna do? Pose with it for a picture?"

"Droll, very droll." Adela smirked at Leanne while Kellie chuckled.

Opening what appeared to be a small, thin antique book, Adela's lips curved into a smile as she took in the first page. "Oh, yes. This is exactly what I wanted."

A vintage passport.

CRSO

Seated in Lady Margaret's Tea House in the village of Stanton Wake, Adela chatted with Kellie and Leanne about their day over afternoon tea. Adela took out her new purchase and examined it. A ripple of brightly colored fabric slid over the page as Leanne flung her Celtic scarf around her neck. She glanced up. "What *are* you doing?"

Kellie answered, "Being ridiculous, as usual." She pulled the robe from her bag. "Not fair. I can't wear this around my neck."

Adela ignored their banter and jotted down a few notes in her journal of all they'd done since breakfast.

Leanne huffed. "I can't find my lip gloss." She plowed

through her purse, piling things on the table.

Kellie pointed to the passport. "Why don't we have a look-see? Find out whose past you're delving into."

Adela tugged the leather tab from a tiny slit. The passport was close in size to a contemporary one, but when she opened the cover, the paper was blank, yellowed, and musty.

She noted Kellie and Leanne's disappointed expressions and smiled. They thought she'd purchased something of no value.

Adela gradually unfolded the paper to reveal one sizeable piece folded into ten sections. Two revealed faded black and white photos—one of a man and the other of a woman and a small child.

Leanne squealed with delight, and Kellie grinned.

Adela fixed them with a mock glare. "You both always seem so surprised when I find something of worth."

By the time their second pot of tea arrived, they'd learned the passport belonged to a man from Southampton and his wife and young son. They discussed the places the family had traveled to, then their conversation moved to the upcoming festival.

"I don't know what to expect." Kellie's expression clouded. "I hope it won't be a letdown."

"No worries, Kellie," Leanne said. "We'll have a great time. Just dressing up in those costumes Adela made will get us in seventeenth-century mode. Remember how hard we laughed when we tried them on the first time? All those layers. I thought I'd ache for days at how funny you looked when you got your arms stuck in that chemise, wriggling like trying to escape a cocoon."

"The least you could've done was stop laughing and helped me out of it. Adela had to rescue me while you lay on the floor laughing your fool head off."

Leanne's face lit up. "It *was* fun." She grew thoughtful. "With all those layers, we might need a two-hour start on dressing."

Kellie munched on her scone and nodded.

Adela studied the passport absentmindedly. Her thoughts went to the costume patterns ordered a year before their trip, and the time taken to sew the period garments. She'd been meticulous about the right fabric, colors, and patterns related to the era.

Taking a sip of tea, she glanced at her friends over the rim of her cup.

"Let's finish our shopping before dinner, go back to the cottage and crash," Leanne offered. She stifled a yawn. "Jet lag's still got me."

Adela signaled the waitress to pay and asked her to bag up the remaining scones. She tucked the paper bag in her tote, and they stepped out into the uncommonly warm March afternoon.

She closed her eyes and inhaled the sweet fragrance of wildflowers and foliage. The fresh country scents invigorated her as they strolled the lane toward their cottage.

Her gaze fixed on a pasture full of sheep, little ones running back to their mothers for safety.

Adela froze.

Beyond the field, the perfect example of a seventeenth

century manor house stood at the end of a tree-lined gravel drive. Enough of the house was visible to glimpse its splendor.

Something about the house called to her, inexplicably. She longed to rush up the drive. Foolish, she knew, but the urge was there nonetheless.

"Adela," Leanne called out. "You'll become a sheep if you stand there any longer."

Adela shook her head, awakening from a trance, but the connection, the pull of the house, stayed with her.

☾☽

The tiny tourist office stood at the center of Stanton Wake in a building dating back over three hundred years. Beryl, the short white-haired woman answering their questions, was most knowledgeable about the area. Having lived in Stanton Wake all her life, there wasn't a thing she didn't know about the village. Many of her ancestors had been born in the area.

Leanne whispered, "Let's find out about the Adela Jenks Manor House, so we can get some lunch."

Kellie elbowed her.

Adela ignored them. She had told them about the house and what she experienced, but she didn't expect them to understand.

She didn't even understand.

But maybe learning more about the place would somehow jog her memory about the connection to the house, perhaps one of her ancestors had lived there.

Beryl told them Maximus DeGrey built Dunbar Park about 1600. His father had bequeathed him one thousand acres. "He had no siblings—at least there is no evidence he did. His son, Henry, inherited. After his death in London, his son, Marcus, took charge of the house and brought his young daughter to live at Stanton Wake. The manor has never been out of the family's ownership."

"Do you think there's a possibility for a tour?" Adela's stomach clenched.

"Not likely. They only do tours during the festival and are probably booked. The family is protective of their privacy."

Leanne jumped in. "How can we find out? We *really* would like a tour." She placed a hand on Adela's shoulder. "Adela is a gourmet chef and history enthusiast and would love a tour of the house and its kitchen as research for her cookbook. Would you be so kind as to help us?" She turned on her winsome personality, which had amassed an enormous social media following and a career as an influencer along the way.

Beryl tapped her chin. "Let me see what I can do." She picked up the phone and dialed.

Leanne whispered to Adela, "That's a good sign."

Beryl stepped out of earshot and spoke quietly into the phone. Nodding, she walked back to the counter where they waited.

Adela held her breath.

The woman's mouth stretched into a wide grin. "You, dear American ladies, have an appointment to tour Dunbar Park tomorrow afternoon."

Adela gently took the woman's hand. "Wonderful! I don't know how to thank you."

"My pleasure, dear, my pleasure. It's nice for someone to

take an interest in our local history. Everyone seems bent on tearing things down to put up something modern. Such a disgrace. I prefer visiting places that own morsels of history, not places where everything was built last week."

Adela laughed and bid her goodbye.

Walking along the cobblestone street, Adela marveled at their good fortune to tour the house, and she hoped it would reveal some of its secrets to her.

$$\mathscr{Chapter\ Two}$$

Replica garments lay scattered across their beds in the seventeenth-century thatched cottage at the edge of the village. Adela sorted through everything with Leanne while listening to Kellie read instructions about the order of the clothing.

Each of them would first put on a smock which took the place of the modern-day slip. Adela had made them out of soft white linen. Next, they pulled on the full skirt which hung to the tops of their shoes, fastened by tying attached strips of cloth together. Over this they put on a blouse also tied together much the same as the skirt. A stomacher buttoned to loops on the blouse, forming a stiff front piece and creating a V-shape which ended just below the waist.

Kellie's outfit was Azure blue with a scarlet stomacher. Leanne's was purple with gray, and Adela's the color of a robin's egg and a wheat-colored stomacher. More than a fair share of laughter accompanied their dressing.

"Leanne, you can't take your lip gloss to the seventeenth century," Kellie scolded as she slipped her iPad into her own bag and smirked.

Adela smiled and dropped her cell phone into hers.

What would someone from that era think if they saw modern technology? She guessed it would be like her stepping into the future hundreds of years from now.

Leanne positioned her phone on the mantel and set the timer. "Okay, girls, let's pose the way we practiced."

Adela arranged herself as Leanne instructed to mimic a painting she'd seen in the British Museum.

The phone's camera flashed, and afterward, they left the cottage.

Scattered clouds dotted the sky on their walk. A light breeze fanned Adela's face, anticipation mounting. At the edge of the village, she paused, her breath catching.

Stanton Wake had been transformed. Electric light was replaced with flickering candles in shop windows. Each store had traded their twenty-first century products for only wares of the era. Everyone was dressed in period costume, although a few tennis shoes peeked from beneath skirts.

Only one shop, in a more contemporary-style building, sold items of modern interest, where Adela purchased a slim book on the history of Stanton Wake featuring Dunbar Park.

They stopped by the bakery. Its aroma no different than a modern one. The window displayed a variety of bread, pies, and tarts.

Kellie glanced at her phone. "We need to go to the manor. It's almost time for our tour."

"The day has gone so fast," Adela said, looking up from her study of the spiced pastries. "Come on, girls. I don't want to be late."

"But Adela . . . there's time for a treat—surely?" Leanne begged.

Kellie steered Leanne away from the bakery's door. "Sugarholic, it's Adela's turn. We won't have her miss out because of your carb frenzy."

Adela laughed. "You are too much. I'm afraid to be late in case they turn us away."

Leanne exclaimed in a posh British accent, "We shall not be tardy, my lady." She looped her arm through Adela's and guided her along the path leading from the village, the scent of cinnamon wafting after them.

The sun warmed Adela's back, the breeze blowing her dress collar, as they approached the drive to Dunbar Park. A teenage boy stood at the entrance, dressed in period clothing.

"Good morrow to you mistresses." He bowed. "Please go forward, and ye shall be greeted."

Leanne dipped into a deep curtsy. "Thank you, kind sir."

The young man blushed from cheeks to neck.

Kellie pulled a face and pushed Leanne on ahead.

Adela guided them down the drive. "I can't wait to see this place. Isn't it magnificent?"

Kellie met her gaze. "If your eyes get any wider, we might need the E.R."

"Good luck finding one," Leanne quipped.

"I know I'm not one to show my emotions, but occasionally things take my breath away, and I can't help myself." Joy and anticipation coursed through Adela. "You'll just have to put up with me for now. It probably won't happened again for, oh, another ten years or so."

Leanne and Kellie laughed.

Adela smiled and faced the manor house rising before her. A graveled circular drive with a massive pool in its midst was situated in front of the three-storied structure.

The honey-hued stone sparkled in the afternoon sun as she marveled at the beautiful building. Its gables peered down at her as if friendly eyes bidding her welcome.

A young blonde woman greeted them at the front door. She confirmed their appointment, and they paid the entry fee.

The grand entrance hall spread before them, the floor paved in black and white marble tiles. A red-haired woman stepped up. She wore a pale lavender grown trimmed in white lace.

"Good afternoon. 'Tis a pleasure to meet ye. I am Penelope, your guide." She curtsied. "I am the lady of the house, and I bid ye welcome."

Adela greeted her in return as did Kellie and Leanne.

Her smile was warm. "Ladies, those are lovely gowns."

Kellie patted Adela's arm, blue eyes shining. "Our friend is a wonderful seamstress."

She smiled at Adela. "Ye are talented with the needle."

Adela's cheeks warmed. "Thank you."

12

Penelope launched into her spiel. "This bronze, six-arm chandelier is of seventeenth-century design, well patinated with the original finish and center turned supports. 'Tis a rare find."

She beckoned them to follow. "This entry was likely fashioned some time after the house's construction. You can see the heavily carved panels were added to create an entryway of sorts."

They crossed the spacious area and through wide double doors propped open by large iron doorstops in the image of lions layered with gold-leaf. The doors themselves were works of art, intricate designs of the outdoors—flowers, birds, and trees in fields with horses grazing languidly. A massive staircase, at the farthest corner of the room, curved its way to the upper floors, concave steps worn by time.

Penelope chattered on. "The house has original paneling and flagstone floors except for the entry, doors, ceiling beams, and the ornate oak staircase."

Every room brimmed with an amalgam of upholstery, drapes, cushions, and Persian rugs, but the walls were period with stained wood. Adela absorbed each detail, attempting to commit it all to memory.

The halls, rooms, the entire atmosphere captivated her like no historic house she had ever toured. She longed to slide her fingertips across the furniture, open a window, or sit on a settle.

They entered a large well-appointed bedchamber. The canopied bed stood in the center of the room draped with blue silk damask curtains. A pair of armchairs in front of the fireplace were upholstered in the same fabric. Flanking the hearth were two iron lions, a fire shovel and tongs, a fire screen, and a stool with a tapestry cushion.

"This is Lord DeGrey's chamber. He is away to London for some days, so we shall not disturb him."

Kellie let out a peal of laughter, and Adela sent her a silencing glare, but Penelope took it all in stride.

"If ye would like to join me in the seventeenth century, *my lady*, we may share a jest or two while ye visit with us." She grinned and curtsied in front of Kellie.

Kellie pursed her lips. "Well, *my lady*, I would be most appreciative if you would do us the honor of showing us what appearance Lord DeGrey does take as we have not had the pleasure of his acquaintance." She curtsied, her blue eyes twinkling with mischief. "And I would like to know when he shall emerge from the lake in his white linen shirt so I may be present."

Leanne snickered and tossed her auburn hair over her shoulder. "May I be present as well?"

Penelope's lips curved upward. "I shall see what I may do to appease ye." She turned to Adela. "Are ye to join them in their . . . observations?"

Adela grinned. "I certainly shall."

Kellie and Leanne erupted into laughter.

Penelope bit back a laugh. "Let us move on to the portrait gallery, if ye please." The second-floor gallery was much smaller than Adela had anticipated, stretching the length of the wall on the landing leading to the next floor.

Penelope must have noted her confusion. "On each floor, you will find portraits of the DeGrey family. This collection is the most recent and goes back a few generations. The next will contain the other DeGrey men. Sadly, only two paintings of the women in the family remain."

She discussed the portraits in front of them and moved on, pointing out each of the men.

"This is Marcus DeGrey, the grandson of the builder of Dunbar Park. He returned to his family home in 1665 to repair and reopen the manor. 'Tis most likely the reason we still have Dunbar Park to admire to this day." She stepped back to allow them room to view his portrait. "I do believe he is the most handsome of them all."

Adela studied the portrait, transfixed by his face, piercing light grey eyes, strong nose and jaw, wavy brown hair tied into a queue. The artist had captured the subtle golden-brown streaks threaded throughout.

Based on the height of the fireplace he stood beside with his forearm resting on the mantel, he cut an elegant figure.

"He was rather tall, wasn't he?"

"He was," Penelope confirmed. "A letter mentioned his horse being sixteen hands. Only a tall man could ride such a beast."

"I also see," Adela observed, "he's not wearing the foppish feminine-style attire that was customary of nobility at that time. The voluminous shirts with wide lace ruffles at the cuffs. Some of the ensembles were so absurd."

Marcus DeGrey wore buff-colored breeches, tall dark brown leather boots that hugged his calves, a deep blue vest, and an ivory shirt with full sleeves rolled to the elbows. He was definitely resisting the fashion of the day.

"Yeah," Kellie said. "The costume display at the V&A in London had some pretty outlandish clothes."

"Why was he so conservative?" Leanne asked. "Seems like his peers would have laughed at him."

"That is most likely the case, though it is understood Lord DeGrey was not one to enjoy life at court," Penelope said. "Several pieces of his correspondence express how he detested the preening and prancing within London society. This stance pushed him to spend the rest of his life here in his ancestral home. Are ye ready to move on?"

Adela continued to stare at Lord Marcus DeGrey. What a man of conviction and character. Beyond the seriousness in his expression, she thought his countenance was softened for the portrait yet still held keen intellect and observation. She willed herself to look away and follow the others from the room.

An hour later, she stood on the terrace at the back of the house viewing a long garden enclosed by a high stone wall. The scent of lavender and roses surrounded her. Her gaze eased across the well-kept gardens with longing. If only they had time to walk at leisure among them.

Penelope continued the tour. "The wall is constructed of Portland stone. It has such a lovely white surface, and when the moon is full, it lights the garden. 'Tis the same stone as the Tower of London and St. Paul's Cathedral."

She pointed to the back corners of the garden. "There you will see two squares with low walls to encompass the orchard and a maze."

"An orchard?" Leanne asked.

"Aye. 'Tis but a slight one for the kitchen. There are more extensive ones beyond the walled garden."

Kellie perked up. "A *maze*."

"'Tis merely a curiosity of the era and an entertainment." She added, "Outside the garden walls lie the stable and outer gardens."

She pointed to the left of the terrace toward the kitchen. "There is a small kitchen garden where vegetables are raised for the household staff and family. And on the other end," she pointed right, "there is an herb garden."

Leanne leaned toward Adela. "You'd be in heaven there."

Penelope faced them. "Are ye a lover of herbs?"

Kellie answered, "She is."

"Wonderful." Penelope met Adela's eyes. "Our final stop may be of great interest to ye. The kitchen."

As they stepped into the massive kitchen, Penelope continued her narration. "'Tis remarkably restored but has modern appliances camouflaged as much as possible. Of course, some contemporary conveniences are noticeable, but for a working manor house, it must be so."

Penelope allowed Adela to step into the kitchen first. She was overawed at the cavernous space. A long, massive table split the room.

The dark wood top of the work surface had shallow dips and nicks from centuries of use. She took in each aspect that made up the essence of the manor—the yawning fireplace with iron cauldrons, a bread oven tucked into one end, and the numerous shelves lining the walls. Adela imagined the activity taking place. She pictured herself kneading bread on the magnificent table, and a pot of stew suspended from an iron hook at the edge of the fireplace opening, fragrant steam lifting into the air.

When they had completed their perusal of the kitchen, Adela glanced one last time at the welcoming space. They followed Penelope back to the entrance of the manor.

"This is where the tour ends," Penelope said. "Thank ye for viewing our home. It has been a pleasure." She left them with a curtsy and a friendly goodbye.

Adela stepped into the modest gift shop and flipped through a book about the manor, stopping at a full-page portrait of Marcus DeGrey standing in his simple attire. One hand perched on the mantel, the other tucked behind his back, wearing the intense expression that stole her breath.

CBSO

Back in the village, Adela walked the cobbled street in front of the shop selling women's clothing and hats. The vibration of a cell phone against the contents in someone's purse split the silence.

Leanne touched her bag. "It's not mine."

"It's mine." Kellie fished it out and answered, "Hello . . . oh, fine, Sarah. We're having a wonderful time. You should—" She stopped in the middle of the street and peered into the distance. "I . . . well, I believe you. You're sure it was him? I know. I know. No, I'm glad you called. Thank you."

Kellie stabbed the button to end the call, dropped her phone into her bag, and turned briskly, retracing their path.

Adela and Leanne hurried after her. When they caught up, her face was pale, lips pulled in a taut line.

"What's wrong?" Adela asked.

"Kellie, you don't look so good," Leanne said. "What did Sarah say? Did someone die?"

Kellie massaged her temple. "Yes, you could say that. The death of a relationship." She sighed. "I'll explain later, but first I must make a call. Come back in about an hour. I'll be ripe for crying." She strode up the lane toward their cottage, wiping her eyes.

Leanne and Adela settled in at a nearby tea shop by the window in case Kellie returned.

Adela pulled in a deep breath. "We'll enjoy a cup of tea, give her time to mull over whatever news she received, and in an hour, we'll march back to the cottage to find out what's going on."

Leanne stared at her cup, then glanced up and whispered, "I've never seen her like this. I thought she and Tim were doing fine."

Adela fought back fearful thoughts. "Yes, I know." She noted the sky darkening. She and Leanne would need to leave now to beat the shower. They gathered their purchases and made the short walk to Dunbar Cottage.

When they entered, Kellie sat at the small dining table, cell phone in front of her, along with her purse and purchases. Her cheeks were tear stained.

Adela placed her bag on the table and put the kettle on to boil. Leanne opened a tin of biscuits and put them in front of Kellie.

In no time, Adela poured a cup of tea and placed it in front of Kellie, who sniffed and spoke in a strained voice, "Sarah saw Tim at Sadie's Bistro last night with the woman he dated before me." Her cup shook as she brought it to her lips.

Leanne placated her. "Kellie, that doesn't mean anything was going on."

Kellie's expression hardened. "Oh yes, it does."

Leanne's irritation spilled out. "You've dragged this out long enough. What did Sarah say?"

Adela sensed an argument coming. When backed against a wall, Kellie usually retaliated, but this time she remained calm. She stared at Leanne. "Sarah said they were more than friendly. It was no casual dinner catching up on old times. She saw them kiss."

Leanne's face fell. "I'm sorry."

Kellie choked on a new wave of tears. "I called him. He didn't deny it. In fact, he didn't sound all that sorry. I don't believe this is happening. Now, I know why we've had such a long engagement, and why he always came up with an excuse to delay our wedding."

Adela rested a hand on Kellie's shoulder. Leanne touched the other. The silence and sorrow enveloped them.

A clap of thunder jolted the stillness and shook them in their seats, snapping Adela back to attention. She opened her purse, seeking a distraction, and rummaged through the contents, removing the vintage passport and unfolded the delicate paper. Handling it with care she placed it in the center of the table. "Let's look at this again, shall we?"

Kellie met her gaze, gratitude in her eyes. She bent over it, fingertips against the fragile paper, as they pointed to areas of interest.

Thunder boomed again, followed by a crash, as if lightning had hit something nearby. They shifted in their seats and looked at one another as a tremendous flash brightened the sky. A strange bluish glow surrounded them for a moment, then turned into a mist which quickly evaporated.

The room fell into darkness.

Leanne asked, "Didn't we see flashlights in the pantry?"

"Yes," Adela confirmed. She rose and began to feel her way through the dark room. Her hands came in contact with the wall. By touch, she followed it, searching for the pantry. Instead, her knee connected with a cabinet, and she cried out in pain.

"Adela, are you all right?" Kellie asked through the dark.

"I think so." One hand on the cabinet to steady herself, Adela rubbed her knee. Another dazzling flash of lightning brought the room into full focus. The cabinet Adela touched came into view. It was not one she'd seen before.

This time, the room remained well lit, bright sunlight shining through the uncovered windows. There was no sign of a storm nor rain.

Adela froze, the hair along her arms standing on end, as she stared out the window. A bird sang cheerily in a tree, branches brushing against the pane.

A tree that certainly had *not* been there a few moments ago.

CAROLE LEHR JOHNSON

Chapter Three

Birdsong trilled on as dust motes floated on beams of light streaming into the cottage. Adela grabbed for the countertop that was no longer there and grasped air. She took in the now sparsely furnished room.

Chairs, tables, and stools were arranged as if in a museum display or living history demonstration.

Kellie was the first to speak. "Okay, I know I'm stressed, but are we having a joint hallucination?"

Adela went to the window and looked out toward the village. Her stomach turned, and her skin prickled. "Um, girls, you need to see this."

Kellie and Leanne joined her. The village was quite altered from the one they had strolled through not an hour before—no paved road or utility poles with electrical wires and fewer buildings.

"I don't understand," Kellie whispered.

Leanne cleared her throat and turned from the window. "Well, I say we are dreaming . . . well, at least one of us is."

Kellie scoffed. "But we were sitting there, Leanne. None of us were asleep."

Adela twisted toward the table where Kellie pointed. Everything on the table lay just as it had been a few moments ago. All of their personal items and purchases there. Even the teacups, teapot, and accompaniments were present.

Yet, everything else in the cottage was different.

All modern conveniences from electrical appliances to running water were gone. And the temperature had dropped. Adela returned to her seat followed by Kellie and Leanne. They stared at each other.

After the long silence, Leanne cleared her throat. "We should go out and walk around. Maybe, *somehow,* this is an elaborate joke, or we've really gone off our rockers."

She raised her eyebrows. "After all, we are here to immerse ourselves in the seventeenth century, but this is, um, taking it a bit too far, don't you think? I mean, for goodness' sake, we've been reading, discussing, and nearly living seventeenth-century England for months. And then Kellie has this tragic thing happen that has affected us all. We are so stressed and tired maybe we really are asleep and brought it all into our subconscious."

"Are you talking to yourself, or do you really believe that drivel?" Kellie snapped, her voice laced with sarcasm.

"Kellie, I know this is hard on you—with Tim and all," Adela said. "But there's no need to be rude to Leanne."

From Kellie's expression, Adela expected a sharp rebuttal, but then a slow, repetitive squeaking sound from outside grew closer. She rushed to the window.

"What is it?" The quavering edge to Leanne's voice defied her usually confident nature.

Adela observed a lone figure on the road. "It's an old man in a horse-drawn cart. Looks like he's hauling vegetables."

Leanne came up beside her. The man noticed them and tipped his hat. A bump in the road jostled the cart, unsettling his cargo, releasing a bag to the road.

Once he was out of sight, Leanne bolted out the door and scooped the sack into her arms. She ran back into the cottage, slammed the door behind her, and tightly hugged the sack to her chest.

Kellie's eyes widened. "What are you doing?"

Leanne dumped her treasure onto the table—a cabbage, three onions, and a smaller sack. She hugged the cabbage like a lifeline. Her eyes narrowed. "I figured we'd need food since we're uncertain how long we'll be here. Wherever *here* is."

"I think it's *when* . . ." Adela said with a heavy sigh and sank into a chair, confusion enveloping her.

"Oh, come on. Listen to you two," Kellie said. "You're both absurd."

Adela said, "Okay, let's stay calm."

Leanne held up the cabbage. "Let's cook these vegetables. I'm hungry."

"You would be, Miss Bottomless Pit." Kellie pulled a face and rolled an onion toward Leanne. "Even if it's something as disgusting as cabbage and onions."

They looked at Adela—their resident chef. She smiled, stood, and looked around. "I suppose we should take inventory of any other supplies." She propped her hands on her hips. "I forgot. Our leftover scones are in my purse." She retrieved them and paused. "Maybe we should save them for breakfast."

Leanne reached for one. "No. Let's eat them now. It could take a little while to cook the vegetables." Her dark blue eyes implored Adela. "Please?"

Adela tilted her head. "Oh, all right."

Leanne reached for a scone. "Wish I had a cup of coffee."

"You two enjoy the scones while I poke around a bit." She rummaged through a cupboard and then noticed a stack of wood piled next to the stone fireplace. Inside the cavernous opening hung an iron contraption that contained a hook holding a dangling, dusty iron pot—not unlike in Dunbar Park's kitchen.

Tucked to one side was a half-moon shaped gap about waist high. Upon closer inspection, she realized it was a bread oven. A small cast-iron stove stood next to the fireplace.

"Well, if we can locate water, I might be able to make soup. Unless we're able to find herbs, it'll be a bland meal."

Leanne searched another cupboard. "There are several bottles with stuff in them."

Adela removed the corks of a few bottles and sniffed. "This is rosemary." She took a deep sniff of another that made her cough. Holding the bottle at arm's length, she said, "Whew, I don't know what this is, but I don't think I'll chance using it."

Kellie opened one. "This smells like licorice."

Adela leaned closer and inhaled. "Must be anise. It's used for baking."

After checking a few more, three were revealed to be dried herbs that could be used in their soup.

Adela picked up an empty wooden bucket by the fireplace and started for the door. "I'll go search for water, but I wouldn't mind company. I admit it. I'm afraid of what I may find."

Leanne opened the door. "You're right. It's best to stick together."

Outside, birds twittered, cows mooed in the distance, and the wind rustled through the surrounding trees, lending a sense of calm to Adela's questioning mind.

The village lay below the hill, far enough so they couldn't hear the people going about their daily lives. Smoke drifted from several chimneys. Horses pulled carts or wagons down the main street. Livestock grazed in lush pastures.

Adela absorbed the scene, not sure what to think except the more she saw, the more it proved her theory. She shivered but shook it off and continued her task. She lugged the heavy bucket, uncertain how she would carry it when full. The rope handle already bit into her palms.

Beyond the cottage on a sloping hill lay a large garden in the early stages of fresh blooms by another cottage. A grey stone wall obstructed the view below the grounds. Single file, they walked around the garden to the wall.

"Wonder what's past this?" Leanne looked for an entrance. Seeing none, she climbed a pile of stones heaped against the wall.

"Leanne, please be careful." Adela dropped the bucket and positioned herself at the base of Leanne's makeshift steps.

"If she wants to be reckless, let her go," Kellie said in a flat tone. "You know she's not going to listen."

Adela knew the tone. Kellie had reached her limit of tolerance.

Leanne stood at the top of the wall and gave them a bow of accomplishment, then turned and released a whistle. "You should see this, Adela."

"I don't think so. With my luck, I'll end up headfirst over the wall."

"Oh, come on. Don't be such a wimp."

Adela freed a deep, uncertain sigh and eased her way up the rock pile a couple of feet, stretched her arm upward, and wiggled her fingers. "Help me up." She bunched her skirt with her other hand as Leanne pulled her to the top.

Leanne leaned against the wall and peered over. Adela did the same and froze. Recognition halted her breath.

Leanne turned to her. "What's wrong?"

Adela grasped the top of the wall as her head swam. Her voice was a whisper. "Don't you recognize it?" She met Leanne's questioning stare. "It's Dunbar Park."

Leanne gawked at it. "That is *not* the manor house we toured."

"Yes, the west wing, I think. But it's . . . well . . ." Adela didn't want to voice her thoughts. It was too preposterous. She swallowed. "It's newer."

From below, Kellie exclaimed, "What?"

28

Leanne gasped, and an unnerving silence settled over them along with the lingering question. *What time were they in?*

Adela stared at the manor. "The guide said some ancestors had done improvements through the centuries. Without those additions, this must have been what it was like when it was first built—" She cleared her throat. The words were hard to digest. Her voice came out tense. "—in the seventeenth century."

Leanne's eyes widened. "So, you're saying we're in England four hundred years in the past?"

Adela looked at Kellie, who had slumped at the base of the rock pile, before meeting Leanne's eyes. She spoke with more certainty than she felt. "It would seem so."

Leanne glanced at the manor house, then slowly descended the rocks. She took Adela's hand and helped her down.

Kellie looked up at them with a horrified expression. "You've got to be kidding? Are you nuts? This—" She gestured to their surroundings. "—is the seventeenth century? This isn't a dream. It's an impossible nightmare."

"Don't believe us." Annoyance altered Leanne's voice. She pointed to the top of the wall. "Go. See for yourself."

Something within Adela snapped. The weariness, the uncertainty, all the emotions raging in her came full force. At times, their bickering wore on her, and as the oldest, she always felt pressured to intervene. Her voice rang with irritation.

"I don't want to talk about this any longer. Let's find water, figure out how to start a fire, and make this soup. Okay?" She snatched the bucket, ignoring the rope burning her palm, and glared at them. "And it's not newly built. It's over sixty years old." She stomped away, her chest tightening.

⊂ℑℰↄ

Wind swept Marcus DeGrey's hair behind him as his horse sped through tall grass growing alongside the graceful river. The smell of early spring rose to meet him. As he slowed his approach to the ancient tree atop the hill, Marcus's gaze roamed his favorite spot to meditate.

The place held many memories for him. He'd grown up laying under the gigantic oak—playing as a child, reading as a young man—escaping many turbulent events. The aura of the tree perched on the hill that overlooked his world exuded something he could not explain. He slid from Roman, his massive chestnut, and dropped the reins to let him graze. One whistle and he'd return to his master.

Marcus drew in deeply of fragrant air and eased onto the soft grass, leaning against the tree as he'd done countless times before. His gaze turned skyward beyond the budding limbs.

Boyhood memories surged through him, the fresh earthy breeze invigorating his thoughts. Climbing the tree as a boy, it morphed into an imaginary stronghold to watch for the enemy's approach. The moments of nostalgia eased the ache in his heart.

Nearby chatter met his ears. He pushed himself up and spotted the old cottage. Three women were stooped over the stream, struggling to hoist a bucket up from the coursing flow of water. None of them looked to be of an age they should labor with a lone bucket.

Though spring was near, the air still held a chill, yet they were not clothed with enough warmth. Marcus watched as they worked together until a conversation appeared to be taking place, halting their attempt. One held the bucket in place while the other two grabbed the handle and pulled. The third woman stepped aside as they tugged it out of the water, sloshing their skirts. One squealed in amusement which caught upon the wind and wafted toward him. The sound was musical. The women placed the vessel on a level spot of ground and dropped to the grass, falling backward in laughter.

Roman snorted and dragged Marcus from his watch. "All right, old boy. Let us take a canter to the water." Without effort, he mounted the horse, and they made their way forward. He would steer to a spot far enough from the women, yet close enough to see them better. As they descended the hill, their voices reached him, their accents foreign, but he was unable to place it.

One of them pointed in his direction. "Hey, Adela, look! It's a Mr. Darcy guy."

So much for not being seen, thought Marcus. And who was this Darcy they spoke of? The women were certainly not from this area, or they would likely have recognized him and therefore not mistaken him for another man.

Marcus shook his head and guided Roman farther along the stream and allowed him to drink his fill, then permitted him to return to his desired speed. The manor came onto view. *His manor.*

The truth still struck him, of how life's circumstances brought him home—now as lord of the manor—in charge of all that remained of his family's holdings including the village. Marcus was not suited to life in London. He abhorred the balls and parties, the manners and fashions of court, the pressure to find a bride and produce heirs. It was all too much until he met Gillian.

Her beauty had captured him. The lust he had felt for her lulled him into thinking he must act in haste and on what he thought was, in fact, love. The marriage was quick at both family's urging. Now, here he stood alone.

Marcus returned to his estate as a country squire, a role he was uncertain he could uphold, yet try he would. For the first time in years, he could breathe again, come to terms with what had befallen him, and plan for the future. *For Nan.*

Chapter Four

Adela strolled toward the stream. Bird chatter in a nearby cluster of trees switched to irritated twittering at the human disturbance. A grassy scent permeated the air, like freshly mown hay.

Adela's shoulders rose and fell on a deep sigh. She couldn't quite grasp what they had seen over the wall. "It's so strange to see it new."

"What difference does it make?" Leanne's tone belied the seriousness of their predicament. "It's still an old manor house."

Kellie shot her a glare. "As much as you know how I hate to agree with you, Leanne. You're right."

Leanne moved closer to Kellie, pinched her arm, and jetted away.

"Ouch! I *will* get you back." Kellie dashed after her. They darted back and forth locked in a childish game that warmed Adela's heart. They disappeared over the rise of a small hill.

When Adela topped it, she saw them lying in a field of wildflowers, giggling. They were forever like siblings who argued yet cared for one another.

A deep wrench twisted in Adela's heart. Her misguided choices had steered her away from finding a husband and having children. How she regretted it. Although, no man had ever moved her toward love.

Believing God had intended her to be single for life, she'd given up keeping an open heart whenever another man paid her attention. Any relationships she had entertained over the years had all ended in disappointment whether due to the man's lack of direction in life, or God, or other reasons for which she wouldn't compromise her beliefs.

Why God had chosen not to place a man in her path she felt drawn to—a godly man—was beyond her comprehension. She shook off the sad musings and focused on *her* girls.

If Adela had to be thrust back in time over three hundred years, she couldn't think of anyone else she'd rather be with. The two young women were like daughters to her, and at the same time, her closest friends. She thanked God for bringing them into her life.

Adela stood over them. Grinning, she mimicked a British accent, "All right. Get a move on, you lot."

A horse's whinny drew her attention. About a hundred feet away a magnificent dark chestnut drank from the stream. Its rider watched them closely. He was too far away to get a clear view, but his substantial height was obvious.

Leanne pointed in his direction. "Hey, Adela, look! It's a Mr. Darcy guy."

"Oh, I hope so," Adela promptly responded as the man cantered away.

Adela caught Leanne and Kellie exchange looks and sent them a smug smile.

Kellie blurted, "I bet you're picturing the lake scene from that movie, aren't you?" She and Leanne burst out laughing.

"It wouldn't hurt my feelings," Adela said in jest with a sultry voice. "Guess we'd better get this water back. It'll take forever to boil." She halted and almost lost her balance. "How are we going to start a fire?"

They stared at one another.

"Well, I *may* be able to, but it's been a long time since my scouting days." Leanne's voice lacked its usual confidence. She shrugged. "Come on. We'll figure something out. Don't we always?"

"Yeah, that's what scares me," Kellie quipped.

Leanne and Adela each grabbed a side of the bucket handle, carrying it between them. Kellie stepped in to take a turn as they went, relieving one or the other. The walk back to the cottage was slower, not wanting to spill their precious cargo. Once inside, they collaborated on making the fire.

Kellie looked at Adela. "You should know how to start a fire. You use it every day."

Adela smirked. "Yeah, since I cook over a firepit and not in an industrial kitchen. I'm trying to remember, but I think they used a flint."

"That's it!" Leanne exclaimed. "We need a piece of metal,

then something flammable. Maybe a piece of cloth or dry grass."

They searched for the needed materials, beginning with the area around the fireplace.

Kellie called over her shoulder, "I'll see if I can find some dried grass or leaves." She shot out the door.

"Hey, why can't we use one of these utensils?" Adela held up a long pair of tongs and a ladle, both made of iron. "We could use either of these to bang against a rock to start a spark."

Leanne looked at Adela. "Yeah, but we need a rock to make a spark, don't we?"

Kellie strode in and extended her cupped hands full of dried grass. "I found this outside. Surely it's dry enough to burn." She dropped to her knees in front of the fireplace.

"Wonderful job." Leanne smiled her approval. "I'll see if I can find a rock."

"What's the rock for?" Kellie placed the grass in the fireplace and dusted off her hands. "I sure hope we can get this going. We'll be cold *and* hungry if we don't."

Leanne jutted out her chin. "We need a rock to make a spark with one of these iron tools, silly."

Kellie glanced at Adela, then sent Leanne an exasperated sigh. "You're the silly one—and Adela too, in this case. You can make a spark by banging those iron tools together."

Adela sat back on her heels, the iron tongs resting on her bent legs. She quietly sniffed, a tear trickling down her cheek.

Kellie patted her shoulder. "Oh, I'm sorry. I didn't mean it. You're not silly."

Leanne stooped and put an arm around Adela.

Adela brushed the tear away and held Kellie's gaze. "You didn't hurt my feelings." Her voice was shaky. She looked into the fireplace. "It'll be dark soon, and we don't know if we'll be able to get this fire going. We must have warmth and food."

Adela rose. "I suppose we should explore the cottage and see if we can find blankets while there is still daylight." She rested a hand on the mantel, her fingers brushing something. She picked up a small metal box and removed the lid.

Inside was a piece of curved metal, a rock, and a dark oily piece of fabric. Her eyes grew wide with a sudden revelation. "A tinder box! This is it—how they started fires. It's difficult, but between the three of us, maybe we can get one going."

Kellie and Leanne huddled near her by the empty fireplace. Adela took the first turn at scraping the metal against the flint until her hands ached and passed it on to Leanne, who soon passed it to Kellie. After half an hour, their exasperation mounted.

"Are we doing it fast enough?" Leanne tried again and gave the flint several vigorous hits until she grew angry in desperation and began banging it harder and harder, stopping with exhaustion. Her eyes glistened. "What are we going to do? I can't take this any longer."

Adela was frustrated, tired, dirty, and hungry. They all were.

Kellie stood, placed her hands on her hips, and peered down at Adela and Leanne. "You two are pathetic. This is some stupid, silly dream, and it doesn't matter whether or not we start a fire. Forget the fire." She stomped off to the table and plopped into a chair.

Adela's teary gaze met Leanne's, and they exchanged weak smiles. When Adela made a move to rise, the sound of Leanne's audible gasp stopped her.

A slight puff of smoke rose from the kindling in the fireplace.

CB80

Kellie leaned back in her chair. "Not too bad. Not as flavorful as your usual, but it definitely hit the spot. You did a marvelous job considering what you had to work with."

"The only thing that would've made it better is homemade bread." Leanne sighed with longing as she reached for their wooden bowls. "Too bad we don't have any." She shrugged and asked Adela, "How do we clean wooden dishes?"

"They cleaned them with sand if my memory serves. I'd rather scrub them using water and let them dry by the fireplace. Not sure how that'll work, but I'm not searching for sand in the dark. Hot water must suffice."

They took care of the bowls, searched for bedding, and found it upstairs inside a huge wooden chest.

After surveying the room, Adela said, "I think we should drag those mattresses down by the fire."

Leanne and Kellie struggled with moving the straw-filled mattresses down the narrow stairs. Each time they stumbled, they fell into fits of laughter. Adela shook her head at their antics. In preparation for bed, she stripped down to her shift. Leanne and Kellie did the same, and they all settled onto their beds.

"Good night, girls. I'll probably wake up a lot during the night and will be sure to keep the fire going. We certainly don't want to light a new one." Adela sighed deeply, remembering the annoyance of their failed attempts.

Leanne yawned. "Good night, Adela. If I wake up, I'll check on it too."

"Me too," Kellie added. "I can sleep through a hurricane though, so don't count on me."

A long time passed before exhaustion took over, and Adela drifted off to sleep. Every unfamiliar sound and smell drove home her theory about their passage through time, though her rational mind forced her to cling to hope that come morning it would all have been a dream.

CR୫ର

Marcus DeGrey rode toward the exit of his estate grounds, ruminating once again on the future. As he passed the massive stone pillars framing the drive's entrance, his mind strayed to Stanton Yorke. His steward was away up north purchasing horses. He hoped the trip proved successful as it could be a valuable investment to breed and sell them and could alleviate Dunbar Park's financial state.

Dunbar Cottage came into view, and he remembered it with fondness. The former cook, Mrs. Drummond, had lived there with her husband and family when he and Stanton were boys. The current cook, Mrs. Henshaw, had been her apprentice. Mrs. Henshaw had spoiled him terribly, to his parents' dismay, always baking his favorite sweets and slipping them to him as he passed through the kitchen to the outdoors and a day of discovery with his friends. Fond memories they were.

Roman whinnied, breaking his musings. He looked at the old cottage, smoke drifting from the stone chimney. He spurred the horse forward. As Roman came to a halt, he jumped to the ground with an angry thump and tied Roman to the fence surrounding the cottage.

"I would wager trespassers have settled onto Dunbar's grounds!"

He approached the cottage with quick, long strides and flung the door open.

A woman lurched from a mattress on the floor near the fireplace, her face contorted with fear. Her eyes darted frantically around the room, and she grabbed the closest thing at hand—an iron ladle, waving it in front of her like a saber. Two younger women ran to her side, each wielding similar objects.

He scowled. "Who are ye? What is your business at this cottage?"

No one answered.

"Well?" He roared.

The women started at the sound. The tallest one stepped forward in front of the eldest. "We are letting this cottage." Her chin trembled, yet she held her ground.

He looked them over, seeing they were clad in only their chemises. The woman in the middle shivered, arms clasped across her chest.

Embarrassed, he averted his eyes.

It took but a moment for realization to dawn. "Ah, ye must be the new servants? I was not yet informed Stanton had secured anyone. He is away for at least another fortnight." He glanced around the room. "Ye have no provisions? Most unusual for Stanton to not prepare. I shall send for wood, food, and other supplies at once. Please accept my apology for the intrusion and lack of readiness for your arrival."

Marcus bowed and strode to the door.

Hesitating a moment, he glanced a final time at the eldest woman, meeting her eyes. He would share words with his steward upon his return.

Such carelessness for any member of his staff was not to be borne. He was *not* his father.

CR✿SO

Leanne rushed to the door and slid the bolt into place with a screech. "I can't believe we didn't lock the door last night!"

She shared a look with Kellie, who shrugged.

Leanne pointed to the fireplace. "Hey, we still have a small fire. I'm amazed it lasted all night."

Adela whispered, "I woke early, added wood, and went back to bed." Her chest rose as she took in a deep breath and added, "Until *he* stormed in."

"Yeah, whoever he is," Kellie muttered. "He didn't even introduce himself. Isn't that part of the rules of this time?"

Adela said nothing, her gaze returning to the door, a shiver of recognition moving over her.

"Are you all right?" Leanne asked at her side.

"I can't believe it's *him*." Adela ignored her and swallowed the lump in her throat. "I can still smell his cologne."

"Him who?" Kellie asked, moving to Adela's opposite side.

The man in the portrait. She was sure of it.

"That was Lord Marcus DeGrey."

Chapter Five

Kellie crossed her arms. "Who is that? The fantasy man from your dreams?"

Leanne's mouth gaped. "Oh, Kellie, don't be silly. Weren't you paying attention when we toured the manor?"

"The guide only mentioned about a dozen Lord something or others. Why is that name supposed to mean something to me?"

Adela faced Kellie. "Don't you remember? The tour guide told us that Marcus DeGrey's grandfather built the manor."

Adela exchanged glances with Leanne, then grabbed her purse from the table and pulled the guidebook from it. She thumbed through the pages until she came to the details of Dunbar Park.

"Look at this." She pushed the book toward Kellie and pointed at the page which gave a brief history of Dunbar Park and contained photographs of the paintings of Lord Marcus DeGrey, his father, and his grandfather.

Kellie's eyes grew wide in recognition.

Leanne raised her brows. "He's even hunkier in real life than in his portrait."

Kellie nodded. "Yes, a *real* Mr. Darcy, I'd say."

"Yes, I agree." Adela smiled.

Leanne met Adela's gaze. "And he was rather kind noticing we needed supplies and . . ." She frantically looked around. "We'd better get dressed, put these mattresses back upstairs, and tidy up. He said he was sending someone with food and stuff. We don't want to be caught in our undies by another unsuspecting man."

Adela and Kellie laughed, and scrambled to help each other dress, return the mattresses, and build up the fire. No sooner had they gotten things into shape when a knock sounded.

Adela answered the door. "Good morning."

Two young men wearing rough work clothes held burlap sacks and a wooden box. The shorter man with ruddy cheeks addressed her. "Lord DeGrey bid us bring ye supplies. They be sore heavy. Could we put 'em down now, mistress?"

She nodded, and they dropped their loads. "Lord DeGrey says we must fetch more wood."

The taller, dark-haired of the two tipped his hat and added, "I be Martin, and this here be Timothy."

"Thank you." Adela instinctively offered a little bow in greeting. "I am Adela, and this is Kellie and Leanne. We appreciate your help."

"No trouble, mistress. Good morrow to ye."

As soon as the door closed behind the young men, Adela plowed through the contents of one bag—sugar, spices, and dried herbs. The box contained cooking pots, utensils, chargers, porringers, trenchers, and tankards. Some were made of pewter, some of iron. Another bag held raisins, dried and smoked meats, onions, and a paper package of seeds.

Leanne opened the second bag and screamed. She dropped its contents and backed away. "What is that?"

Adela's gaze dropped to a small lump of moist, brown flesh. "From the looks of it, that would be a rabbit. A fresh one."

Leanne turned away in disgust. "How medieval!"

Kellie's eyes were averted, but her voice was sarcastic. "Well, you're not too far off, only by a few hundred years."

Leanne gagged. "Ugh, just plain gross!"

Adela snorted. "Don't you buy raw meat at the grocery store? It'll make a tasty stew with the vegetables and the other stuff from Marcus—" She cleared her throat. "—Lord DeGrey."

Kellie squinted. "All I can say is I'm glad that's your department." She spun around as Martin and Timothy entered with loads of wood.

"We will be bringin' in more." They hurried out, glancing shyly at Leanne.

"Leanne, you have admirers, Martin in particular," Kellie stated with a smirk. "Since he's missing so many teeth, you won't have to worry about what a poor cook you are."

Leanne slapped Kellie's arm, which prompted her to grab the rabbit and began chasing Leanne around the room dangling it in the air. Leanne screeched.

45

Martin and Timothy entered with their second load of wood and froze in the doorway, witnessing the scene with wide eyes and mouths ajar.

Adela smiled. "Boys, don't pay any attention to them."

Timothy asked, "Is she 'afeared of a rabbit?"

Adela laughed. "I'm afraid so."

The young men entered the room and stood beside Adela. Martin added, "And it not be live either!"

Leanne glared at Martin. He quickly backed out the door with Timothy following.

Adela looked at them with hands on her hips. "Done now?"

Both Kellie and Leanne were breathing hard, facing off on each side of the table, and nodded. Kellie returned the rabbit to the bag and quickly washed her hands. Adela oversaw the organization of their supplies.

A knock sounded on the door. Adela opened it to Timothy and Martin once more, who meekly placed their loads of wood on the stack near the fireplace. She whispered to Leanne and Kellie, "You two be nice to them. They're only trying to help."

Leanne and Kellie dipped their chins and muttered, "Okay." When the young men finished stacking the wood, they thanked them.

Martin looked away bashfully. "Mistress Adela, should you be makin' any sweets or such, 'twould not be refused by me and Timothy."

"You and Timothy are welcome anytime." She held up a strange-looking iron utensil. "As soon as I can figure out how to use some of these things, I'll try my hand at a pie or something."

Both men beamed. "Thank ye, mistress."

Once they left, Kellie asked, "Should you have told them you didn't know how to use some of this stuff? I get the feeling we're supposed to be maids or something."

"Good point. I'd better get busy trying to figure this out, and I'm getting hungry. Are you?"

Leanne's growling stomach echoed in the room.

Kellie grinned. "Well, Leanne can eat 24/7."

"Please don't start. I need help with this. Kellie, since you're enamored with that rabbit, wash it in this pan, cut it up, and put it into our soup pot. Leanne, peel these potatoes and carrots."

Adela filled the iron pot half full of water. Kellie added the washed and dressed rabbit. Leanne chopped vegetables and added them to the mixture. Adela added dried herbs, then sat on the stool and looked at them. "I'm not sure how long this will take over an open flame." She wrinkled her nose. "I hope it'll be done before we starve."

Kellie placed a sack of flour on the table. "Could you make bread or biscuits?"

"Unless that's self-rising flour, I'm not sure I can do it. We may be eating unleavened bread."

Leanne dropped into a chair with a thud. "What are we going to eat for breakfast?"

Adela surveyed their supplies again. With a hand on the flour, she had a sudden idea. "What if I make pancakes? Well, without syrup."

She offered a weak smile and held up the sack of coarse sugar. "We have sugar. Though, we must use it sparingly. I think sugar was—*is*—rather expensive in the seventeenth century."

It didn't take Adela long to present her version of pancakes with their limited resources sans syrup. They ate as if it were a gourmet meal.

Leanne dabbed the edges of her mouth with a rough cloth. "That wasn't bad. Pancakes sprinkled with a bit of sugar is a lot better than unleavened bread."

"Yeah, I take my hat off to you. They were pretty good." Kellie sipped her weak coffee. "Wish we had cream for this nasty stuff."

"Thanks, but I hope rabbit stew tastes much better than this." Adela grimaced. "It'll likely take all day to simmer. Let's eat apples for lunch and hope it holds us until dinner."

A horse's whinny captured their attention. Leanne sprinted to the door and opened it to Martin and Timothy holding two live chickens. A rooster scratched the dirt at their feet.

Martin gave them a gap-toothed grin, but his eyes were on Leanne. "We brung ye more goods from Lord DeGrey. He says we need to build ye a pen to hold 'em."

Timothy extended a bottle toward Adela. "We brung ye some ale fer the bakin'."

Adela blinked in confusion until she realized it was for yeast. "Oh, thank you so much." She grasped the bottle gratefully. Now they could have bread.

Leanne turned to Adela, her eyes pleading, before addressing the men. "Thank you both. We appreciate your help."

Adela instructed, "Leanne, please stir the stew."

Leanne headed for the fireplace, Martin watching her. Adela addressed Timothy and Martin. "Thank you. I suppose you could go to the back of the cottage and get started. Where can we put the chickens while you work?"

"No need, ma'am. We can toss feed near where we be workin'. They stay close." Martin glanced in Leanne's direction, but she had busied herself stirring the stew. "Come, Timothy."

The moment the door closed, Kellie's laughter filled the cottage. Leanne's glare cut like ice.

Adela waved the bottle of ale. "We have yeast for bread, and we may have eggs soon except I don't know a thing about raising chickens. Other than giving them food and water, I just remember someone telling me roosters could be terribly mean. And sometimes a hen would peck a rooster to death."

Smiling, Leanne shook her head. "Tough neighborhood."

"We should get some tips from Martin and Timothy." Kellie darted behind Adela. "Maybe if Leanne speaks sweet nothings in Martin's ear, he'll help."

The remainder of the morning they stirred the stew, cleaned, and took turns peering out the window at the progress of the chicken pen. Leanne elected Adela to carry water to the men along with crudely made cookies.

Martin gladly accepted a cookie, then gazed at his feet. "Mistress Adela, be Mistress Leanne betrothed?"

"I'm afraid so, Martin." Adela added, "And Kellie also." She asked God to forgive her for the lie, but they didn't need any more complications than they already had.

"No need to be 'pologizin', mistress. It never hurt to ask."

She laughed. "No, it certainly doesn't."

Martin grinned. Timothy returned with more wood and a bundle of hay for the nesting boxes. "Look, Timothy. Mistress Adela brung us water and sweets."

Timothy's eyes widened. "Thank ye, mistress. We 'preciate the kindness."

"I hope you enjoy these. I'm rusty at cooking right now, but I'll hopefully get better with time."

Adela returned to the cottage. Her thoughts strayed to her use of the word *time*. *Like I know how much time we have here.*

Kellie and Leanne grilled Adela on what she said to Martin. Adela teased as she paused at the bottom of the stairs. "I told him you two were free to marry, and he and Timothy had my permission to court you both."

Leanne's mouth dropped. "Adela, you didn't?"

Kellie glared and after glancing at Leanne began to laugh. "You should see your face. It's redder than a tomato."

Leanne stormed off and stayed clear of the door and windows. She checked her empty pockets and groaned. "Oh, what I wouldn't give to play hours of Candy Charade on my phone right now! Anything to distract me from this horrible reality. A 300-year-old suitor without a full set of teeth. No modern conveniences. Women are mere property. Why couldn't this just be an awful reality TV show?"

Adela and Kellie exchanged concerned glances. Adela mouthed, "Just let her be."

Kellie nodded, and Adela beckoned for Kellie to follow her

upstairs to offer Leanne some space. In about an hour, she had recovered, and they all set about their tasks.

Surprisingly, Adela found the rabbit stew not half bad, though Leanne gagged a little before tasting it.

The next several days passed uneventfully. It took all day to go about their chores of meal preparation, washing, and cleaning, ending with a routine of collapsing on the oak settles each evening in front of the fireplace to chat about the day, exhausted from their labor. Adela always pulled out her daily planner to remind them of the date and day of the week.

When one of them began to nod off, they trudged up the steep, narrow stairs to their beds.

They never forgot to bolt the door again.

CAROLE LEHR JOHNSON

Chapter Six

A perfect spring day dawned with birdsong, and early flowers in bloom perfumed the cool morning. Lord Marcus DeGrey stepped onto the graveled drive in front of Dunbar Park and stretched lazily, inhaling the fragrant air. Footsteps on gravel behind him swung his gaze around to Martin. He gave the young man a welcoming grin. "Good morrow, Martin. How goes your day thus far?"

Martin bowed. "Good morrow, my lord. All is well on this fine mornin'. How be ye today?"

"Fine, Martin." Marcus changed direction to stroll down the drive, hesitated, and turned back. "May I have a word?"

"Aye, my lord."

Marcus clasped his hands behind his back and rocked on his heels. "How goes it with the women in Dunbar Cottage? Are they well ensconced in their new positions?"

"Well, my lord, I wouldn't know about that. Timothy and me took them supplies just as ye telt us. We not been back since."

"I see . . . so ye have not seen them at the manor, or on the grounds?"

"No, my lord."

Marcus pondered the situation while Martin patiently awaited instruction. "I shall seek out Mrs. Brimberry and inquire about the women. Good morrow."

"Good morrow, my lord." Martin scurried away.

Marcus ambled down the drive toward Dunbar Cottage. His rising anger muddled his thinking. He needed to speak with his head housekeeper and cook first. Still clutching his hands behind his back, he halted and turned toward the servants' entrance to the manor.

Thrusting the door open, he almost ran into someone. "My apologies, Mrs. Brimberry. I was looking for ye."

She steadied herself from their near collision. "Aye, my lord, ye found me."

"Have the three women now living in Dunbar Cottage reported for service?"

She pressed her hands to her waist against the crisp apron. "No new servants reported to me, my lord."

"I shall go to the kitchen and inquire there. They may be aiding Mrs. Henshaw, yet methinks they should first have reported to ye. Good morrow."

Halfway down the long corridor he heard the housekeeper reply, "Ye too, my lord."

The aroma of fresh-baked bread and sweet pastries greeted him, a reminder he had not broken his fast. "Mrs. Henshaw, I should have married ye years ago. The smells that come out of this kitchen are enough to bring any man to his knees."

He dropped onto a stool by the worktable where the wiry gray-haired woman furiously worked an enormous lump of dough.

Her laugh was robust for such a petite woman. "Oh, go on, ye. Flattery will get ye *everywhere!*"

Marcus reached for an apple tart fresh from the brick oven. "Have three women come to the manor inquiring where they are to work?"

The cook paused, hands deep in the dough. "When did ye stop sayin' grace before eatin'? Your dear mother, God rest her soul, would be most unhappy."

The tart froze inches from his lips. "I do apologize." Marcus bowed his head and said a silent prayer of thanks, looked up at her, and laughed.

"That's better. Now, let me think . . . no, not seen a soul be new 'round here. Should I?"

"When I passed Dunbar Cottage a few days ago, I took notice of smoke rising from the chimney and went inside to find three women. I assumed Stanton had hired them before he departed north. Mrs. Brimberry has not seen them either, so I must be certain they are not trespassers. If they are, they now have most likely fled."

"Please be kind to them, me boy . . . mayhap they be women alone. We know not what hardships they may have endured." She wiped her hands on her apron and continued, "Women who have no protection or connections can be desperate."

"I shall, Mrs. Henshaw. I shall."

The kindly woman had been with the DeGrey family for as long as he could remember. Her mother had been a servant in the DeGrey household when they lived in London. She had grown up in their service and was as a member of the family—someone Marcus trusted like a second mother.

He rose from the stool, reached for another pastry, and strode toward the door. "If they are not trespassers, I had best find out why our new servants are not at their posts."

"Marcus."

"Aye, Mrs. Henshaw." He pivoted and offered her a friendly smile, waiting for the words of forthcoming wisdom.

She kept her eyes on the dough and began pounding it with one fist. "Mind your temper. Your mother be watching."

Marcus hovered in the doorway and said over his shoulder, "Aye, Mrs. Henshaw." It was as if he were but a lad swiping tarts from her kitchen, and his own mother was a room away focused on her needlework.

The bittersweet memories tugged at his insides, and he pushed them aside before they could be drowned out by the bad ones that were sure to follow.

CB80

The walk to the stables provided Marcus time to ponder what he would say to the women. Why had they not done as instructed? He tried to recall what he had said to them. Possibly, they had misunderstood. If they were trespassers, they may have run away since their discovery.

The pleasing scent of hay reached him. He had to hand it to Stanton Yorke. The man was a talented manager of the estate. The stable hands knew if they didn't keep things shipshape they would answer to Stanton.

Timothy approached. "Good morrow, my lord."

"Good morrow, Timothy. Things look splendid here."

A flash of pleasure crossed Timothy's face as he bowed. "'Tis nothin', my lord, but my task." He straightened. "Would ye be lookin' to ride Roman? 'Tis a fine mornin' for it."

"Aye, 'tis my aim." Marcus strode to his favorite horse and was met with Roman's sleek chestnut head and a whinny. After Timothy readied him for the ride, Marcus mounted and eased out of the stable, basking in the crisp air.

Gravel crunched under Roman's hooves as he cantered down the drive. An early spring had arrived. The gardeners had done a fine job with the planting of new flowers and trees. Splashes of vivid color dotted the manor grounds. Marcus concentrated on the beauty to keep his anger reined in as he spotted smoke rising from the cottage chimney once more.

He tethered the horse to the wooden fence and swung the gate open, ready to barge in, and demand to know why they had not presented themselves for work.

A recollection struck him like a kick from a horse. His step faltered on the path, realization coursing through him as he recalled he had not *told* them to report to the manor. He was stunned to have seen them in their sleeping attire, and the thought had become merely that—a thought unspoken.

The door to the cottage jerked open, and the younger woman with dark hair burst out. "They're everywhere! I guess

God brought me to the seventeenth century to die of shock!" She came to an abrupt halt in front of him on unsteady legs.

"Oh, Mr. Darcy . . . uh, I mean, Lord DeGrey, I'm so sorry. I didn't know you were here. I, we, were just having a bit of a problem." Her voice shook. "Lizards!"

He did not await an invitation and shoved his way past her through the open doorway. The eldest woman stood on a chair, waving a broom in the air. Marcus's eyes followed her movements. "I imagine that implement is used to sweep the floor," he stated wryly.

She brought her green-eyed gaze to his, lost her balance, and tumbled toward the floor.

The broom flew through the air. A scream sounded behind him. Marcus made one long stride and caught her. Her arms wound around his neck, and she clung to him, warmth emanating from her.

"What were you doing in a chair waving a broom like a madwoman?" He nodded toward the stone. "You could have split your head on this floor."

The tall, fair-haired woman held nothing back. "It's all because that twit over there—" She pointed to the dark-haired one. "—is deathly afraid of lizards. Adela was trying to coax him from the rafters and into this bucket, so we could put him outside." She scowled in the other woman's direction. "Baby."

"Oh, you just shut up," the other woman retorted. "You hate—" She hugged her waist. "Well, you hate a lot of things, so you can't say anything about me."

"Yeah, and what do I hate?" She placed fists on her hips and stared at the other.

"Girls, please. Lord DeGrey will think we are imbeciles."

An unbidden bark of laughter escaped him, a reminder of he and his brother, Christopher, when they were boys. "Well, I must inquire of their years as they quarrel like children."

Her breath on his face reminded him he still held this stranger in his arms. She looked at him in a most peculiar way. Almost as if she'd just seen something completely foreign. He quickly placed her onto her feet but didn't pull away.

"My apologies, mistress. Are you quite well?"

Her palms were fiery against his chest, seeping through his linen shirt. When he glanced at them, she jerked away as if burned, her eyes wide with fear. She shook imaginary wrinkles from her skirt, avoiding his gaze.

"Yes, sir. Thank you. You may have saved me from a nasty bump."

"Indeed." His mouth quirked as their eyes met, hers a sparkling green.

"I am not coming in until that lizard is out of here." The woman at the door screeched.

Marcus cleared his throat, his mirth growing. "Let us see what we may do about that." He retrieved the broom and searched for the lizard. "Ah, there he is. A tiny one, I might add." He smirked. His height allowed him to use the broom to reach the frightened creature hiding in a crack on the ceiling beam.

"Mistress, please hand me the bucket."

Adela complied and stepped back to watch. He nudged the lizard into position above the bucket. One brush and the creature fell into the container, eliciting a squeal from the one who feared it. She ran down the path away from the cottage.

Marcus handed the broom to the green-eyed woman and walked out. He turned and found her watching him as he strode toward the woods.

When he returned, he said, "There. Seems we have taken care of your problem. I apologize, but I do not know your names since we were not properly introduced when we previously met." He proceeded to introduce himself.

The fair-haired woman spoke up. "Sir, I am Kellie Welles. The fearless lizard hunter is Adela Jenks," she pointed to the woman with the green eyes, "and the coward hovering on the path is Leanne Harcourt."

He looked at Adela. "Ye are of no relation?"

Adela answered with hesitance, "No, sir, we are friends."

Marcus looked from one woman to the other and bowed. "'Tis a pleasure to make your acquaintance. I am here to inquire why ye have not reported for your assigned duties."

He read distress in Mistress Adela Jenks's eyes which had nothing to do with lizards.

Of a truth, he was certain.

Adela took a tentative step toward him. "Lord DeGrey, I must apologize for our neglect. But you, um, when we sailed into London, our bags, um . . . portmanteau was stolen. We only have the clothes we now wear." She lowered her gaze. "We were too ashamed to appear at the manor inadequately attired."

Marcus studied her. He clasped his hands behind his back. "Upon which ship did you arrive, mistress?"

Without hesitation, she brought her gaze to his. "The

Tristan and Jane. A merchant ship sailing from Boston."

Marcus's regard stayed fixed on her lovely green eyes. He wanted to ask how they came to be so far from London and how they had discovered Dunbar Park was in need of servants, but something held him back.

This woman's presence touched him. Not since . . . *No.* He would not entertain those thoughts.

The last time he had encountered a woman who had affected him so, it had cost him, *dearly* cost him, and he dare not allow it to happen again.

Marcus broke free of the woman's gaze. He muttered they would receive appropriate attire when they reported for duty on the morrow and then fled without another glance at the captivating Adela Jenks.

CAROLE LEHR JOHNSON

Chapter Seven

Adela stood in the doorway of Dunbar Cottage and met the dawn, staring over the magnificent spring countryside. Fresh buds opened, unsullied air stirring new growth on the trees near the cottage, and she marveled at the lack of noise pollution.

"Adela." Kellie stood behind her and yawned loudly. "What are you doing up so early?"

She brought her gaze around to her friend. "I'm nervous about going to the manor and given a job I'm not up for. The role of a servant in this era is grueling." She closed the door and bolted it with a clatter. A shudder racked her body, and she went to the table where she'd begun preparing their breakfast before the sunrise cast its warming glow through the window.

The creaking stairs brought her attention to rest on Leanne. "How'd you sleep?"

"A little better—" A yawn broke her words. "—I think." She dropped into a chair at the table.

Kellie moaned as she made her way to sit beside Leanne. "What time do we have to go to the manor?"

"Soon, I'd imagine," Adela said. "We should discuss the possible jobs before we go. Formulate a plan."

Leanne and Kellie nodded.

Leanne jumpstarted the discussion. "What skills do I have that could be used here? I'm a social media influencer and photographer for Pete's sake." She shrugged and looked at Adela. "It's a given you'd be best in the kitchen."

After shoving a bite of biscuit into her mouth, Leanne talked around it, considering Kellie. "You'd be good in the stables since you love horses, or I guess maybe you could work for an apothecary or in some sort of medical job. You're nearly a doctor. That's got to count for something."

Kellie shrugged and retrieved another biscuit. "I don't think they'd allow a woman to work in the stables, much less in medicine. We're in the same boat. I'm a nurse practitioner, and as far as I know, that's not a job description at a manor."

Adela heaved an exasperated sigh. "I suppose it all depends on what's needed. They may need a chambermaid or kitchen help. Who knows? We don't have any options until we figure out how we'll get home." She picked up her plate and put it in the small tub they'd chosen to use as a sink and washed it. Kellie and Leanne finished eating and cleaned their items too.

Moments later, Adela walked with them down the lane toward the manor, tiny white flowers carpeting the ground beneath the trees.

The day was pleasant enough with a slight chill in the air. Timothy and Martin passed by in a wagon and greeted them. Martin grinned at Leanne, and Kellie poked her in the ribs, prompting a loud 'Ow!' from her.

"You two are something. You know that?" Adela said good-naturedly. She sighed and broached a subject she'd been pondering while making breakfast. "You need lessons on appropriate behavior for this time." They stared at her wide-eyed. "Yes, I'm afraid if we don't watch our step, we could have a serious problem. Servants are held to different standards in each historical era. We'll go over all of the ones I can retrieve from my memory bank."

She sent them a nervous smile. "For certain, Leanne, you need to rein in your dramatics, and Kellie your sarcasm must be brought down a few notches. It will not be tolerated."

They gave her a skeptical look, and she glared at them. "Fancy a day in the stocks then?"

Kellie grimaced, and Leanne gasped.

All joking and laughter halted as they approached Dunbar Park's imposing structure. The manor house wore a massive stone façade built to impress. Warm honey-colored sandstone glinted in the morning sun, the windows gleaming. Adela paused at the curve that circled to the main entrance, peering up to take in the picturesque building. A series of wide steps led to grand, black-stained oak doors that had been polished to a luster. The same building they'd seen only days before but over 300 years earlier. Remarkable.

Adela started for the door but quickly stopped. "Servants are *not* allowed to go through the front."

Footsteps on the gravel drive brought their gazes around to see a tousled-hair boy leading a brown pony.

"Excuse me," Adela inquired. "Will you please show us to the servant's entrance?"

The boy paused. "Aye, mistress. Folla me." He dropped his gaze and walked on.

He led them to the west side of the house past a large hedgerow. A right turn took them to a narrow drive that ran parallel to the manor. The youth pointed straight ahead. "There be the stables." His arm swung toward an iron gate attached to the corner of the manor. "And through the gate be the kitchen door." He touched his hat and continued on his journey.

Adela called out her thanks and led the way past a modest garden full of infant vegetables. She inched the gate open, and they found themselves on a stone-studded walkway, a variety of herbs lining the path. They stopped at the kitchen door and shared nervous glances.

Leanne held up crossed fingers, smiled, and rapped on the door.

"Well, I never!" A wiry, grey-haired woman stood in the doorway. Her face was red and pinched with anger.

Adela stepped closer. "We're sorry to bother you, ma'am, but we were told to ask for Mrs. Brimberry."

The rage seeped out of the slight woman. "Aye, ye must be the sarvants His Lordship said would be comin'." She ushered them inside.

A plump girl entered the kitchen from the door across the room.

The grey-haired woman strode to her and asked, "Charissa, where have ye been gurl?"

Her fingers twitched as she clasped her hands against her apron. "Sorry, ma'am. I did not mean to shirk me duties." Her cheeks turned a pretty shade of pink. She leaned closer to the elder woman and whispered, "The privy. 'Tis where I been."

Kellie's uncontrolled laughter filled the enormous kitchen. Leanne jabbed her in the side, and Adela shot her a look of horror. The stare silenced her, and she had the good grace to appear embarrassed and mutter under her breath, "Sorry."

The older woman tsked, but Kellie's laughter had an effect on her that surprised them all. Her laugh was low, sweet, and musical. "Take these gurls—" She surveyed Adela. "—ta see Mrs. Brimberry."

Clarissa bobbed a curtsy and left the room expecting them to follow. When the kitchen door thumped to a close, she stopped and turned to introduce herself. "I suppose ye heard me name, but would ye telt me yours?"

They gave their names, and Adela said, "It's nice to meet you, Clarissa. What's the name of the woman in the kitchen?"

"That be Mrs. Henshaw. She be all nonsense and wind. Nice 'nough most the time. Soft on the inside like." She turned and pointed down the hall. "Will take ye to Mrs. Brimberry 'afore I be scolded."

After a few twists and turns, Clarissa halted in front of a door at the end of the hall and gently knocked.

A firm voice answered, "Come in."

Clarissa opened the door and stepped inside, curtsied, and announced them. "Mrs. Brimberry, here's the sarvants Lord

DeGrey bid come to ye for work." She backed out of the room and closed the door behind her.

The housekeeper stood behind a large desk which had seen better days. Visible among the stacks of papers and ledgers, chips and scratches scarred the surface. A white vase of daisies and ferns perched on one corner.

"Aye. Well." Mrs. Brimberry returned to her seat, not offering them a chair.

Adela glanced around and spotted only one other chair—a stuffed armchair by a tiny fireplace. She supposed *sarvants* were to stand when addressed by their superiors.

Silence hung while Mrs. Brimberry pulled a ledger toward her and opened it to a blank page. She brought her gaze to Adela. "Would ye be their—" She waved a hand at Kellie and Leanne. "—mother?"

"No, ma'am." Adela cleared her throat. "We are close friends and traveling companions."

"What are your names?" She dipped the quill into the ink and scratched it over the page as they answered.

"Now, let us begin with ye, Adela. What are your skills?" The quill went back into the well with precision, no drops of ink falling.

"I am a che—cook. Having worked in . . ." She searched her memory bank to be certain to answer in a way that wouldn't have her scrubbing the kitchen floor and fireplace for however long she'd be here. She was getting too old for that kind of labor.

"I was the head cook in a grand restaurant in Boston . . . in America." She stammered, "The Colonies."

Mrs. Brimberry's attention snapped from her ledger to Adela. "In truth?"

"Yes, ma'am." Adela nodded. "And after a decade, I began teaching."

Eyes wide, she returned to the ledger and began writing. Finished with Adela, she looked at Kellie. "And ye mistress?"

Kellie stood tall, back straight. "I appreticed with a doctor. To aid him in healing and surgeries." Her stance allowed no room for argument. She was her usual confident self.

The housekeeper raised her thick eyebrows but didn't question her. "Well." She brushed the top of the quill against her chin. "I am uncertain what to do with ye. Your skills are most valuable, but there is no day-by-day work associated with them." She leaned back in her chair, releasing a creak in the leather. Her eyes sparked with promise. "Ye may be useful in the brewery."

Kellie's face fell. "What?"

Adela speared Kellie with a stern look.

"Aye. Ye are accustomed to making potions and tinctures and such, are ye not?"

"Mrs. Brimberry, if I may . . ." Adela took in a breath and continued when she wasn't interrupted, "Kellie is most aware of medicinal potions and the like, but she's never brewed ale. That's why she's so surprised by your suggestion. I'm sure she'll take to it well."

Adela looked at Kellie with pleading eyes, and Kellie gave her a reluctant nod.

"Now, for you, Leanne." Mrs. Brimberry twisted the quill

from side-to-side. "Where might your talents lie?"

Leanne stared out the window. Adela felt her friend's pain but couldn't come up with a practical solution to help her. What did you do with a social media influencer in the 1600s?

"Methinks ye would do nicely as a chambermaid, and mayhap, work in the laundry."

Adela heaved a sigh, praying Leanne would accept this and move on. She watched her eyes flicker to Mrs. Brimberry, still vacant as if she peered through the glass.

Mrs. Brimberry studied her porcelain skin, Adela noted, likely realizing they were the hands of a gentlewoman and not a servant. But the woman said nothing.

Leanne said quietly, "Yes, ma'am."

Mrs. Brimberry stood. "Let us locate uniforms. Ye are free to alter them for a proper fit. We will supply ye with what ye need. This way." Her frame was tall, rigid, and strong. No leeway would be given here. This drill sergeant would well oversee their jobs, Adela was sure.

They trailed behind her, winding their way through the maze of corridors, rooms, and storage closets, obviously expected to remember everything as she pointed out and described the use of each. When completed, they stopped in the kitchen.

"Mrs. Henshaw, I am leaving Adela with ye as she has some cookery skills that may be of assistance." A wave of her hand motioned Adela to step further into the room. "I will have Patience find a uniform for her." She nodded with vigor and peered at Kellie and Leanne. "Come along, girls. I shall see to your uniforms."

Adela watched them go, noting the fearful look in Leanne's eyes, and gave her the brightest smile she could muster before turning toward the cook. "I hope I may be of some help to you."

No response came from the tiny woman. Adela sniffed the air. "Oh, that smells heavenly." Her stomach growled in agreement.

Mrs. Henshaw sent her a distrustful look. "Well, you be a cordial gurl . . . woman."

She returned to her bread-making and gestured toward a steaming loaf on the table. "That'd be what ye were sniffin' like a dawg. Cut yourself a piece. Butter be over there." She motioned with her head again, wisps of grey hair floating about her slender face.

The knife lay next to the bread along with a crockery of butter. Adela's mouth watered at the sight.

"Jest put that bread on the napkin." She curled her lips. "No need to soil a dish."

"Thank you." She sliced off a healthy chunk of the crusty bread, broke off a piece, and stuffed it into her mouth, eliciting a moan of pleasure. "Oh, my. This is delicious." Adela tore off another piece and slathered it with the fresh butter. "I don't think I've ever tasted anything so divine."

The declaration brought a wide smile from the woman. "Ah, go on wit ye. Flattery will get ye everywhere."

Adela laughed. "If you continue feeding me things like this, I'll flatter you until I own Dunbar Park in no time."

"Oh, will ye now?" A deep, pleasant male voice answered from the doorway. Marcus DeGrey crossed his arms over his broad chest. "I suppose Mrs. Henshaw has a great deal of power of which I was unaware." He gave them a smile that made Adela's knees weaken.

"Master Marcus! Ye gave me a fright. Still slippin' up on your old Bertie?"

Marcus pushed away from the door with his shoulder and strode to the elder woman and kissed her cheek. "Mrs. *Bertie,* you shall never be old."

She patted him on the cheek with her aged hand, leaving a smudge of white.

He looked at Adela. "May I assume ye are to assist Mrs. Henshaw in the kitchen?"

Adela struggled not to chuckle at the white spot on his cheek—the lord of the manor. She gave him a slight nod.

His gaze rested on her, but her eyes could not stray from the white smudge. She longed to reach out and wipe it away. Something in his look shifted as if he'd noticed something in her gaze.

"Mistress Adela, is there something wrong? Ye appear to be on the precipice of humor."

There was nothing for it—Adela laughed. Her hand came up with speed and clapped it over her mouth, shoulders shaking. Mrs. Henshaw looked at her as if she'd lost all of her senses, then brought her stare to Marcus before she joined in.

"Methinks I have become green or some unsightly color to have provoked such amusement."

"Master Marcus, ye have a bit of flour on your cheek."

He brushed at his face but kept missing the mark.

"My hands will do ye more damage. Adela, wipe the flour from Master Marcus's face."

Adela's smile faded.

Mrs. Henshaw pointed to a cloth, and Adela picked it up and cautiously stepped toward Marcus. She had to stop thinking of him as *Marcus*. He was her employer. She was his servant. He *was* lord of the manor.

The napkin came up of its own volition. He held still while she brought a corner of it to his face, trying to keep her fingers from making contact.

He stepped closer, and she held her breath. The flour did not come off.

He said, voice wary, "Perhaps ye should apply more pressure, or we shall stand here until Mrs. Bertie is preparing the evening meal."

Adela stepped closer, wrapped the napkin around her finger, so she could apply more pressure, and pressed it against his cheek. She began to rub the flour away, and the warmth of his skin caused the heat to rise in her own.

Oh, Lord, please don't let me turn the color of an apple.

Her mind strayed, and she found herself watching his lips. She kept rubbing, lost in time—in more ways than one.

A cough sounded from the cook. "Methinks ye have rubbed a hole in his cheek. The flour be gone."

Marcus didn't seem to hear, his gaze on Adela. She pulled back, bumping into a chair. "I'm sorry, *Mar*—Your Grace."

He frowned. "Your Grace? I am an Earl, not a Duke."

My lord, Adela chided herself.

His eyes held something undefinable. Was it suspicion?

A chill raced up her spine. The thought of being burned at the stake as a witch entered her mind.

Shuffling footsteps on the flagstone floor caught their attention, all eyes focused on the maid in the doorway. A tall, red-headed girl curtsied and said, "Sorry to interrupt, my lord." She held out her arms. "I brung the lady's uniform as Mrs. Brimberry telt me."

Mrs. Henshaw answered her. "Thank ye, Patience. Give it to Adela."

The girl obeyed and curtsied her way backward out of the room.

Adela hugged the clothing to her like a shield, eyes fixed on the clothing. Marcus stood shoulder to shoulder with her. She pulled in a deep breath and heard him sigh, the heat of his breath fanning her face.

He turned to her, eyes questioning. "I shall leave ye to your duties." He gave Mrs. Henshaw another kiss on the cheek, turned on his heel, and left them.

"That lad has taken an interest in ye, gurl. I can see it in his eyes." She washed her hands and dried them on her apron. "Will come to no good end, so watch yourself."

Adela placed the bundle of clothes on a stool and looked at her. "What do you mean?"

She heaved a longsuffering sigh. "Please do not take me wrong, gurl, but Master Marcus be like all men. They do get lonely and sometimes seek the company of a young woman."

"I am his servant and not a woman looking for a good time nor a husband." She smiled at the woman. "Nor am I young."

The older woman raised her eyebrows. "Ye must be some years younger than the master."

Adela asked, "How old is Lord DeGrey?"

The woman squinted at the ceiling in concentration. "Oh, in a fortnight or so he will be eight and forty. Why do ye ask?"

"I'm fifty. Well, I will be in a few weeks."

A frown further creased the cook's face. "Ye do not say!"

"Yes, ma'am." Adela retrieved the clothes. "Where may I change?"

The woman led her to a compact room off the kitchen and helped Adela with her uniform. It wasn't a terrible fit except for the length. Mrs. Henshaw summoned Patience to bring her sewing implements, so Adela could take it to the cottage to make the alteration that evening.

When they'd returned to the kitchen, the cook gave Adela a piercing stare, "My child, I know Master Marcus well. No one is better able ta read his moods and know his fancies. I been with him since he was learnin' ta walk." She turned to stir the contents of the large copper pot and spoke over her shoulder. "Mark my words. Keep your distance if ye know what be good fer ye."

CAROLE LEHR JOHNSON

Chapter Eight

Adela strode to Dunbar Cottage alongside a lagging Kellie and Leanne as the sun set before them, sending shards of brilliant red and orange across the horizon.

It had been a long, grueling day of labor.

Leanne carried the sewing kit while Adela gripped a basket laden with food. Mrs. Henshaw had insisted upon it when she remarked how exhausted Adela appeared at the end of their kitchen duties.

Kellie moaned as she rotated her shoulders. "I'm done in. Heaving burlap bags and stirring a wooden paddle in an iron pot of a putrid-smelling concoction isn't for the faint of heart."

Leanne gagged. "At least you weren't emptying chamber pots all day long. I thought I'd throw up from the smell until Patience gave me an ointment to dab under my nose to suppress it."

Adela patted her back. "It won't be easy, but all this back-breaking work will offer further incentive to find a way home."

Kellie and Leanne nodded in agreement, continuing their shuffle to the cottage.

Leanne lifted a corner of the cloth covering the basket. The aroma of herbs and roasted vegetables escaped, and she closed her eyes, inhaling. "I'm so tired all I want to do is eat and fall into a dead sleep."

"Amen to that." Kellie ended on a groan.

Adela opened the cottage door and dropped the basket on the table. "I'll get the plates."

Kellie unpacked the food. "I'm so glad she's kind and had pity on us. You must have made a wonderful impression, Adela."

"Not sure about that, but she is loyal to Marcus." Too late to take back her slip of the tongue. "I've got to stop calling him that, even in front of you two. We can't afford to be too familiar with anyone here and appear disrespectful. Who knows what the punishment is?"

Kellie and Leanne shot her a look of interest.

Adela narrowed he eyes. "What's that face for?"

Leanne nudged Kellie. "I wonder what happened in the kitchen?"

Adela busied herself arranging the food.

Kellie grinned. "She's blushing."

Adela sighed with feeling. "Lord DeGrey came into the kitchen while I was talking to Mrs. Henshaw, and things, well, became a bit complicated."

Leanne sat and clasped her hands on the table as if waiting for her favorite sitcom. "Do tell."

Kellie nodded.

Adela dished out the food, said a prayer, and told them what happened. She straightened when she was through. "I don't know what to think about any of it. But, then again, I feel like I'm living in a surreal sci-fi movie and can't escape."

Leanne grinned. "Trapped in time with Mr. Darcy. What a dilemma."

Kellie chuckled and said, "Ah, yes, *what* a dilemma."

"You two are gonna be the death of me." Adela smiled and changed the subject. "I'm glad Lord DeGrey provided us with eating utensils instead of only a knife. I never thought I'd say this, but I'm truly thankful the fork has been invented." She held it up like a sword.

Leanne and Kellie snickered. They finished their meal in silence, too weary for more words, and not long afterward went to bed, drifting to sleep in seconds.

03&0

Adela bolted from bed, unsure if a nightmare or a sound awakened her. Lying still, she willed her heart to slow its rapid pounding and tried to reconstruct what could have awakened her. The house was quiet with only the sounds of Kellie and Leanne breathing across the room.

Troubled and unable to return to sleep, Adela slipped downstairs, rekindled the fire, and made a cup of tea.

Marcus was a generous employer. If she remembered her history, tea was an expensive commodity in this era. She almost choked on the next sip as it brought clarity to her thoughts. He'd been *very* kind, extremely so, including how he'd responded to the incident in the kitchen. Many of the aristocracy considered servants their property, especially the females, with whom many exercised brief dalliances.

Anger gripped Adela's insides. She surged from the chair and paced the room, venting her frustrations out loud. Mrs. Henshaw's words echoed in her mind.

"How dare he assume such!" She slammed the iron poker into the flaming logs and began her tirade anew. With the last jab, she heard the creaking stairs and looked up to see Kellie and Leanne, their eyes wide with fear.

"What's going on?" Kellie asked.

"I'm so sorry to wake you. I've just had an epiphany." She banged the poker into its place by the fire. "Marcus, yes, *Marcus* is an aristocratic snob and a male chauvinist."

Leanne placed her hands on her hips. "Are we talking about him again? I . . . *we* assumed there was a burglar. You scared the life out of us."

"I woke up and couldn't calm down, so I made tea."

"Tea? In the middle of the night?" Kellie snorted. "Caffeine will *not* help you sleep."

Adela slumped into a chair. "What's wrong with me? These suspicions came over me with such force. Am I right about him? Why else would he show me attention? Is Mrs. Henshaw right? Does he have a history of womanizing?" She looked at them.

They sat beside her, uncertainty in their expressions.

Kellie whispered, "*Nothing* is wrong with you. Let's face it.

This is a weird time for all of us. We've been thrown three hundred and fifty years into the past, and we're clueless how to handle it. We're not even sure how to begin finding our way back. But we will certainly try."

Adela massaged the back of her neck. "How do we unravel this mess?"

Leanne slapped a hand on the table. "We'll work it out with pen and paper. Formulate ideas to return home."

Kellie's brows furrowed. "A process of elimination?"

"Yes." Adela mused, pushing thoughts of Marcus into the back of her mind. "We'll begin with where, when, and how we got here. All the elements present at that time."

Leanne's organizational skills kicked in. "We need to write down everything we remember from the day. No detail is insignificant. Let's put it all down on paper, and we'll see where we are then."

Adela smiled, hope surging through her. Together, they would find a way home.

ᏨᎦᎦᎩ

Adela watched as Leanne marched across the room and shook Kellie with intensity. "Wake up!"

Adela shoved her arms into the sleeves of the brown linen top, securing each tie in place. She stifled a yawn. "I know she's tired, but aren't we all?"

Rising before dawn each morning, the days had blurred with their routine of a quick breakfast and lengthy walk to the manor, full workday, brainstorming in the evenings over a possible return, lessons on how *not* to behave, rinse and repeat. They'd been at it for a week now, and the interminable days of hard labor were getting to them.

With no time for relaxing, before or after work, tension had wound its way into their usually amiable friendship.

Kellie rolled onto her back, a painful whimper escaping her lips. "Please don't make me go back. I've worked twelve-hour shifts in the E.R. for days and not felt this bad."

An exasperated puff of air left Leanne's mouth. She fell onto the edge of Kellie's bed and let her forehead drop to her knees. "This has to get easier once we build up our stamina. If these people can do it day after day, so can we."

Adela sank onto her bed and began pulling on her boots. "She's right, you know. We need to hang in there and keep going."

Leanne struggled to rise, fatigue written into her every move. "But we're out of paper. How can we map out a plan if we are out of paper?"

Determination coursed through Adela. "Don't worry. I'll ask Mrs. Henshaw how to get more."

Kellie slid out of the bed and ended up sitting on the floor with her back against it. "I have one idea."

"Only one?" Leanne teased.

"Yes . . . for now." Kellie stood and began pulling on her clothes. "We need an energy boost. Like a power drink."

"Excellent idea," Adela said. "Another thing to discuss tonight."

Leanne whirled. "Wait. Isn't today Saturday?"

"Yes," Kellie answered. "Why?"

Leanne clapped her hands. "We're off tomorrow!" She laughed, pirouetting around the room and bowing with a flourish. "Don't you remember Mrs. Henshaw told Adela we have a full day off once a month?"

Adela nodded. "Great! We need some serious down time to think and rest, and a full twenty-four hours off is the answer."

The walk to the manor infused Adela with more hope than the day before, with the expectation of time away from their labor.

Mrs. Henshaw greeted them as they entered the kitchen. "Ah, gurls, I know ye have already broken your fast, but please try the fresh bread." Her smile widened. "'Tis somethin' Adela telt me about and wanted to try."

After they had a taste of the warm, dense bread and reached for seconds, Mrs. Henshaw's face lit with pleasure. Adela praised her. "This is wonderful. The rosemary brought your already perfect bread to another level."

She slapped Adela's arm. "Oh, go on, ye."

The cook's pleasure delighted Adela more than the bread maker herself. Kellie and Leanne continued to stuff their mouths. They thanked her and stepped toward the door, but Adela stopped them.

"Wait, girls." She turned to the wiry cook. "Is tomorrow the Sunday of the month we're off work?"

"Aye, 'tis the day."

Leanne leapt into the air, arms raised high, and gyrated around the room.

Mrs. Henshaw stepped back, shock etched on her face.

Leanne lifted Kellie off the floor. Adela laughed and patted

Mrs. Henshaw's arm. "Not to worry. They're just happy."

She pulled a face. "'Tis a strange way to show pleasure."

Adela agreed, watched the girls go their separate ways, and turned the corner to get her apron. She bumped straight into Marcus DeGrey.

His quick reflexes brought his arms around her, and she responded in kind. They were out of the cook's line of vision— *alone.*

The moment suspended between them, Marcus looking down at her.

His light grey eyes lit with something Adela had never seen before. Was it interest or suspicion? The pull of those eyes held her, powerless to look away.

Memories of her anger surfaced like a buoy. She shoved him away. "Please let me go."

"I believe *ye* were holding onto me, Mistress *Adela.*" His voice dripped with humor. "And I believe 'twas ye that did run into me." He frowned but released her and asked, "Who is Mr. Darcy?"

"I . . . I beg your pardon?"

He raised his eyebrows. "Mistress Leanne called me Mr. Darcy before."

"Uh," Adela stuttered. "My mistake, my lord." She curtsied and rushed to collect her apron, muttering under her breath, "Rogue."

Chapter Nine

Adela rolled onto her side, the bright April sunlight slanting through the flimsy curtains warming her face. Her sigh was deep, pleasurable.

Sun? *Oh, no. We've overslept.* She bolted out of bed and shouted, "Girls, girls! Hurry, we're late and who knows what Brimberry will do to punish us. I've heard rumors."

Both women shot from their beds, grabbed their clothes, and shoved them on without thought. Leanne stood, tripped while putting on her boots, and landed on the floor with a thump.

"Wait a minute!" Kellie waved her blouse at Adela. "It's our day off."

Adela staggered to her bed and collapsed onto it. She brought a trembling hand to her temple. Her body ached, and she felt she could sleep for days and still not be well-rested.

Kellie sat beside her and placed a comforting arm around her. "I'm sorry. Your outburst surprised me."

Leanne stood over them with folded arms. "I agree. But I don't suppose that's what's going on here. Is it, Adela?"

Adela rubbed her temple. Sniffling, she said, "No. I'm sorry I woke you. We've been at this for what *seems* like months, and I guess the routine is ingrained in me. My internal clock is completely messed up." She patted Kellie's hand. "You didn't upset me. I have so much on my mind, and I'm worn to the bone."

"Something's happened again, hasn't it?" Leanne asked, her eyes narrowing.

Adela drew in a deep breath and released it. "Yes. I had a run-in with Marcus DeGrey yesterday."

Kellie gave a mischievous smile. "A run-in?"

"What was he angry about?" Leanne asked.

"No, I mean I *literally* ran into him. He grabbed me to keep us from falling, and I did the same." She shivered. "It's the way he looked at me with those ... those grey eyes." Unshed tears burned. "And his tone when he spoke to me."

Kellie bobbed her head from side to side. "*So*?"

"I'm afraid he is an aristocrat who thinks his servants are his property and if I don't *comply*—" She raised her eyebrows. "—he'll dismiss us, and then where will we be?"

Leanne sat beside them. "Does the way he looks at you make you uncomfortable?"

She looked at Leanne. "What do you mean?"

"You know. Creeped out."

Hesitating, Adela answered, "No."

"Oh, I get it," Kellie said with a gleam in her eyes. "You find him attractive, but—"

"Kellie!" Adela crossed her arms.

"Come on," Kellie said. "Just because he shows you a little attention doesn't mean he's a monster. He's been nothing but kind to us."

"Yes, he has," Adela said. "But he may want me to return the favor, and we need these jobs until we can find a way home."

"There's no way we're going to let him take advantage of you," Kellie stated in a firm voice. "If we have to sleep in the woods and eat berries until we figure this out, we will. You need to stand up to him. The next time he makes an advance tell him you will not tolerate it." She stuck her nose in the air. "So, there."

Leanne turned to Adela. "Let's not ruin our day off."

Adela offered a weak smile. "We'll make the most of it, shall we?" She rose, finished dressing, and as she drew the blanket over her pillow, her gaze fell on her small Bible. She picked it up and hugged it to her chest. "I think we've forgotten the most important thing we should be faithful in doing." She held the Bible in front of her, and they stared at it.

Kellie's mouth fell open. "I am so ashamed. We haven't even mentioned the Bible since we arrived in this seventeenth-century pit."

Leanne averted her gaze. "We haven't even prayed together."

"We've dropped the ball, but we are human," Adela said. "How often does anyone get plunged into the middle of another century? The trauma has overwhelmed us. Let's ask God to forgive us and move forward."

Kellie's face brightened. "I know how we can spend our day off—well, part of it. After all, we do have laundry, cooking, and cleaning to do."

Leanne said, "Okay, tell us your plan."

Kellie ignored the dig. "Let's make a picnic, go to the river, and spend the morning with Bible study and prayer. It's such a glorious day. The air smells so sweet—not like that stinkin' place I slave in." She wrinkled her nose in disgust.

Leanne pulled herself to her full five-foot, three-inch height. "Got to hand it to you, Kellie. That's genius." She looked at Adela. "So, what can we take to eat and drink?"

Adela's spirit lifted. "Let's see what the larder holds." She led the way to the kitchen, maneuvering the narrow stairs with care.

She rummaged through the cupboard and found enough to carry them through lunch, thankful for all of Mrs. Henshaw's leftovers. Their food consisted of shriveled apples from the cellar—last year's crop, oatcakes, cheese, apple tarts, meat pies, and ale.

Adela had questioned the ale until Kellie educated them on the brewing process. She assured them she had removed some before it fermented to create alcohol.

On the walk to the stream, Adela looked at Kellie. "I'm so glad you made our special ale. I wouldn't be able to handle the regular brew."

"Yeah, and you definitely couldn't stand making cock ale. It's by far the sickest thing I've had to do so far." Kellie gagged, bringing a hand to her throat. "It's revolting. They actually kill a rooster, do the disgusting ritual of cleaning it, then boil it for a few minutes—before it's cooked completely." She looked at Adela for the right word.

"Parboil."

"Yes. We steep the rooster in some sort of wine called sack and soak it with raisins, dates, and nutmeg. Once it's cooled, we put a lid on the cauldron and let it sit for about a week. Then, they strain and bottle it. But you can't drink it for a month." She winced at the memory. "If I have to stir that foul-smelling brew one more time, I'll hurl." She put her basket down, retrieved the coarse brown blanket, and shook it out hard, releasing her frustration.

Leanne exhaled loudly. "At least you don't have to empty chamber pots." She choked and sat on the blanket beside Kellie. "I'll switch with you."

Adela knelt and retrieved items from the basket. "I'm starved."

After saying the blessing, they ate in companionable silence, enjoying the breeze and pleasant temperature. A mother duck and her chicks paddled across the river, soft fluffy downs of yellow gliding through the water.

Leanne sighed, her gaze following the ducklings. "What is it about a picnic that brings the best flavor out in food?"

Kellie laughed. "I think you may be on to something." She nudged Leanne on the shoulder. "That and the fact you're not having to schlep chamber pots."

"True." She grimaced. "I've certainly developed a deeper level of empathy for the people who have to clean out the portable toilets at outdoor events. Bless them."

Adela smiled, relishing the hint that her usually cheeky friend had returned to them.

⚖️

Marcus urged Roman over the hills surrounding Dunbar Park, his mind whirling with unanswered questions. Nan would arrive tomorrow—his precious child, his reason for living. He was anxious for her to depart London and relieved the manor was ready for her arrival. The governess would accompany her and then depart as she had given her notice some weeks before. He had paid her handsomely to stay until it was time to escort Nan to the country. She would be away to the Colonies to meet her intended.

Until he could employ another, Nan could become acquainted with the estate, the workings of the manor, and settle into country life.

Voices carried on the breeze—ones Marcus recognized. He twisted in the saddle and peered through the trees leading to the river. The new servants were sitting on a blanket, surrounded by food and drink.

He eased Roman to a small copse of trees by the water and tied him to a bush where he could reach grass and water. Marcus eased his way toward the women and crouched behind some brush. The tall, light-haired woman read from a small book. If his memory served, her name was Kellie.

"The steps of a good man are ordered by the Lord, and He delights in his way." Her pale hair glinted in the sun. "I get what it means, but I can't say I've met all that many people God would actually delight in."

"You mean *men,* not people," the dark-haired woman interjected. He couldn't recall her name. "You're letting your bad relationship with Tim color your judgment, Kellie."

Adela joined in. "I know how she feels, Leanne. I've always held back my feelings because whenever I tried to draw close to a man he always disappointed me. Maybe it's a failing on my part. Trust is a valuable thing. Something that must be earned."

Marcus rose without sound and returned to Roman. Shame ate at him for eavesdropping, but he needed answers. They were three of the most unusual women he had ever chanced to meet. Common laborers they were not.

Their speech, manners, and bearing proclaimed a much higher station than mere servants. Something was amiss.

CB&D

Adela woke, momentarily uncertain where she was. The gentle wind played with her hair, sending wisps of waves across her eyes. She took in the stream bordered by delicate white flowers and dotted with trees. A bird flew overhead.

A snore invaded the peace. She looked at Kellie, who slept beside her. Leanne scribbled with speed into her journal.

Adela whispered, "I've never seen you that intent on journaling."

Leanne's pencil paused over the page. "Yeah, go figure. I've seen things here that may be useful in my business. Better to put it on paper and not trust my memory when I get home." She tapped the pencil against her chin. The light in her eyes dimmed. "*If* I get home."

Adela raised onto an elbow. "We'll get home." She nodded with emphasis. "Once we've done whatever God brought us here to do."

"Yes. As you've said, 'God doesn't have to tell us every step to take as long as we are willing and available to take a step when He shows us.'"

Kellie rolled to one side, propping her head on her bent arm. "What are you talking about?"

Adela ruffled her hair. "We're back on the subject of why God brought us here."

Kellie smiled sleepily and stretched like a lazy feline. "What should we do now?"

Adela sprung to her feet and scooped up their items. "Let's visit the village. It'll be amazing to compare it to its modern counterpart."

Leanne pursed her lips. "Sure, why not." She nudged Kellie with her foot. "Come on lazy-bones. Help us."

Kellie rolled onto her back, closed her eyes, and released a loud puff of air. "But I'm so comfortable. This is heavenly."

Adela tugged on Leanne's sleeve and motioned to Kellie. Leanne nodded in understanding. On the silent count of three, Adela and Leanne grabbed one of Kellie's arms and hefted her up.

"You two! Leave me be. All I want is to sleep."

"Kellie, if you sleep all afternoon, you won't be worth shooting." Leanne scowled. "Let's get exercise and explore. It'll be a month before we get another chance."

Leanne and Adela towered over her until she yielded.

After returning leftovers to the cottage, they walked to the village, taking in the new spring foliage and wildflowers. A pungent scent met them as they walked down the narrow road.

White blooms stood atop tall stems rising from scattered dense clumps along the lane.

Adela plucked a long-stemmed blossom and a few leaves from the plant. She sniffed and passed it on to the others. "What do you make of it?"

Leanne leaned away from the flower, easing it back to Adela. "Garlic. Strong garlic."

Kellie smiled. "I love the smell of garlic." She took the specimen and carried it.

Leanne harrumphed. "Bet you wouldn't like it so much if a man who'd eaten it tried to kiss you. Yuck."

"Hmm . . ." She shrugged. "Maybe not."

They reached a fork in the road but recognized nothing and took the road on the right, spotting the village church ahead.

The grey stone structure blinked in the bright sunlight, its tower looming over them. Since it was late afternoon on a Sunday, they found no one about, so they let themselves into the churchyard, the gate clicking shut behind them. Noting the Roman numerals cut into its pediment, they marveled at the long history of the church, dating back to the fourteenth century.

"Do you think we can go inside?" Leanne asked Adela.

Adela shrugged. "I don't see why not. I doubt they lock the doors." She gripped the handle and eased the door inward. In front of them stood a font and to its right church pews were arranged in two rows, each flanking the outer walls. Silence engulfed them as they stilled, transfixed by the history that had passed through this small country church for centuries.

Kellie sat on the closest pew and spoke in hushed voice. "Can you imagine the lives spent here worshipping century after century?"

Leanne and Adela settled into the pew in front of her. Adela closed her eyes in silent prayer.

Heavenly Father, please guide us as we embark on whatever task You have set before us. We don't know why You've brought us here, but we know that time is in Your hands. You are beyond time—past, present, and future. We belong to You. Keep us strong and faithful. Amen.

She lifted her head to see Leanne and Kellie standing in the aisle gazing at the altar before them, serene expressions on their faces.

"This is a peaceful place," Adela said. "I can feel God's presence here. On our next Sunday off, let's come to church. I only wish I'd thought of it before now."

She looped her arms through theirs and left the tranquility of the sanctuary, going back the way they had traveled. This time they took the other fork in the road that led them to the Blackhorse Coaching Inn.

Adela stared at it from a distance. "I'm not sure if women went into taverns or inns without male companionship during this century. Let's play it safe for now."

She guided them past the inn, enticing aromas wafting toward them of cooking meat and vegetables.

Leanne sniffed. "That smells so good. I'm hungry."

Kellie elbowed her. "What else is new?"

"I know. I can't help it. Seems it's grown worse since we got here."

Adela laughed. "I'm sure it's all that heavy lifting and walking you're doing now."

The next landmark they recognized was the market cross at the center of the village. It stood proudly, shimmering in the afternoon sun.

Kellie shrugged. "Doesn't look any newer than when we saw it in the past. Ha! I mean *future*."

Leanne ran a hand over the pitted and worn white stone. "I suppose it's old even by today's seventeenth-century standards. Can you imagine what this cross has seen? Wish it could talk."

They walked on, noting the thatched cottages, some built of stone and some with a plaster façade. All were surrounded by gardens of budding flowers, vegetables, and herbs.

Adela's thoughts drifted to the old church, realizing no one had suggested they tour the cemetery behind it. Perhaps their thoughts mirrored hers.

Would someone in the twenty-first century find *their* graves among its stones some day?

CR∞

Marcus paused in the open doorway of the library. The morning sun slanted through the large paned windows as Adela Jenks ran her finger along the spine of his family's Bible, a look of awe on her face.

Brown leather with gold-etched letters spelled out the title. Her lips moved as she read, her other hand sliding a cloth over the table's surface. The brass lantern-clock on the mantle chimed the hour.

Marcus cleared his throat. "And what brings ye to be dusting rather than working in the kitchen with Mrs. Henshaw?"

She started and quickly curtsied. "A maid is ill." Their gazes held. Another curtsy and she said, "Excuse me, sir."

He nodded, and she left the room, her footsteps echoing down the hall.

Marcus searched for the book he'd come to find and mulled over Adela and the other women. As servants, they certainly did not fit the mold—soft hands, refined posture, uncommon speech even to his ears, the lack of knowledge for their tasks.

And Adela always met his eyes when he spoke to her. They were never downturned as servants were instructed to do.

From whence did they *truly* come? And how could he discover this?

Chapter Ten

Mrs. Henshaw occupied a chair next to the fireplace, deftly mending a tear in the hem of her skirt. "If I rip this another time, I shall be wearin' nothin' but thread."

Adela gave her a warm smile. "You sew almost as well as you cook, Mrs. Henshaw."

Her fist pressed into the colossal lump of dough, releasing the pungent scent of yeast. As an afterthought, she said, "You've been tripping on your hem lately. Do you think you've lost weight?"

The elderly cook brought her gaze to meet Adela's. "No, my clothes fit as they always did." She bit the thread in half and stuck the needle into the cushion by her chair.

Adela grimaced. "Oh, how can you do that?"

Mrs. Henshaw stood and shook out her skirt. "Do what, my dear?"

"Bite the thread. My grandmother used to do it and the first time I tried, I shivered. The feel of the thread against my teeth is, well . . . creepy."

The wiry woman laughed with delight. "Ye are a strange gurl." She blew a strand of hair from her face and continued with her kitchen duties, chuckling.

"Who is a strange girl, Mrs. Henshaw?" Marcus DeGrey ambled into the kitchen with a buoyant spring in his step. He dropped into a chair and observed the two women at work, arms crossed against his chest.

Adela tried to stay focused on her task, but his presence was unsettling. Why did this man make her feel so awkward? Like a beetle under a microscope.

Whenever she saw him, something within her stirred. She couldn't determine if it was apprehension or fascination. Not having control of her emotions was maddening. Her inner thoughts halted as she caught the end of something said to Mrs. Henshaw. When she looked up, his eyes were still on her.

"Aye, she arrives tomorrow."

"Good. We shall make a batch of her favorite treats." The cook stood and strode to a shelf above one of the worktables. She removed a wooden box, scarred with age. With a grunt, she perched on a stool at the table where Adela kneaded the bread. "My memory 'tis not what it used to be. Glad to have these recipes scratched onto paper."

Marcus placed strong hands on the chair arms and pushed himself up. "I shall leave ye two lovely ladies to your work." Again, his gaze settled on Adela. This time, his eyes held no mischief or humor, only a glint of—was it uncertainty? He stood there for a moment biting his lower lip and with a nod left the room.

Mrs. Henshaw was still focused on her collection of recipes when Adela asked, "Ma'am, who is coming tomorrow?"

The woman brought her grey head up. "Oh. His daughter, Nanette. Yet, we call her Nan." Her eyes held a faraway look. "Sweet little thing. She has been with her governess since her mother did leave them. But now the master has the house in workin' order, she be comin' ta live with him. Shall be good for them both." She turned back to her search.

Adela plopped the ball of dough onto a floured board and covered it with a clean cloth to rise. "How old is she?"

"She will be five the comin' month." With a stack of aged papers in front of her, she slammed the lid shut and stood. "Best be gettin' to it."

Adela eased into a chair to rest her weary feet. "I'll be glad to help you. Baking is my favorite pastime."

Mrs. Henshaw pushed a cup toward her. "Drink up and rest a bit before we start."

Adela sipped the drink and leaned back into her chair, drew in a deep sigh, and released it. The little spitfire of a woman darted around the kitchen gathering baking supplies.

CB&O

Gravel crunched under the cart as it approached Dunbar Manor. Adela, Leanne, and Kellie moved to the side of the drive and watched its approach.

A short, dumpy man with close-set eyes and disheveled reddish hair drove the horse-pulled cart.

Kellie moaned. "Oh, no. That's Mr. Leckle. He brings dried oats and hops to make the ale. They'll start growing this year's crop now, but he stores the dried stuff and sells it until they harvest this fall."

"So, why the 'oh, no'?" Leanne asked.

Kellie shivered as he passed and tipped his hat, the cart slowing. She whispered between clenched teeth, "Walk faster. Just wave and keep moving, or we'll be late for work. Do *not* make eye contact."

Adela and Leanne sped up as they were told. When out of earshot, Adela asked, "Why did we do that?"

Leanne interrupted, "Hey, isn't he married to Violet, the pretty blonde woman that works in the washhouse?"

"Yeah. Right. About *that*." Kellie's eyes grew stormy. "You should hear the way he talks to her. He's always demeaning her, telling her she's lazy and stupid. I could knock him into the middle of next week!" She clenched her teeth. "Let me tell you—anyone who works in the washhouse is *not* lazy."

"Poor woman," Leanne said.

They kept their pace until they'd reached the manor and said their morning goodbyes, having avoided the odious Mr. Leckle.

Before Adela reached the kitchen, she heard the mingled laughter of Mrs. Henshaw and Marcus DeGrey. Her hand on the door, Adela paused. She didn't want to be late, so she steeled herself, pulled in a ragged breath, and trudged inside.

Marcus was saying, "Nan will be very pleased to find this treasure of sweets awaiting her." He leaned over and kissed the woman's wrinkled cheek. "Ye are a rare talent."

The cook's hand came up and cupped his cheek. "Marcus, ye shall always be me little lad. Come waddlin' into me kitchen every day for a sweet." Her eyes watered. "Cute as a kitten."

Adela looked on, embarrassed to interrupt the touching scene. She was about to step back when Marcus took the old woman into a gentle embrace.

"Ye have always been like a mother to me."

As he turned, he saw Adela. His eyes were moist, but he didn't shy away from her gaze. He released the woman and patted her shoulder.

"Thank ye for this wonderful display for Nan. Her arrival should be before the noon hour." He nodded in Adela's direction and left the room.

Mrs. Henshaw wiped her eyes with the corner of her apron. "Good mornin'. Hope ye slept well."

"Yes, ma'am." Adela tied on her apron and began looking over all the things they'd baked the previous day, now displayed on the vast worktable. "I think you've made a feast fit for a princess."

"No, Adela. *We* did. Nan will love the things ye did create for her. Never seen the likes of a cake with a name written upon it. Shall send her into one of her happy fits."

A chuckle left Adela. "What's a happy fit?"

The woman presented Adela with a look of amusement. "Much like your gurls did when I telt them they had a day from their chores—except Nan be near five."

"I see your point," Adela mused. The sight of Marcus DeGrey holding the older woman with affection seared in her memory. The man was an enigma.

101

"Me dear, will ye please help me cover the treats?" Her eyes warmed with fondness. "When me boy wanted a peek at them, I could not telt him no."

"I'd be happy to." Adela retrieved a cotton tablecloth, and together they covered the food, then returned to their tasks.

Adela peeled and chopped vegetables at the kitchen's long worktable when Kellie came in. "What are you doing here?" She glanced at Mrs. Henshaw who never looked up from stirring a pot of soup.

"Good day to you, Mrs. Henshaw." Kellie gave an awkward curtsy. "I was wondering if you'd mind saving some table scraps for me. A stray kitten is hanging around, and I want to feed him."

The old cook perused Kellie with interest. "Ye want to feed it?" Her voice held curiosity. "A soft heart for small animals, have ye?" She offered a smile.

Kellie clasped her hands in front of her. "Yes, ma'am. I do."

The cook turned and strode to the opposite end of the worktable.

Kellie leaned toward Adela and whispered, "Have you seen that guy in the stables? I saw him bringing a horse past the brewery. He's the proverbial tall, dark, and handsome—in a rugged sort of way."

Mrs. Henshaw gathered small bits of meat and put them into a chipped dish. "Here. Take this. Will gather more and give them to Adela to bring home at day's end."

Kellie's face brightened. "Oh, thank you, Mrs. Henshaw. You are a dear." She hugged the old woman, bringing a blush to her withered face.

"Oh, go on wit ye." She waved her out of the kitchen just as the door from the hall burst open with a bang.

"Miz Bertie!"

A small girl rushed into the room, arms outstretched and blonde curls bouncing. She launched herself into the woman's embrace.

"Nan, me dear! 'Tis so good ta have ye with us. And ye are no more a mite of a gurl. All growed up ye are." She peppered the child's face with kisses. "Me pet."

Adela tore her gaze from the heartwarming reunion to see Marcus also watching the touching moment, his face relaxed, light grey eyes bright.

Mrs. Henshaw rose, tugged Nan to the table, and lifted a corner of the cloth. Nan's eyes widened, her mouth dropping. "Miz Bertie, did ye make this?" She pointed a small finger at the elaborate cake with swirls of pink icing.

"No, me sweet." The corners of her eyes crinkled. "Mistress Adela made it."

Nan crooned with delight. "Mistress Della?"

Marcus's deep voice sent a tingle through her. "*Adela*, my dear."

She looked at her father with adoration. "*Aa*dela."

"Correct." One side of his mouth lifted into a crooked grin.

Adela had not seen that particular smile before. Amazing how a grin could reveal many emotions. This one was undeniable. Total and complete love without reservation.

No one had ever looked at her that way. A tug on her sleeve grabbed her attention.

"Mistress Aadela, my name is on the cake. Why?" Beautiful round eyes, the color of the Caribbean, peered up at her in awe.

Adela stooped and took the girl's small plump hand. "Well, you see . . . Mrs. Henshaw told me you were coming, and you will now be living here, so I thought I'd make you my special cake. It's reserved for birthdays and special celebrations, but I figured this must be a special occasion for you—" She glanced at Marcus. "—and your father."

The child cocked her head, deep in thought. "But my papa's name is not on the cake, so it must be just for me." Her eyes widened, and she added, "And it's such a big cake. I think we should give some to the poor in the village. After all, we are to give with a large heart and an open hand. Right, Papa?"

Marcus's flowing laugh filled the room. Adela liked the way it sounded—genuine and open.

Adela crouched to her level and patted her strawberry blonde curls. "Yes, I suppose you're right."

"I like ye, Mistress Aadela, yet ye speak most strangely." The sweet face held pure innocence, nonetheless for such a small child she was poised and refined. "From where do ye come?"

The girl's father cleared his throat. "Aye, mistress, please enlighten the child."

Adela noted the inquisitive tone in his voice. Her head swam. She closed her eyes and fought the wave of anxiety, swaying on her haunches. A distant buzz sounded in her ears. When she opened her eyes, Marcus knelt beside her, a warm hand on her shoulder. His gaze held alarm. "Are ye unwell?"

The cook spoke over his shoulder. "The witless thing did not stop for a bite all the day." She handed a small glass to Marcus. "Make her drink this. Shall bring color to her cheeks."

Marcus held the glass to Adela's lips, pressing it until her head tilted, allowing a few drops to trickle into her mouth.

Her hand came up to grip his, controlling the flow of the biting liquid. She sputtered as the fiery drink took hold of her senses, her grip on his hand tightened, face aflame.

"Please forgive me, Nan, Lord DeGrey. Mrs. Henshaw is correct." She struggled to rise. "I have eaten little today, and it has left me dizzy."

"Are ye certain ye shall be well?" He put an arm around her waist, led her to the nearest chair, and eased her onto it. He handed her the glass and gave her a formidable look that demanded obedience.

Her frown did nothing to sway his silent order. She took the glass in trembling hands and sipped. He stood over her until she drank it all.

"Thank you, sir. Your help is appreciated." She glanced at Nan who clung to the cook, gripping her leg, eyes wide. "I'm much better."

"Nan, I will be fine," Adela said. "That'll teach me to skip a meal." She stretched out her hand to the child and wriggled her fingers. Nan ran to her and to Adela's surprise crawled onto her lap and hugged her.

"Nan, my dear, be gentle with Mistress Adela," Marcus said. "She must needs rest. We shall leave her to the care of Mrs. Bertie. Perhaps it would not be amiss for her to partake of this wonderful feast they have prepared for your arrival."

"Oh, aye, please. Mistress *Aadela*, eat as much as ye want, so ye shall be well enough to attend my party. Please?"

Adela peered at Marcus, but her words were for Nan. "No, my dear, I cannot attend. I am a servant. This party is for you and your family. Not the people who work for your father."

Nan's face fell. She looked to her father, pleading in her eyes. "Papa, Aadela must come—and Miz Bertie too." She waved her pudgy arm toward the table. "After all, they did prepare this for me."

"Oh, Nan, ye must see . . ." His words trailed off before he continued, "Of course, they may come. And so shall all the staff. Ye need to become acquainted with everyone and they with ye."

The child squealed and danced around the table, her beautiful curls bobbing.

Mrs. Henshaw replied, "Humph! Marcus, ye cannot be serious. 'Tis not done—this mixin' of classes."

Marcus patted her shoulder. "Now, Mrs. Bertie, there is nothing amiss in this household with the master having a bit of merriment."

She gave him a smile of admiration and left the room, calling over her shoulder. "Adela, best be gettin' some food in that belly of yours. We have a lot of cookin' to do if we are ta feed all the staff."

Nan continued her dance around the table until her father intervened. "Nan, please stop. You make me unsteady with your twirling. Let us see you settled into your room and take a rest. The festivities are not til this eve, and we must allow Mrs. Bertie and Mistress Adela to resume their duties."

The girl nodded. "Aye, Papa." She curtsied to Adela. "Thank ye, Mistress Aadela. We shall see ye this eve." She took her father's hand, and they strode toward the door.

Before they crossed the threshold, she twirled to face Adela. "Thank ye for the loveliest cake. I have seen nothing like it in my entire life."

Marcus chuckled and met Adela's eyes. "After all, she is *very* old."

Adela smiled and reached for the meat pies that she and the cook had made before their world was invaded, but her thoughts were on the precious girl and her handsome father.

CB❧SD

A fine mist accompanied Adela, Kellie, and Leanne to the cottage, flowing around them like a fog. The temperature dropped, and they shivered as they walked, the sun beginning its decent on the horizon.

Kellie held the new kitten in her arms, cooing and rubbing its tawny dappled fur.

Leanne said, "She is adorable. What did you call her?"

"A tortoiseshell." Kellie snuggled the tiny creature closer, eliciting a loud purr. "And, my friend, she'll get rid of your lizards."

"Oh, my sweet kitty." Leanne stroked the kitten's fur. "You are now my new BFF."

Adela petted the kitten. "What did you girls think of Nan? She's a darling child, isn't she?"

They agreed and talked about the party. Marcus's kindness to allow the servants to join them was shocking, and they marveled at the abundance of food prepared by Adela, Mrs. Henshaw, and the kitchen maids.

Leanne asked, "What was the chicken dish Mrs. Henshaw made?" She rolled her eyes back in delight. "It was divine."

"Green chicken."

Leanne grimaced. "Sounds gross."

Adela laughed. "It's the parsley sprinkled on top that gives it the name. Were you afraid you were eating lizard?"

Leanne gagged. "Oh, that's just wrong."

Adela nudged her shoulder. "You know I'm kidding." She looked at the kitten and cringed. "I guess we'll leave that to her."

Kellie raised her brows and speared Adela with a look. "*I* noticed Lord DeGrey's eyes on you most of the evening. You may be right about his assumptions as lord of the manor. Just don't let him intimidate you. Okay?"

Adela gave a sharp nod. "He'll get an earful if he tries anything." Her voice held confidence, but she cringed at the thought of a confrontation. "I'm sorry if the situation causes us any problems."

Leanne frowned. "It's not your fault the man is attracted to you. And you said in this time, it's a common thing and well-accepted in the aristocracy. But it doesn't make it moral."

"No, it doesn't." Adela's eyebrows furrowed. "And I'll be certain to point it out to him should the need arise."

Leanne fisted her hands. "We have your back. Plus, I did have those self defense classes. I'll show him some twenty-first century moves. Take that, Mr. Darcy!"

Adela laughed and put an arm around Leanne. If she had to be stranded in time with anyone, she was glad it was with them.

CR&O

Adela woke the next morning to the sound of whining. *Whining?* She sat up in bed and listened intently, glancing at Kellie and Leanne's empty beds. She slipped into her clothes and darted down the stairs. The girls sat on the floor in front of the fireplace playing with the kitten *and* a puppy.

"Oh, no. What have you done now?" Adela plopped into a chair. "Isn't a cat enough to care for?"

"Adela, lighten up. This little puppy was hanging around with the kitten yesterday, and I guess he found his friend. He was whining at the door this morning." Kellie's eyes were moist. "We couldn't turn him away, could we?"

Leanne said, "No, we're not turning him away. He now has a home with his little tortoise cat." She hugged the puppy, and it attempted to lick her face. "You'll be my hero too if you catch lizards."

Adela rose to prepare breakfast. "You'd better figure out where to keep them while we're at work. They can't run loose in the cottage without supervision." She huffed. "Unless you're willing to clean up the aftermath."

Leanne frowned but nodded.

"Ah, I didn't think so. We don't have long, so you'd better come up with a plan while I make breakfast. And don't forget to hang up your unmentionables you put in to soak last night."

Kellie and Leanne scrambled to take their wash and hang it on the makeshift line near the cottage before taking great care to fashion a bed out of a wooden box and tattered blanket.

Adela smiled at her friends, though it held a touch of sadness. She recognized the importance of something so mundane as caring for stray animals that offered much-needed comfort to them in such a time of uncertainty.

 CXEO

That evening as dusk swiftly approached Adela, Kellie, and Leanne returned to the cottage, the usual fatigue enveloping them, though they attempted conversation.

Leanne nudged Adela. "Nan is smitten with you."

Kellie waggled her eyebrows. "And so is her father."

"Don't joke about such a thing." Adela frowned. "I told you what Mrs. Henshaw said. I'll not have him thinking I am at his beck and call just because I am his employee." She harrumphed and strode ahead of them.

A streak of brown fur sped across her path with something flapping on each side of its mouth. *The puppy?*

Another blur of earth-toned fur slipped by giving chase to the first. "Leanne, is that the bra you hung up this morning?"

"My limited-edition bra!" she screeched and sped after the thieves toward the cottage. "Come back here, you little devils!"

Kellie sprinted after her. "Don't you dare harm them. They're just babies!"

Adela watched the scene play out, fighting the desire to laugh. The thought of a bra as a limited-edition item was the felling blow, and she burst into sidesplitting laughter.

"Ah, the noble art of bickering."

Adela swung around at the sound of the deep melodic voice. Marcus DeGrey leaned against a tree a few feet off the path.

"'Tis quite amusing." He nodded toward the pair chasing the animals. His gaze held hers. "But your laughter is not. 'Tis pleasing."

A shout pulled their attention from one another. Kellie waved the bra like a flag. "I have the special edition bra!"

Leanne groaned. "It's *limited* edition, you moron."

Adela returned her gaze to Marcus, uncertain what to say, and shrugged. "They may not be sisters nor my daughters, but I do love them."

Marcus inclined his head in acknowledgment, and then he hesitated, his expression perplexed. "Mistress Adela, what is a limited-edition bra?"

CAROLE LEHR JOHNSON

Chapter Eleven

The day dawned with rain. Gentle though it was, it put a damper on their plans for a picnic and Bible study by the river on their precious day off.

Kellie stomped her foot. "I am not spending my only free time in this cottage. I have to get outside, or I'll explode."

Leanne sat on the floor in front of the fireplace rolling a ball of yarn for the kitten and puppy to chase. "Well, go explode somewhere else. I'm making the most of it by *not* having to empty and clean chambers pots nor haul heavy buckets of water up a million flight of stairs." She grimaced. "I intend to be a slug and do as little as possible today. At least my laundry can hang in here where these two little monkeys won't carry it across the estate."

Kellie put on her secondhand cloak and pulled the hood up. "I'm going for a walk."

Adela looked up from writing in her journal and pointed to the window. "In this?"

"Yep." Kellie walked out in the drizzle and closed the door. She paused in front of the cottage. "Where to?" She surveyed the rolling hills, vivid with the green of springtime. A horse stood on the rise just left of the manor—no, two horses—with riders. She walked down the path toward the manor, away from the men.

The distinct freshness of the spring rain, a blend of foliage, floral, and herbal elements filled her lungs. It invigorated her, unlike the putrid stench of the brewery. How much longer could she cope with this sense of having no actual purpose?

Her life of helping others was everything to her.

Kellie's thoughts jumbled as she turned over their dilemma of how to return home. Each evening for several weeks, after a grueling day's work, they discussed the possibilities and recreated everything they could remember about that moment from arranging all their items in the same way to sitting in the same chairs. Leanne had written down their every idea and theory, but it had all come to nothing.

Kellie found herself at the edge of the manor's front lawn, facing the hedgerow that blocked the kitchen garden from view. She slipped between the tall plants and walked through the outer gardens toward the stables. If she could only borrow a horse and go for a ride. Rain did not concern her.

A small boy catapulted from the open doorway, a rough sack over his shoulder, his wavy caramel hair floating after him. She took a tentative step into the stable and called out, "Timothy, Martin. Is anyone here?"

A quiet whinny sounded from a nearby stall. The scent of manure and hay filled her senses as she strode over to it and peered inside. A beautiful black horse munched on hay, wary large brown eyes examining her.

Kellie stroked the horse's forelock. "You're the loveliest colt I've ever seen." The horse leaned into her hand. She glimpsed his long slim legs. "Look at those fine legs. You're likely to be seventeen or eighteen hands. I bet your sire is tall."

"Aye, so ye know somethin' aboot horses?" The voice was male, low, and cautious.

Kellie turned and saw the man she'd mentioned to Adela. He was even more handsome up close.

"I . . . I was just . . . He's a beauty." She petted the colt's velvet nose and moved away, her bravado returning. "Is there some reason I'm not supposed to be here?" She lifted her chin a notch. "I do work here you know."

He chuckled. "Ye may come anytime ye like. Jest do not go nigh that beast." He gestured toward an enormous horse at the back of the stable. "He is sure to take a plug from your arm."

"I've seen Lord DeGrey on him. He doesn't seem so mean."

He wrinkled his brow and crossed his arms over his broad chest. "So, ye have watched the master ride, have ye?"

Kellie drew back. "Well, no. I've just seen him ride by the cottage a time or two."

The man relaxed his stance, face reflecting understanding. "Oh, aye, so ye are one of the new sarvants at the manor?" He gave a slight bow. "I am Stanton Yorke, manor steward."

Kellie curtsied. "Kellie Welles."

Their gazes held a moment until Kellie broke the contact.

Stanton leaned against the nearest stall and pinned her with a questioning stare. "So, Mistress Welles, what do ye do at the manor?"

She frowned. "I work in the brewery."

He laughed. "I take it ye are not pleased with the task?"

"Ha! To say the least. It's the most horrendous job ever. How anyone can drink that gross liquid is beyond me." She clutched her middle in mock disgust. "Just knowing what's in it makes my stomach churn."

His deep laugh filled the stable, white teeth flashing. The horses whinnied in their stalls.

Kellie put her hands on her hips and glared at him. "What's so funny?"

Stanton's dark grey eyes crinkled at the corners, holding her captive. "'Tis humorous ye feel thus when many find it so pleasin'. They never question what it does contain."

"Well, I put nothing in my mouth until I know what it's made of. That's just common sense. Don't you think so, Mr. Yorke?"

A crack of thunder sounded close, and Kellie jumped.

Rain gushed down in sheets, and a blast of wind drove a wave through the door and drenched them, Stanton catching most of it on his back. Kellie sputtered as it hit her in the face, soaking her hair. She was thankful her dress wasn't saturated since her chemise was drying at the cottage. The glint in Stanton's eyes was still there when she looked at him. He stepped to a cabinet on the far wall and returned with a towel. She thanked him and dried her face and hair.

116

"Afore we were rudely interrupted, I do believe ye were telling me the disadvantages of the brewery—and the drink ye do make there." He gave her a charismatic grin and continued in a buttery voice, "So I take it ye have not sampled the brew?"

"Absolutely not." She grimaced. "Do you mean you actually *like* it?"

The rain grew louder. She didn't hear his response, though she attempted to read his lips. Dangerous move. He had nice lips.

He moved closer and spoke into her ear, "Mistress Welles, would ye like a proper tour of the stables?"

She stepped back and bumped into the stall gate, startling the horse. "No. No, I think I should get home before the rain worsens."

The rain grew deafening. She cringed.

"No, I think not. Ye shall sure be drowned before ye arrive." He pointed to an open door. "Ye can dry and rest there, and remove yourself from the odor, until the rain slackens. I would not want ye to catch your death on the walk home."

Kellie protested, but when she looked out, the rain was a proper waterfall. She agreed and allowed him to lead her.

"'Tis my office for record-keeping. Make yourself at home. I need to care for my horse after the long ride. There's drink there." He pointed to a beautiful stained cabinet against the far wall, polished to a high sheen. "Help yourself." He closed the door behind him.

It was a snug office with a brick floor, paneled walls, a desk and chair, and two comfortable-looking chairs facing the walnut desk. *Cozy.*

Kellie went to the cabinet and surveyed the drinks, sniffing each decanter. Most reeked of pungent alcohol, the nasty stuff she was making, or paint thinner—except one. It had a slight woodsy scent to it, not alcoholic. She took a pewter cup from the shelf and poured enough for a sample. It wasn't bad and definitely wasn't fermented. She filled the cup and made herself comfortable in a chair facing the desk, her gaze taking in the room. A few paintings of landscapes with horses and their riders graced the walls. A tiny unlit fireplace was tucked into an alcove near the desk.

The back of the chair rose high, so she rested her head against it, suddenly weary. Where had the day gone?

Frustrated at her loss of freedom and the inability to use her true profession, fatigue claimed her. Eyes slowly blinking, she drew in a deep breath which brought the pleasant scent of rain, eyelids fluttering shut.

The door creaked, and Kellie jumped, the empty cup clattering to the floor. Stanton's solid form filled the doorway.

"Sorry ta keep ye waitin'. Marcus brought his horse back, and I had to attend him." He retrieved the cup and placed it on the desk. "Would ye like more?"

Kellie smoothed her skirt and instinctively patted her hair into place. "No. I should be going. Has the rain stopped?"

"Aye, 'tis but a light mist at present. Your cloak shall be enough to see ye home dry." He stepped aside, so she could pass but touched her arm. "Would ye want a tour?"

Before she could stop herself, Kellie blurted out, "Yes, but I'd like to ride too. Would that be possible?" She stammered, "I mean if Lord DeGrey doesn't mind."

Stanton studied her face. "Aye, 'tis possible. No need to ask. Ye may ride one of my horses."

"You own horses *here* at the manor?"

"Aye." He lifted a dark brow. "Is that strange to ye?"

"Well . . . I mean, you're an employee of Lord DeGrey's. Doesn't that make a difference?"

"No. As long as I take care of me own horses."

"Then I accept. It'll be a while before my next day off. What time should I be here?"

"Early is best. Shall give us more time." He added, "Unless ye care to ride after your duties at day's end. 'Twould be dark but with a new moon the evening would be a fine one."

Did she detect a twinkle in his eye?

"No. Day is better, so I may admire the countryside." At least, she wouldn't have to worry about being pressured into something like Adela. After all, Stanton Yorke was not lord of the manor but a paid servant just like her.

೮౩ೞೞ

Adela, Mrs. Henshaw, and Clarissa chatted amiably while working at various tasks. Mrs. Brimberry entered the kitchen and stopped in front of them with hands folded demurely at her waist.

"Mrs. Henshaw, I am sorry to put ye in a predicament by relieving ye, although temporarily, of one of your help." She cleared her throat. "Miss Winthrop, Nan's governess, has left us to be wed, which was expected, but Lord DeGrey has yet to find a replacement."

Mrs. Brimberry turned to Adela. "Lord DeGrey has noticed

the fondness the child has for Mistress Adela and asks she divide her time between her kitchen duties and Nan's care."

Adela stopped peeling potatoes. She was to care for Nan? Did the request hold an ulterior motive?

"A maid will assist the child in dressing for the day and take her down to break her fast with her father. They shall pass the morn together, so Adela may continue to help in the kitchen." She pulled in a deep breath. "Adela, ye shall guide the child with her schooling. Miss Winthrop has left ye a list of duties and the complete schedule for each day, therefore I shall not go on." Mrs. Brimberry paused and looked a question at Adela. "Well, what say ye?"

"Um, I . . . Mrs. Brimberry, I have only—"

"Ye have only . . . *what*?" Mrs. Brimberry's voice rose to a higher pitch on the last word.

"I will do as instructed," Adela quickly added.

The housekeeper's face relaxed. "I am pleased to hear it. Go to the small parlor to collect Nan and make haste to the school room. When her lessons are complete, escort her to Lord DeGrey's study where he will await ye. Ye may then return here."

Adela nodded, but Mrs. Brimberry was not finished. She chewed on the inside of her lip, a malicious glint in her eyes. "Ye must needs go to the attics now as the morning sun will light the room and retrieve some items for the school room. I do believe there is a box of implements of use to ye in instructing the child. Ye shall find the box in the furthermost corner from the stairs. Take Clarissa with ye, so ye may have assistance."

She added, "Clean everything well, and once ye settle Nan into her first lesson take into account the list the governess left. Your schedule of the day accompanies it. Carry it with ye as a reminder of when and where ye shall need to be each day." She sent them a condescending glance and exited the room without waiting for confirmation.

"*Pfft!*" Mrs. Henshaw exclaimed. "'Tis a fine mess. How shall I make do?"

Adela dropped onto a stool and met the cook's gaze. "Oh, my word. I don't know how to teach a small child. I've never been a mother nor an aunt."

Clarissa chimed in, "Oh, but Mistress Adela, Nan loves ye. Shall not be a problem teachin' her because she be a sweet child and all."

Adela patted the girl's shoulder. "Thank you for the vote of confidence, Clarissa. I appreciate it."

The girl gave her a curious stare.

"What?" Adela asked. "Did I say something wrong?"

"No, ma'am. 'Tis just ye do speak strangely."

The cook told her, "Gurl, do not be rude. 'Tis that she be from Amurika."

"My apologies. No disrespect meant."

"I wasn't offended. Honestly." Adela received a bright smile in return, though it did nothing to quell the increasing uneasiness of her new task. She wiped her hands on her apron, considering removing it when she realized the attic would be dusty and left it on. "Shall we go and see what supplies Mrs. Brimberry wants us to find?"

Clarissa spun to face Mrs. Henshaw. "Sorry ta leave ye."

121

The girl curtsied.

Mrs. Henshaw dismissed them, and they made their way to the attic, chatting amiably until they reached the narrow stairs leading to the uppermost floor of the manor. Clarissa's eyes flickered nervously from side to side.

"Are you all right?"

The girl stuttered, "Aye, mistress. Fair afraid of what does lie there." She wrung her hands. "There be tales of ghosts and such."

Adela placed a comforting hand on her shoulder. "Nothing to be afraid of. God will protect us."

Her words appeared to comfort the girl as they entered the dimly lit area. Adela made her way to the corner where Mrs. Brimberry said the box would be located. After a few minutes of peeking inside wooden boxes, they found the supplies. Propped next to the box was a large portrait partially covered with a heavy cloth, revealing one side of a woman's face.

Clarissa went to recover the painting but instead the cloth fell to the floor. She gasped. A raven-haired woman stared back, her features mirroring those of Nan. A distinct slash cut across her face as if sliced with a razor-sharp blade.

☾☆☽

Adela located the small parlor near the kitchen and knocked. A maid opened the door and gestured her inside. After Adela entered, Lord DeGrey met her gaze. In mid-curtsy, Nan bolted from her seat and threw her arms around Adela's waist, nearly toppling them both.

"Mistress Aadela! I am so delighted to see ye." The sweet face peered up at Adela, blue eyes wide and twinkling with joy.

"And even more delighted ye shall be my teacher."

Lord DeGrey stood upon her entrance, a move Adela found odd since she was a mere servant. He signaled for her to take a seat at the table.

"I am sorry, but Nan has not finished. I feel she is growing and must needs a small meal at mid-day. She has chattered incessantly and glanced every other moment to the door awaiting your arrival."

A glimmer of humor touched his handsome face. "Not that I do not love the sound of her musical voice, yet perhaps ye shall instruct her to moderate her speech while dining."

Adela smiled, sat next to Nan. While the child ate, Adela took in the room's décor. Lovely shades of blue with cream accents lent the space a calming, restorative ambience. Fresh white daisies graced the center of the table, and wide windows overlooked the front lawn and drive, a perfect vantage to observe a visitor's approach.

"Mistress Adela," Lord DeGrey said, and she hesitantly met his steady gaze. "Please teach Nan how to properly pronounce your name." He sipped his coffee, its heady aroma permeating the room.

"I will, my lord." Adela looked from his unnerving stare and observed Nan shoveling food into her mouth.

Marcus sighed. "Nan, please do not gobble food like a wild beast." He gave Adela a longsuffering look. "I am uncertain what that governess did teach my daughter, for it was most assuredly not table manners."

"I understand. She is only a little girl, but she will learn."

He stood. "I am certain ye are a patient woman and have

given evidence of it thus far. I am sorry to depart, but I must needs meet with the steward." He kissed Nan's cheek. "Ye be a good girl. Do not give Mistress Adela any troubles, or I shall hear about it." He gave her an indulgent smile, then presented Adela with a slight bow. "Good morrow to ye."

Adela watched him stride from the room. His lean frame encased in an ensemble befitting his station—black overcoat, white shirt tucked into buff trousers, and tall black boots. Yet, he wore none of the preening wigs of this time nor the lace cuffs, likely a rebellious move among his fashionable peers—as in the painting they'd seen on the tour.

A twinge of admiration fluttered within her.

A small hand waved in front of her face. "Mistress Aadela. I called your name many times." Her eyes widened. "Were you looking at Papa?" She squinted. "'Tis all right. He is quite handsome. My governess said so often."

Adela laughed and hugged the child to her, though the mention of what the governess said struck her. Had their relationship gone beyond her duties to Nan?

⊗⊗⊗

The sun barely met the horizon, and Kellie marveled at how her luck had changed that day after a fire erupted at the alehouse and allowed her an unexpected day off. Smells of horse, hay, and leather met her at the door of the stables. Over her shoulder the coming light rose above the manor roof, bathing it in an ethereal glow. She sought out Stanton among the stalls with more than a little trepidation.

She jumped at the sound of his voice and turned to face him. "Good morrow to ye. What brings ye to the stables this morn, mistress?"

"We say 'good morning' in America," Kellie told him, then wondered if that was correct in seventeenth-century America. She made a mental note to ask Adela.

"Aye." One side of his mouth lifted. "Good mornin' to ye then."

Was he mocking her? His smile was unreadable.

"I happen to have a day off and was wondering if you'd be up for our ride now?"

Stanton smiled. "Aye. 'Tis could be arranged." He moved to prepare two horses and ducked into his office, returning with a basket.

He led the horses out, halted the white mare next to Kellie, and released the reins. The well-trained beasts remained still while Stanton intertwined his fingers and bent low for her to put a booted foot into his hands to help her mount. He sent her a questioning look.

"Are ye ready?" His eyes sparkled with amusement.

Kellie huffed. "Mr. Yorke, do I amuse you? Do you think I cannot ride?"

A flash of irritation crossed his strong features. "No. Am I not allowed to assist a lady onto her horse?"

Kellie shrugged and placed her foot onto his cupped hands and expertly lifted herself to the saddle. When she tried to throw a leg over the horse though, her skirt would not allow it. Her face heated with the realization. She was supposed to ride side saddle. She quickly bent her knee and slipped her leg to rest against the pommel. This was going to be a long day.

Stanton pulled his horse to stand by her and stalled. "Are

ye ready? We shall take it slow at first. 'Til ye get used to your mount." He leaned over to pat the mare on the neck. "She be a fine one. Ye will have no trouble with her."

"I'm not used to riding side saddle, so I need to take it easy for a while."

His mouth parted but morphed into a wide grin, a hint of disbelief on his face. "Aye. Where ye come from do all the ladies ride astride?"

Kellie raised her chin. "Yes." A thought came to her. "I borrowed my brother's breeches, wore them under my dress, and rode every day." She shrugged. "I made sure no one saw me. It was invigorating." She urged her horse on until she was leading Stanton out of the stable yard, the sun now warming her face.

He drew up beside her and tapped the basket tied to his saddle. "We have refreshment, should we be gone the day."

She laughed. "Looks like enough to last several days."

"Aye." His eyebrows rose, a mischievous glint shone in his eyes. He prodded the horse into a gallop and called over his shoulder, "See if ye can keep up, Mistress Welles."

Kellie grinned, his wit pleasing her, and took off after him.

CB₴

As Kellie walked back to the cottage, her mind filled with this new man in her life. She reminded herself she'd be leaving soon—*she hoped*—but why shouldn't she have some male companionship until then?

The memory of Tim kept invaded her thoughts, trying to outshine the handsome steward. She pushed it away and recalled the near perfect day, except for the side saddle. That was near torture. He'd laughed out loud when she'd asked him over their picnic lunch if he could find some breeches that would fit her because she'd never put herself through that again. He told her he'd see what he could do.

When Kellie entered the cottage, a barrage of questions flew at her.

"Kellie Welles, where have you been? We've been worried to death about you," Adela said with a frown.

Leanne's arms were tight over her chest, eyes blazing with indignation. "How dare you keep secrets after all we've been through?"

Kellie heaved a sigh. "After the fire, I went to the stables for a ride."

Leanne narrowed her eyes suspiciously. "Why did you say that with a smile on your face?"

Adela rested her hands on Kellie's slender face and looked her straight in the eyes. "Who were you with?"

Kellie started. "What?"

"You heard me. You were with a man, weren't you?"

Leanne straightened. "Oh, my! I know who it is. It's that guy from the stables. You said he was good-looking."

Kellie couldn't keep from grinning. "Okay. I was with him. We went riding and had a picnic. It was perfectly innocent."

Adela's face paled. She closed her eyes and swayed. "Oh, Kellie. What have you done?"

"I didn't do anything wrong." She gripped Adela's arm and led her to a chair. "What's the matter?"

Adela propped her elbows on the table and massaged her temples. "That's Marcus's steward. Don't you remember he thinks the steward hired us before he left to go north to buy horses?" She shivered. "His name is Stanton, isn't it?"

Kellie nodded, dread coursing through her.

Adela gripped her hand. "When he and Marcus talk, it's sure to come up. Then he'll tell him he had nothing to do with hiring us. What will we do?"

Kellie swallowed hard. She pictured the smiling steward, who had been kind to her. If he discovered their lie, could he become dangerous?

Chapter Twelve

With Nan's lessons completed for the day, Adela returned to the kitchen and put on her apron. Mrs. Henshaw and two maids were chopping, stirring, and doing various tasks. "Well, ladies, what are we making for the evening meal?"

Clarissa slapped a cleaned fish on the worktable with a moist thump and heaved a forlorn sigh. "Mistress Adela, we be havin' more food than the staff can eat."

Mrs. Henshaw gave the girl a menacing stare. "Stop your complainin' and wrap the fennel stalks 'round the fish for the oven." She slapped two more fish onto the table in front of Clarissa. "And mind not ta put them in the oven 'til I says so."

"Aye, ma'am." Her eyes darted from the cook to Adela, one corner of her mouth lifting.

"Mrs. Henshaw, what do you need me to do?"

A thoughtful expression played across her wrinkled face.

"Since you are so good at bakin', try your hand at one of them cakes with writin' on it. Shall impress the master's guests."

"Guests?" Adela asked.

"Aye. Some of his old friends from London sent word of their arrival this eve." She tsked. "Some how-do-ye-do! Not givin' any more notice than that."

"How many guests?"

"There be five, I believe. 'Tis why we be scramblin' 'round like headless chicks."

Adela gathered supplies for the cake and began measuring ingredients. She hesitated when a thought struck. "What do you want written on the cake, Mrs. Henshaw? Is it someone's birthday or another occasion?"

The cook spoke over her shoulder, "'Tis the master's birthday. S'pose his friends thought it right and proper ta surprise him on his special day."

Adela's insides twisted, creating a birthday cake for the lord of the manor intimidated her more than she would've guessed. "But . . . Mrs. Henshaw, it's a special occasion. I don't know if I'm up for the task. Don't you want to find someone more experienced? What about the bakery in the village?"

The woman turned and sent her a peculiar look. "A bakery in Stanton Wake?"

Adela's stomach fell. She'd remembered the bakery in the twenty-first century Stanton Wake. "I'm sorry. I'm just stunned you'd want me to make a cake for such an important occasion."

"After seein' the cake ye made Nan, I know ye will do a fine job of it."

"What should I write on it?"

Mrs. Henshaw shrugged. "S'pose happy birthday?"

Adela's laugh echoed through the room. They turned to stare at her with questioning gazes. She shook off the censure and continued with her task until the cake was in the oven.

Mrs. Brimberry's entrance interrupted preparations for the icing. She cleared her throat to get their full attention. "Excuse the intrusion, but I must needs have assistance with Lord DeGrey's guests. Matilda has become ill and cannot assist with the serving of the meal."

Her gaze met Adela's. "Please dress in one of the serving maid's uniforms and be ready to attend the guests. Ye are aware of the proper way to serve—" The woman furrowed her brows. "—am I correct?"

The wooden spoon froze in mid-stir. "Yes, ma'am."

"Good. Finish what ye are doing, change, and make haste to the dining room." She turned but before reaching the door, stopped, and addressed Clarissa. "You need to change as well." Her heels clicked as she exited the kitchen.

Clarissa's face paled, and she reached for the nearest stool and fell onto it. "Oh no, what ta do?" She wrung her hands, and tears slid down her cheeks.

Adela placed an arm around her. "Don't worry. It'll be fine. Really. All you do is remove a plate, bowl, or glass from their right with your right hand." She straightened and looked down at her with a confident smile.

Beads of perspiration broke out on the girl's forehead. "I shall never 'member that! I be dismissed!"

Mrs. Henshaw grabbed her by each shoulder and gently

shook her. "See here, gurl. Ye got ta stitch yourself together. Ye can do it."

Adela nodded. "Clarissa, you stay there, and we'll have a lesson." She placed dishes in front of her to mimic the table settings and removed things the way she'd told her.

After several attempts, the girl appeared to warm to the duty. She beamed at Adela. "Oh, Mistress Adela, ye are a gem. Would not have been able ta do that with someone who jest telt me about it. 'Tis easy tha way ye showt me. Thank ye."

"My pleasure, Clarissa. You're a natural." She nudged the girl on the shoulder. "I imagine we'll work well together."

Adela wondered if she was trying to convince the girl or herself. The task set before her made her insides stir, and she prayed her knowledge of the time's etiquette proved correct.

◌҉◌

Adela and Clarissa strode into the large dining room and stood shoulder-to-shoulder, giving one another confidence. Mrs. Brimberry directed men to place chairs around the table. She tapped a thin stick against her leg as she watched. When they'd completed their task, they stood back and waited while the housekeeper used the tool to measure the space between each chair, nudging one until it met with her approval.

When she finished her inspection, she told the men, "Ye may depart for now. I shall call when the flower urns are to be brought in." She turned toward the waiting women. "Now, I shall instruct ye."

Clarissa piped up. "Mistress Adela showt me how, ma'am."

Adela poked her in the ribs, but the girl's enthusiasm got the best of her.

Clarissa peered at Adela. "But, Mistress Adela, ye knows how ta do it. No need in Mrs. Brimberry teltin' us agin."

The housekeeper glared at the girl, and she shrank next to Adela, her chin dropping to her chest.

Mrs. Brimberry swung her gaze to Adela. "Is this true, Adela? Ye have taken it upon yourself to instruct her in the art of serving at Lord DeGrey's table." She glared. "Hmm?"

Though her stomach tightened, Adela held her ground and refused to let the woman intimidate her. "Yes, ma'am. I know how to serve and remove dishes."

"We shall see." From the sideboard, she retrieved a plate, utensils, and a glass and brought them to the table. Once arranged, she stepped back and gestured to Adela. "Show me."

The silence in the room could have been dissected with one of Mrs. Henshaw's meat knives.

Adela strode to the table, picked up a plate, stepped away, and returned the plate to the table. She served the imaginary guest from the left. After a brief hesitation, she removed the plate from the right and placed it on the sideboard. While there, she picked up a pitcher, took it back to the table, and poured invisible liquid into the glass on the right. She rejoined Clarissa, her gaze focusing on the mural across the room.

Mrs. Brimberry craned her neck, now an uncomely shade of purple. She turned and created a place setting at the head of the table. When finished, her face had returned to normal. She motioned for the women to join her. "This is how I would like each place setting arranged. Make haste, and I shall return to review your work."

Her heels tapped a tattoo on the polished floor and echoed down the hall, fading like the tension in Adela's stomach.

Clarissa glanced around to see if anyone was listening before turning to Adela. "She do put on airs, our Brimberry."

Adela chuckled. "One day you must tell me her story."

The maid brought a few plates to the table and worked as she asked, "What ye mean—her story?" A plate clinked into place, and she winced.

"Oh, Clarissa. Please do not chip a plate, or Mrs. Brimberry will have our heads on one of those gigantic platters." She gestured toward the sideboard.

The girl laughed and clamped a hand over her mouth.

"Not a pretty picture, is it?"

Clarissa's hand slipped away, and she whispered, "Aye. But what do you mean about her story?"

"Like where she came from? How long has she worked for the DeGrey family?"

She nodded, and as they worked companionably, she spoke in a hushed voice, telling her that Mrs. Brimberry had worked on the estate when Lord DeGrey was a boy, before his father had put them into debt and left the manor abandoned until his death when his son returned to set it to rights.

"Mrs. Brimberry was still livin' in the village, having a hard time of it I was telt, so she came back ta work here."

Adela straightened a plate. "She doesn't seem old, her hair so dark and all."

"Aye, she be a comely woman. Jest too . . ." Clarissa's voice trailed, searching for the right word.

"Pinched?" Adela offered.

Another laugh threatened the maid, but she'd learned her lesson now and quieted it.

By the time she and Adela completed the place settings and gained a nod of indignant approval from the housekeeper, she excused them for a brief respite. Upon their return to the dining room, they were awed by the transformation.

Two huge urns filled with flowers in a rainbow of colors stood guard at the door. Interspersed among them was a variety of greenery, creating a cascade around the rim with the flowers standing tall in the center. Smaller versions of these arrangements graced the sideboards that held enormous platters of food.

Mrs. Brimberry came to their side. "Stand by the sideboard until the guests have entered and been seated. I will signal when to begin service. Do not speak unless spoken to first. Keep your answers brief and respectful. Never say more than is expected of ye." She presented them with a firm, tight-lipped regard and walked away.

Clarissa looked at Adela and mouthed, "Pinched."

It was a struggle for Adela to hold in her laughter, and her shoulders shook for a moment while she bit her lip. She distracted herself by looking at the glittering tablescape before her.

Gold-rimmed crystal glasses sparkled in the candlelight. There were no windows in the room, only walls of beautiful landscape murals painted in soft tones. High-backed dining chairs upholstered in tapestry with gold threads running throughout the design glistened festively, along with the three-pronged forks and their companions.

Adela had to hand it to Mrs. Brimberry. She'd created a magnificent table setting in such a short notice.

A cough captured her attention. She saw Marcus DeGrey enter the room with a lovely, young red-haired woman on his arm, followed by the remainder of his guests, but his eyes were on Adela.

There were nine guests in all. A motley crew of seven foppish men—one much more so than the rest—and two heavily made-up women, including the petite woman Marcus escorted.

Clarissa giggled, and Adela prayed Mrs. Brimberry hadn't heard. She angled her eyes toward the girl who nodded at the peculiar gentleman who wore one of the most outlandish costumes she'd ever seen in any history book. She coughed lightly to suppress her laughter and took in a deep cleansing breath, squeezing Clarissa's arm in warning.

Then, the strangely dressed man in the chartreuse waistcoat trimmed in brilliant blue spoke, "My deeah, Maacus." His tone was slow and nasal. "What could ye have been thinking? Moving to this backwata place in the center of no wheaa." He twisted a lace-cuffed hand in the air. The adornment flapped beyond his fingertips and closely missed taking a swim in his wine glass.

Adela pressed her arms to her sides and bit her lip at the spectacle, getting through the evening would be absolutely impossible. How could she stand it? And poor Clarissa was in the same boat. She was afraid to glance at the girl. If she did, they'd both be in deep trouble.

The housekeeper whispered, "The male servants will pour the wine, but when they finish and stand aside, Adela, go to the sideboard for the first course. Take two plates and begin serving Lord DeGrey and then the person to his right and so forth until all the guests are attended. Return here and await the second course."

A round of laughter sounded from the guests. When Adela peered at Marcus, his mouth tightened, resignation on his face.

The nasal *Mr. Pompous* commanded attention. "Oh, aye, 'tis maavalus, indeed!" He presented a toothy smile, his chin held high, sleeves flapping.

Adela wished she'd heard what displeased Marcus yet made *Mr. P* so happy. As she pondered the absurdity of the situation, her eyes met Marcus's scrutinizing expression. One side of his mouth quirked up as if he'd read her thoughts. He abruptly turned as the woman to his left placed a hand on his forearm.

Clarissa elbowed Adela and gestured in Mrs. Brimberry's direction. Adela discovered the housekeeper was motioning her to serve.

Adela gulped, telling herself she could do it. It wasn't like she was taking a meal to a king but simply delivering food to the table. Servants were invisible. But if she dumped a bowl of hot soup in the lap of the lord of the manor . . .

She closed her eyes for a moment to clear her mind and asked God to help her through it.

Tiny ripples crossed the surface of the broth, the bowls trembling in her hand. When she placed the bowl in front of

Marcus, he whispered, "Adela, please smile. They shall think I beat my servants into submission."

She could only nod and scurry back to serve the other guests.

After she completed the first round and returned beside Clarissa, she blew out a puff of air.

Clarissa leaned in. "What did Lord DeGrey say to ye? Your face is liken ta a tomato."

Adela stilled. "You saw him speak to me? Oh my. What if Mrs. Brimberry did too?"

"Niver fear. No one was watchin' ye but me because they was lookin' at that strange man."

Adela released a breath. "You're right. Thank you."

Clarissa smiled before being summoned to pick up the bowls along with another maid.

Each time Adela served Marcus, she averted her eyes, mortified he'd say something else to upset her poise. The only thing he said was 'thank ye,' each time she served him, but kept his voice low enough for her ears only.

After the last dish was presented, Mrs. Brimberry excused Adela. Not only was she grateful to be leaving the ridiculous Mr. Pompous but also Marcus's unnerving gaze. One minute she was flushed to find his eyes on her, the next she wanted to burst into laughter at the man with his elaborate powdered wig, high-pitched nasal voice, and lacy frills.

The moment she found a place to sit—a well-hidden spot by the entrance to the kitchen—she dropped onto the bench and pulled her boots off. Walking for miles never bothered her, but standing still in one place for so long did her in. She wiggled her toes and arched her feet.

Footsteps interrupted her break. She tried, and failed, to shove a foot into her boot when the steps grew closer.

"Aha."

The toes of shiny black boots stopped inches from her feet. With dread, she brought her gaze up to Marcus DeGrey towering over her.

"Adela, what shall I do with ye?" He crossed his arms over his chest and stood with a self-possessed air. "Ye remain a mystery."

When she found her voice, she said, "I don't know what you mean, my lord." Was this the moment he fired her for laughing at his guest? She'd tried so hard to hide her amusement, succeeding so with Mrs. Brimberry.

A flash of uncertainty flared in his grey eyes.

"I'm so sorry, I would never laugh at your guests, but . . ."

His shoulders quivered, and he laughed.

Startled, she dropped her boot, flinching at the crash it made when it met the floor.

"Your *regard* for Lord FitzJames went unnoticed—except by myself. It seems I have come to read ye quite well." He moved as if to sit beside her on the bench. Hesitating, he regained his position above her.

Adela, realizing she was still shoeless, scrambled to pull her boots on but found her feet had swollen. Heat engulfed her as she struggled to make them fit.

Then, Marcus did a most extraordinary thing—he knelt before her. "Allow me to assist ye." He gripped the boot she held, their fingers touching.

"No." She jerked away from his grasp and said with less force, "No, Lord DeGrey. That would be unseemly. I am but a servant."

"Aye." His eyes held hers. "But 'tis because of me ye have injured feet, waiting upon my guests. And myself." He pried the boot from her, gripped her heel in his hand, and gently placed her foot inside.

Adela's stomach clenched. What was he doing?

He repeated the action with her other boot, placed his hands on his thighs, and asked, "What do ye find the most humorous about Lord FitzJames?"

The warmth of his hands on her feet had distracted her, and she could barely form a sentence. A memory of the lace-adorned sleeves flapping above the wine glass brought a smile to her lips, and she chuckled.

"Please share your thoughts. I find a great deal amusing about the man. He is a fop and a dolt. And that is a kindness."

Adela looked a question at him.

"He does trust by dressing in the latest fashions of men he is superior—no matter how ridiculous his appearance—and he is foolish in both deed and thought."

She grinned, a touch of mischief claiming her. "'Tis a *maavalus* explanation, my good fellow!"

Marcus released a full-throated laugh.

Adela's eyes widened, and she clasped her hand over her mouth. "I'm so sorry. I shouldn't have said that about your friend."

He patted her hand. "He is no friend of mine, my dear. Lord FitzJames insinuates himself upon any unsuspecting person of the nobility without invitation, within the whole of the kingdom. Good manners, being what 'tis, most refuse him not. If given any hint of his impending arrival, they hide in their chambers and instruct the servants to announce they are away."

It was Adela's turn to laugh. "I can't say I blame them." Her hand warmed where his still lay atop hers. They looked down simultaneously and pulled apart.

She cleared her throat. "I suppose I'd better see if Mrs. Henshaw needs anything further before I go home." She rose and he followed, standing too close for comfort.

"Good eve, mistress." He studied her face. "I am pleased to have found ye alone, so I might reassure ye all is well. Now, I must needs depart to see what birthday surprise I am to feign delight in from my uninvited *friend*s. I suppose they are in the parlor drinking all of my spirits as we speak." He bowed and turned to leave, then faced her. "Thank ye for taking such excellent care of Nan. I do believe she is smitten with ye."

Again, he turned, and she could've sworn he whispered, "As am I."

CB&O

Lord DeGrey had insisted on a footman escorting Adela to the cottage since night had fallen. Her thoughts went to the missed lessons with Nan, the attention from Marcus, and the preening man at dinner. When she arrived at the cottage, the door stood open with Kellie and Leanne peering out, the golden light from candles spilling onto the path.

141

Martin and Timothy shut the gate behind them and nodded in greeting to Adela. She approached the door, and Kellie asked, "Must've been some dinner if you're just now getting home. What did they make you do?"

Leanne relieved Adela of the basket and plunked it on the table to peek inside. "Wow. This looks great. Leftovers?"

Adela slid onto the settle by the fire and removed her boots, reliving the sensation of Marcus's hand on her foot. Her face warmed as she answered Leanne, "Yes. Mrs. Henshaw insisted. I suppose it'll be okay to have as leftovers for a day or so. It's mostly pies and breads." She moaned in relief as each boot slipped to the floor. "By the way, what were Timothy and Martin doing here?"

Leanne and Kellie shared a mischievous look.

"Well?"

Kellie told her, "Mrs. Henshaw gave us cookies, so we gave them to the boys—" She cleared her throat. "—for killing and cleaning a chicken, chopping firewood, and fetching water."

Adela could not hide her amusement. "Cookies—for all that work? You should be ashamed."

Leanne said, "Well, we kinda told them we'd give them a few coins from our pay too."

"You two are incorrigible." Adela smiled and added, "But pretty smart."

With a laugh, they led Adela to the table and served her roasted chicken, vegetables, and freshly boiled and cooled water. She settled back and told them all about the formidable Lord FitzJames, though she did not dare tell them about Marcus.

Chapter Thirteen

Leanne secured her makeshift face mask before gripping the handles of two buckets. She skirted the outer east wall along the path from the manor to the privy pit. Her teeth clenched and she shivered as she contemplated the contents of her burden, thankful they were covered with heavy fabric. She moved with greater care as she set them on the path to rest her aching arms.

The daily trip began as soon as she arrived at work. Her breakfast having digested on their walk to the manor was a blessing. Although, this chore did stop any desire to eat for hours. She'd lost weight, something she'd never struggled with—always maintaining her ideal weight for a five-foot, three-inch frame.

The thunder of horse's hooves exploded from the edge of the forest. A massive chestnut erupted from the trees and reared, front hooves dangerously close to her face. Her attention went to the buckets, grateful she no longer held them. She screamed and dropped to the ground, covering her head with her arms.

A man's voice swore with feeling. The thump of booted feet moving toward her with quick, firm steps drew her gaze up to peer into eyes the color of the sky before a storm. He dropped to his knees beside her, straight caramel hair falling across his brow.

"Are ye injured?" He raised a tentative hand toward her. "Please assure me ye are unharmed."

Leanne stared, mouth ajar, eyes wide, and eased to a sitting position, her gaze focused on his. He laughed. A pleasant, lyrical, *beautiful* laugh.

Irritated beyond measure, she narrowed her eyes and exploded. "What are you laughing at you, you thoughtless moron? You could've killed me, and all you can do is laugh?" She stood, brushed the dirt from her skirt, and stomped her foot.

"I know not what a *moron* is, but I deem it not a compliment," he responded, humor still intact, as he looked at her. He rose and clasped both hands behind his back. "I do apologize. 'Twas beastly of me. 'Tis just that your expression was quite comical. Pretty, though comical."

"Do you have a clue what I'm carrying in these buckets?" She pointed to the odious things, her finger shaking franticly. "You'd better thank your lucky stars I had just put them down when you tried to trample me to death!" She sucked in a breath and released it. "If I'd dumped that, that disgusting stuff on me I would've murdered you on the spot." She growled, turned, and marched down the path, leaving the buckets of refuse behind.

The man cleared his throat and called out, "Methinks ye have left your wares behind, mistress."

After a dizzying turn, Leanne glared at him, stalked back to the buckets, and forced herself to pick them up with composure. She muttered under her breath, "Be calm, Leanne. Don't spill a drop of this vile stuff because of this idiot." She refused to look at him as she made her way to the cesspit, the man's dark grey eyes a burned image in her mind.

CR&SO

Kellie stepped into the kitchen at the end of the workday to find Adela removing her apron. "You look beat."

Adela released a sigh. "Yeah. We did a lot of baking for the week, and with the heat outside—and the oven inside—it was a furnace." She wiped a handkerchief over her damp face. "I'm so hot I may take a swim in the *pond*. Would it raise a scandal, Mrs. Henshaw?"

The cook bent over a heap of bread, placing the loaves carefully, one-by-one, into a cotton sack. She cackled. "Gurl, ye would be the talk of the village. Every man in the county would be out walkin' the hills at all hours lookin' fer ye to swim agin. And the vicar would be givin' a lesson outta the pulpit for sure." Her laughter faded, and she frowned. "Ye would not do such a thing, would ye?"

"Well, in my . . ."

Kellie's eyes widened, and she dragged a finger across her throat in warning.

Adela pulled a face. "No, Mrs. Henshaw. I'd not do that.

145

I'm only jesting." She moved to leave with Kellie but turned back. "I've been meaning to ask, Mrs. Henshaw. Why doesn't Lord DeGrey go to church? Do any of the servants attend?"

"Oh, aye, well . . ." The woman avoided Adela's eyes. "He does not go, but some servants do upon occasion." She shoved a stubborn loaf into the bag. "I attend when able."

It was obvious she was uncomfortable discussing the subject. They bid her good evening and stepped out into the fresh, warm air.

Kellie turned to Adela. "I'm going to the stables for a bit, so I won't be walking home with you and Leanne."

Adela's brows rose, and her eyes narrowed.

"I'm going to check on a mare about to foal." Kellie stepped onto the path. "I want to see if the mare is doing all right. This is her first colt, and Stanton is a little concerned. He wants my help should something go wrong. After all, I did tell him about my experience with horses."

Adela's mouth was a grim line. "I understand, but I don't think your association with him is a good idea. You just got out of a long relationship. I don't want you to get hurt again." She shrugged. "And we don't even know how long we're going to be *here*."

Kellie's face warmed, thinking of the fateful phone call, her eyes moist. She said in a small voice, "I'm aware of that."

Adela put an arm around her.

Kellie met her eyes. "Thank you for caring. I promise I'll be careful. Although I do find Stanton attractive, I only want to be friends. We both love animals, especially horses, and from what I've seen, he's a kind man."

Adela lightly squeezed Kellie's shoulders. "Please be careful with your heart. It is a fragile thing that breaks easily."

They shared a knowing look and parted company at the kitchen gate just as Leanne crept up, her face wearing a *I just lost my last friend* expression. Kellie waved to her, then heard Leanne ask, "Where's she going?" She didn't wait for Adela's reply.

A few moments later, the sound of male voices reached her as she arrived at the entrance to the stables.

"When will he arrive?" Stanton asked.

"This day. I know not when."

Is that Lord DeGrey? Who are they talking about?

Kellie hesitated, reluctant to interrupt. A deep guttural moan sounded.

"What am I to do with him? He is a self-seeking charmer and most assuredly cares much about women and gaming," Lord DeGrey gritted out the words, then his tone changed. "Where is Roman?"

A brief silence followed before Stanton responded, "In the east paddock. I took him there this morn. With the mare about to foal, he was much too restless."

Boots shuffled closer to the stable entrance, and Kellie darted behind the open door.

"Perchance he be visitin' for a brief time then be on his way. Did he say why he comes?"

Lord DeGrey sighed. "His letter said not."

The men now stood a short distance from Kellie's hiding place. After a few parting words, Lord DeGrey strode slowly toward the manor, arms clasped behind his back. Stanton's footsteps shuffled against the straw. Kellie eased from behind the door to entered and bumped face-first into him. She reeled sidelong and landed against the doorpost with a whack. His quick reflexes steadied her, hands gripping her arms. She grimaced as pain shot through her shoulder.

"Are ye all right, lass?" His hands remained on her.

She stretched her neck to one side. "I'm okay. It hurts a little, but I don't believe I've done any damage."

Stanton led her into the stables, used his booted foot to haul a stool closer, and eased her down onto it. "Stay." He strode toward his office. When he returned, he handed her a pewter mug. "Drink."

Kellie sipped with care, uncertain what foul beverage he'd given her. It was not disagreeable and warmed her as it slipped smoothly down her throat. She cradled the mug and peered up at him. "Thank you. It's not . . . unpleasant."

In his smile, she read relief. He dropped to his haunches. "Are ye certain ye are not in pain?"

"I'm fine. Honestly. I'm a nurse after all, so I'd recognize a serious injury."

The moment the words left her mouth, she was aware she'd messed up again. Were there even nurses in this century? Or were they merely *wet nurses*? Oh, no!

His eyebrows pinched together. He opened his mouth to say something, a flash of bewilderment flickering across his face, but he said nothing.

She feigned a headache. "I . . . I may need to go home and take a rest."

Stanton gripped her hands, pulling her up. "Come rest in my office. 'Tis much more comfortable."

She rose and allowed him to escort her to one of the comfortable chairs.

"Rest here for a bit. Keep sippin' that." He walked across the room, lifted the lid of a trunk, and retrieved a rough woven blanket, draping it across her lap. Once he'd arranged it, he sat in the chair across from her. "Ye do appear a mite pale."

She rested against the back of the chair and closed her eyes. "I'll be fine in a few minutes. Please see about the mare. I came to help if you need me."

"If ye are sure it shall be all right to leave ye."

"Yes. Please take care of her." Relief at the sound of his fading bootsteps calmed her. She had to consider what a nurse was in this time and try to repair the damage she'd done by revealing her profession. If only Adela was here to advise her. Kellie closed her eyes and tried to concentrate, but the day caught up with her. Weary, she drifted into blissful sleep.

Splintering cracked the peace. Kellie lurched from the chair. How long had she slept? It seemed only seconds. She shook the cobwebs from her mind, yawned, and left the peaceful confines of the office for the aroma of fresh hay and leather. A soft whinny met her.

"There now, gurl." Stanton muttered softly. "Have a care and not harm your new daughter."

Kellie found him kneeling beside a beautiful sable filly, rubbing her dry with clean straw, the mare on the other side licking the newborn. Such a heart-warming sight. Was she thinking of the horses or Stanton? She took a step back and unsettled an empty bucket. He turned toward the noise.

"Have a good rest? I could not bring myself to wake ye. Ye did appear weary."

Kellie blew out a breath. "That's very kind of you. Yes, it has been a tiring day. How long was I asleep?"

"Oh, aye. Ye were gone for nigh on two hours."

She peered out the door and found the sky lit with stars one rarely saw in the twenty-first century. Well-lit cities and their pollution blotted out the beautiful night sky God created.

"Sorry. I didn't mean to sleep at all. I really should go home. Adela and Leanne will be worried." She turned to leave when the crunch of hay underneath boots garnered her attention. His calloused hand halted her departure, and she looked down at the sun-bronzed skin. Most women in her time would kill for that tan. Her gaze had no trouble sliding up to meet his. Was Adela right? Had she grown too attracted to him?

Oh, good grief, Kellie. Get a grip.

She pulled away. "I really must go. I'm so glad the mare is okay, as well as her newborn. I'll look in on them tomorrow." Her legs wobbled, and she forced strength enough to sprint into the night.

◈

Leanne pored over the papers littering the cottage's table, one elbow resting on its surface with fingers entwined in her hair. She tapped the pen against her chin and looked up at Adela. "Addie, this is like a Rubik's cube. I'm so frustrated I want to toss all of it in the fire."

Adela brought her gaze from the stove. "You only call me Addie when you are at the end of your wits. Why?"

Leanne heaved a sigh. "I have no idea. Maybe it's my subconscious throwing out a signal for help." She pulled a face and returned to her work.

"I wonder if we should reenact, one more time, exactly what we were doing at this table when we were transported here." She held up a paper with a sketch of where items were on that fateful day.

The door flew open on a burst of wind, and Kellie stormed inside. She slammed the door and leaned against it, her face flushed. "Oh my gosh! What was I thinking?" She struggled to untangle her cloak from her shoulders, smashed it onto the peg by the door, and dropped into a chair next to Leanne.

"What's got you in such an uproar? Addie—" She threw Adela a smirk. "—told me you were going to the stables to see that hunk of a man."

Adela stiffened. "I said no such thing."

Kellie glared at Leanne. "You're unbelievable." She picked up a handful of papers and waved them in Leanne's face. "By the way, what the heck are you doing?"

Leanne grabbed the papers, tapped them into an even order, and stacked them with the others. "I'm trying to find a way home, you dolt."

"Oh, is that Leanne's new word-of-the-century?" Sarcasm dripped from each of Kellie's syllables.

Leanne rose, hands flat on the table, and shoved her face into Kellie's space. "Why, you . . ."

Adela stepped in and pressed Leanne's shoulder, forcing

her back into her seat. "We're all on edge. I've lost count of how many weeks we've been here, and it's getting old. But we have to stick together and get along. She brought her gaze to Kellie. "What has got you in such a dither?" She raised her arm and pointed. "You were itching for a fight the moment you came through the door."

Kellie's head fell, tears darkening her bodice. "I'm so sorry. To both of you. I've messed up, and we may be burned as witches." She sobbed into her hands.

Leanne grimaced. "What are you talking about?" She hesitated. "And I'm sorry I called you a dolt." She shoved Kellie on the shoulder playfully. "I don't even know what it means. I overheard one of the chambermaids call Christopher one."

Kellie asked, "Christopher? How did you learn about him?"

Leanne glanced at Adela. "All I know is he's Lord DeGrey's younger brother, and he's come for a visit. Apparently, he's quite a looker but a real womanizer." She shrugged. "So, I guess a dolt would be a jerk of some sort."

"No, a dolt is an idiot." Adela sat by them. "So what have you done that's so horrific to get us burned at the stake?"

Kellie's gaze inspected the tabletop. "When I was going into the stable, I overheard a conversation between Stanton and Lord DeGrey and didn't want to interrupt. I hid behind the door against the stable and waited until they finished." She halted. "I just realized what you said about Lord DeGrey's brother, Christopher. They were talking about him. Marcus said he was a self-seeking charmer, who loved women and gambling."

Leanne huffed. "Guess calling him a dolt was accurate enough."

She resumed her confession. "Anyway, when he left, I went into the stables, ran headfirst into Stanton, and hurt my shoulder. He was concerned, and when I tried to reassure him, I slipped up and said I would tend to it since I am a nurse." She rubbed her shoulder. "He had the strangest expression on his face and started to say something, then stopped."

Kellie brought her gaze to meet Adela's. "What *is* a nurse in this century?"

Leanne watched the exchange, wide-eyed, taking it all in. She knew as little as Kellie did about this century. Before Adela could answer, a thought came upon her with such force, she stood and looked down at them. "Could he be the jerk who nearly killed me this morning?"

Both women stared at her in surprise. Adela pulled her back to her seat and asked, "What? The man on the horse you told me about?"

"Yes. If that's who it is, he's everything the chambermaid told me, plus what Kellie overheard in the stables." She placed her hands on her waist. "He thinks he's Mr. I-Got-It-All-And-More, too good-looking and charismatic for his own good. He laughed at me."

Kellie frowned. "What are you grumbling about?"

Adela patted Kellie's arm. "She told me on our walk home a horse bolted out of the woods and nearly ran her over. I'll dish up dinner while she tells you." She resumed the meal preparation and tossed over her shoulder, "Will you please clear the table while you discuss the jerky Christopher?"

Leanne nodded. "I'll be glad to tell you about the idiot. I actually called him a moron and an idiot, and he didn't know what a moron was. Can you believe it?" She kept up her tirade until Adela served them.

Kellie said, "I'd still like to find out if we're headed to the stake." She glared at Leanne. "But who could find out with the diatribe that has raged on about Christopher DeGrey. It may not have been him. Lord DeGrey said he didn't know when he would arrive. If you saw the man early this morning, surely it couldn't have been Christopher. Where would he have been all day?"

Leanne blew out a deflated breath. "Hmm. Maybe you're right. I won't jump to conclusions. Okay. Back to Kellie's question about nursing."

Kellie glanced at Adela, who said, "I imagine you're okay. Nurses at this time mostly took care of the insane and those who had the plague or smallpox. That's probably why he shot you a strange look."

Leanne howled. "He may be afraid you'll infect him." She grabbed her sides, shaking with laughter.

Kellie relaxed and smiled. "I'm sure glad we have you to keep us informed, *Addie*."

An hour later after dinner was cleared and laughter dissipated, the latter doing them all a world of good after so much stress and weariness, they again settled at the table with all of Leanne's research spread before them.

Adela pointed to the sketch of the placement of items. "What's this one, Leanne? I can't quite make it out."

Leanne squinted, held the paper closer to the candle, and huffed. "This light is so awful. It's a wonder these people don't go blind at an early age."

"They usually went to bed at dark and rose at dawn." Adela yawned. "Let's go to bed. The *orange of daylight* comes way too early."

Kellie asked, "Where did that saying come from? It's odd."

Leanne nodded in agreement, a rare occasion with her.

Adela shrugged. "My grandmother used to say it. Methinks we should call it a night, shall we?" She rose, gave them an awkward curtsy, and laughed. "Even my curtsy is off-kilter."

Leanne sent her a sympathetic look, but Kellie said, "You may have been born for this century after all. For such a time as this."

Adela gave a weary nod and trudged upstairs.

The words struck Leanne. *She* was certainly not born for this century. She missed her family and friends, technology, a hot shower, her car, and Starbucks. She surveyed her papers again in the waning light and prayed for God to show them the way home.

CB&D

Adela knelt by the herb garden on the east side of the manor. The aroma of fresh herbs always took her to another place. But now, it was to another *time*. She couldn't discern what to make of the reason God had brought the three of them there.

Her eyes closed as she contemplated their destinies. What was to become of them? She didn't dislike her day-to-day routine. Cooking and baking were her life, and teaching Nan was a delight. Yet, the long strenuous days were difficult.

Adela's thoughts strayed as she mulled over the past. Marcus's face forced itself into her mind's eye, which set her to questioning past relationships. She'd always tended to rush things rather than savor each experience. She dove into attraction and abandoned all caution. Since coming to Christ, that flaw in her character had faded. Afterward, she'd been attracted to men, but her senses had been keener. Her standards had been raised, but no man had measured up.

Her shoulders rose and fell on a sigh as she clipped several herbs for drying. Mrs. Henshaw had given her permission to take them back to the cottage. The dried herbs they discovered when they first arrived at the cottage were diminishing quickly.

The lavender, rosemary, and mint in the basket reminded her of Leanne's complaint everything in the seventeenth century smelled bad. She laughed as her gaze glided to meet the horizon scattered with amber-tinged clouds.

Adela stared at the pure beauty before her, praising God for all He'd created. "Thank you, Lord. I don't know why I'm here, but You have Your reasons. They're not for me to comprehend—or to question."

She finished her task and strode toward the kitchen to continue her morning duties before Nan's lessons began. The quiet reprieve of sitting and teaching Nan and not standing on her feet for so long was a welcome break. And she did care for the sweet child.

Her face was filled with such wonder at discovery. She loved to learn about anything Adela suggested. She prayed Nan would not lose her zest for knowledge. And the girl did adore her father.

Adore—this brought back the word *smitten* to her memory. Marcus had said Nan was smitten with Adela, then his whispered words returned to her, *"As am I."*

CঔৰৎD

Marcus DeGrey sat at his desk in the study and shoved the stack of leather-bound ledgers away, sliding them to the edge of his polished mahogany desk. He pressed his thumbs against his temples and massaged away the building tension.

Beams of sunlight danced through the long row of windows and across the Turkish rug in front of the desk. His gaze moved from the light spilling into the room. He was torn between the drudgery of accounts or a ride on Roman over the rolling hills in the fresh air.

Marcus rose and strode to the row of windows which spanned the entire east wall of his study. He clasped his hands behind his back, peering out at the garden. Since his arrival at the manor, he had worked diligently to bring the estate back to its former glory. His father had left it on the precipice of decline. At the least, he'd confessed and sought forgiveness from Marcus—and God. The only advice he offered to Marcus on his deathbed was to restore the manor, which spurred Marcus to do just that. For his sake as well as for Nan.

The winter had been mild, and they continued to prosper. Stanton had been a tremendous help, as his father predicted and suggested. Then why was he now so restless? After his mother's death, his father slipped into despair and sought solace in drink and gambling. Marcus dealt with his own grief of his mother's death and his brief failing marriage. He had been young and headstrong, ending up pressed into service while overindulging at a tavern in Plymouth, and found himself in Barbados.

Escape had not been easy, but he found his way back. Upon his return, he was met with a letter from his wife saying she had left him—and their daughter. A daughter he was not aware existed. The child was with a governess at their London townhouse.

His image reflected in the glass and made a mockery of him and how he had spent his life. Movement outside shifted his attention to the herb garden. Adela strolled to the plants and knelt. He watched while she clipped herbs and placed them in a basket. She brought the clippings to her nose each time and closed her eyes as if savoring the scent.

The morning sun glinted off the auburn streaking through her brown hair. When the clouds shifted and left amber trailing the sky, her gaze eased upward. Her words caught on the breeze and drifted through the other window, which was open. Her prayer and his image in the glass collided, the mocking resuming. Her faith was evident from the women's talk of Scripture in the meadow by the river to her prayers over meals and now this prayer of thanksgiving to God.

Marcus's thoughts flew to another time in his life before Nan was born and gave him purpose. What kind of man had he been? What kind of man was he now? He'd long since abandoned God—just as God had abandoned him.

His attention returned to Adela. She rose from her undertaking, a secretive smile on her lips. Her perfect, full, rose-colored lips.

Marcus turned and strode to his desk, dropping into the

chair and jerking an account book from a stack. He slammed it down in front of him and began fitfully turning the pages. "Dullard!" he reprimanded himself.

What was wrong with him?

He'd flirted with her shamelessly, and it must stop. She was in his employ. He was no addlepate. Then, why did he act thus? He must needs go for a ride. Aye, that would do.

He had foregone his ride the day before after he and Stanton had discussed his brother's pending arrival. But he would do so now.

Just as Marcus was about to rise to leave the study, a knock sounded at the door.

"Enter," he called out in irritation.

The door creaked open, and a tousled honey-colored head popped around. The wayward had returned.

"Good morrow, brother."

Adela stopped, in awe at what lay before her. Each time she entered this sanctuary, she had the same overpowering sense of belonging and comfort, the smell of leather, paper, and beeswax surrounding her. The library housed hundreds of books from floor-to-ceiling and wall-to-wall.

Her cloth floated from shelf to shelf, pausing often so she could take in the gilded titles. She gasped and trailed her finger lovingly along the spine in reverence—*First Folio*, a collection of Shakespeare's plays. It was a first edition from 1623. *Incredible.*

When she reached one of the long tables, the massive Bible

spread open before her on a pedestal, opened to the Psalms. It was published in 1611. She always saved it for last, so she could stop and read for a minute. Psalms was one of her favorite books of the Bible.

The squeak of the door startled her.

Nan stepped into the room and dipped an adorable curtsy. "Good morrow, Mistress Adela."

Before she could respond, Nan lifted her skirt and ran out, slamming the door behind her. Moments later, the door creaked open again. This time, Marcus entered with Nan in his arms.

"Adela, did this child come in here, interrupt your work, and slam the door on her way out?" His gaze flicked to the child.

"Yes, my lord. She did come in, curtsied, and left."

His brows rose, and he tilted his chin. "And did she not slam the door with force?"

Adela didn't want to get the girl in trouble, but she couldn't lie. "Yes. But it may have been an accident."

"No. I think not. She came to tattle on ye."

A tear glimmered in the light and slid down Nan's cheek. She turned her face and buried it into her father's neck.

Ah, that my face was there.

Adela straightened, her cheeks heating. Where had that come from? She cleared her throat. "Tattle? For what?" She stepped closer. "Nan, did I do something wrong? Please tell me if I did."

Nan raised her arm and pointed a small finger across the

room and whispered, "You read our family Bible. I heard ye." She jerked her accusing arm tightly to her chest.

Adela looked into Marcus's eyes to find a glint of humor. "Is it a punishable offence?"

The corners of his mouth turned upward. "Indeed. And we do have a witness. The penalty would be severe I do believe."

Nan's head popped up. "Oh, no Papa! Not Mistress Adela."

"Then why, my child, did ye determine to tattle on her?" He eased her away from him, settled her into a nearby chair, and lowered to his haunches. "My dear, ye should never be so swift to pronounce judgment." His slender fingers caressed her cheek. "Do ye understand?'

Her blonde curls quivered with her nod. "One of the maids did tell me it was not proper for a woman to read the Bible."

Marcus peered at Adela, looking a question at her.

She wasn't sure what he wanted, so she knelt beside him. "Nan, I am sorry if I offended you by reading your Bible. It's such a lovely thing and so full of God's promises. I could not resist. Will you forgive me?"

The child nodded.

"Nan, Mistress Adela can read any book in this house she desires. Do ye understand? No one is ever to be forbidden to read. After all, she is your teacher until we find another to replace her."

Nan catapulted to her feet and pressed her hands onto her hips. "We shall never replace her! I love her!" She ran from the room, leaving them to stare at the empty space.

Adela returned her gaze to Marcus, who wore the most unexpected expression—one of admiration.

Chapter Fourteen

Marcus watched his brother as he brought a glass to his lips. "So, my long-lost kin, what have ye been about of late? We have not seen ye for quite some time."

Christopher DeGrey speared a piece of venison with his fork and brought it to his mouth. An impish smile lingered as he chewed.

Marcus surveyed him carefully, attempting to solve the mystery of his wayward younger sibling. The man lacked direction, ambition, and scruples. Was he truly like their father? Had he inherited the deep-seated makings of a man with no character?

Yet even their father had some semblance of virtue. He supposed their mother had a hand in guiding Christopher into ruination as well. Their youngest child had been a surprise to them all, and both parents had coddled and spoiled him shamelessly, even forcing Marcus and Stanton to allow Christopher to tag along as they roamed the countryside, slowing their pursuits.

"Well, brother, I have had adventures which have gained coinage enough to keep me in the lifestyle I would *like* to become accustomed to."

Marcus huffed.

Christopher believed his over-charming countenance would obtain anything, or anyone, he desired. He had probably obtained the *coinage* from gambling. He had the most amazing luck. Or was he simply a talented cheat?

"Christopher." He took another sip. "Ye are what—four and ten years my junior?"

His brother nodded, still chewing.

Marcus placed his glass on the table. "That would make ye four and thirty?"

"Not until October." He smirked. "Please make me no older than necessary."

Marcus raised an eyebrow. "Aye." He took a bite, chewed, and swallowed. "Do not ye consider 'tis time to grow up? Take responsibility for your actions—your life of leisure?"

Christopher ran a hand through his light hair. "Jack, I see no reason to alter my methods of earning a living. It has worked quite well for me thus far."

Marcus narrowed his eyes. "Do not call me that."

"Why ever not? 'Tis your nickname."

"My name is Marcus *Jackson* DeGrey." He growled. "*Not* Jack."

A high-pitched squeal stalled their conversation. Nan sailed into the room, her night-gown floating around her like a gossamer cloud. "Uncle Chris!" She jumped into his arms. "Just now this very moment have I found ye were here."

"My little peacock! Are ye not the pretty thing?" He hugged her with a tenderness Marcus knew was reserved only for his niece. He drew back and surveyed her. "Are ye just come from the bath? Your hair, 'tis wet, and now ye have ruined my shirt."

Nan's face fell. Before she burst into tears, Christopher's grin, and the sheepish glint in his eyes, returned the joy to her face. "Oh, uncle, ye are a rogue, just as Papa says." She hugged him with vigor.

Christopher sent a wounded glance his way, but Marcus returned it with a knowing nod.

C3ED

The next morning, Adela slipped into an empty kitchen. Something that had not occurred since her first day of work. Mrs. Henshaw could always be found busy at some task or another, a song on her lips or muttered words to one of the kitchen maids to 'make haste' about something.

As she donned her work apron, she took in the polished pewter, brass, and copper utensils gleaming from hooks scattered about the space. On the windowsills, small pots of flowers or green plants, supposedly keeping flies at bay. The scent of plants, fire, and cooking meat were pleasant, homey, and lent the room a cheerful ambience, the white-washed walls lightening an otherwise dim atmosphere.

Adela breathed in deeply, the solace and familiarity of the

kitchen enveloping her. She thought of Kellie's words the other night—the quote from the Book of Esther.

For such a time as this.

The more time she spent in this world so unlike her own the more she seemed to fit it. Could Kellie's words be more prophetic than she realized?

Adela shook her head to clear it and dove into her daily routine, busying herself until the cook's cheerful song echoed from the hall.

Here in this song you may behold and see

A gallant girl obtain'd by wit and honesty

All you that hear my song and mark it but aright

Will say true love's worth gold and breeds delight

Mrs. Henshaw bustled in and met Adela's eyes. "Good morrow. Are ye tired of that tune, me gurl?" The woman thumped a bag onto the worktable. "I been ta fetch some cabbages for Christopher. The boy do like forced cabbage. I have not made it for so long, methinks I need the cookery book." She pointed a crooked finger to the shelf behind Adela. "Will ye please hand me the large brown one?"

Adela retrieved the well-worn book and placed it in front of the cook, who found the recipe. Adela glanced over her shoulder, trying to read the old text with its curling letters.

"If ye will gather the things whilst I read them, would be a great help ta me."

"I'll be happy to." Adela stood at attention like a soldier and shot the woman a salute, which made her wrinkled face glow with amusement, eyes sparkling.

The cook patted the sack of cabbage. "We have this, and the pig be simmerin' on the stove already, so we need the hard cheese ta grate, a big onion, and that old bread there." She motioned toward a hard loaf on the counter by the stove. "Grate it to make the crumbs, then add salt, pepper, and a pinch of nutmeg."

Adela gathered each item and brought it to the worktable. Mrs. Henshaw read each step of the process, ending with— "Potatoes smashed good and proper be the way young Christopher do like it."

"This mixture with the pork and cabbage is something we'd call a casserole where I come from," Adela said. "And the potatoes would be called *mashed potatoes*. Sometimes they're served with gravy on top." Talk of twenty-first century cooking did cause a pang of homesickness—and the memory of a warm shower with lavender soap.

"Sounds like one of them fancy Franch words, does this *casserole*." Mrs. Henshaw spat out the word like a curse.

"Got something against the French?" Adela asked.

"Eh. Suppose so. Been at war with them for nigh on five hundred years. Off and on about somethin' or another."

Adela sighed. "Yes, I suppose you're right. Men just can't seem to get along. Got to flex those muscles."

The cook belted out a laugh. "Right, ye be my gurl. Right, ye be." She grinned at Adela. "Ye do make me laugh, and I like ye all the more for it."

They spent the rest of the morning preparing Christopher's favorite dish for the mid-day meal. As Adela crumbled the dry bread, she wondered if Marcus or Nan would like it. She wouldn't as she wasn't a fan of the smelly vegetable. An idea struck her. "Mrs. Henshaw, why don't you add your own touch to this casserole? Sauté mushrooms and add to it. Or does Christopher not like them?"

"Aye, he does. Maybe 'twould be a good idea. Let us try." A mischievous smile spread to her lips. "If the boy does not like it, I'll skelp that purdy head of his." She chuckled. "'Tis because of him we do now have a mid-day meal. When he was a wee one, he asked why did we not dine half through the day. Telt me 'twas a long while from morn til eve."

It was Adela's turn to give a boisterous laugh just as Mrs. Brimberry stalked into the jovial atmosphere.

"Mistress Adela, why are ye not in the school room?" The housekeeper placed her hands on her bony hips. "I happened upon the child dancing around the room singing some ridiculous song about true love being gold. Mrs. Henshaw, is that not the nonsensical song ye are constantly singing?"

Mrs. Henshaw met the housekeeper's look with a stormy one. "Aye, 'tis so. *Love in a Maze.*"

Their gazes held for a time while the silence in the room grew more tense by the second, but Mrs. Henshaw did not waver.

The housekeeper swung her angry stare to Adela. "Ye will tell the girl she shall not sing it again. 'Tis not becoming of a lady. Now go attend to the child's education. Ye are late." She threw a hard glare at the cook and stomped from the kitchen.

Mrs. Henshaw hmphed. "Wonder what has her drawers in a twist?"

Adela pushed away the mental image of Mrs. Brimberry in

underwear and rushed to attend Nan. She'd lost track of the time this morning. When she arrived and asked Nan about the song, the little girl said, "Sorry, Mistress Adela, I like the song. Why shall I not sing it?" Her blue eyes widened with innocence.

"Sweetie, I cannot say. I don't find anything wrong with it, but Mrs. Brimberry thinks it unladylike." She reached across the table and patted the child's hand.

"I will tell Papa ye approved it and will continue singing until my throat has become hoarse." She flipped strawberry curls over her shoulder and crossed small arms over her chest, defiance bright in the serious eyes.

"Nan, I'm sorry, I should not have said I didn't find anything wrong with it. Mrs. Brimberry has been under your father's employ far longer than I have. Her word is more important than mine. Let's not buck the system."

The child blinked with confusion.

Adela chuckled. "It means we have to follow the rules. And we don't want to get the housekeeper in trouble. She's like me—she needs her job."

Her lovely little face fell into deep concentration for a few moments. "Ye do?"

"Yes, my pet. I do. How else can I clothe and feed myself if I don't work? In this ti—" She began again. "In our world, women have little choice in the matter. If we do not have a father, brother, or husband to care for us, we must labor to survive. It's not fair, but there it is."

Nan propped her chin in a cupped hand and appeared thoughtful.

"Don't worry," Adela said. "One day, many years from now, women will not have to live like this. They will be able to go to the same schools with boys and learn alongside them and be able to take on any profession they choose. All they must do is study hard and contribute to society the same way men do."

The child's mouth dropped.

"Come here, my sweet." The little girl obeyed, and Adela pulled the child onto her lap and hugged her.

"Mistress Adela, will women be doctors and lawyers and poltishuns too?" She leaned on Adela's shoulder and wound small arms around her neck.

"Yes, my dear," she said without thinking, "Women can even be president of the United States."

Before Nan could question this final revelation, footsteps resonated near the door, and a tall, slender man she had never seen entered the room. Adela recognized that smile. It was the embodiment of a self-assured man, one used to get his way in the presence of the opposite sex—young or old.

Nan threw herself out from Adela's embrace and ran toward the man. "Uncle Chris, did ye come to see where I learn things?"

He crouched in front of the child, and she threw her arms around him. "Twirl me, twirl me!"

Her uncle rose, grabbed her hands, and began to swing her into a wide circle, her body parallel to the parquet floor as she spun wildly in the air. Nan's gleeful screeching must have reached the kitchens on the opposite side of the manor.

Adela watched in amusement until the housekeeper stormed in and halted in the doorway.

"What is the meaning of this? Child, your father shall hear of this." She glared at Christopher, apparently not fearful of his standing in the household. "Master Christopher, this is most unbecoming of a young lady. I shall tell Master Marcus immediately. Ye, sir, are a devil!"

For a second time, the housekeeper's rigid frame departed a room in fitful anger.

Christopher DeGrey lifted his gaze from Nan to Adela. There was definitely a roguish glint there. Adela hated to pass judgment on someone based merely on appearance, but she'd seen the expression many times through the years. Whether the seventeenth century or the twenty-first, it was the same.

"What say ye, mistress? Am I a devil?"

Nan answered for her. "No! Ye are my favorite uncle, and no one shall call ye that again. Do ye hear me? I care not what she—" An adorable finger pointed at the empty doorway. "—says. What can she know? She thinks the *Love in a Maze* song is . . . is nonsen . . . bad and forbids me to sing it." Her face pinked with indignation.

Christopher's laugh was hearty and, admittedly, beautiful. Just like the man. What woman stood a chance if he turned on the charm? Certainly not Nan. Thank goodness she was a child and not a woman of no relation to the man. Leanne came to mind. But her encounter with the man had not captured her in a good sense. At least she was safe.

Marcus DeGrey walked in, wearing a frown. "What in thunder is going on? I just met Mrs. Brimberry, and she was positively seething with rage. Something about *Love in a Maze*, then she informed me Christopher is a devil and was influencing my child with improper behavior." He stood beside his brother, a couple of inches taller than him.

Side-by-side, Adela saw the resemblance between them, particularly in the eyes.

Nan looked up at them. "Papa, Uncle Chris was twirling me. Ye know how I like to be twirled. And he does it best." She pinched her lips. "Sorry, Papa. Ye do it very well indeed."

"Aye, my dear. He's the best twirler in the family. I have no issue with allowing him the title."

She hugged her father's leg. "But you are the best papa ever. Uncle Chris has no child to twirl, so I must allow it."

Christopher flinched at the child's remark. He dropped to her level. "Nan, ye are so adorable I need no child but ye." He hugged her, and she beamed at him.

Marcus peered at Adela, then back at Nan. "Now, what about this song of which Mrs. Brimberry spoke. Mistress Adela, have ye taught it to her, or has she picked it up directly from Mrs. Birtie?"

Adela rose as Nan rushed over to take her hand. "Please, Papa, do not be angry with Mistress Adela. She did not teach me. I heard it in the kitchen and 'membered it. I am a good 'memberer."

They all chuckled with Adela's being the loudest. "I'm sorry for laughing. She is such a good girl, and I cannot understand why Mrs. Brimberry finds so much censorship in her actions. She has done nothing wrong, but if you judge she has, I will take the blame and her punishment for whatever you consider proper, Lord DeGrey."

Christopher went to her side. "I stand with Mistress Adela. This child is an angel and should not be punished. Mrs.

Brimberry is the one who should be reprimanded. A proper dunking in the river should suffice."

"Christopher, we are not tossing her in to see if she is a witch. She has merely erred in judgment. I do not think suffering is due anyone. I shall instruct her accordingly." He tugged his sleeve down at the cuff, gave them a crisp nod, and exited the room.

Christopher looked to her. "Ye were magnificent, mistress. Most would not stand against the powerful Lord DeGrey." There was a hint of sarcasm in his tone.

"Thank you, but I was not trying to stand *against* your brother." She stroked the girl's thick hair. "I just wanted it on the record Nan had done nothing wrong."

He squinted at her, curiosity in his expression. "Ah, do I see admiration in your eyes for my *old* brother?"

"I do not consider forty-eight old nor does he look it."

Why had she said that?

"I do believe he became nine and forty most recently." Christopher glanced at his niece. "Did he not, Nan?"

Adela remembered the book she'd purchased at the manor. She answered, "No, he did not. He was born in 1618."

Christopher reeled in surprise. "In truth, how came ye to know this?"

Adela's response wasn't a lie.

"When I first saw his painting, I was told the information." She lifted her chin in a challenge.

He pursed his lips for a moment. "Well, no matter. I am still the younger and more handsome." His eyes danced with humor. "If ye have no further need of Nan's company, mayhap she can accompany me to the stables to see the new foal."

Nan looked up at her teacher, hands clasped under her chin, eyes shining.

Adela would not break the child's heart. Who knew how long the errant uncle would be visiting? She looked at Christopher. "Certainly. Who am I to keep you two apart?"

Christopher took one of Adela's hands in his, bent over it, and placed a soft kiss on her knuckles. "My thanks to ye, lovely *Adela*." When he rose, one side of his mouth quirked upward in a seductive smile.

She leaned into him, so Nan couldn't hear. "Master Christopher, I don't want to jeopardize my position here, but I'm aware of men like you. You are a flirt, and I'm old enough to be your mother." She patted his hand as if she were speaking to Nan. "Your charms do not affect me."

His gaze held a hint of disbelief and something more— perhaps approval or censure?

He released her hand and took Nan's. "We bid ye good day, Mistress Adela. After we see the foal, I shall take Nan for a turn in the garden before we meet Marcus for our mid-day meal." He flashed her a daring smile before leaving with Nan.

Mrs. Henshaw's words about Christopher being the reason they had a midday meal returned to her. Yes, Christopher certainly had a way with women from an early age. She would be sure to warn any women there he set his sights on.

γδ

Leanne stood by the gate waiting for Adela and Kellie. She arched her back and stretched her neck from side-to-side, working out the knots from the day. The happy squeals of a child came from the garden, revealing Nan's nearby presence. That was the happiest child she'd ever met. Marcus must be doing something right.

"Uncle! 'Tis not fair, I travel the maze the best. Ye may be lost without me."

The wayward uncle had arrived.

Leanne looked toward the maze at the east corner of the garden. She was well-acquainted with it since she passed close by every morning on her way to the pit. *Yuck!* The daily memory pained her.

A laughing Nan catapulted from the maze, and a tall, fair-haired man emerged. There was something familiar about him. She inched her way closer to the west flower garden that ran parallel to the inner courtyard wall, attempting to get a closer look.

A sudden burst of energy brought the two of them running in her direction, and a flash of recollection erupted. It was *him*! The idiot moron who nearly killed her with his horse.

"Uncle! Ye play ill. 'Tis ye I must chase." The girl sped after him, and he feigned injury, dropping to his knees, hands on thighs, head bent. When he caught his breath and lifted his gaze, Leanne found herself looking directly into his grey eyes.

Recognition shone on his face. She retreated two steps and fell backward into the brilliantly, blooming flower bed. Her feet stuck up and arms flailed in an attempt to push herself upright.

The man had the gall to approach her as she struggled. "We meet again."

His smirk was so condescending Leanne wanted to pummel him. "What are you doing here, you—?"

He completed her sentence. "Idiot moron?" His hand hovered, gesturing to aid her. "Or shall ye conjure up some other means of shaming me?"

Leanne rolled onto her side, knelt, and pushed herself upright. "I wouldn't accept your help if you paid me!" The moment the words were out, she wished they weren't.

"Mistress, ye do me harm. I do not consort with women of low caliber."

Her mouth dropped. "To what are you implying? I . . . I'll have your head." She struggled to leave the confines of the edged garden bed and faltered, straight into his arms.

How much worse could this get?

His chest quaked with laughter as she shoved him away. Nan raced over and stood with hands on her hips.

Voices and laughter came from the gate, and Leanne glanced in that direction. Adela was attempting to quieten Kellie without success. Christopher had the audacity to join them followed by Nan.

Leanne's anger skyrocketed, and she lost control. She punched him in his middle, knocking the wind out of him, and he fell to the ground, clutching his stomach, eyes tearing in pain.

Nan ran to his side and threw her arms around him. She shrieked at Leanne, "Ye mean old lady. Ye hurt my uncle. I hate ye!"

Leanne took in a deep breath and dropped to her knees beside them. "I—I'm sorry. You are just so insufferable. I was defending myself."

"Leanne! What have you done?" Adela crouched beside Nan while Kellie hovered over them.

"This is the man who nearly killed me on his horse. I didn't know he was Lord DeGrey's brother."

Nan cried, "And my uncle. Ye have killed my uncle." She sobbed uncontrollably while she hung onto Christopher's neck.

He said between clenched teeth, "I'm fine, sweetling, 'Tis truth." He put an arm around her and pulled her close to his chest. "Methinks I had this coming."

Leanne stood. "Yes, you did." She turned to Kellie. "Let's go home." She leaned down to grip Adela's hand and pulled her up.

Adela turned to Christopher. "I am sorry about this. She shouldn't have done that. Please accept my apologies."

He nodded, rose, and picked Nan up to soothe her.

"I don't like that old lady, uncle."

He responded, "Methinks I *do*."

Leanne narrowed her eyes and sent him a scathing glare. He better think twice before crossing her again.

CAROLE LEHR JOHNSON

Chapter Fifteen

"Mrs. Henshaw really knows how to make a tart." Kellie licked the sticky fruit filling from the tips of her fingers.

"Girl, that will be your third." Adela lifted her cup to her lips. "Where do you put it?"

Leanne chimed in. "Are you kidding? With the manual labor we're doing, we can eat anything we want and never gain a pound. I've lost weight, and I've been eating like one of Stanton's horses."

Kellie smiled, a smudge of dark purple berry on her chin. "Yeah, and these have to be healthy. After all, this is before we processed our food within an inch of its life. Has to be in a pretty natural state if you ask me."

"True. Guess I hadn't thought of that." Adela shoved the plate closer to them. "Eat up. At my age, it still doesn't matter. I can *look* at a cheesecake and gain five pounds. May as well just glue it to my stomach and bypass the process."

"Ha! Might as well enjoy it first." Kellie licked her lips and reached for another tart.

Adela faced Leanne. "I'm sorry your twenty-ninth birthday had to be celebrated with berry tarts. But I am glad you didn't have to spend it in the stocks after punching the lord of the manor's brother."

Leanne grimaced. "Yeah. Sorry." She changed the subject. "You've a birthday coming up soon. Let's see . . ." She tapped a finger against her chin. "You'll be fif—"

Adela feigned hurt. "No need to remind me."

Leanne began to speak, but before she could, the door vibrated with vigorous knocks followed by high-pitched calls. "Help, Mistress Kellie! Please help!"

The plea repeated until Kellie opened the door and found the boy she'd seen around the stables.

"Andrew?" He stood there, shaking, eyes brimming with tears.

He grabbed her hand and tugged. "Mistress, please. Will ye come?"

"Why? What's wrong?"

"'Tis Master Stanton. He be ill and telt me to fetch ye. Said he wanted nowt to do with the quack in the village. Said ye was a narse."

Kellie felt the blood drain from her face, her knees weakening. She glanced at Adela and Leanne and opened her mouth, but nothing came out. They were at her side in an instant.

Adela placed a gentle hand on the child's shoulder. "Andrew, are you certain Master Stanton said to fetch her?"

His Adam's apple bobbed as he swallowed. "Aye, he did. Can she come?"

Kellie held Adela's gaze and nodded. "Yes, I'll come." She glanced around.

Oh, how she wished for medical supplies. What would she need?

The boy tugged her out into the early morning light, its chill clung to her. "Andrew, let me get my cloak." She darted back into the cottage and returned, wrapping the cloak snugly around her shoulders.

Kellie glanced back at Adela and Leanne. "Check on me when you have time between duties. I don't know what I'm in for."

They nodded, and Adela said, "I'll inform Mrs. Brimberry."

The child led her to the stables, up a narrow set of stairs, and into a well-furnished room that smelled of bay rum cologne and a tallow candle burning on the bedside table. Stanton sat propped on several pillows, his shirt clinging to him, face damp with perspiration.

A small fire warmed the space. Kellie removed her cloak and asked Andrew to bring a pitcher of cool water, clean cloths, and soap. He nodded vigorously and dashed out the door.

She kneeled beside the bed. "Stanton, can you hear me?"

With effort, he opened his eyes. They were red, glassy, and dull.

Kellie drew in a sharp breath and touched his forehead

wishing for a thermometer. He definitely had a fever, but she wasn't sure how high.

"Can you open your mouth wide please?" He complied, his eyes never wavering from hers. She drew closer to see red spots on the inside of his mouth. She groaned. Was it measles—or worse—smallpox?

The boy returned, bits of cloth hanging from his pockets, a pitcher in one hand, and a lump of soap in the other.

"That was very fast. Thank you, Andy. Do you mind if I call you Andy?"

He placed the implements on the dresser next to a copper basin and shook his head.

Kellie poured water into the basin, soaked a cloth, and placed it across Stanton's neck, her mind whirling as how to proceed without a fever reducer.

"Andy, do you know what he has eaten today? When he started feeling poorly?"

The child shook his head.

Kellie said gently, "I'm afraid you cannot be in here. What he has is highly contagious, and you must not catch it. Do you understand?"

His eyes grew wide, and tears formed on his lashes. Unable to speak, he pointed to her and then to Stanton.

She understood. "No, I cannot catch it. I've already had this disease and recovered, so I cannot get it again."

Relief shone in the child's eyes.

"Now, I need you to do something for me please. Go and wash your hands very, very well with soap. Then go home and change into clean clothes and have these—" She tugged on his sleeve. "—washed right away."

He nodded, sent Stanton a sad look, and backed out of the room.

"Oh, and Andy, please tell my friends what has happened and for them to come as soon as they can." His dark head bobbed again as he left.

Stanton croaked out painfully, "Kellie, am I ta die?"

Her stomach lurched. "Oh, Stanton, not if I can help it. I'm not a doctor . . ."

"Not . . . not ta worry." He grimaced as he tried to swallow. "Wan . . . want ye." He reached for her hand and clasped it weakly.

She gave it a reassuring squeeze, closed her eyes, and prayed, "Lord. You alone are the Great Physician, please guide me to help this man."

When she opened her eyes, he watched her carefully, his gaze roaming her features. "Thank ye for comin'."

The warmth from his hand affected her, yet she was unsure why. At times, her patients made her heart break with sympathy. This was different. Yes, her heart held compassion, but there was something more she felt as he looked at her.

ଓଖ

At day's end, Adela made her way to the stables, Leanne accompanying her as they discussed the history of the plague in England.

"Are we in danger?"

"I really don't know." Adela's voice dropped. "I feel so

183

helpless right now."

"What are we going to do when we get there? All Andy said was Kellie needed us to come to her. What if we're walking into the plague? Andy said it was contagious, and he wasn't allowed back until Stanton is well."

They approached the stables to find Andy perched on a stump of wood next to the door. He pointed them upstairs to Stanton's living quarters and hurriedly left.

Filing up the narrow stairs, Adela stood at the closed door and glanced at Leanne before knocking. A soft voice said, "Come in."

Kellie leaned over the bed mopping Stanton's forehead and neck with a damp cloth. She glanced up at them with a pained expression. "I'm so glad you're here. I need some things if you don't mind gathering them."

Leanne pulled a scrap of paper from her apron pocket and the stub of a pencil. "Of course. What do you need?"

"I need an iron pot for the fire, more water, clean cloths, and food. Preferably sweet potatoes or liver." She sighed. "Or fish, spinach, carrots, kale . . . any combination of these will do." She continued bathing his neck and face. "I'm not sure what's available in this time, but I need to get some vitamin A into his system."

The rhythm of scratching pencil upon paper and Stanton's heavy breathing resonated in the stillness. Adela breathed a silent prayer. The man was gravely ill, and Kellie was determined to save him.

"Also, please ask Mrs. Henshaw if she has any herbs to help curb a fever? The only thing that sticks in my memory are the hips from a dog rose plant."

She drew in a deep breath and released it, exhaustion evident in her posture. "Thank you both. You must be tired from a long day, but I can't do this alone. You're both immune to the measles—and I pray that's all it is." Her eyes clouded. "Bad enough, but smallpox would be the kiss of death."

Adela embraced her. "We're here for you. No matter what."

Leanne voiced her agreement and patted Kellie's shoulder before they turned to leave.

As they reached the door, Kellie spoke, "I thought of something else. Something much harder to achieve. Will you convince Mrs. Brimberry that I be excused from my duties so I can stay here and monitor Stanton's recovery? I don't trust anyone else to do it. I'm afraid they'll call the local whatever-they-call-them, and he'll be bled or given some other barbaric treatment that will likely kill him."

Adela nodded. "We'll see what we can do. And we'll pray for you both."

Kellie nodded and offered a grim smile.

When she turned to resume her ministrations, Adela saw Stanton's eyes were on Kellie, a hint of clarity in them. How much of the conversation had he heard—and understood?

A half hour later, Adela and Leanne returned with the supplies with the exception of food containing vitamin A. Mrs. Henshaw immediately set about cooking some of the items, saying she would deliver them to the *boy* as soon as they were ready.

Leanne held out her palm to reveal a linen bag tied with twine. "She said to steep this in a pot of boiling water and have him drink a cup every hour or so."

Kellie took the bag and sniffed it. "Lavender." She looked at Adela. "Don't you drink lavender tea?"

"Yes, but it's mixed with black tea. Should be good though. You may save a tablespoon out of that bag to put in the water you're using to bathe him. It has a calming effect."

Adela watched Stanton's gaze follow Kellie as she filled a kettle to boil water over the fire. "Mrs. Henshaw did have some leftover sweet potatoes." She rummaged in the basket they'd brought from the kitchen and pulled out a small crockery dish. "They've been mashed, so it won't irritate his sore throat."

"Like baby food," Leanne chimed in.

"Leanne!" Kellie reprimanded her.

"What?" Leanne's eyes brightened in understanding. "Ah, yeah."

Adela turned to Kellie. "Mrs. Brimberry will not allow you to be gone every day but said she would tolerate it if we took turns, then each of us would only miss our chores every other day."

Kellie's face flashed to a deep, angry red. "You have got to be kidding?" She flopped into the chair by the bed. "What is so darned important about brewing ale *every* day?"

Stanton rested his hand on hers. His voice rasped. "Nowt ta be concerned . . ." He strained to push himself up on the pillows but collapsed. He raised a finger and pointed to his chest. "Am better."

Adela surveyed the scene, saddened to see a strong, healthy man reduced to such a weakened state. She stepped forward, unsure about intervening, and spoke timidly, "Stanton, I'm Adela." She nodded toward Leanne. "This is Leanne. We are Kellie's friends and don't mind taking turns to help you. You are a *very* sick man, and Kellie is more than capable of nursing you back to health. She will tell us what to do." She cleared her throat. "We've already had this disease and cannot catch it again. Others at the manor may not have had it, and we can't risk them catching it."

His brows rose. Whether impressed with her knowledge, or that she was willing to care for a stranger, she couldn't tell.

A moment passed before he nodded.

"Okay, so it's settled." She peered at Kellie. "You've been here all day. Let me stay tonight, and Leanne can come and relieve me in the morning. You can switch with her the next morning."

Kellie and Leanne nodded.

"Now scoot. Get some rest." Adela retrieved the dish of sweet potatoes, nudged Kellie from her seat, and took her place. She draped a napkin under Stanton's chin and sent him a reassuring smile. "Kellie, please bring me a cup of tea before you leave."

Kellie did so, her gaze lingering on Stanton, conflict in her eyes.

Adela gently touched her arm. "I will take good care of him. Now go. Get some rest."

Kellie sighed and whispered in Adela's ear. "If his condition worsens, send for me immediately." She looked at Stanton once more, and left, closing the door gently behind her.

Adela brought a spoonful of the sweet potatoes to Stanton's lips. Their eyes met briefly before his twinkled, and he opened his mouth. He swallowed and grimaced.

"It's uncomfortable to swallow, but you must eat to keep up your strength and get these vitamins into your system."

His eyes narrowed.

It took her a moment to realize he had no idea what a vitamin was. "Oh, yes. Well, it's the um . . ." She blew out a breath and gave him another bite.

While he swallowed, she tried to sort out how to phrase it.

"Honestly, I'm not sure how to explain it. Kellie would be able to much better than me." A phrase flashed in her mind. "An old saying where I come from is, 'an apple a day keeps the doctor away.' There are some foods that have healthy benefits, and the sweet potato is one of them. Surely your mother encouraged you to eat—or not eat—certain foods?"

At the mention of his mother, he winced and said huskily, "Died in childbed." He turned away, but not before she saw the pain in his eyes.

Adela placed a hand on his forearm. "I'm sorry. Even though it's been ten years, I still have trouble coping with the loss of my parents." She patted his arm before pulling away.

When he faced her, she glimpsed a mutual expression of sympathy on his face.

After finishing his meal, Mrs. Henshaw arrived laden with a cloth-covered tray. "Well, well, well, me boy. What have ye gone and done? Feelin' poorly, are ye?"

Concern marred his features. She held up a hand. "Not ta worry. Mistress Kellie telt me about your sickness. I did have it as a little un."

Stanton looked at the woman and patted the chair Adela had just vacated. The cook sat with a moan of relief.

She removed the wet cloth from the basin, rung it out, and wiped his face. "No need ta speak, me boy. These women will take care of ye. Do as they say, 'specially Mistress Kellie. She do know what she be talkin' bout. Mistress Adela says so, and I trust her. Them girls may be speakin' a odd way, but they hearts be in tha right place. 'Tis a good thing ye did in hirin' them ta work here."

Adela froze.

Afraid to meet Stanton's eyes, she kept her back to them while preparing another cup of tea and saying a silent prayer for strength. She attempted to keep her voice light. "Stanton, I'll join you with a cup of this delightful tea. I've always had a liking for anything lavender." She schooled her features before facing them.

When she turned, she asked Mrs. Henshaw, "Why don't you have a cup as well? I'm certain you could use a breather before going to your room for the evening." She handed the woman her cup.

The cook's eyes softened and glowed with gratitude. "Are ye not kind, me dear? No one but me little Marcus ever showt me as much kindness 'cept ye and your gurls."

Adela sat on a stool on the opposite side of the bed, leaned in, and brought the cup to Stanton's lips. He accepted but with a questioning glint in his eyes as he sipped a few times before holding his hand up and pointed to her cup across the room.

She retrieved her tea and sat again, keeping her eyes on

Stanton, while Mrs. Henshaw chattered on about what she'd brought and admonished him to *eat up.*

Adela assured her, "I'll be sure to feed him as much as he can hold. You are a dear to cook so much after a full day in the kitchen. Thank you, ma'am."

The woman set her cup down. "I best be getting' to me bed 'afore I drop." She groaned as she rose. "Almost forget to telt ye there be a surprise for ye on the tray. A favorite treat."

Adela's heart warmed at the gesture. "You are so kind." She kissed the old woman's cheek and escorted her to the door. "Thank you again. I'll see you in the morning."

"Will not be tellin' if ye are a bit late on the morrow, me dear." She winked and inched her way down the narrow stairs with care.

Adela turned, hoping Stanton had drifted off, but his eyes were on her, narrowed with suspicion. She took a deep breath and dove in. "You must have questions but cannot speak well. Shall I try to answer them without you asking?"

He nodded.

"My friends and I were stranded here." She repeated what they'd told Marcus about their ship's arrival from the Colonies and stolen luggage. She realized he would question why they were trying to return home and not go forward with the reason they'd come.

An idea popped into her mind.

"There was a letter waiting for us at the pier from my distant relation's solicitor. He died, and we had nowhere to go. We went to his home, and they turned us away. When we discovered the abandoned cottage, we chose to stay until we could figure out how to return home."

Adela shrugged. "When Lord DeGrey found us in the cottage and assumed you had hired us, we thought we could work to earn enough money to get back to the Colonies."

During the telling, his eyes held hers. His face revealing nothing other than more questions lingering behind his dark gaze, but he seemed content with her words.

She rose from her perch. "I'll get us a fresh cup of tea."

As she prepared it, she told him, "Please forgive us for our deceit. Women are so vulnerable in this—" She coughed. "—in a country far from home."

While giving him a sip, he reached out and lightly touched her shoulder.

"Thank you for understanding. I realize you may feel the need to tell Lord DeGrey." She dipped her gaze away.

He pointed to his throat and shook his head, then pointed to her mouth and shook his head again.

It took a moment for her to understand that he wasn't going to tell Marcus. She thanked him and squeezed his hand.

One side of his mouthed quirked.

"All right, tea and food it is."

Half an hour later, having eaten more than she'd expected, Stanton slept. Adela meditated on why he'd agreed not to tell Marcus. And, furthermore, what might hold him to that promise?

CB80

Kellie mused over how the days and nights melded into one as Stanton improved and was now in the final stages of recovery. The itching had been an issue, but Mrs. Henshaw had boiled hops in water to make a decoction to relieve it.

When Kellie told Stanton she needed to spread the liquid on his rash—which covered most of his body, he attempted to rail at her. If he'd had a voice, it may have been effective. When she tried to unclothe him, he pushed her hands away. With hands on her hips, she told him in her profession, she'd seen her share of half-clothed men, and if he scratched, he would be scarred for life.

What concerned her most was the chance of it morphing into pneumonia or encephalitis.

Two weeks passed before he could speak without pain nor had a fever. Thanks to Mrs. Henshaw's knowledge of herbs and such, the itching had almost subsided. He sat up in bed watching Kellie clear the remnants of their meal.

"Come sit. Ye are weary, and 'tis me to blame." He coughed, but it was lighter than before. "I can take care of meself."

Kellie folded her arms. "Oh, can you now? When you can stand up and not fall on your backside, I'll believe it."

He gingerly slid one leg from the covers and let it dangle over the side of the bed. He glanced at her, chin high, and moved his other leg.

She waited.

With quivering arms, he eased himself to sit at the bed's edge. This time his smile was self-assured. The muscles in his well-formed arms tensed as he pushed himself to a standing position. His smile verged on arrogant.

Kellie moved toward him.

He lifted a hand. "No. Am fine."

She ignored him and stepped nearer.

His first step was like a newborn colt on spindly legs. The next move was as Kellie anticipated, and he tumbled toward the floor. She braced herself to stop him, but they both fell with a thud and groans.

Kellie sat up, rubbed her neck, and glanced at Stanton, who rolled onto his back. He appeared winded but otherwise unharmed. She helped him up and back into the bed.

"Stubborn man," she muttered while tucking the blankets around him.

Stanton placed a hand atop hers, its warmth spreading up her arm. She met his eyes but was unprepared for the mixture of penitence and admiration in his gaze as he drew her hand to his lips and gently kissed it.

CAROLE LEHR JOHNSON

Chapter Sixteen

Adela ruminated over the extent of Kellie's concern for Stanton's recovery. She insisted someone be with him at all hours. Was she simply being overly cautious because of who the patient was or was there more to it?

She turned to bring Stanton his breakfast, placing the tea and porridge laden tray carefully on his lap.

He stared at her. "Ye do know 'tis not necessary." His voice cracked with disuse. "I am capable of doin' this for meself now."

Adela settled herself into a chair with a cup of tea. "Yes, I know. But Kellie is the nurse, and she knows what is, and is not, necessary. I trust her." She brought the cup to her lips, smiling over the rim. "She'll be here in a moment, so if you have something to tell me, you'd better do it now."

He chuckled, eyes shining. "The three of ye are most

uncommon women." He took a bite of porridge and grimaced.

"Throat still tender?"

He reached for his cup of lavender tea and held it up. "This helps."

"Yes, it does. I love the flavor." She took a sip. "Stanton, what are your intentions toward Kellie?"

He flinched, almost spilling the hot liquid, and cleared his throat.

"I'm sorry. I should have cushioned that by telling you I had a sensitive question for you." She shrugged. "Those two girls are like daughters to me, so I guess you could say I'm being an overprotective mother, and you're on the hot seat."

A bark of laughter escaped him, and he grabbed his throat. Wiping his mouth with a napkin, he shifted on the bed. "I must say the three of ye are most direct in your speech. Somethin' I confess I *do* prefer."

Adela laughed. "You, sir, are an *uncommon* man for this time in history. Most men want a subservient woman who complies with their every demand. No questions asked."

His brow furrowed. "*This time in history?*"

Adela surveyed the handle of her cup, chewing on her lower lip. "I merely meant that in general men don't care for a strong woman with her own opinions. Tell me it's not true."

His face relaxed. "Aye. 'Tis of a truth." He finished his meal. "I must admit my br . . . *I* do not agree with that nor Marcus or Chris. We are of a similar mind. Women should not withhold their speech unless in a crowd. Yet in the company of close family should be free to speak."

"I'm surprised, pleasantly so, that you are of this opinion."

She studied him. "But you have not answered my question about Kellie."

A corner of his mouth raised. "Ye, mistress, are most astute. But I—" He paused as the door opened.

Kellie breezed in and removed her cloak. "Is all well? Do we have a fever today?"

Stanton shot her a telling smile which reaffirmed Adela's need for him to answer the question—and soon.

Adela stood. "He's doing quite well. I'd say today should be your last to attend him."

In Kellie's eyes, Adela caught a fleeting glimpse of regret, not of his getting better, but that she was no longer needed to care for him.

Adela took her leave, descending the narrow stairs into the crisp morning. She and Kellie needed to have a heart-to-heart. She walked to the manor and paused at the herb garden, breathing in the cool air infused with the scent of herbs.

The sound of footsteps on gravel reached her. Marcus approached, his countenance pensive.

"Ah, Mistress Adela, just the one for whom I am seeking." He stopped within two feet of her, his hands clasped behind his back. "How does Stanton fare this morn?"

"He is doing well. He should be up and about by morning. Although, he will require a few half-days at his chores before resuming a full schedule."

Marcus nodded. "Aye, excellent." He drew nearer to Adela, her breath catching. "I have need of ye . . ." His eyebrows rose. "Pardon me, I mean, I have something I must needs ye to do for me—and Nan."

Her curiosity piqued. "Anything I can do for Nan is not a problem." She stated her words carefully, and by the glint in his eyes, he'd taken it as meant.

"Aye. I see." He stood shoulder-to-shoulder with her. "Would ye walk with me through the garden?"

Adela's mind whirled. What was this man's aim?

She nodded and followed his lead toward the rose garden along the courtyard wall. She brushed her fingers against the petals, releasing their diverse fragrances—one spicy which reminded her of her grandmother's favorite rose and the next strong and sweet much like Leanne's perfume. She hesitated. "Lord DeGrey, would you mind if I pick a rose?"

"Allow me." He retrieved a small knife, rapidly sliced several stems, and presented them to her with the flourish of a bow. "My lady."

She thanked him, her gaze on the bouquet. When she took it, a drop of blood fell from his hand onto the soft pink bloom. Her hand instinctively sought the wound to halt the flow of blood, her fingertip pressing the injury. Another drop fell and slid into the center of the rose, merging with the pale pink backdrop. An artist could not have painted a more flawless effect of red on pink, rendering a faded streak of blood to the heart of the rose.

Memories of her grandmother's instruction returned to Adela. A pale pink rose conveys grace, gentleness, joy, and happiness. A red rose signifies passion, true love, romance, and desire.

Words etched on a stone bench in a garden she'd once visited were on her lips in a flash. "*If I had a rose for every time I thought of you, I'd be picking roses for a lifetime."*

Her hand flew to her mouth, her gaze seeking his, and noting a glimmer of interest in his eyes. "I—I just remembered that. It was carved on a garden bench." She struggled to gloss over the situation. "There was a pink rose there with red streaked throughout the petals. It was said to mean *'I'll always remember you."*

She sucked in a breath, going from bad to worse. "I believe it was an old Swedish proverb."

Marcus whispered, "'Tis of no concern."

"What?" She wasn't sure what he meant. Was he speaking of the roses, the romantic words she'd spoken, or something else?

His hand shifted to interlace their fingers. "The wound. 'Tis a trifle. Mayhap ye can educate me on the meanings of these red and pink flowers."

The touch of their intertwined hands jolted Adela's senses along with the early morning breeze encircling them with the heady scent of the garden. A horse whinnied in the nearby stables, and Mrs. Henshaw's voice rang out in search of a kitchen maid.

Adela regained her senses and pulled her hand away. "Perhaps." She swallowed. "Some other time, my lord." She hugged the blooms to her chest, this time pricking her own finger, and winced.

Marcus made to attend her, but she backed away.

"Good morrow." She dipped into a slight curtsy and strode in the direction of the cook's voice.

Once on the kitchen threshold, she glanced over her

shoulder and found him watching her. She realized he'd never told her what he'd wanted her to do for Nan—*or him.*

ᴄ₃₈ᴐ

Leanne strolled at a leisurely pace on her return from the cesspit, reveling that she made it through another day of the revolting task. When she rounded a curve in the path, a young boy trudged in front of her, waving a stick in the air like a sword. She coughed to make herself known.

When he turned, she recognized him as the boy who had brought Kellie to Stanton. "Good morning, Andrew."

He waited for her. "Good morrow, Mistress Leanne."

She placed the empty buckets at her feet. "How do you know my name?"

"Mistress Kellie telt me ye was her friend."

The large eyes were a pale blue and penetrating. She'd seen those eyes before, only darker in hue. She crouched to his level. "Oh, and what else did she say about me?"

"'Twas nothin' bad. Said she 'twas a friend of yours. She 'tis a good lady. Takin' care of Stanton and such. Ye and Mistress Adela too." He dipped his chin. "I thank ye for doin' it. He be as a papa to me." When he brought his head up, his eyes held unshed tears.

Leanne couldn't help herself. She gathered the little boy into her arms. "You are most welcome. We are glad to help. Stanton is a fine man." She released him, but he did not move away.

A glimmer of humor shone on his sweet face. "Mistress Kellie calls me Andy." He dug his toe into the dirt, making small circles. "I like it."

"I do too. Is it all right if I call you Andy?"

He nodded vigorously and took her hand in his. "May I walk with ye?"

"You may. I could use a strong boy to protect me. I was walking on this path the other day, and a big, mean man on a wild horse nearly trampled me to death. You can be my look-out in case he comes back."

Andy straightened and held the stick up. "I shall protect ye, mistress."

She released his hand and presented him with a deep curtsy. "I thank you, kind sir. May I also ask your aid in helping me with one of these buckets?"

"Aye." He grabbed one and retrieved her hand in the other.

They walked hand in hand, each swinging an empty bucket at their side, when they met Martin and Timothy driving in a small empty cart.

Martin waved. "Good morrow, Andrew, Mistress Leanne!"

Andrew pulled Leanne to the side of the path. "Where ye goin'?"

"Ta get firewood," Timothy said. "Cook says we about to have a cool bit of night for a while."

"Andy, how does she know that?"

"Because she got ta rumtism." His eyes followed the cart as it passed. "Mistress Leanne, would ye be all right takin' the buckets? Think I may ride with them and help. Totin' wood is a powerful hard job, and they may need me."

Leanne chuckled. "Yes, little man, you run along. I'm sure

they will be glad to have your help." She ruffled his hair and took the bucket from him. He grinned and bounded off after the cart, shouting for them to wait.

He jumped aboard and waved to her. A delightful child, she thought. Just like Nan.

Leanne smiled and continued on her way. But the spring in her step faltered when the next bend brought her face-to-face with Christopher DeGrey, who whistled a tune that sounded suspiciously like Mrs. Henshaw's song. She averted her eyes and rushed past him.

The whistling continued behind her, and it grew closer the further she walked. *Is he following me?*

"Mistress Leanne, may I walk with ye?"

She smelled his cologne—aftershave—whatever they called it here.

Without looking at him, she spoke over her shoulder, "No, you may not. I don't walk with men who try to murder me with their horse, dump me into flower beds, and laugh at me."

He sighed, and she turned to face him.

"I did apologize for the horse incident. However, ye cannot blame me for the bed of flowers ye sought." He rested a hand on his flat stomach. "And methinks ye have repaid me, though 'twas not my fault."

"*Methinks*, you had it coming after the horse incident."

He stepped closer, the wind ruffling his honey-hued hair, and peered at her with teasing blue-grey eyes. "Perhaps."

Yep, she knew why women swooned over this charmer. *But not her.*

Leanne wheeled and briskly walked away. He easily kept pace.

His hand returned to his stomach. "May I compliment ye on your sparring skill? Ye have quite the punch."

She glared at him, yet the corners of his mouth lifted into a disarming smile. She stopped at the entrance to the walled gardens. "What do you want?"

He extended his arm. "Would ye please accept my offer of friendship?"

Her gaze dropped to his outstretched hand. She narrowed her eyes and with a deep sigh of resignation took it.

Warm, soft lips on the back of her hand flashed a current of heat up her arm and neck. He met her eyes and offered that *blasted* smile. Could he read her reaction?

She broke their contact, a slight tremor running through her.

Christopher straightened, clasped his hands behind his back, and rocked on his toes. "So, Mistress Leanne, may we begin anew?"

Leanne couldn't stand the sight of the man, yet she couldn't shake his effect on her either. She cleared her throat. "Yes, I suppose we can try."

But, deep down, she wasn't so sure it was a good idea.

CB&ED

"Adela, my dear, take yourself away," Mrs. Henshaw said with concern. "Ye look most weary. 'Tis been a hard day and all."

"I'm okay, really." Adela dusted flour off her hands, then went to the basin and gave them a thorough scrubbing. Over her shoulder, she told the cook, "I would love some of your famous tea though."

Mrs. Henshaw brewed the tea, prepared just the way Adela liked it, but as she reached to take it the kindly woman said, "Ye take it to the garden and ease yourself 'til the gurls come ta take ye home." She handed her the steaming cup, her eyes twinkling. "And take your strange words like 'okee' with ye."

Adela smiled. "You are such a sweet lady, Mrs. Henshaw. I don't know what I would do without your kindness."

The woman blushed and gently slapped Adela's shoulder. "Oh, go on. Take your tea ta the garden and smell the roses ye are so fond of."

"Superb idea." Adela removed her apron, hung it on the peg, and reclaimed her tea. "I'll see you in the morning. Hope you get a good night's rest. Please tell Kellie and Leanne where to find me."

"Ye as well, me dear. Will be leavin' meself shortly. I be certain to tell the gurls."

Adela stepped out the kitchen door into the early evening air and strode toward the long, narrow rose bed which followed the east wall. She and Marcus had stood there only yesterday. What he'd wanted to ask her still niggled in her mind. She walked to the end of the bed near the maze and sat on a white-washed wood bench under a small tree.

She took a sip, leaned against the trunk, and closed her eyes, the pleasant breeze drifting over her. Mrs. Henshaw was such a thoughtful woman—and so hardworking. Adela wasn't sure how she did all the work she took on each day at her age.

The bench shifted. Adela gasped and opened her eyes to

find Marcus beside her, no guile or agenda in his expression.

"Good eve, Mistress Adela."

Adela began to rise, but he placed a warm hand on her forearm.

"Please sit with me. I must needs ask ye the question that was interrupted yesterday." His lips twitched. "Ye appear to hold your breath when I am in your presence. Do I unsettle ye?" Genuine concern dashed across his face. He crossed his arms. "I hope I do not frighten ye."

She gripped her teacup with trembling hands and stared into the brown liquid. "No, my lord, I . . ." Her voice faded as she saw Kellie and Leanne approach. She rushed to her feet. "I'm sorry, but I must go now." She shoved the cup toward him. "Will you please give this to Mrs. Henshaw for me? Good night." She rushed toward Kellie and Leanne.

He called to her, his voice solemn yet expectant. "Mistress Adela."

She started. *Now I've made him mad. Will I ever say—or do—the right thing in this time?* When she turned, he was on her heels.

"I'm sorry. I wasn't thinking." She reached for the cup. "I'll take it to her in the morning."

He touched her arm and said with firmness, "No." Marcus looked toward Kellie and Leanne. "Please do not concern yourselves. There is something I wish to discuss with Mistress Adela. Ye may go home now. I will escort her and be assured she comes to no harm."

Though their eyes held surprise, they nodded and left. Marcus placed the cup on the bench. He offered his arm.

Adela stared at it in astonishment.

"Mistress Adela, do ye refuse me?"

"Um, no, I, um . . ." She hesitantly looped her arm through his and rested her hand on his forearm, a very muscular forearm.

"'Tis the favor I would discuss with ye."

Afraid to look at him, she focused on her feet as they walked the garden path, and he took the route that led toward the fountain at the end of the walled gardens.

Adela took the opportunity to study him—the shape of his tightened jaw and Roman nose to his dark, wavy hair tied into a queue at the nape of his neck. She was glad he didn't wear the ridiculous wigs of the era like the preening creature who had dined with him.

"Mistress Adela, will ye accompany us to Somerset to visit an old friend of mine? He has inherited a castle and is rather excited to show it off. I must needs have a companion for Nan." The muscles in his jaw clenched. "Ye will carry on with her studies while there."

Adela stared at him, wide-eyed. Was this some sort of ruse to get her alone? Heat crept along her neck.

"Mistress Adela, are ye unwell?" He placed his free hand on top of hers.

She stumbled into him.

With quick reflexes, he pulled his arm from hers and wrapped it around her shoulders, pressing her yet closer. Her breath caught.

Adela stammered her apologies and uncharacteristically steeled herself, no longer a lamb facing a lion. It didn't matter that he was the lord of the manor. She pulled from his hold and stepped backward, her gaze meeting his and her words tumbling out with surprising steadiness.

"What do you wish of me, Marcus? To be a caretaker for Nan, or is there more you have in mind? I would appreciate full disclosure. I won't play coy with you. I need this job to survive. I also do not want to jeopardize work for my friends."

His eyes held satisfaction, admiration, and perhaps a touch of desire in their depths. "Adela," his voice rasped. "Please say my name again."

She froze, realizing too late her mistake.

He brought his hand to her cheek, his fingertips a butterfly's touch. She shivered but warmed to his touch, his grey eyes mesmerizing her.

A child's cry sounded from the terrace. "Papa! Papa! Where are ye?"

In a matter of seconds, Nan was upon them, the tail of her white gown flapping behind her.

Marcus heaved a frustrated sigh, dropped his hand, and turned to his daughter. "Nan, what are ye doing out of bed?" He dropped to his haunches as she approached.

Nan flung herself against him and clung to his neck. "I was not sleepy, so I was sitting by the window and saw ye and Mistress Adela walking. It was lonely in my bedchamber. I sneaked down the stairs to see ye." She threw a bright smile up at Adela. "I love ye both so much I could not stay away."

The adorable tiny face melted Adela's heart. She dropped to kneel at Marcus's side and smoothed the child's hair. "I love you too, my sweet. But you need your rest."

She bent, bright curls veiling her face. Her whisper came out shaky. "Papa, did she say she would come with us? If she does not, I shall die."

Marcus barked out a laugh. "I am to be undone by two beautiful women. I can see that in my future."

Beautiful—is he talking about me?

Adela sat back on her heels and once again stared at this mysterious man.

He settled Nan on his hip and rose, grabbing Adela's hand and pulling her up with them. "Ye, my sweet child, are irredeemable." Nan lay against his shoulder, and he nuzzled his lips onto her neck, then blew against her skin eliciting shrill giggles.

"Papa, ye know that tickles." She gave him a glowing expression of adoration. "Do it to Mistress Adela. I would hear her laugh."

Adela looked at Marcus and took a step back as Nan grabbed her sleeve to pull her toward them. Marcus eased the child's hand away. "No, my dear. Ye have frightened Mistress Adela beyond reason. It would be improper for me to do such a thing." He continued to watch Adela. "I shall take ye to bed and then walk Mistress Adela home."

"No . . . that's unnecessary. I know the way well." Once again, she turned to go, but he seized her hand with gentleness.

"No, ye shall not walk in the dark alone. Come with me and we shall put Nan to bed."

She followed along, uncertain why she'd given in so easily. Once they had tucked the child in with a placid reprimand not to rise until morning, they left her.

The sun had not quite dropped behind the curving hills beyond the village when Marcus and Adela reached the path to Dunbar Cottage. He tucked her arm under his and placed her hand on his forearm, resting a warm hand atop hers.

Why is he so familiar with me?

She also noted he had not answered her question about any intentions toward her. He talked about the visit to his old friend at Nunney Castle.

Adela swung toward him. "Nunney?"

His grey eyes dropped to meet hers. "Ye know of it?"

She nodded, fearful to speak. She had visited the small castle with Kellie and Leanne before coming to Stanton Wake. Most of it lay in ruin from disrepair after it was first damaged by the Parliamentarians during the English Civil War. She swallowed the lump in her throat.

That was in 1645, only twenty-one years before.

ભ🙊

Marcus watched Adela, captivated by her features shifting from uncertainty to surprise. What was it about her he found so appealing?

Oh, aye, she *was* lovely, yet no noble beauty to be sure. Not like . . .

His thoughts betrayed him. *She* had been exquisite, but he had quickly come to know she had no substance. No depth of character. Adela embodied such qualities he now understood he desired. She was kind, thoughtful, and unselfish. He swallowed. The warmth of her arm through his muddled his thoughts. She was staring at him as if he had lost what few senses remained. "Aye, mistress. What say ye of this venture to Nunney Castle?"

"I suppose that is fine."

Her hold tightened, a pleasant sensation warming his arm. "Very good. We shall leave two days hence. Please pack as lightly as possible."

Her deep sigh reverberated against him, and he shifted to walk closer by her side, the waning light impeding his sight. If only he could read her expression. What would it reveal? He took a different tactic. "Please tell me again how ye came to be here? I have yet to ask Stanton how he found ye."

She stiffened and did not answer him at once. "As I said the day we met . . ."

The clip-clop of horse hooves and a cart's rattle halted their conversation. Mr. Leckle pulled up beside them, tipped his hat, and moved on. By this time, they had arrived at the cottage, candlelight flickering in the windows.

He released her, turned, and standing a hair's breadth away whispered, "What was the name of the ship on which ye arrived? I have forgotten."

She took a half-step away from him toward the door and in a low voice said, "It was the *Tristan and Jane* from Virginia. Good night, my lord."

A brief flash of light met him as she opened the door and quickly shut it behind her. He didn't leave immediately but mused over the fact she had previously told him the ship had sailed from Boston.

The woman was an enigma—one he would most certainly

figure out. When they returned from Nunney Castle, he would ride to London to seek information, but first he had questions for Stanton.

Chapter Seventeen

Adela held tight to Nan as the little girl leaned from the carriage window and squealed, "Papa, look! The castle—the castle!"

She laughed. "Nan, you'll fall out of the window then there'll be no castle for you to see because you'll be knocked senseless."

"Oh, Mistress Adela, ye would never allow harm to come to me."

Nan's sweet words of honest affection warmed Adela's heart. How could she get so attached to this child in such a brief period? When she went back to her own time, it would break her heart. She placed her hand on the tousled strawberry-blonde curls and smoothed them into order releasing the lavender scent.

Nan peered at Adela, blue eyes wide with excitement only

a child can express with complete innocence.

The carriage jolted as they crossed the moat. Brackish water stared up at them, bright green duck moss so thick it appeared the ducklings were walking rather than paddling across it.

"Oh, look at the towers." Nan took Adela's hand and clasped it, pulling her to peer out.

"Yes, pet, they are quite amazing, aren't they?" Excitement colored her words.

If only she could tell Nan how special this trip was to her—to see the castle while people lived and thrived there. Marcus told her King Charles II had returned it to the Prater family after he'd gained the crown, and his friend was now restoring it to its former glory—before the 1645 damage from the civil war.

Nan pointed toward a stone wall next to the moat's bridge. "What are those men doing?"

Adela glanced out at Marcus, who rode close enough to the carriage to overhear their conversation. A corner of his mouth tilted upward. "Ye now know why I chose to bring Roman rather than ride in the carriage. I lack the skill to answer such a rapid fire of questions."

Instinctively, Adela's hand rested on Nan's hair again. "She's merely excited and curious." Nan beamed at her. "And, children like to share their happiness with those they love."

Marcus's smile faded, sadness dimming his eyes. He gave her an approving nod and spurred his horse forward.

Adela considered the cause of his pain. He was a kind, generous man, but the history between he and Nan's mother was a mystery.

The carriage halted inside the courtyard—a small area roofed high overhead and supported with huge beams. Servants bustled about, removing their trunks and scuttling away to disappear through a doorway.

As they left the carriage, Marcus handed Roman's reins to a stable hand, and he came toward them. Nan fell into his arms, giggling.

Adela placed her foot upon the step to depart unaided from the conveyance.

He placed Nan onto her feet and turned to help Adela. His brow furrowed. "Wait until someone assists ye, should ye misstep. 'Tis not safe."

She gripped the sides of the carriage as he placed his hands on her waist to bring her to the cobbles.

The independent nature within Adela surged. "I'm fully capable of climbing down from a tiny carriage. Women aren't helpless, you know."

Marcus's hands froze around her, his grey eyes squinting as he met her gaze. "Ye, Adela Jenks, are a curious woman. I merely wanted to make certain ye did yourself no harm. The cobbles here are uneven, and a fall could result in injury." He released her, stepped back, and gave her a bow. "Pardon me."

"Marcus, old fellow!" A deep voice reverberated across the courtyard as a tall, fair man approached them.

"George! 'Tis good to see ye." Marcus embraced the man and patted him heartily on the back.

After introductions to George Prater, Nan and Adela were handed off to servants to escort them to their rooms to freshen up before the evening meal. Adela looked back to see the two men walking side-by-side, Marcus the taller of the two. Their stride was the same—confident, bold.

Over the next hour, Adela settled into her chamber next to Nan's. She was, after all, playing governess to the child at her father's request. It was a lovely room by her own shabby-chic standards.

Based on seventeenth-century norms, it was probably the room for the governess, being adjacent to Nan's, but not of the same quality. She strode to the door connecting their chambers and peered inside to find Nan curled up on the small, canopied bed. Her hands clasped together and tucked underneath the pillow, knees pulled to her middle.

Adela's chest tightened with fondness as she watched Nan's gentle breathing. Pale, reddish curls fanned out on the white pillow and counterpane, pink cheeks on ivory skin. She went to the bed and bent to touch the girl's arm and found it chilled. A blue chintz blanket lay folded on a trunk at the foot of the bed. Quietly unfolding it, she placed it over the sleeping child and tucked it with care. Adela knelt by the bed, arms folded in front of her, as she prayed for this precious little girl and her father.

∞

Marcus followed the servant up the winding staircase to Nan's room. All he could think about during his visit with George was Adela's remark about how children merely wanted to share their happiness with those they love.

Nan's incessant questions had always been a struggle for Marcus. Guilt regarding her mother's departure had plagued him and placing distance between he and Nan helped ease his conscience. He was the reason Nan had no mother. If he had been the husband she needed, she would still be with them.

He paused at the door. Silence met him, so he eased it open. What he saw took him aback.

Adela knelt at Nan's bedside. His daughter slept while she had one hand resting on Nan's arm. Adela's lips moved, eyes closed. Was she *praying*?

Her lips stilled, and she leaned in to kiss Nan's cheek, a tear slipping onto the reddish curls. Adela then rested on her folded arms atop the counterpane, inhaled, and released a breath that was more a sigh.

Marcus retreated from the room, but his boot caught on the Turkish rug. He stumbled forward but righted himself with ease. Adela's head snapped up, her mouth forming an O. A few glistening tears clung to her cheeks.

"My lord, I . . ." Adela stammered as she pushed herself from the floor.

"No need to rise. I am sorry to have disturbed ye," he whispered and gestured toward Nan. "I merely wanted to see how Nan faired—" He attempted a smile. "—and ye as well."

Adela stumbled, and Marcus reached out to assist her and froze, unsure whether to offer aid. Her hands shot out, clenching tightly to his arms. He grasped her waist. Inches apart, he searched her face. She averted her eyes to his cravat.

The warmth of her hands through his sleeves was tantalizing. Reticent to break his hold, he leaned near and murmured, "I would not have ye afraid of me."

Startled eyes met his. "I am not afraid." Her lips trembled

on the whispered words.

He could not look away, and it seemed, nor could she.

The air between them warmed and flowed as if it had a life of its own. Marcus moved a fraction closer and brought a hand to her face, brushing away the tears with his fingertips, her cheeks reddening at his touch, eyes downcast. When he spoke, his voice was hoarse, foreign to his ears. "This I am glad to hear. Nan cares for ye a great deal and . . ."

A yawn sounded from the bed followed by a squeal, halting his words. They drew apart.

"Papa!" Nan bounced on the bed, then catapulted toward them. "Oh, Papa, I dreamed I was a princess asleep in a great bed of brilliant silks and tapestries covering the canopy, and there was food like I have not seen served on platters as big as me!" She held her arms wide and grabbed him around the legs in an affectionate embrace. "I love ye, Papa. Thank ye for bringing me to my first castle. Mistress Adela has been to a lot of castles, but she said she likes this one best because I am with her."

Her lively voice quickened his heart. He bent and pulled her to his chest, closing his eyes as tiny arms wound around his neck. When he opened them, Adela stood against the bed, her face lit with pleasure.

Nan leaned back in her father's arms, her bright eyes squinted up at him in curiosity. "Papa, were ye about to kiss Mistress Adela?"

༺༒༻

"Nan!" Adela said in horror. "Your father would not do such a thing. He kept me from tumbling to the floor." Her thoughts betrayed the desire she *had* wanted him to kiss her.

Nan heaved an irritated sigh. "I saw ye. It did take a long time for ye to steady. Timmy the gardener tried to kiss Amy, the kitchen girl, and he touched her cheek like Papa did. So, I think he was."

She turned in his arms. "Papa, were ye were about to kiss Mistress Adela?"

Marcus's lips twitched in amusement. "Well, my dear . . . Adela takes such great care of ye. And I appreciate it. So, aye, I aimed to kiss her cheek in gratitude." He demonstrated by pulling Nan close and quickly kissing her cheek. "Ye see?"

The little girl laughed. "Very well. So, when are ye going to give *her* one?" She giggled.

Adela bit back a smile as Marcus set Nan on her feet and beamed at his daughter. "I came to escort ye to dine."

"But Papa, ye must kiss Mistress Adela, *and* she must come and eat with us."

Adela captured Nan's hand. "Let us get you freshened up so you may eat with your father. I am to eat in my chamber, Nan. A servant is not to eat with you in the dining hall."

Marcus's face was guarded. "Nan, we are guests in my friend's home. We will go down and dine with Lord Prater and his family. Ye will do as Adela says, and quickly, then we shall eat. Food will be sent up to her."

Nan stamped her foot. "No." She pursed her lips and crossed her arms.

"Nan, do as your father says, or I will be the one in trouble. Where do you get the idea you may speak to him in such a disrespectful way?"

Before Adela continued, Nan whimpered, "I heard what ye said to Papa when he tried to help ye out of the carriage. I am not helpless either, and I want him to kiss ye because I love ye and preecheeate ye too."

Marcus dissolved into laughter. "Adela, your behavior has come back to bite ye. She is only following your example."

Adela's face heated. She lowered to Nan's level. "Nan, I am so very sorry. It was not very nice of me to say that to your father. He was only trying to help. Just like a few moments ago when he tried to keep me from stumbling. So, you see, all is well, and you must obey your father because he is doing what is right and proper, which is to greet and be cordial to his friend and family."

She rubbed the child's arms. "I am uncertain, but he may have children who would like to play with you."

Nan's face puckered as she considered all Adela said. A long silence later, she looked at her father. "All right. But ye *must* kiss Adela before I freshen myself." She stood her ground once more, hands on hips.

The discomfort on Marcus's face pained Adela. Fright overtook her as he approached with measured steps.

"All right, Nan. For ye."

He closed the distance between them and brought his hand to her cheek once again. She held her breath in anticipation, her gaze on his, as he slowly leaned in to place his soft, warm lips to her cheek.

Oh, my traitorous heart, but it's only a peck on the cheek done out of obligation.

It was no mere kiss though, the warmth coursing through

220

her from his nearness, his touch, unnerved her in a way she had never experienced.

Marcus lingered, his lips hovering near her ear to whisper, "'Tis done not out of duty, Adela."

She closed her eyes, inhaling his clean, woodsy scent, the strength radiating from his tall form, the gentleness in his touch. Then, he eased away, held her gaze for a long moment before saying, "Nan, be down promptly, please," and strode to the door.

When Adela faced Nan, she met the little girl's smug expression with her hand propped on a small hip, she couldn't help but smile.

What a little imp indeed.

CB&C

Kellie followed Leanne as she stomped down the stairs. "I cannot believe Lord DeGrey hauled Adela away." She took the last step with a leap into the room. "Jerk!"

"Leanne! What's come over you?" Kellie touched her shoulder. "Go sit down. I'll start breakfast while you fume."

Leanne obeyed, plopping into a chair at the table. "I know it's silly, but we have so little time together to talk and work on getting back home."

"Yeah, I know." Kellie put water on to boil and pulled out the day-old bread Mrs. Henshaw had given them.

"I'm sorry to be such a grump. Between Adela leaving us and that, that brother of Marcus's, this has not been a pleasant week." She rested her head on folded arms and sighed.

Kellie sliced the bread and put it on the stove to warm, then brought butter, honey, and Mrs. Henshaw's berry preserves to the table. She loved the woman like a sister, but she could be a drama queen at times. "Tea will be ready in a flash."

Leanne popped up. "Kel . . . thank you."

Kellie pulled a face. "What did I do to deserve that?"

Leanne erupted into laughter. "Your face reminds me of the little boy, Andy. His eyes are the same shade of blue."

Kellie returned to the table with their tea, handing Leanne a cup to which she added honey in hers and Kellie's.

"Thanks." Kellie chuckled. "He is a sweet boy. Sometimes I could just pinch his cute little face. I've been meaning to ask where he lives. He's always at the stables."

Leanne shrugged. "I don't know." She sipped her tea with care. "Why don't you ask Stanton? I met Andy on the way back from the *pit* the other day, and he thanked me—and all of us—for taking care of Stanton. Said he was like a papa to him."

"What?" Kellie's eyes rounded. "A papa?"

"That's what he said." Leanne shrugged, took a sip of tea, and wrinkled her nose. "What's that smell?"

Kellie bolted from her chair. "The bread!" She grabbed a cloth, then the handle of the iron griddle, and set it aside. "I got it just in time. Thanks to your sensitive nose."

She wiggled her eyebrows. "My nose and I are glad to be of service."

Kellie brought generous slices of bread on two plates to the table and said grace, then a possibility struck her.

"Um, Lee, do you suppose Andy is Stanton's son?"

Leanne froze, bread near her lips. "*Son?*"

"Well, Andy told you Stanton was like a papa to him and was grateful to us for helping while he was sick."

Leanne huffed. "I suppose it's possible." She grew pensive and toyed with the cup handle. "He would have to take after his mother, whoever she is, because they don't have any distinguishing features in common."

"Hmm, no. Andy has blue eyes, Stanton's are grey."

Leanne shot her a glare.

"Don't look at me like that. I was saying they don't have the same eye color or hair color. Andy's are more like . . ." Her eyes widened, realization hitting her.

"What?" Leanne asked, clutching her bread. "Like *who*?"

"Christopher DeGrey."

Leanne gasped, dropping the bread to the plate. "Oh my, you're right. I can't believe I didn't see it before."

CB&ED

Leanne hummed as she walked back from the pit. It took her mind off her troubles. Temporarily, at least.

"Mistress Leanne! Wait for me!" Andy shouted behind her, his sturdy little legs surging to catch up with her.

When the boy reached her side, she tousled his hair. She settled her empty buckets on the path and lowered to her haunches, not a minor feat in the cumbersome dress. "How are you today, Andy? I've missed seeing you the past couple of days. What have you been up to?"

"Oh, aye. Stanton has been most busy with a new foal. Mistress Kellie has been helpin' when she be done with her chores."

Leanne stood, and he grabbed her hand, swinging it between them. He looked up at her adoringly. They each retrieved a bucket.

His faced flushed, and he looked down at his feet. "I have a question for ye, mistress."

She squeezed his hand. "What would that be?"

He blinked a few times and drew himself to his full height. "I know ye have some years on me, but would ye wait 'til I be as tall as Stanton and marry me?"

Leanne halted in the middle of the path. The conversation she'd had with Kellie the night before came to her. Who was this child, and where did he belong?

She drew him to the side of the lane and sat on a soft tuft of grass, pulling him down beside her. "Where do you live, Andy?"

Without releasing her hand, he scooted closer, tears welling. "I live with Timothy and Martin since me mother died."

Leanne lifted his chin, so their eyes met. "I'm so sorry your mother died. That must have been very hard."

He nodded and swatted the errant tear from his cheek.

"But what about your father? I'm sure he loves you very much."

Another tear escaped. "I know not who my sire is."

She drew him onto her lap and held him, gently rocking, and tucked his head under her chin.

An unknown father indeed. A careless one who was too charming for his own good. No good. Her blood boiled.

They sat for some time before he spoke again. "Well, will ye?"

Leanne's heart lurched. "Oh, my sweet. I am much too old for you. By the time you grow as tall as Stanton, I will be an old woman. You'll be wanting a pretty girl your own age."

"No," he said with powerful conviction. "I shall always love ye. Ye saved my . . . Stanton."

"I only helped. Mistress Adela and Mistress Kellie helped as well. Especially Mistress Kellie. She's a nurse you know."

"Aye. But she does love Stanton. And I think Mistress Adela does love Lord DeGrey, so ye see . . . it must be ye." He studied her face with a serious expression, much older than his years. "Mrs. Henshaw is the only other lady I do know that be kind to me. And she be much too old for me."

A spirited laugh sounded, interrupting their conversation. "Oh, child, Mrs. Henshaw would make ye a much better wife. This one is a rare breed, and I do not wish ye to come to any harm. Break your heart she would."

Andy jumped to his feet and glared at Christopher DeGrey. "No! She is perfect. Leave her be." His bright blue eyes flashed with anger, and he clasped his small hands into fists, then bolted down the path toward the manor.

Leanne had an idea he was going to the stables. She crossed her arms and gave Christopher a scowl. "How could you be so cruel? To laugh at that boy. He has no family. His mother died, and he doesn't even know who his father is. Probably some low-life who jilted his mother."

Something flickered in his eyes—his brilliant blue-grey eyes. She certainly believed Kellie right in her assessment.

Christopher turned on his heel, hands clenched at his sides. He strode a few feet, then abruptly turned and marched back to her. "Mistress Leanne, ye judge harshly when ye know nothing of a situation. I am not at liberty to educate ye on Andrew's story, but I assure ye he is well cared for. He resides with a respectable family in the village who are well paid to care for him. In future, I would appreciate no *assumptions* about anything until ye know all the facts. Good morrow."

Leanne's mouth dropped. *What was that all about?*

How she wished Adela would return. She would probably have some excellent advice on this sordid subject. And how was she to handle poor little Andy's broken heart? The beast, Christopher DeGrey, had hurt him deeply with his words. Why had he done that?

The more she thought on it, her anger ignited. She jumped to her feet and left her buckets, forgotten, at the side of the path.

When she caught up with Christopher, she grabbed his arm and twisted him to face her. "Why were you so cruel to Andy?"

His eyes bored into her, wetness glazing their depths. She stepped back, shocked at his tears.

"I . . . I'm sorry." She moved to back up, but he grasped her upper arms.

"Don't be. I had it coming. In truth, cruelty was not my intention. It was in jest. I did but jest in hope he would laugh. After all, he is but a boy." He sighed, dropping a hand from her arm. When he ran trembling fingers through his hair, it looked just as Andy's only moments before when Leanne had tousled it.

Her words came out as a whisper. "Are you Andy's father?"

He didn't answer.

Releasing her, he strode into the woods before turning back. "Follow me not. I must needs think."

The truth was evident in his pained expression and tense bearing.

Leanne watched him, shoulders weighed down as if burdened, and she longed to comfort him, yet she stayed her ground.

What was his story? Truly, who was Christopher DeGrey?

CAROLE LEHR JOHNSON

Chapter Eighteen

The sun slanted over the manor, shooting red and yellow streaks across the sky, as it began its descent behind the stables. The end of June was fast approaching, and the weather had been mild with just enough rain to nourish the countryside but not as warm as Kellie would have expected for summer. She picked up her pace, nearing her destination. The rolling green hills and fresh country smells surrounded her at every turn.

Honey-scented vegetation abounded, lush leafy plants and trees filled with twittering birds left her with a sense of calm.

In Stanton's message, he requested she come to the stables when her duties were done for the day because he had something to tell her. The possibilities danced around in her mind. She advised Leanne she would be late, and Stanton would see her home.

The warmth of lanterns already lit for the coming night greeted her when she entered the stable along with the whinnies and snorts of the horses settling in for the evening. She closed her eyes, the scent of hay mingling with bay rum welcoming her. Stanton was near.

When she opened her eyes, he stood a few feet from her, leaning against a stall, eyes dancing with amusement. "Would it be improper for me ta ask what ye were doin'?"

Kellie grinned. "Yes. It would be most ungentlemanly of you." Her skirt swished against the hay as she strode toward him. "Why have you summoned me?"

"'Tis not for me to summon ye. I am not the lord of the manor. 'Twould be Marcus's job." His eyes narrowed. "Would you rather *he* summon ye?"

Her cheeks burned. "No. Why would I? It would be—"

Stanton leaned toward her. "Aye?"

"Oh. Never mind."

He gripped her upper arm though his touch was gentle. "Who would be wantin' Marcus to summon them?"

Kellie paused. She'd messed up *again*.

An unlikely rescuer entered the stable.

"Stanton, have ye seen Mistress Leanne? I—" Christopher DeGrey's voice preceded his appearance in the open doorway. "Pardon me. I was not aware ye had—" He coughed. "—a visitor."

He released her arm. "No, Chris, I have not seen her, but Mistress Kellie has I am certain."

"She's home. I'm to join her shortly. Would you like for me

to give her a message?"

Christopher closed the gap between them and bowed. "Good eve. We have not formally met."

Stanton moved to stand beside her. "Mistress Kellie, this is Marcus' brother, Christopher DeGrey."

She curtsied. "A pleasure to meet you." Her lips curved upward. "I saw you in the garden with Nan when you came upon Leanne."

A flush crept across his cheeks. "Indeed." He cleared his throat. "It appears the bushes have eyes."

Stanton crossed his arms over his chest and frowned at Christopher. "Sounds like a story I may need to hear."

"No need, Stanton. I am confident Mistress Kellie will be most glad to share it with ye." He bowed again. "I shall take my leave. Please tell Mistress Leanne I must needs speak with her. I have no wish to create a scandal by appearing at your cottage door whilst she is unchaperoned." He strode to the door, his shoulders slumping.

Stanton huffed. "The lad shall never grow up."

"I'm not sure, but there may be something going on between him and Leanne. She talks about him way too much. Not in a flattering way, which reminds me of the saying, 'The lady doth protest too much, methinks.'"

"Ye do impress me, Mistress Kellie. I was not aware ye know Shakespeare."

Kellie couldn't suppress a sneer. "I do not. Adela has quoted it numerous times, and it stuck in my brain."

His chuckle warmed her insides.

The rugged man had a soft side for literature? She looked at him quizzically. "Are you a fan of Shakespeare?"

The laughter faded, and his expression grew puzzled. "Fan?"

"Um . . . it's a term for someone who likes something or someone a great deal."

Stanton seemed appeased by the explanation, his features relaxing. "Just as ye are a *fan* of riding?"

"Exactly." She sighed in relief. "Now, *why* did you summon me?"

"Come this way." He bowed with a wave of his hand toward the stalls. "I have something to show ye."

Kellie followed his direction. He opened the gate and ushered her in. The beautiful mare they'd attended for a few weeks stood in the corner munching hay, her huge brown eyes surveying her guests.

Stanton led Kellie to stand by the mare, speaking soothing words to the horse as they approached. He brought one of Kellie's hands to splay it against the horse's stomach, laying his hand atop hers and gently sliding their connected hands over the prickly hair.

Kellie looked a question at him.

"Close your eyes. The way ye did earlier. Do ye feel a difference between here—" His warm hand guided hers and stopped. "—and here?"

Her eyes flew open, and she gawked at him. "Really? Do you mean . . ."

"Twins." His eyes gleamed with pleasure. "'Tis a rare thing."

"Yes, it is."

He nodded, too transfixed on the horse, his hand still on hers.

"So, this is what you wanted to tell me?"

"Aye, and ta ask if ye would care to assist when they arrive?"

"Yes. How much longer will it be?"

"Methinks a fortnight or so."

Kellie had trouble remembering if that were seven days or fourteen. Her gaze slipped to their hands, his eyes still on the horse. The heat against her skin, his nearness, brought her back to the present. She pulled away.

"I need to go. Leanne will wonder where I am. I assume she's holding dinner for me."

"Aye. I suppose so." Concern flashed in his eyes. "The hour grows late. I shall walk ye home."

"Totally unnecessary. I've been traveling the path for weeks."

"Aye, but not at eve whilst alone. 'Tis not safe."

"On manor grounds?"

"No. A woman must never be without a chaperone."

Kellie raised her eyebrows. "*You're* going to chaperone *me*?" She teased.

His white teeth flashed against his tanned face.

She stepped from the stall and held the gate for him. "If you must."

"I must." He clicked the gate shut and stayed at her side as they walked out into the dusk.

Doves cooed in the distance, a gentle wind with the scent of foliage in it tousled her hair. They ambled in companionable silence for a time before he spoke.

"We were interrupted earlier. Now tell me who would wish for Marcus to summon them."

Kellie stared, unsure how to respond.

His gaze steadied on hers. "'Tis Mistress Adela, is it not?"

Fear welled, and her stomach roiled. She faced him and lightly gripped his bicep. "Please do not tell anyone. Adela would never admit it, and I don't want to get her into trouble. She . . . she admires him, respects him."

Stanton rested a comforting hand on her shoulder. "Not to worry yourself, mistress. I will say naught. Yet, I must needs tell ye somethin'. 'Tis not my place to share the reasons, but ye must needs help Mistress Adela not to lose her heart to Marcus. Even if he returns the feelin'. She must turn him away."

Kellie sniffled. "I know. He cannot have a relationship with his servant. I mean, he *could*, but it would not be proper. Adela would never take him on those grounds anyway. Her faith would not allow it. And he cannot marry a servant with his status."

"'Tis true." He looked away, a hint of sorrow in his eyes.

"Stanton, is there something I should know about Lord DeGrey?"

He observed the stars just appearing. "'Tis not my tale. I would not have your friend hurt—nor ye . . ." His voice trailed off, gaze softening, as he embraced her. She rested against his shoulder, a faint whisper of leather and hay clinging to him.

234

The strength of his arms comforted her in a way Tim's never had. Breathing in his scent, she released a contented sigh as if she'd waited for this moment her entire life.

He pulled back abruptly. "My apologies. I should not have done that."

"I didn't mind." Her hands still rested on his chest, then she realized the gravity of her words. It was true. She *hadn't* minded, but she could not, should not, be swept up in any man's arms. Her fiancé just dumped her for crying out loud.

Kellie dropped her hands, turned, and walked briskly along the path, leaving him behind. He caught up with her but did not utter a word.

What was she thinking! This man, this time, it was all getting to her. She couldn't begin to wrap her mind around it all. It didn't make sense. Why were they here?

The cottage came into view, light spilling from the downstairs window. She longed to bury herself under the scratchy covers of her uncomfortable bed and have a good cry. "Thank you for walking me home. Have a good night."

Kellie meant to leave Stanton without another word, but when she opened the door, what she saw made her stumble back and clutch his arm for support.

⋘⋙

Leanne slammed the door behind her, angry with Kellie for leaving her to walk home alone *again*.

Since Adela's departure, she'd gone to the stables to help Stanton with something or another nearly every evening. Leanne hated walking the creepy lane at night by herself. Yeah, she could take care of herself. She'd taken martial arts for several years for that very reason. It gave her confidence.

She banged the kettle onto the stove wishing she had a strong cup of coffee, not tea. What was it with these people?

Adela had told her coffee houses were the *thing* in London, so why didn't they have one in the village? What she wouldn't give for a cup the size of those disturbing buckets she carried every morning. She pictured herself in her convertible going through the drive-thru of her favorite coffeeshop, almost able to taste the vanilla in her latte.

Her list of withdrawal symptoms was getting longer with each passing day—coffee, social media, shopping, indoor plumbing. She wanted to bay at the moon in distress!

A teapot stood at attention on the table, waiting for the brew. The chair beckoned her, so she dropped onto it, planted her elbows on the table, and stared at the kettle.

Her thoughts strayed to the uppermost question that filled her thoughts every single day—how would they get home?

Steam drifted toward her, caught on a draft likely from under the kitchen window in the old cottage. Most days, she pretended she was the heroine of a fairy tale—a ragged servant awaiting her glass slipper, but more times than not she told herself this was all a horrible reality TV show prank. An elaborate one, yes, but those Hollywood producers had millions at their disposal. She whispered into the empty room, "Okay, I give up. You can come out of hiding. Joke's on me."

Wearily, she smoothed her straight hair and stood to collect the kettle. Once the boiling water filled the teapot, she grabbed the honey and re-claimed her seat. Before she could take the first sip, a firm knock sounded.

She scowled, unkind thoughts filling her mind. "Kellie, the door is unlocked."

The door creaked open.

Without turning, Leanne wrapped her fingers around the steaming cup. "You sure took your sweet time. I ran into the nice lady with the horrid husband. She didn't seem well. Maybe I'll take her a basket of food tomorrow. Certainly Mrs. Henshaw would be okay with that." She sipped, the heat a little more intense than expected. "Come on and have a cup before we eat." She twisted in her seat, and her mouth dropped.

Christopher DeGrey stood in the opening, the darkness framing his tall physique. A rush of cool unsullied air flowed into the space. "Good eve, mistress."

Leanne glared. "Why are you here?"

He closed the door and strode to the table taking a seat without an invitation.

She crossed her arms and glared at him. "I didn't invite you in nor did I ask you to take a seat."

"No, ye did not. I am to assume I must force my attentions on ye." He stammered, "No, I mean—I didn't mean in an unsavory way." He crossed his arms, mimicking her posture. "What I mean to say is I would like to tell ye about myself *and* Andrew." He released a heavy sigh. His face was pale, blue-grey eyes dark with underlying emotion.

An unknown sensation tugged at Leanne's heart. She rose, retrieved a cup, and placed it in front of him with a clink.

With slow deliberation, he prepared his tea and brought his gaze to hers. "When ye scolded me about Andrew's care, I was all astonishment. His mother died in childbed. I do not pretend we were wed for we were certainly not."

A pained expression marred his handsome face. "At seven and twenty, I was not in a situation to care for a child. A village couple with no children agreed to care for him. Money is provided for his needs, and I have kept myself away so as not to be a hinderance." He combed his fingers through his hair.

Leanne nodded and prepared herself another cup of tea as he continued, "Though I believed I left Andrew in capable hands, this burden has consumed me since morn, and I have now discovered duplicity. The couple used the money to line their pockets. The child—*my* child—sleeps in the cottage with Timothy and Martin and spends his days in the stable with Stanton."

He gulped the tea as if for fortification. "Please do not misunderstand. I am most grateful to them for meeting his needs. Yet 'tis not sufficient. Andrew has had no education beyond Stanton's modest lessons and learning the skills of a groom." His eyes glistened. "I desire more for him."

Leanne's heart melted for this man she'd held in contempt. Mostly because he'd hurt her pride and laughed at her. How ridiculous she now felt.

"Christopher, why are you telling me this. I feel your pain, but why me?"

His brow creased, a struggle of emotion crossing his features. He slowly reached for her hand and nestled it in his. Leanne stilled, every nerve within her on alert at his gentle touch.

"The moment I met ye I sensed a joining. I angered ye, and

ye hesitated not to reveal it." Color rose from his neck to stain his cheeks. "I have never met a woman who attempted not to seduce me. Until ye."

She recoiled, pulling her hand from his grasp. "So, this is about your bruised ego?"

He jumped to his feet. "No! I say, no. 'Tis about destiny. Do ye not believe in that?"

"Oh, sit down and chill." She stood and paced the room, her hands waving. "Destiny? Really? Do all the women you know fall for that line?"

His puzzled look made her question his sincerity. "Do you honestly believe destiny brought us together? What about Andy? He deserves more. How could you abandon your own son?" Disgust filled her, but she maintained eye contact.

His face lit with awe. "Aye, I do believe destiny brought ye and Andrew together. He is taken with ye or else he would not have asked ye to marry him."

Leanne laughed. "He's a child wanting a mother-figure."

His brows furrowed. "Mother figure?"

"It's psychology." She waved her hand in dismissal. "I don't want to get into that right now. Suffice it to say he *needs* a mother, and I'm the first woman to show him any affection or attention. The *woman* you have paid must be a real piece of work to neglect such a sweet child."

The light in Christopher's eyes reminded her of Andy. Was he somehow more like his father than she believed?

"You know you two look alike?" Leanne smiled. "Someday, he'll likely be as handso—" Nope. She was not going there. "Never mind."

"Ye say that quite often, Mistress Leanne."

His captivating smile twisted her insides, the feeling not altogether unpleasant. It had charmed many a young woman though, including Andy's mother.

Oh, what did Adela call men who were womanizers in this era, or maybe it was another time . . . a rake?

She narrowed her eyes and sat. "You still haven't answered my question. Why are you telling me this?"

"Ye are most lovely when ye are angry."

Leanne scoffed. "Flattery will get you nowhere, mister." Where was Kellie to rescue her?

Christopher reached across the table and stroked her hand with tenderness. "I intend not to flatter, merely to state what I perceive. Ye are, indeed, lovely."

Her breath caught, but she drew her hand away, leaving his resting in the center of the table.

"If you refuse to tell me why you have enlightened me with your sordid past, you should leave, Christopher."

He flinched at the insult, but the hurt in his eyes shifted to a look of determination.

Christopher stood, rounded the table, and dropped to one knee. "Mistress Leanne, will ye marry me?"

Leanne gasped, her eyes wide, lips parted. She rose to rush from this man who both beguiled and angered her.

But he rose with her, cradling her cheek in a gentle caress, his arm slipping naturally around her waist. She leaned into him as he eased his lips onto hers in a warm, reverent kiss that reverberated through her.

Christopher deepened the kiss, and she responded with equal fervor, her arms slipping around his neck.

The door swung open, and Kellie cried out, "Leanne!"

Leanne drew back, Christopher's arms still around her.

Stanton spoke, his voice laced with a hard edge. "Ye said ye would not come here with no chaperone."

Christopher cleared his throat but did not release Leanne. She still reeled from the headiness of the kiss and his words. "I could contain myself no longer. I wish not for this woman to slip through my fingers and have asked for her hand in marriage."

Leanne had never seen Kellie so wide-eyed, and she had also never seen her cling to any man—most certainly not to Stanton Yorke.

Stanton raised his chin. "And pray tell has the lass agreed to this proposal?"

Christopher stilled, his gaze on her, genuine affection in their blue-grey depths.

As her heart hammered in her chest, all Leanne could think was—*oh, how she longed for all this to be reality television.*

CAROLE LEHR JOHNSON

Chapter Nineteen

On Nunney Castle's uppermost floor, Adela peered from her chamber's window over the moat to the tiny village, savoring a quiet moment while Nan napped next door. She, Leanne, and Kellie had toured this castle's ruins and grounds a few days after their arrival in England, so this visit was her second trip to the structure with its four towers, conical roofs, and battlements.

To be standing here, seeing it in its prime, was like living a dream.

A knock drew her out of her musings. She opened the door to a small thin girl, who bobbed a brief curtsy and presented a toothy grin. It was with talent she'd managed a curtsy wielding such a heavy tray laden with food and drink.

"Good eve, mistress."

Adela opened the door, and the maid placed the tray on a

table by the window. She followed and pulled out a chair.

"This is a tremendous amount of food for one." Her gaze sought the girl's face. "What is your name?"

The girl drew back and shot her a wary look. "Me, mistress?"

"Yes." Adela lifted the pitcher and sniffed the contents.

Face red, her chin dipped. "I be Catherine, mistress."

"Such a pretty name." Adela poured a tiny portion of the liquid into a stemmed glass and held it to the light. "What is this, Catherine?"

"'Tis watered wine, mistress." She coughed. "Lord DeGrey said ye was a lady and did not care for powerful drink."

It was Adela's turn to draw back. "Oh, he did, did he?"

The girl's face paled.

Adela placed a hand on her arm. "Oh, please don't misunderstand me. I'm sure he did it out of kindness."

The color returned to her ivory skin. "Aye, mistress. Do ye be needin' anythin' more?"

A knock sounded, and the girl hurried to answer it.

Lord DeGrey stood with his fist raised to knock again. He nodded at the maid. "I wish to see Mistress Adela. Ye may leave us."

Catherine scurried away.

Marcus strode to the table, pulled out the second chair, and seated himself across from Adela. He glanced at her glass. "Do ye not find the wine to your liking?"

"Yes. It's good. Thank you for requesting it watered." Her lips curled with amusement. "I assume *you* assumed I could not handle it full-strength."

A low laugh escaped him. "No. As I know ye to be a woman of faith and—" Warmth radiated in his gaze. "—I dare say a virtuous one. I believe ye likely abstain from potent drink."

"A wise assumption."

When she set her half-filled glass on the table, he reached for the pitcher and refilled it before she protested. "Please, do not allow my presence to hinder your dining. I shall collect Nan shortly, so we may dine with the Praters."

Adela's stomach quivered at the thought of eating under his watchful eye. She had proper manners, but, in this time, table etiquette was most likely poles apart from twenty-first century guidelines. She reached for the three-pronged fork, much larger than what she used in her time. It had *heft*.

He drew in a deep breath, eyes never wavering from hers.

Perhaps she could distract him with conversation.

"M . . . Lord DeGrey. I want to formally apologize for my outburst at the carriage. It was not a salutary lesson in manners for Nan to witness." She gently speared a piece of meat, lifted it to her mouth, and chewed slowly. It was so tender it almost melted in her mouth.

"Mistress Adela, ye have thus issued such an apology in Nan's presence, do ye not recall?"

Still chewing, she nodded.

He rubbed his chin and bit his lip. "Furthermore . . . that is not the only time ye have begun to call me Marcus."

Adela felt the blood drain from her face. She brought the glass to her lips, swallowed air, and coughed, which turned into a fit that seemed to never cease. Tears pooled along the curve of her cheeks and blotched the dove-grey fabric of her dress. She dabbed her eyes with a napkin and peered at him with another apology. His features blurred through the tears, and she was glad his expression was hidden.

His chair scraped over the slate floor, then she felt his warmth beside her. He lightly pulled her to stand, placed a hand on her shoulder, and with the other rubbed her back in firm circular motions.

"Most times, this works for Nan when she does choke."

His warm wine-scented breath tickled her cheek, distracting her from the coughing, which subsided. Adela closed her eyes, breathed in and out several times, willing her mind—and her heart—to remain calm. "You may stop now. Thank you for your help." She reclaimed her seat and carefully sipped her drink, pushing away the electrifying effect of his touch.

His voice was thick with emotion when he returned to his chair. "Methinks we must speak."

She schooled her features. "About what, Lord DeGrey?"

His eyes shone, seemingly affected as well. When he spoke, his voice was edged with impatience. "I am weary of these games we play. There is something between us ..." His stare bored into her. "We must identify it. Will ye help me?"

Adela dropped her gaze to her lap, hands clenching until her knuckles whitened. "I don't know what you mean. You are my employer—my *master*."

His chair scraped across the floor in a flash. Pale grey eyes peered into her very soul.

"I am *not* your master." He enunciated each word. "Is this

246

what ye think of me?"

Her throat constricted. All she wanted was to flee the room and have a gut-wrenching cry.

Adela rose, eased her chair under the table, and with every ounce of grace she could muster, told him, "Good evening to you, Lord DeGrey. I shall retire the night. It has been a long day."

He closed the space separating them and pulled her toward him.

His expression softened as he drew her into an embrace and pressed his lips to her neck. "Please let us not part whilst angry, Adela."

She closed her eyes, savoring the tender way he said her name, and allowed herself to be held, knowing it was not right, yet . . .

Please, Lord, help me for I am afraid. Not of this man, but of this time You have brought me to. What am I to do?

Marcus eased back, straying only a breath from her face, his eyes imploring hers. "Ye mystify me, Adela. I know ye harbor some feeling for me. 'Tis written on your face, in your voice, and your actions, yet ye resist." He brought his lips to hers, delicate, soft, like the brush of a rose petal. It took her breath away, and she was lost.

Her arms wound around his neck, and she breathed in the scent of rosemary.

No man had ever kissed her this way.

She sensed his passion, the restraint of a gentleman, not the improper attention of a lord to his servant.

Chivalry was most certainly choking on its last breath in

the twenty-first century. She had seen it die firsthand with each of her failed relationships over too many years. Now, she was too old to care, and here she was in the arms of a bona fide lord, but it wouldn't matter if he'd been a stable hand. His station in life had nothing to do with her feelings.

He murmured her name against her lips, and she came to her senses, dropping her arms, and stepping back. "No." She swallowed hard and with force said, "*No.* This cannot happen."

He appeared stunned, his voice assuring. "I am not asking anything further of ye. I would never compromise ye in such a way."

Though trembling, Adela stood her ground with folded arms. She had let the men of her past control her. It ended now. "Your presence in my chamber alone is enough by today's standards. Is it not so, Lord DeGrey?"

He rubbed his forehead. "My thoughts are amiss. Ye speak truth."

Neither of them moved, both staring at the other, locked in a small eternity. A few strides took him to the door. "Please forgive me for coming to your chamber while ye are without a chaperone." His hand on the door, he faced her. "Adela, I am not sorry for the kiss, and of a certainty, neither are ye."

After he left, Adela leaned against the table, turmoil within her. She squeezed her eyes shut, his words washing over her anew. This time, he was the one who had spoken truth.

CO80

Leanne met Kellie's incredulous stare. Her friend clung tight to Stanton, who guided her to enter the cottage. His voice was nearly a growl. "Chris. What have ye done?"

Christopher pulled Leanne tighter. "I have done naught."

Kellie aimed narrowed eyes at him. "Oh, yes, you have."

Her face blanched as she turned to Leanne. "You were kissing the man, and he asked you to marry him, and you stand there like a mannequin in a department store window." She blew out a frustrated breath. "Wipe that love-sick grin off your face."

Anger shot through Leanne, and she released Christopher and pointed at Kellie. "What do you mean?"

"You want to say yes, don't you? I see it in your eyes."

Stanton gently took Kellie's arm. "'Tis not our affair. They are both of an age, but methinks I shall take Christopher with me." He looked at the man and jerked his head toward the door.

Christopher took Leanne's hand. "Please consider my offer. We shall speak on the morrow." He brought her hand to his lips, then followed Stanton out the door.

With the warmth of his lips lingering on her hand, Leanne turned to Kellie, whose face was still flushed with anger. She took a seat at the table and peered up at her friend.

"Let me explain."

"Do tell." Kellie snarled. She removed her cloak and joined Leanne at the table. "What in the world just happened?"

Leanne wasn't exactly sure. She sighed and attempted to relay all that happened from the moment Christopher stepped over the threshold to the proposal and kiss that nearly brought her to her knees.

The man and the kiss still lingered on her mind and heart, and that's what worried her.

⋞⋟

Marcus approached Nan's chamber just as the sun passed over Nunney Castle the next morning. He tapped on the door.

"Come in, Papa."

Nan sat at a dressing table with Adela holding a length of leaf-green ribbon, preparing her hair for a day of adventure. Her long curls tumbled down her back.

Adela looked in the mirror at Nan's reflection. Marcus met her eyes, and they stared at one another until she looked away. He faced his daughter. "Mistress Adela has made ye even more beautiful than ye were, my child."

Nan flew into his arms. "My sweet," he said, then peered over her at Adela.

The memory of the night before flashed across her face. His sleep was plagued with thoughts of her pliant in his arms, her lips soft against his. He had to find a way out of his circumstances, so he could have this woman.

If she agreed to have *him*. He would seek Stanton's counsel upon their return to Dunbar Park.

He rose, settled the child on her feet, and took Nan's plump hand in his. "Ladies, we are to have an out of doors feast today."

Nan squealed, bounced on her heels, and tugged her father's hand until he was at her level. Her arms enveloped him, and he squeezed his eyes shut, tucking this memory away for when he was a doddering old man sitting before a fire.

A glimpse of the scene flitted through his mind like lightning in a tempest. He hoped, with any good fortune, he would not be *alone*. His gaze caught Adela's.

Yet he must needs discover her secret. He feared another entanglement that may cause Nan harm. Just as Gil had caused them both.

He stood and eased Nan toward Adela. "Ready yourselves. We shall leave within the hour."

Fingers entwined at her waist, Adela twisted them nervously. "Lord DeGrey, since you will be with the Prater family, would I perhaps be able to remain here and take care of Nan's laundry."

"I think not, Mistress Adela. Ye shall attend Nan should she have need of ye. The Prater children will have their governess in attendance." He bowed and left.

Marcus shut the door, rested his back against it, and allowed a deep exasperated breath to escape. Far too much mystery surrounded Adela—and her friends. The unanswered questions railed through him, frustrating beyond measure. He must get to the bottom of it. He would inform George that pressing business must take him to London, therefore they would depart two days hence.

Marcus shoved himself away from the door and strode down the hall with purpose in his steps. Aye, he would find the truth about Adela Jenks.

CRITICAL

Adela was in awe of their entourage for the picnic—two horse-drawn carriages and a cart with food and supplies as well as furniture and carpets. They rode along bumpy lanes she would not call roads. Nan had ridden in the carriage with the Prater children and their governess, while she was told to ride with Lord and Lady Prater and Marcus.

With each jolt, she bumped into Marcus's thigh, but he made no move to slide closer to the window out of which he constantly stared.

In one instance, the lurch was so severe she thought surely, they had lost a wheel. The jolt slammed her into him, her chin hitting his shoulder. He grabbed her before she fell to the floor, and she clung to his arm. Lady Prater held tight to her husband, her face pale as her ivory gloves. A moan escaped her, and Adela realized the woman had motion sickness. Not a glorious feeling to be sure.

Marcus's arm intertwined with Adela's, pulling her closer to his side. The frown he'd worn the entire journey had softened when she looked at him. Something akin to pleasure glinted in his pale eyes. "It shall not be long."

The jolting eased, but he did not let go. He kept his gaze on her, and she sensed had the Praters not been with them, he would've kissed her again. If only she were able, she would will herself to the twenty-first century. Everything was growing increasingly more complicated.

The carriage stopped with a final jolt sending Adela's neglected book to the floor and her prayers ceasing for safe travels. Her whole body ached, not unlike the one and only time she had ridden a rollercoaster. Was a picnic worth such discomfort? Was this really what people enjoyed subjecting themselves to in this time?

No one moved until a servant opened the door to report a shady spot had been found and to wait while they unloaded.

Marcus spoke up. "George, ye and Mary please go first. I believe your wife needs fresh air at once."

The man thanked Marcus and exited the carriage. Marcus retrieved Adela's book and extended it to her. When she grasped it, his grip held firm.

In a low voice, he said, "I slept very ill last night thinking on how to address ye, mistress." His shadowed eyes implored her. "Please allow me into your life. I wish ye no ill. Let us begin this day to know one another more. Once we are settled, let us go for a walk. I shall begin by telling ye about myself, of what I do not share with others, what ye must needs know."

The servant coughed, holding the door open.

Marcus stepped into the bright sunlight and reached up to assist Adela. When she stood, her legs quivered for a moment until she gained her bearing. Rather than taking her hand, he lifted her from the carriage with strong hands at her waist.

She nodded her thanks and smiled.

The servant pointed to a copse of trees about a hundred yards from the carriage. Adela took in the surroundings—the top of a knoll overlooking lush, rolling hills in an astonishing array of green. Sheep dotted distant fields while other land held rippling rows of crops. Large grey rocks, stacked into walls separating fields, formed an uneven checkerboard design across the land. The pastoral scene resembled a masterpiece like a painting that graced the walls of the Louvre or the Met.

"Where are ye, Adela?" Marcus spoke low at her shoulder.

Her eyes flickered to his. She hadn't moved since leaving the carriage. "I'm sorry. I was simply admiring the landscape."

They stood alone. The Praters had taken Nan with them to the trees where they were reclining on blankets, the children squealing in delight at their release from confinement, chasing butterflies. No one was near enough to see him take her hand in his and give it a light squeeze.

She looked at their joined hands and back at him. "This is improper, Marcus." Even as she said the words, she longed to take them back but refused to be a dalliance. She swallowed a sigh. It was impossible, and for heaven's sake, the man was three hundred years her senior. The realization almost made her laugh aloud.

Marcus's grip tightened. "They cannot see from their post. Will ye answer my question before we join them?"

Her thoughts muddled. "Question?"

He squeezed her hand again. "Do not play coy with me."

"Hmm? Oh, yes, your question." Adela drew in and released an unsteady breath. "Yes, Marcus, I will try. But when I reveal all, you won't understand. I hardly believe it myself." This time *she* gripped his hand tighter. "But I cannot tell you today. I must ask Leanne and Kellie. It is not my story alone to tell."

A moment passed before he said, "If ye must. I understand. Yet it does not hinder me from beginning my story, does it?"

Adela shook her head. The man baffled her more each day. What would happen when—*if*—she told him the truth? And, furthermore, what was he going to reveal to her?

CB80

Throughout their meal, Marcus's attention gravitated from Adela to Nan as their group spent a leisurely two hours with a delicious lunch of cold meats, pasties, apple cider, fruits, cheese, and tarts.

The governess for the Praters stood. "Come along, children. Let us explore." Her gaze turned to Adela. The woman had a kind, engaging smile that lit her face. "Will ye join us, Mistress Adela?"

Adela rose and brushed the wrinkles from her skirt. "I'd be happy to." She seized Nan's hand.

Marcus hoisted himself to stand. "Thank ye for your kind offer, but Mistress Adela and I have a matter to discuss." He patted Nan. "My dear, will ye please excuse Mistress Adela for a brief time? I shall send her to ye the moment we are finished."

Nan nodded, and the governess corralled the children to follow her to a nearby meadow teeming with wildflowers.

George Prater's eyes clouded. "Marcus, tarry not. My wife and I would have ye join us in a game of pall mall."

Marcus nodded and extended his arm toward Adela, who curtsied before the couple, and accepted it.

Once out of earshot, Adela asked, "Was that rude?" Her voice held no derision, merely curiosity.

He watched her face, searching for censure, but found only curiosity. "No. Why do ye ask?"

She shrugged. "I'm a servant, and you're leaving your host and his wife to walk with me. Is that not unseemly in this . . ."

Her voice was lovely, and although she spoke English, he was unaccustomed to her pronunciation. Her speech revealed that she was no commoner. Educated, she was.

The woman had captivated him, and now was the time to

find out if it were real or only the longings of his lonely heart.

A brilliant orange butterfly fluttered across the path away from the children who busily picked daisies and wildflowers. His eyes followed the clumsy, jagged pattern of the insect's flight and wondered how they survived at all in their short life so wrought with danger and uncertainty.

Life was much the same, his in particular.

They walked in silence for a while, distancing themselves from the rest of their party. "I suppose I should begin as we have little time."

His arm tensed, drawing her closer. "Adela, please do not judge me harshly, although I take full responsibility for my wayward life. I have been—*I was*—a most unruly young man. I spent years imbibing spirits, seeking comfort in women, and gambling each eve away whilst my father funded my escapades." He sighed. "Regret is my constant companion."

"We all sin, Marcus," Adela said, compassion lacing her voice. "None are exempt."

His eyes sought hers, but he saw nothing apart from empathy within their green depths and the glimmer of unshed tears.

Does she truly feel my pain? But what could so gracious a woman have ever done to hold such a burden as his?

The intoxicating mix of vegetation and flowers comforted him as they eased their way to the edge of the clearing and entered the forest. A trail wound its way through the dense foliage. Splashes of green ferns mixed with bluebells dotted the forest floor.

Adela put pressure on his arm and eased them to a stop.

"Do you mind if I pick a few bluebells?"

"No." He removed his coat and strode toward a large tree.

He lay the coat, lining side down, on the soft undergrowth and sat, leaning his back against a tree. He rested his forearm on his knee and watched her graceful movements. She knelt and rose, selecting flowers and bunching them into a bouquet.

When she returned, she stood over him. "Would you care to continue our walk—and conversation?"

Hesitantly, Marcus took her hand and pulled her to sit beside him. "Adela, my father was a good man, but troubled. My mother was of a weak constitution, which weighed on him. Being the eldest son, they pressured me to marry and provide an heir. I was not of a mind to do so as I was enjoying the lifestyle wealth and position allowed."

He exhaled a painful sigh. "They indulged me much. I see now. My mother was pressed to follow my father's directive. With her ailing, I yielded, fearful to cause her more anguish."

Adela nodded, urging him to go on.

He peered into the forest as if seeking strength of his words among the trees. "I wished not to marry. The relationship between my parents was troublesome in the beginning, yet, later, they loved each other, though 'twas too late. An ill impression of marriage was made upon me."

Her hand lay in his. When he brought it to his lips, she shivered. "Are ye chilled? We may return to the others."

She turned her face away. "No."

Marcus pressed on. "A friend of my father introduced me to a French woman a few years my senior. She was exquisite. I was smitten at first sight." He ran his hand through his wavy hair. "In haste we married. My father obtained a special license, but 'twas not long I realized my error. She was not what I expected. Suffice it to say she sought a husband with wealth to supply her with expensive clothing, jewelry, travel, and all she desired." He hung his head. "And she desired other men. Any man that cared to offer her more baubles."

Adela's eyes widened, her hand clutching his more firmly. "Oh, Marcus. I'm so sorry. You must have been heart broken."

Marcus relished the compassion in her eyes. None had ever looked at him that way. He rubbed his furrowed brow, stilled for a moment, and then brought his gaze to hers. "My mother died, and my father fell into despair. He drank and gambled away most of his fortune, leaving me with a title and an almost derelict estate. Upon his deathbed, he recanted the error of his ways and asked for forgiveness from me and God."

He inhaled sharply. "I mourned my mother's death and my failing marriage. Young and headstrong, I overindulged at a tavern in Plymouth and awakened aboard a ship, pressed into service, which took me to Barbados. Escape was not easy, yet I found my way home at last, only to find a letter from my wife. She had left me, along with our infant daughter, who I knew not existed."

Adela gasped. "How horrible."

Marcus ached to pull her close and hold her, yet he restrained the longing and stood. "Let us rejoin the others. Please accept my apologies for putting your reputation in jeopardy once more. I shall speak to George, so therefore your repute be not marred."

Her expression was unreadable, yet in her posture he sensed tension, a wall rising between them.

Marcus spoke not again but escorted her back to the group, the call of a lone dove echoing in the distance. A low, mournful cry Marcus felt deep within his spirit.

Chapter Twenty

The carriage ride from the picnic to Nunney Castle was mostly a silent affair. Marcus exchanged sparse conversation with the Praters while Adela watched the rain pour in sheets from the heavens, obscuring the countryside. It pounded as a waterfall against boulders and reverberated inside the small conveyance, which hindered conversation.

The recounting of the past filled his whirling thoughts. When the time was right, he would conclude the story.

He stared into the darkened sky. From time to time, he glanced at Adela, who attempted to read a small leather-bound volume she had selected from his library before their departure from Dunbar Park.

The jarring would have driven him to distraction whilst attempting to read, but she persevered.

He prodded her. "Does that not affect your eyes?"

Adela met his gaze. "Not really. It helps pass the time." A jolt threw their shoulders together for a moment. She gave a half-hearted shrug.

Marcus returned his attention to the window but not before he registered George watching them.

George had admonished him about walking unchaperoned with Adela. He said Marcus should be thankful no one of concern was in their party, and his servants were most loyal and gossiped not. Marcus expressed his gratitude and assured him he would be more circumspect in the future.

What had he been thinking? Obviously, he had not.

His mind had been too full of Adela.

☾☽

Adela rose early to prepare for their return to Dunbar Park. Nan slept while she packed their belongings. It had been a pleasant trip and the Praters, and the children's governess, were delightful. At times, she'd seen George Prater eyeing her warily, but there was friendliness in his gaze. His wife was a kind woman, although oblivious to her surroundings, but she always had a ready smile, even for the servants.

A soft knock brought a maid to tell her a footman would arrive shortly to collect their trunks.

She went to Nan's room. The child slept peacefully, her cherub face in relaxed repose. "Nan, sweet thing, it's time to rise." She smoothed her thick hair away from her face and kissed her cheek.

"Oh, Mistress Adela, please allow me to sleep." She stretched her arms and yawned. "I was having a delightful dream of playing in a field full of daisies."

"I'm sorry, dear, but you must dress and have breakfast with the Praters."

"If we must," she said with exasperation and rose, allowing Adela to prepare her for the day.

Adela escorted Nan to breakfast. Marcus was absent. The Prater's governess said she could watch Nan until her father arrived.

Back in her chamber, a tray had been delivered, and Adela ate a hurried meal of bread, cheese, and eggs. She surveyed the rooms a final time for anything left behind.

A few moments later, Nan burst into the room with Marcus on her heels. "Mistress Adela, the carriage is ready. We depart posthaste." He gave no greeting, bowed, and left the room.

"Nan, clean your teeth." She did so while Adela retrieved their cloaks to ward off the early morning chill.

As they left the room, Adela asked Nan, "Is your father feeling well?"

Nan took her hand and looked up at her. "I suppose. He appears a bit *preocuplied*." Her little face scrunched with concentration. "Oh, what is the word?"

"Preoccupied."

"Yes. That one."

"I suppose he's simply considering the journey. The ride is unpleasant."

"Aye. 'Tis why I sleep."

Adela laughed. "Yes, my sweet, you are able to sleep on a boulder in a storm. I cannot."

Nan smiled. "I suppose neither can Papa nor else he would

not be so *procupied*."

Adela patted her shoulder. "You are so right." She wondered what held the man's thoughts—and how much of it concerned her.

Over an hour later, Nan slept nestled on Adela's shoulder. Marcus chose to ride with them in the carriage rather than on Roman as he had done on their journey to the castle. With each bump, his eyes flew to his daughter to be sure she was not flung from her seat.

Adela revisited all Marcus had shared of his life. He had shown no hesitancy in revealing his pain, yet she sensed he withheld a vital part of the story.

She absentmindedly stroked the little girl's hair, a gesture both familiar and comforting—like a mother's touch of a daughter. She sighed, her fondness for the child *and* her father exceeded logic.

This was *not* her place in time.

Marcus rose and gently moved Nan to the padded seat he vacated, using his jacket for a pillow. He moved to sit next to Adela. Her breath hitched.

What was it about this man that transformed her into a blithering idiot? Words had difficulty leaving her mind, much less her lips. She had steeled herself against his charm after their walk the day before, but any wall she raised tumbled at his nearness.

Marcus leaned against her shoulder and whispered, "I have something for ye."

She brought her gaze to his, the piercing grey of his eyes unnerving her.

From his coat, he retrieved a small tissue-wrapped package tied with brown twine, the green wax seal bearing the impression of a globe.

"'Tis for ye. It seems I have missed your birthday whilst Stanton was ill."

He placed it on her lap.

His breath was warm on her neck. She took the package with care and closed her eyes, fighting the emotions that betrayed her. In the twenty-first century, men did not act in such a way. They did not capture her heart and soul. They were not . . . *Marcus*.

Rain pattered on the carriage roof, the sound a solace until his warm hands touched hers. She opened her eyes slowly, fearful of meeting his gaze.

His eyes were sad, almost mournful. "Please open it."

She sluggishly tore into the paper.

The smell of leather wafted to her. She uncovered a supple, brown book. A small brass key dangled on a slender leather cord wrapping around the book, which tucked into an inch-wide strip braided into the cover. Not a lock, but a splendid decoration.

Adela drew in a shaky breath. "It's beautiful."

His breath was too near, tickling her jawline. "As are ye." She tightened her hold on the book.

"'Tis a diary. I have seen ye writing."

This brought her eyes to meet his. "You have?"

"Aye. Most surely when ye have been sitting by the river." One side of his mouth lifted. Humor edged his tone. "When

Kellie and Leanne have been sleeping."

The smile came easily. Yes, the girls were there. Always by her side, encouraging, uplifting, and dear to her.

Marcus slid his fingertip across the diary's cover. "See, 'tis engraved for ye."

"This is too precious a gift for me to accept. I am merely the governess."

"Ye are not *merely* anything," he said, his words resolute. "Ye are much more than a governess to Nan."

She caressed the soft leather and read the inscription, *Adela Mary Jenks*. It was beautifully crafted and embellished with gold, a tiny angel etched into its dark surface next to her name. Her lips parted in awe.

"Why is there an angel here?" Her finger touched the image, gently brushing against his hand.

Marcus leaned closer and whispered, "Because God has sent ye to me."

All her senses stirred. She swallowed hard, her heart gripped with emotion. A sob caught in her throat. His strong arms surrounded her, comforting and understanding.

"What have I done?" His voice choked.

Adela brought her gaze to meet his and lifted a hand to his cheek. "You have done nothing. And you have done *everything*." Her head fell to his shoulder, and she wept.

Adela kept telling herself it was all a dream. She would awaken soon and be back in her bed with the rude sound of the alarm clock telling her to rise for work. Another day, another year.

Her life was full with a career she enjoyed, friends she adored, and good health. God had blessed her more than she deserved. She'd accepted there had never been a man in her life to make her feel cherished, loved, and accepted as she was.

Gravel crunched beneath the wheels of the carriage, and it slowed. Nan popped up from her makeshift bed and peered out the window. "We are home!"

A footman prepared the steps. Nan fidgeted in her seat and gathered her doll, book, and blanket.

Rain pelted the roof of the carriage. The weather had slowed their journey, so it was now dark. Outside the carriage window, lightning flashed, illuminating the manor. She flinched, sending the diary to the floor.

Marcus retrieved it and whispered, "The last few miles of our journey, where were your thoughts?"

More lightning brightened the inside of the carriage, revealing his weary features.

Adela took the book from him, tried to form a response, and dropped her gaze to her lap. "You did not seem happy when we left Nunney Castle. Nan said you were preoccupied." She smiled to herself, remembering Nan's attempt to pronounce the word.

"Forgive me. 'Twas not my intention to withdraw. At present much weighs on me." He turned away from her as the footman opened the door and extended a cloak above them. "Wait here."

Marcus pulled Nan, who still clutched her belongings, into his arms. He stepped under the cloak and sprinted toward the manor's door, where a servant held it open.

Moments later, Marcus jumped into the carriage with the cloak in his hand, his hair dripping. He bent over her in the confined space. "'Tis too late for you to return to the cottage. Ye shall sleep in the manor tonight by Nan's chamber."

Adela made to protest, but he was right. It was late. She nodded.

He placed his arm around her and draped the cloak over their heads. The servant held the door as they exited. Marcus gripped her against him, picked her up to keep her feet dry, and carried her to the manor.

When they were at the threshold, Marcus let her slide to her feet yet kept a firm hold on her.

Adela avoided his eyes. Another flash split the night sky, sending unease rippling through her.

His breath tickled her ear. "At first convenience, please speak with your friends of our discussion. I care to know as soon as possible." His arm lingered a moment longer at her waist before releasing her. "Ye are not to return to your duties on the morrow. Today has been most taxing, so ye must needs rest. We shall speak at day's end."

The smile he offered weakened her resolve. "Good eve, Adela."

She strode wearily to the chamber next to Nan's, the diary hugged to her chest, her heart in turmoil.

CB&CD

The morning broke to a cornflower-blue sky, remnants of storm clouds skittered past like dandelion seeds on the breeze. Adela sat on a bench next to the kitchen garden, watching dew sparkle on the leaves of herbs.

Familiar voices rode in on a soft wind. Adela stood to meet Kellie and Leanne on the path to the manor. When they rounded a curve in the lane and saw her, they sprinted the distance and threw their arms around her.

Adela drew back. "I missed you girls too."

Kellie folded her arms. "Where were you last night?"

With eyebrows raised, Leanne touched her arm. "We thought Lord DeGrey had whisked you off for good." She smirked. "To say—Gretna Green?"

Adela opened her mouth to protest, but instead laughed. "Oh yes, that's exactly where Marcus and I were." She ignored the not altogether unpleasant thought. "I'm only joking, of course. Leanne, I'm impressed you know of such a famous elopement location, even if you're almost one hundred years too early."

Leanne shrugged. "TV."

Kellie leaned forward, studying Adela. "You come back from a castle, and it's *Marcus* now?"

"I—well," Adela fumbled for an explanation. "Only a slip-up." She ignored the comment and moved forward. "Our trip was delayed due to weather, so Lord DeGrey arranged for me to stay in the room next to Nan's last night. He also gave me the day off to recuperate from the journey."

Kellie and Leanne shared a questioning glance.

With hands on her hips, Adela narrowed her eyes. "What?"

"We have to talk after work," Kellie said, uncertainty in her tone. "It's important."

"I have something to talk to you about tonight as well." Adela said goodbye, eluding their piercing gazes, and left them to see Mrs. Henshaw. She tried to shake the sense of foreboding lingering after Kellie's words. What did they need to talk about, and furthermore, how would they react to her news?

Adela found the kind-hearted woman kneading dough amid the strong, inviting scent of yeast wafting from the oven. Matilda, one of the kitchen maids, chopped vegetables.

"Good morning, ladies." Adela eased the door closed behind her. "You sure have the kitchen smelling delicious."

The cook dropped the dough with a splat onto the worktable and hastened, with the speed of someone far younger, toward Adela and enveloped her into a motherly embrace.

"I have missed ye, gurl. Was wonderin' when the master would bring ye home." She released Adela at arm's length and peered into her eyes. "Are ye well?"

"Oh, yes, Mrs. Henshaw. Thank you for the warm greeting. I have missed you too." She kissed the old woman's cheek and sat at the worktable. "How are you?"

She returned to her dough, a smudge of flour on her nose. "Doin' fine, jest fine."

Matilda threw over her shoulder with a cackle. "Aye, Adela, she be skelpin' me ever which way she can."

The cook and Adela laughed. Mrs. Henshaw shoved a cup of tea and a plate of warm bread toward her, followed by butter and homemade berry preserves.

Adela thanked her and tucked into the scrumptious breakfast, savoring the yeasty bread. "Mrs. Henshaw, this is divine. Heaven on a plate."

The old woman chortled with pleasure. "Ye are too kind, my child."

"No, ma'am. You are an artist in the kitchen."

A rich male voice answered, "Aye, she is."

Marcus leaned against the doorframe, arms across his chest.

The cook crossed the room and tugged him to her level and kissed his cheek, no thought given to the flour she left on his lapels. "Me boy, glad I am ta see ye home again. 'Twas a right powerful storm last eve." She went back to bread-making. "Felt it in me bones."

"'Tis good to see ye, Mrs. Bertie." He placed an arm around her stooped shoulders. For a moment, she lay against him and closed her eyes. One lone tear followed a crease along her face.

Adela pretended to concentrate on slathering her bread with more butter. When she looked up, Marcus still had his arm around the woman, but his eyes were on Adela. He gave an imperceptible tilt of his head toward the kitchen door that led to the gardens. She thought she'd imagined it until he mouthed the word *outside*.

"I'll gather flowers for the kitchen. It always brightens your day, Mrs. Henshaw."

"Thanks be to ye. Sounds lovely."

Marcus sat in Adela's place and picked up the buttered bread she'd left and nibbled on it.

"Adela," Mrs. Henshaw called to her.

Adela paused and turned back to her. "Yes, ma'am."

"When ye return, stay a bit and have another cup of tea."

"I'd love to." She grabbed the shears and basket hanging on a peg by the door. It thudded shut behind her, and she was careful not to glance over her shoulder.

Adela cut enough flowers to fill half the basket before footsteps crunched on the walk. The sound stopped, but she didn't turn. "You wanted to speak to me?" she asked, a flower in her hand.

"Aye. Have ye spoken with your friends?"

She cleared her throat. "No, not yet. I had planned on meeting them down the lane, but I overslept. I'm sorry."

His hand rested on her shoulder. "Are ye avoiding what ye have promised to do?"

Adela faced him. "No, Marcus. I'm not." She took a step back. "I fully intend to ask them, but I must convince them to let me tell you." She brought the flower to her nose, drinking in the honeyed scent, and breathed a prayer for strength.

Marcus dropped his hand and gave her an understanding nod. "What reason do they share for not allowing *ye* to tell me?"

Adela's gaze roamed the garden, seeking a bench. "May we sit? Somewhere no one will see us."

He led her to the small orchard at the northwest corner of the garden. They sat under a duke cherry tree, its fruit hanging in rich red clusters above them. Bees, busy with their morning routine, hummed around nearby blooms.

Adela struggled to answer his question without giving away anything of importance. It was a fine dance she must perform, but perform she would to keep them safe.

"I do not wish to give ye pain." His voice was low, throaty, and held compassion. "I am merely trying to understand."

She re-arranged the flowers in the basket. "It's difficult. As I've told you, I—*we*—cannot jeopardize our positions. We are strangers in a strange . . . land."

"How did ye come to travel—three women alone? 'Tis not seemly."

Adela wanted to crawl under the stone bench. What could she say? She prayed for an interruption. Anything. She had to talk to Kellie and Leanne. At that moment, the pressure of their plight and the confusion of their trip through time as well as her growing fondness for the man overcame her.

Unbidden tears flowed in a torrent, not the dainty tears of a gentlewoman.

Marcus leaned toward her, eyes imploring.

Her shoulders shook with quaking sobs. "*M . . . ar . . . cus.*"

He handed her a handkerchief. She dabbed at her cheeks and wiped her nose. "It's such a long, incredible story." She hiccupped. "Please don't make me say more until I speak with them."

Gripped with fear and so many indefinable emotions, Adela stood and the basket spilled its colorful contents at his feet. She knelt before him, her hands on his knees.

Shame coursed through her.

"I beg you," Adela sputtered. "Please allow me to speak with them first."

Her chin dropped to her heaving chest. She was begging the man when what she wanted to do was rail at him for being so stubborn and authoritative. But she must do all in her power to placate him for she feared what would become of them if they were removed from their positions.

The world outside Dunbar Park would be loath to welcome three women lost in time.

છ૪૦

Marcus was ashamed and stunned at once. Ashamed he had pushed this precious woman to respond thus and astonished at her humility.

Was she afraid of what she must needs tell him? Why? Had they done something unforgiveable? A sudden thought seized him. Had they committed a crime?

He attempted a gentle tone, but his emotions were caught in a whirlwind, not sure where they belonged. "*Adela.*"

His hands found hers. He eased them to his lips, tenderly kissing them. "Please rise. Ye have naught to fear from me. No matter what your account reveals. 'Twas not my intent to upset ye thus. Please accept my regrets—no matter what ye have done wrong. I shall not judge ye."

She looked into his eyes.

Marcus retrieved the handkerchief and wiped her face. Her wide eyes stayed on him. When he'd finished, she remained on her knees and brought her hands up to cup his face, searching his eyes with intense regard.

Adela leaned in and placed her lips on his with a feather-like touch, the unexpected contact and soothing scent of lavender in her hair rendering him senseless.

He recalled their kiss at Nunney Castle, and even though he continued to chastise himself, he longed to repeat the offense.

Her shimmering eyes held gratitude and relief. "Thank you."

He helped her rise, gather the fallen flowers, and replace them in her basket. "I shall return ye to Mrs. Henshaw. A cup of tea will restore ye."

Adela smoothed her hair. "I cannot go back yet. My face is puffy, and my eyes are red." She released a shaky breath. "I'll wash my face in the stream."

She moved to walk away, but he caught her arm. "No. Not alone."

Her eyes shone with concern. "If someone should see us going to such an isolated place without an escort, there would be gossip. Please let me go."

He nodded. "Against my better judgment." He sat. "Leave your basket here and make haste. If ye have not returned shortly, I will come for ye."

Adela's lips curved into a teasing smile, and she dipped a curtsy. "Yes, my lord."

Marcus entwined his fingers with hers. "Have a care."

The rustle of skirts and footfall on gravel brought his gaze to the path, where Mrs. Brimberry stood, her eyes betraying all she had seen pass between them.

Marcus felt Adela's fingers slip from his grasp.

Oh, what had he done?

CB 80

Once Adela delivered the flowers to the kitchen, she carried their evening meal back to Dunbar Cottage, her mind on Mrs. Brimberry, and awaited Kellie and Leanne's return.

What would happen now? The woman already despised Adela without any ammunition, but now she had a keg of gunpowder at her disposal.

The door banged open. Adela jumped, clutching her chest. "You scared the life out of me."

"Sorry." Leanne tossed a sack onto the settle by the cold fireplace. "We were eager to get home."

"Leanne!" Kellie picked up the sack and peeped inside. "Don't bruise the fruit Andy gave us."

"Fruit?" Adela asked.

"Yeah. Stanton told Andy he could harvest a bit of the ripe fruit from the garden orchard."

Adela settled back in her seat. "That was nice of Stanton—and Andy."

Leanne grinned. "Andy is like a monkey in those trees. It was fun just watching him. I so wanted to join him."

Kellie laughed. "That would have raised eyebrows."

With a shrug, Leanne sat beside Kellie. "This meal looks amazing."

Kellie filled her plate and pinned Adela with a serious look. "What happened at the castle?"

Adela sighed. She wasn't ready to dive into it. "It can wait a moment. What do you want to talk to *me* about?"

Leanne exchanged a glance with Kellie before saying, "Christopher DeGrey." She cleared her throat and looked at Adela. "While you were gone, Christopher shared with me that Andy is his son." She coughed. "And he, uh, asked me to marry him."

Adela's mouth dropped. "What?" She blinked a few times.

Leanne filled her in on the entire story including the couple who had been paid to take care of the child.

"Poor Andy. That's horrible." Adela shifted from sorrow to concern. "Now, what about this proposal? Did you give him an answer?"

With a sigh, Leanne said, "No, I haven't." She threw up her hands. "It all happened quickly and took me by complete surprise. He was kissing me, and Stanton and Kellie walked in." She sagged in her chair. "I'll deal with Christopher soon."

Kellie cleared her throat. "Now, that's out of the way. What happened at the castle?"

Adela looked at her plate. She took a deep breath and spilled all that occurred between she and Marcus.

Kellie and Leanne listened intently, eyes wide, until she spoke of Marcus's request. Kellie's fork fell onto her plate with a clang, her expression incredulous. "You cannot be serious. We *can't* tell him. We'll be burned as witches."

"I'm with Kellie. How can you trust him? You're the one who said he wanted you for his mistress."

When Adela spoke, her voice cracked. "I was wrong about him." She straightened, summoning any shred of strength she possessed. "I've seen so many sides to him, and it always comes back to being honorable. He's kind-hearted, gentle, forgiving, and a great father to Nan."

Kellie's eyes widened. "Oh no. You have fallen in love with him." She folded her arms. "It started on the tour when you saw his painting at the manor, didn't it?"

Adela pushed herself from the table. "Don't be ridiculous.

You can't fall in love with someone by looking at a painting." She huffed and strode to get the tarts. "I mean *seriously*."

When she returned, they gawked at her as if she'd turned into a flying pig. She plopped into her chair, the breakdown in front of Marcus returning. Those same feelings surged again.

"I'm so sorry. No matter what I do . . . it's just wrong." She shuddered. "Everything is my fault. I would never put you in danger, no matter what I feel about Marcus."

Kellie and Leanne put an arm around Adela, but she was beyond comforting. She sent a feeble plea to heaven.

God, please help us.

CO&O

Marcus found Stanton in the stables mucking out the stalls. He glanced up at his approach, shooting him a relaxed smile. "Aye, Marcus. Come ta help?"

"Oh, most certainly," Marcus said with an edge.

"In truth, ye look as if ye lost a friend." He tossed the shovel aside and pointed toward the office.

Marcus followed him into the space and sat next to the desk. Stanton poured warm ale for each of them and perched on the edge of the desk, meeting Marcus's gaze. "Ye slept ill."

Marcus eyed his friend over the rim of his cup. "Aye."

"Where did ye find the three women in Dunbar Cottage?"

Stanton flinched. "I did not find them anywhere. Why do ye ask?"

He froze, realization hitting him like a punch in the jaw. "I *assumed* ye had employed them—asked them as much—and they did not deny it."

Stanton pushed from the desk and stood at the window. His intake of breath audible.

"What is it, Stanton?"

He turned and surveyed Marcus. "Why do ye ask?"

Marcus narrowed his eyes, something else dawning upon him. "Do ye have feelings for Mistress Kellie? Is that why ye withhold truth from me?"

A woman's voice called out from the stables. "Stanton, are you here?"

Marcus smirked. "Seems I have conjured up the woman in question."

Stanton rose swiftly and strode to the door. "Aye, Mistress Kellie. I will be out in a moment." He turned toward Marcus, his graveled voice resonating through the small room. "Foals about to come."

"*Foals?*" Marcus echoed with eyebrows raised.

"Aye." Stanton glanced at him. "May be a difficult birth." He rubbed the back of his neck with his free hand. "Mistress Kellie has agreed to help me."

Marcus stood. "Acquainted with horses, is she?"

"Aye." Stanton moved through the doorway toward the stalls.

Stanton did not have to answer the question to reveal its truth for he saw the tenderness in the man's expression when Kellie called to him.

Marcus exited the office and strode toward the tall blonde, who rubbed the mare's neck and spoke soothing words to her. "Ah, Mistress Kellie. How do ye fare this eve?"

"Well, my lord." She bobbed an awkward curtsy.

Stanton nodded. "My gratitude for assisting me tonight, mistress."

Marcus watched the interaction with interest. "Ye are busy. I shall return on the morrow." He fixed Stanton with a stare. "And we shall resume our discussion."

The following morning brought Marcus once more to the stables where smells, pungent and earthy, surged with the wind blowing through the open door. He entered, his mind drifting to the past. He loved the smell of leather and hay. Although, if truth be told, he could do without the scent the horses left behind.

He and Stanton had spent much time there as lads after Stanton, two years his junior, had come to live on the estate when his father was hired as manor steward. The two of them had been inseparable ever since.

Marcus's eyes adjusted to the dimness. Silence greeted him. A horse whinnied from behind. He turned, shielding his eyes from the sun, and watched as Stanton approached, leading a limping horse by the reins.

Stanton raised his hand in greeting and called out across the stable yard. "He threw a shoe, but all is well." He led the horse to a stall.

"What brings ye here, Marcus?"

Marcus rested against the stall and gave the injured horse a pat. "Ye know well why I have come. We were interrupted yesterday." He cleared his throat. "There is something I must needs do, and I wish your assistance."

Stanton continued his ministrations to the horse and

nodded for Marcus to continue. He did so after ensuring they were alone.

"There is something most unusual about the women. No one knows from whence they came, and they speak most strangely, certainly not as servants." He rubbed the back of his neck. "And Adela evades my questions."

Stanton's lips parted as if to ask a question, but he returned to his task, not meeting Marcus's gaze. "How may I help? I know no more than ye."

"I will travel to London to investigate the little knowledge I have gleaned of them. Adela said they arrived on the *Tristan and Jane*. I would care to know the name of the man ye are acquainted with at the Navy Office in the Admiralty."

An uncomfortable silence filled the space until Stanton spoke. "Aye. Samuel Pepys is his name. A mere acquaintance." He gave Marcus a hard stare. "Why do ye pursue this? Are the women not workin' out? Are they not doin' their jobs well?"

Marcus stammered, "Well, aye . . ."

"Then why?" His eyes bored into Marcus. "Methinks ye have somethin' more ta tell me."

"No." Marcus turned and paced the length of the stable.

"Ye are in love with her then?"

Marcus whirled, met Stanton's scowl, and squared his shoulders. He was lord of the manor and was in control, though at present he did not credit it.

"Stanton, try to understand. Adela is as a mother to Nan. A mother she's never had. There is . . . there is something different about her. I cannot explain it. But I am tired of living by convention."

281

Stanton scoffed. "Convention? Her plight goes far beyond that, *my lord*." He narrowed his eyes. "Ye are still wed."

Marcus leaned against the stall, the truth he didn't want to acknowledge, hadn't acknowledged for some time, hitting him full force, knocking the breath from him. He closed his eyes as the pain flooded in.

Gillian. Oh, how he despised the woman.

Stanton cleared his throat.

"Ye do not speak reason, Marcus. Ye cannot marry Adela even if ye desire it. In the eyes of the law, ye are bound to another. And ye *chose* to marry Gillian—even at your family's insistence."

Marcus sighed. "Aye, they pushed, and I accepted. I lusted after her and mistook it for something different—better." He gripped the stall. "Had I waited, surely I would have realized it could never work between us. Her fanciful notions did not include me."

"I know this, but do ye not think ye mayhap be makin' the same mistake this time as well?" Stanton resumed tending the horse while he spoke. Marcus watched his hands work deftly at the task. "And she is not of your class. This can bring only heartache. But the truth is ye are still wed to Gillian and know not where she be. Ye cannot ask Adela to marry ye even if just to provide Nan with a mother!"

Marcus clenched the wood until blood seeped from his palm. "How am I to prove anything when I know not where she is?" He fought to rein in his temper. "Perhaps she is dead, considering the life she desired—overindulging in spirits, men, and laudanum."

He turned to walk out. "'Tis none of your business how I live my life."

"Marcus!" Stanton bellowed, blocking the path. Rage turned his eyes black. Marcus had once seen him angry when a man threatened a widowed tavern maid. The young woman attempted to support her child in this unseemly profession, when a drunkard accosted her and began to slap her face before Stanton stepped in to correct him.

Marcus scowled, his chin held high, staring Stanton eye-to-eye.

Stanton pushed a finger into Marcus's chest. "Ye have your own life ta live, but I will not stand by and watch my brother do somethin' else ye shall regret the rest of your days." He clenched his fists until his knuckles whitened. "'Tis an ungodly thing ye are about."

Marcus's blood chilled. He felt as if someone had dashed him with a bucket of icy water. "What did ye say?"

"Ye heard me." Stanton turned to walk away, but Marcus grabbed his arm.

Stanton struck Marcus in the face with his fist.

Marcus stumbled backward into the wall and rubbed his jaw. "I said, what did ye say—about being your *brother*."

"Marcus, ye cannot be so foolish to not know."

"No! I want to know *now* what ye mean."

Stanton led a brown gelding from the stable into the sun. He mounted the horse and looked down at Marcus. "Have ye not wondered how the son of a Scotsman came to be here as a lad and raised alongside the master's son?" He turned the horse toward the surrounding green hills when Marcus's arm

283

shot up to take the reins.

"Stanton, how can this be?" He ground out the words. "What proof have ye?"

Their eyes met, and Marcus saw the affection reflected in Stanton's dark grey eyes, the anger dimming. He'd always been as a brother to him. *Could it be?*

"*Our* father named me after this village." Stanton nodded, regaining the reins. "Ask your barrister." He urged the horse to a gallop and then a full run.

Marcus stared at the retreating figure of his *brother*. Thoughts of going to London to investigate Adela's tale now forgotten.

Chapter Twenty-One

Scattered grey clouds tinged with ocher splashed across the morning sky. Marcus urged Roman faster along the road to London. He pushed the horse, and himself, to the limit, determined to reach West London, acquire answers, and return to Dunbar Park by the morrow.

He stopped only to allow Roman to rest, drink, and eat as did he. The journey was tiresome but not unachievable. When he arrived at his London townhouse, he left Roman to his groom, bathed away the dust of the road, and made his way to the docks. He enquired of Samuel Pepys but was told he would not be in his office until two days hence.

"Where may I seek merchant ship records?" He stared the timid man down until sweat beaded his forehead.

"Lord DeGrey, I shall be most happy to send ye to someone who be of aid." His hand trembled as he scribbled a name and address onto a scrap of paper.

Marcus bowed, thanked him, and strode from the building. He peered at the writing. The name was barely legible, but the location was plain—Blackwell Dock.

He took a hackney to the docks, instructing the driver to wait for him. When he opened the door, the bell's chime announced his entrance. A surly man limped to the counter. "Aye, sire, how may I assist ye today?"

"Good morrow. I am enquiring of a merchant ship—the *Tristan and Jane*—arrived this spring past." He rubbed the back of his neck. "It was to have sailed from the Colonies— either Boston perhaps or Virginia."

The man pulled a heavy ledger from under the counter. Its hardboard cover thumped against the wood. Using his index finger, he flipped several pages, dust puffing into the air. He took great care in perusing the records, his bony finger moving slowly down each column. When he finished, he shook his head. "Sorry, sire, but there be only one vessel near that name. The *Tristram* and Jane. Has not been in port since 1637. Sailed from Virginia."

Marcus's heart skipped a beat. "Are ye certain?"

"Aye, our records are well kept. There is no account of the *Tristan and Jane.*"

Marcus braced himself against the counter, gathering his thoughts. He thanked the man, placed a half-crown on the counter, and left.

His stomach sank, a pain welling from deep within his soul.

Why had Adela lied? What could she—*they*—perchance be hiding?

When he returned to his townhouse, a servant brought a meal to his study. Although late and he had eaten little on his journey, his appetite was scarce. He ate enough to keep up his strength and retired early.

Determination bit at him like an angry dog. He would leave early on the morrow, return to Dunbar Park, and confront Adela.

૱૪

Leanne stretched out beside Adela and Kellie on a blanket by the river, staring into the summer sky. Fluffy clouds drifted overhead, white puffs of cotton against a sapphire canvas. A warm, woodsy scent wandered by, lulling her into a lethargic slumber.

"Kellie?"

"*Hmm . . .*"

Leanne lolled her head to one side, her eyelids at half-mast. "Whatever happened to the blonde woman who works in the washhouse? I haven't seen her in a while." She yawned. "The one you said had the horrid husband."

Kellie grunted as she rolled onto her stomach and pushed herself onto her elbows. "Oh, yeah, I forgot to tell you. Seems they were taking care of an orphan. *Well . . .* they were paid to, but the truth came out they weren't helping him. Just pocketing the money."

Leanne jerked to sit upright. "Who was it?"

Kellie shrugged. "I don't know. Just heard gossip in the alehouse. Didn't ask because you know how gossip is."

"What happened to them?"

"Christopher found out and sent them packing." She rolled onto her side, reached in their basket for an apple, and took a crunchy bite. One cheek protruding, she said, "Figured Lord DeGrey would've been the one to do that—not his brother."

Leanne fidgeted with the corner of the blanket. "No idea who the child is?"

Kellie chewed and swallowed. "Not a clue, but the child has an ailment. No one knows what. Since I don't know who the child is, I can't check him or her." A light glinted in her eyes. "Say, why don't you ask Christopher who it is?"

With all the casualness she could manage, Leanne agreed, but when she twisted to face the river, Adela sent her a questioning look. She sighed, feigning her usual distress over the lack of modern convenience. "I could sure go for a vanilla latte with an extra shot right now. It's the first thing I want when we get back. I can picture myself now at the drive-through in my car." She stretched out a hand. "As though I'm about to accept my drink."

Kellie laughed. "Only you would think of coffee first after going back through centuries."

She wasn't truly thinking of coffee, but of how she might locate Christopher without raising suspicion. She had to find out the truth about Andy.

The next morning, she took her time on the walk of shame to the cesspit. She met no one along the path.

Where *was* Christopher?

Ever since the infamous proposal, and her subsequent rejection, she'd seen little of him. It still didn't seem real. How was it she had failed to secure even one real suitor in the present day, yet she'd already almost gained a fiancé, the brother of a lord at that, over three hundred years in the past?

Leanne tossed the buckets down beside the crumbling stone wall leading to the manor's servant entrance. How tedious the chore was—*everything* was.

She longed for modern day, where her life made sense. She knew how to navigate that world. She missed her thousands of social media followers. No one in this time would be able to fathom her job nor was there a real place for her skill set. What was she going to do if they were stuck here forever?

Andy popped from behind a tree. "Good morrow, Mistress Leanne."

She jumped. "Andy, good morning. I didn't hear you."

The little boy crept toward her, grabbing her around the waist in an affectionate embrace. She tousled his unruly hair. Was this sweet child ill? The thought squeezed her heart.

When she pulled back to look at him, his face was pale and the usual spark in his blue eyes dull. "Are you feeling okay?" She pressed a hand to his cheek and noticed the skin around his lips was blue.

He nodded, his shaggy hair bobbing. A lone tear escaped and inched its way along his cheek. "'Tis of no great consarn, Mistress Leanne. I just be weary for now. Shall pass."

Leanne cupped his thin shoulders in her hands. "This has happened before?"

"Aye, mistress. Ever' so often." He shrugged. "Tho' 'tis been happenin' more of late."

Her insides clenched, and she took his hand. "We will go Kellie and have her take a look at you. You'll be right as rain in no time."

Andy peered at her curiously. "What do it mean—*right as rain?*"

Leanne laughed. "I have no idea other than you will feel much better." She grabbed the buckets and walked on, but he lagged behind as if he had no energy.

She motioned for him to climb onto her back. "How about a piggyback ride?" He grinned and climbed aboard, wrapping his legs around her middle.

His slight weight made carrying him easy, though she was certain he'd lost more in the past few days. She turned her head, so he couldn't see the tears welling in her eyes and pointed to a beautiful bird perched in a nearby tree. His head lay on her shoulder, and he snuggled against her.

God, please heal this precious child.

They walked to the kitchen and found Adela and Mrs. Henshaw wrestling an enormous piece of meat onto a spit. Their heads came up at the sound of the door.

Leanne smiled. "You need some muscle." She unloaded Andy, settling him on a stool. "I've had my warm-up."

"Aye, Leanne, where be the men when we need 'em?" Mrs. Henshaw chuckled, but her expression sobered studying the boy.

"Is there somewhere he can lie down for a little while, Mrs. Henshaw? A bit of rest would do him a lot of good." She didn't mean to alarm the child. "And perhaps Kellie can come by to check on him."

"Of course, of course." The woman washed her hands, wet a clean cloth, and wrung it out. "Aye. Ye can put him abed on the cot in the stillroom. 'Tis where I go when the aching head comes upon me. What be ailin' ye, Andrew?" She ushered the boy toward her and bathed his face, looking him over as she led him from the room.

After they left, Adela frowned. "What's going on?"

Leanne dropped into a chair. "There's something seriously wrong with him. He's lethargic and has lost weight. If I get Kellie now will Mrs. Brimberry have my head on a platter?"

Adela sighed. "Probably so."

Mrs. Henshaw re-entered the room. "Be off with ye. Mrs. Brimberry has gone ta the village and will be gone a while." Her expression turned solemn. "Methinks Andy is a very sick lad."

Leanne sighed. Adela squeezed her hand. "I'll get Kellie. We have to do whatever we can to help Andy."

Adela nodded, and Leanne rushed outside, the wind whipping her hair and skirt. She ground her teeth to quell her rising ire as she ran to the alehouse.

Where in the world was Christopher DeGrey when his son needed him most?

ᘓᙏᙎ

Night fell over Dunbar Cottage. Adela sat beside a sleeping Andy on a settle by the fireplace. It was a pleasant summer evening, and the boy rested peacefully, his narrow chest rising and falling evenly.

"It breaks my heart to look at him." Leanne sniffled. "I can't find Christopher to tell him his son is ailing." She rested her head on the table, her gaze on the child.

291

Kellie placed a hand on Leanne's arm. "I'm so sorry I can't give a definite diagnosis."

She dabbed her tears. "What's your best guess?"

Kellie paled. She entwined her fingers, and when she spoke, her voice was low, serious. "A congenital heart defect. I'd wager aortic stenosis, but I don't work in cardiology."

Leanne's chest constricted.

Adela rose and went to the door, reclaiming her cloak from the peg. "I'll find Marcus. Christopher needs to know what's happening." She trudged up the lane to the manor, her thoughts on the poor child.

The sharp clip-clop of horse's hooves on gravel tore her from her sorrow. She stepped off the drive and into the thick pasture bordering the road. The moonlight revealed Roman and his master coming at a gallop.

Marcus slowed his mount and sprang to the ground. She gasped as he stalked toward her, his face drawn into a hard mask.

"Why did ye lie to me, Adela?"

She took a step back, attempting to school her distress.

He drew so close his breath fanned her face. His cologne filled her senses as she peered into his eyes, their coldness haunting her. She cowered, and the grief resurfaced. She buried her face in her hands.

He grasped her wrists. "No. A sad countenance shall not fetch my mercy. I would have the truth."

Something in Adela shifted. She yanked her wrists free. "You are not why I'm upset, you great oaf!" A shuddering breath was all she managed. "A dying child is more important than what you think of me."

His chin lowered, flinty eyes softening. "Of whom do ye speak?"

"Andy is terribly ill." She drew in a shaky breath. "Kellie believes she knows what ails him, but there is nothing she can do."

His voice calmed, but his gaze was still hard. "How came ye here in the night?"

"To find you." She jerked her chin up and glared at him. "I know you're a kind-hearted man and will do something to help us, to help Andy, especially since he is your brother's son."

He crossed his arms. "How do ye know this?"

"Because your brother told Leanne." She narrowed her eyes. "Right before he asked her to marry him."

Shock registered on Marcus's face. He had certainly not been aware of his brother's actions.

Adela's legs buckled, the stress of the day wearing on her, and fell against Marcus.

His arms encircled her. He whispered near her ear, "I am sorry, Adela. But we must needs talk as soon as ye are well. I shall return ye to the cottage and fetch Christopher."

He braced an arm around her shoulders, supporting her as they walked to the cottage, his free hand leading Roman.

At the cottage, Adela called out, "Leanne, Kellie, let me in."

The door burst open, and Leanne's eyes widened at the sight of Marcus.

"I ran into Marcus on the lane."

Somehow, Adela felt no hesitancy, nor shame, in calling him by his Christian name in front of her friends. When she looked at him, she saw no censure. He surveyed the room, stopping at Andy's sleeping form.

Kellie rose from his side and helped Adela to the settle opposite the child. She looked over Adela. "You're pale. Are you okay?"

Marcus answered, "Of a truth, she near swooned."

"What?" Kellie placed her hand on Adela's forehead. "You don't feel feverish, but you're clammy. Are you dizzy?"

Adela nodded. "But I haven't eaten since breakfast."

Kellie scoffed. "No wonder. Leanne, find Adela something to eat."

Leanne scurried to the kitchen and quickly brought her a piece of bread and cheese.

Marcus stood over Andy, his brow furrowed. "Is he greatly ill?"

"As far as I can tell from the symptoms, and the things I found in my examination, his heart is failing. But only further medical attention would determine a prognosis."

Marcus frowned. "In truth, I know not of this prognosis of which ye speak. However, we shall make haste to summon a physician."

Kellie looked at Adela, worry in her eyes.

Adela finished chewing and placed the plate on the small stool next to the settle. "Marcus, it will not help Andy. If Kellie isn't able, then no one can."

Marcus sank next to Adela. "How came ye here—the three

of ye?" He rubbed the back of his neck. "I know ye did not arrive by ship." His eyes bored into Adela's. "'Tis why I rode to London. There is no *Tristan and Jane*—merely a *Tristram and Jane* that has not docked in London for more than thirty years."

Adela kept her gaze on his stormy grey eyes, though he appeared in control of his emotions at the moment. "I haven't spoken with Kellie and Leanne." She shivered. "We had an agreement, Marcus."

Silence engulfed the room like a heavy fog, all eyes on Lord Marcus DeGrey, who swiftly rose and headed for the door with clomping bootsteps. He turned, his jaw set. "I shall return in haste with Christopher. And, Adela, I shall have the truth this eve." He rushed out into the night.

Adela dropped her head into her hands. "Oh, what to do?" She puffed out a breath, her solemn gaze rising to meet those of her friends. "He will not give up. We must tell him."

Kellie sighed in exasperation. "How in the world will he ever believe us?"

Leanne dropped into a chair, her face softening. "I agree with Adela." She patted Adela's arm. "Besides, our *Lord Marcus DeGrey* is smitten with her, so it's doubtful he'd allow an angry mob to burn us at the stake." She shot them a smirk. "The way he looks at you, Adela, confirms everything I need to know. He doesn't care where we came from or how we got here. He just wants the truth."

"You certainly are self-assured," Kellie spat out.

"*Shh . . .*" Adela admonished her. "You'll wake Andy.

Kellie hung her head. "Sorry."

Leanne's face crumpled. "Poor little guy. If only we could take him back home with us."

Adela sank lower onto the settle, the food replenishing her, yet the fate of the child still burdened her heart.

CBSO

Marcus jumped from Roman's back before the horse halted at the stable entrance. A light warmed the window of Stanton's office. Without knocking, he stepped inside, Stanton sat behind his desk, chair tilted back, one booted-foot balancing against the edge of the desk. His lips were poised to sip from his cup.

Christopher stood by the empty fireplace, one forearm on the mantle, a drink in his other hand.

Both men faced Marcus when he swept in. "Christopher, Andrew is sickening at Dunbar Cottage. I would have ye come with me."

Christopher stiffened, his face flaring red, as he lowered his pewter cup onto the mantle with a thud.

Marcus's jaw clenched. "Did ye think me unaware ye were the boy's father?" He swung his gaze to Stanton, who eased his foot from the desk and let his chair fall with a scrape against the floor.

Stanton's gaze went to Christopher. "Let us go see the boy."

"After all this time, he knows not I am ..." Christopher's voice trailed off, a blank stare upon his face, and he sputtered, "What am I to do?"

Marcus fixed Christopher with a stern gaze. "Ye shall be a father."

Chapter Twenty-Two

Adela's stomach clenched as she gathered their twenty-first century items. They agreed it was time to reveal all—come what may. She settled at the table alongside Kellie and Leanne, and they placed everything in front of them.

The time of reckoning was at hand.

Before them was a package of tissues, a blue comb, Adela's Bible, the manor house book, the antique passport, their own passports, Adela's planner, Leanne's lip gloss, Kellie's iPad, and three cell phones.

Adela stared intently at the collection before covering it with her shawl.

A rap on the door made her jump, a hand flying to her chest. "Well, this is it." She forced herself from the chair on wobbly knees, strode to the door, and opened it to discover three tall, imposing men standing before her.

Three?

Marcus stepped in first and gently touched her arm. "I would not have ye afraid. If ye are willing to share your story, so shall I listen."

Adela glanced toward Andy, who slept soundly. She turned to Stanton. "Would you mind carrying Andy upstairs and put him to bed? He'll be more comfortable, and we can speak freely without disturbing him."

He went to the child with Kellie on his heels. "I'll go with you."

She caught Christopher's gaze on the stairs and then on Leanne. When they returned, he asked Kellie, "How is he?"

"He's resting. It's the best thing for him. I understand the fatigue doesn't last long, but it returns more frequently now. The longer he rests, the better he'll be for a time. Trust me. Where I come from, we know of this illness quite well."

"Thank ye, mistress, "Christopher said with a slight bow of his head.

Adela patted Kellie's arm. "You're doing everything in your power to help him."

Kellie nodded, but her expression was grim.

Adela faced the table. "Please have a seat everyone." She sent a silent prayer to God to make the men understand—and believe—what they were about to divulge.

With everyone seated, Adela pulled in a deep breath and began, "Lord DeGrey has asked that we disclose the truth about who we are, why we are here, and how we arrived."

Marcus spoke up, concern in his eyes. "I would have ye keep this between ye and me, Adela. 'Tis of no concern to

Christopher and Stanton."

"Marcus." She stopped, knowing she shouldn't address him in so familiar a manner, but, at the moment, she didn't care. "This concerns each of us here, as well as Andy."

Marcus nodded, urging her on.

Adela cleared her throat. For years, she had stood in front of a classroom and taught hundreds of cooking classes, but to say what she must in this room of men—from the past at that—it was impossible and absurd.

"There is no easy way to explain . . ." Her voice shook, and she fought to steady it.

Leanne and Kellie rose to stand at her side. Their presence further urged her onward. They were in this together whatever the outcome. She was not alone.

"What we have to tell you will be hard to believe." She looked at Kellie and then Leanne. "We still have a hard time believing it ourselves." Her focus went to Marcus. "But it is the full and honest truth."

Adela straightened. "Leanne, Kellie, and I did not come to England by ship nor did we come to this cottage by accident. We planned to come here."

Marcus's eyes narrowed, taking in her every word. She willed him to prepare himself for what she said next. *Please believe me, Marcus.*

"It is no surprise we are not accustomed to the work of servants nor the customs of this place and time." Leanne took Adela's hand and squeezed it as she pressed on. "In fact, we are *not* of this time. We are from the future—the year two thousand and twenty-one to be exact—and we can prove it."

Marcus stilled in his seat, eyes widening. She heard the other men's sharp intakes of breath and could only imagine what went through their minds.

Adela removed her shawl from their modern items and picked up the antique passport. "This passport started it all—or so we believe." She gently opened it, pointed to the issue date, and held it out for the men to see in turn. "It is an important form of identification in our time. It was issued in nineteen hundred and fifteen—over two-hundred and forty years from now."

Adela paused to let the information sink in.

"I bought it in a shop in this very village—the building that houses the bakery. In our time, it's a charity shop. Kellie, Leanne, and I were in Stanton Wake on holiday. We paid to stay in this cottage. When we returned from a day of sightseeing in the village, we looked over this old passport and suddenly everything shifted to what we see now. We traveled through time."

Christopher looked as if Leanne had slugged him in the stomach again. Stanton leaned back in his seat, his face like stone, gripping his knees with strong hands. Marcus blinked and stared intently at her.

Adela pushed her Bible toward Marcus. "Please open this and read the first few pages."

After a moment's hesitation, he did as instructed and read aloud—"*Published by Thomas Nelson, The Holy Bible, King James Version, 1970.*" He looked at her, bewildered.

"Now turn the page and note the inscription."

He returned to the Bible. *"Presented to my daughter,*

Adela Mary Jenks, on her sixteenth birthday, July 9, 1984. Love, Mom."

Marcus's lips parted, grey eyes questioning, perhaps seeing truth within her gaze.

"There's more." Adela picked up the manor book from the gift shop and turned to the page with the portrait of Marcus. She laid it in front of him.

"How can this be?" He shook his head. "A superstitious man I am not—nor believe I in witchcraft, yet this is beyond my understanding." He hesitated and pointed to the page. "Why is the date under my portrait inked out?"

Adela swallowed. "No one should know the date of their death."

Stanton reached for the book, and Marcus showed him. He stared at it and then at Marcus as if to make sure it was indeed the same man. He looked at Kellie. "I knew ye had secrets, but I never thought 'twas this."

Adela laid her hand atop Marcus's. "We didn't ask to be here. It's beyond our understanding. In all these weeks, we still do not truly know how or why we were brought here from our time. But it did happen, and we know God brought us here for a reason. Until tonight I didn't realize it, but I believe it's Andrew. We must try to save his life."

Christopher dropped the manor book onto the table with a thud. "Stanton says ye are a nurse, Mistress Kellie. Can ye not save him?"

Kellie's head dropped. "It will take more than I can offer here. He needs surgery. Medical technology of the future."

Leanne interrupted, "If we can find a way back to our time,

we will take him with us and get him the help he needs." She turned to Adela. "But how would we return him to this time?"

Adela's thoughts raced. "I don't know." She suddenly felt so weary, her strength giving way. She lay her head on her arms. "Oh, God, please help us. We don't know what to do?"

A warm, gentle hand caressed her hair. She brought her gaze to look at Marcus, tall and strong by her side. "Adela, hear me. We shall figure this out together."

Kellie's voice cracked. "We've tried to figure it out. We want to go home."

Stanton's intense dark gaze surveyed the items on the table. "Kellie, 'tis truly this secret ye were keepin' from me—from us? 'Twas not, in truth, only the feelin's Adela has for Marcus ye wanted me to keep to meself, was it?"

Marcus's head shot up, and his gaze found Adela's. Heat flared in her cheeks.

Kellie offered Adela an apologetic half-smile. "Sorry. It was a slip of the tongue."

Christopher's voice broke into the moment. "If ye take Andrew to your time, ye can get help for him there—'tis so?"

Kellie nodded and attempted to explain the procedure as best she could. When she finished, he squared his shoulders. "Then we must discover how this shall be done, and I shall go with ye."

Leanne gasped.

Silence fell over the room.

Marcus took Adela's hand and squeezed it. "'Tis late. We must needs rest." He rose and drew her with him. "His gaze swung to Christopher and Stanton. "Speak no more of this.

Tomorrow eve we shall gather in the library and discuss the matter." He faced Kellie. "I shall tell Mrs. Brimberry ye are not to work for some days while ye attend to Andrew."

Stanton and Christopher took their leave after bidding them a good night, Christopher's gaze lingering on Leanne, Stanton's on Kellie.

Marcus remained, his hand gripping Adela's. "Let us step out-of-doors a moment." They stood in the dark, away from the light splaying from the window.

He released her hand, slid his arms around her, and gently tilted her face up. "Adela, I care not how ye came to be here. I do believe ye, and it does my heart good to know ye have affection for me. Yet, there is something I must do before—" He kissed her cheek. "I shall explain soon."

His thumb softly caressed her face before he leaned in and pressed a delicate, tender kiss on her parted lips.

Adela closed her eyes and melted into him. For the first time in her life, she felt cherished—*treasured*.

"Tomorrow we shall begin our research." His voice grew hoarse. "I shall advise Mrs. Brimberry ye shall spend extra time assisting me in the library and . . ."

"Marcus, won't it be seen as inappropriate?"

He brought a finger to her lips. "Aye, perhaps ye are correct." His resigned sigh mingled with sadness. "We shall have Nan aid us as a lesson in her letters."

Adela nodded. "No one will question it."

A languid smile curved his lips. "Ye have mesmerized me, Adela Mary Jenks. And 'twas before I knew ye were a woman of the future."

Tears escaped Adela's eyes. He brushed them away with his finger. "I would not have ye sad, my dear. And . . . I would have ye not go back to your time. Please stay with me."

Adela stilled, drinking in his gaze filled with tenderness. She touched his cheek and felt the stubble of his unshaven skin beneath her fingertips. "Marcus, I . . ."

His eyes saddened. "Ye have someone to go back to?"

"No."

The light returned to his eyes. "I do not flatter myself to imagine I am perfect. There are many things I am not proud to have done in my life, but I shall make it right before I—"

"What are you not telling me, Marcus?"

"My dear, 'tis late." He rested his chin on top of her head. "I shall tell ye soon." He lowered his head until their eyes were inches apart. "When ye have broken your fast on the morrow, fetch Nan and come to the library. We shall gather what books may aid us in our discovery."

Adela nodded, and before she could respond, he brought his lips to hers with such sweetness she quite lost herself in him, her heart reeling at how this man was able to so undo her, and furthermore, how she could ever leave him?

೦೪೫೦

The next day, Adela found Marcus standing over the massive globe by the table in the library. Nan left her side and ran to him.

"Papa!" She flung herself into his arms. "'Tis a lovely idea to have Mistress Adela and ye teach me my letters in the library." She giggled. "*And* to help ye as well."

304

"Aye, dearest. Ye shall make a wonderful assistant." He kissed her cheek and put her down. "'Twould be most helpful if ye begin by sitting at this table." He pulled out a chair, gently ushered her in to it, and stood behind her.

Adela stood with hands clasped at her waist watching the interaction between father and daughter. Marcus was a doting father, not timid to show his affection.

Marcus's eyes sought hers, and he gave her a brilliant smile and motioned her forward. When Adela reached them, he kissed her cheek, then dropped his lips to her neck and left a soft lingering kiss.

"Marcus!" Her breathy whisper reprimanded him.

Nan's head popped up to peer at them, her eyes wide. "Did ye call my papa by his Christian name?"

Marcus dropped to his haunches. "Aye, Nan, she did so. We have become good friends. Do ye not call your friends by their Christian names?"

The child's face scrunched in deep concentration before she nodded. "I suppose." She crossed her arms. "Aye. Let it be so." She gave a more forceful nod and added, "Now we must needs begin to learn."

Marcus roared with laughter.

Adela shook her head. "You are such a precocious child, my sweet girl."

"What does pre . . . pre . . ." She frowned. "This word is most difficult."

"It means you are very intelligent." Adela dotted a quick kiss on the top of her head. "Let us get to work then."

Marcus took Adela's hand and tugged her to one of the

305

shelves and began to remove books. "As I locate books on the subjects that may assist us, I shall hand them over to ye. Take them to Nan and instruct her how to put them in order, alphabetically, by title. She may stack them on the table while we collect more." He lowered his voice. "This shall keep her occupied for some time."

"Good plan, *my lord*." She teased. The glint in his eyes held mischief as he looked over her shoulder and presented her with a swift kiss on the lips.

"Be careful," Adela hissed.

"Not to worry. She is busy."

Adela turned to see the child engrossed with the globe. When she faced Marcus again, he placed another book in her arms. "Ye were looking at the globe when we arrived. For what did ye search?"

He swung back to her with a copy of Robert Hooke's *Micrographia* in his hand. "The land ye came from?" He handed her another book. "'Tis a long distance. How did ye come to travel here—in your time?"

Adela caught sight of a familiar title on the shelf above Marcus's shoulder. "May I have that book?" She reached over him and tapped it with her finger, bringing their faces closer.

He pulled in a breath. "Ye smell lovely."

"Marcus, stay focused."

He shook his head as if clearing it of all thought and removed the book. "This?"

"Yes. I have a copy at home."

His eyes widened as he handed it to her. "The Complete Herbal?"

"Well, an edited and updated copy. It has the modern uses of the herbs he'd included in this original." She handled it carefully, though it was obviously new.

"Herbs are still used for healing though ye have such advanced medicine?"

"We do. Mostly by individuals—for use at home. Herbs and essential oils will always have health benefits."

"Though neither will help Andrew?"

Sadness swept over her. "No. His ailment is severe."

She took the books he'd gathered and placed them in front of Nan. "Ready to begin?" The girl's grin melted her. She returned to Marcus. "Where did you get Nicholas Culpeper's book?"

Marcus flipped through a volume, his face intent. "From his apothecary shop in London. We were at Cambridge together. I visit his shop on occasion."

"You were at university with Nicholas Culpeper?" Adela's voice held awe.

He glanced at her, eyebrows raised. "'Tis of no concern. We were mere acquaintances of a friendly nature. Nothing more. Does this concern ye?"

"Oh, no." Adela shook her head. "I'm still amazed I'm living in a time when there were—*are*—so many eminent people who have been long dead in my time."

He gave her a thoughtful look. "Aye. This I can see. A feeling of which I am unfamiliar, of a certainty."

Adela felt a nudge and jerked with a start. Nan clung to Adela's leg, large eyes gazing at her. "Mistress Adela, I am finished, and I need more books." She huffed and stalked back to her seat. "Methinks the two of ye talk too much."

Marcus and Adela laughed. Adela knew it was not only Marcus whom she would miss when she returned home. Both father and daughter were bound forever to her heart.

⋘∞⋙

Adela took in each concerned expression that evening around the library's table. It was apparent no one knew what they were doing. In front of each lay paper, quills, a bottle of ink, and a book.

Marcus stood at the head of the table, uncertainty in his tone. The last ray of sun had crested the manor, and the library filled with flickering shadows from candles glowing throughout the room.

Kellie said, "I'd like to report Andy is feeling better—for now—I have left him with Timothy and Martin with strict instructions to keep him in their cottage tonight and have him rest as much as possible. Mrs. Henshaw made a wonderful dinner for them to share with a special dessert."

Christopher straightened in his chair. "Thank ye, Mistress Kellie, for your kind attentions to—" He dipped his head, candlelight glinting off his golden hair. "—my son."

"You're welcome, Christopher." Kellie paused. "Or should I call you Lord Christopher?" She grinned at him.

Christopher barked a laugh and sent her a broad smile. "No, Christopher shall be fine." He turned to watch Leanne, who tried to *not* look at him. Adela saw the affection in his eyes.

Marcus cleared his throat. "Let us begin. *The Sceptical Chymist* is one volume which may shed light on what we seek, perhaps more than the others." He nodded. "Mistress Kellie has the most knowledge regarding chemistry, therefore she shall take any volumes pertaining to the subject."

He assigned each person a subject, and before they set to work, Marcus asked Adela, Kellie, and Leanne to recount their individual memories of the fateful night of their arrival.

Stanton asked, "What was the most significant thing ye remember about that eve?"

Without hesitation each of them said it was the intense lightning strike.

Leanne tapped her fingers on the table. "It seemed more concentrated than any I've ever heard. Almost like it struck the cottage but didn't harm anything."

Kellie nodded. "That's exactly what it was like." She smiled at Leanne, who responded with a grin.

Adela admired the women. No matter what, they always managed to put aside their differences. She looked at them fondly. They were her family.

When her gaze slid back to Marcus, he looked at her with a trace of understanding in his eyes. She released a shaky breath. "I do remember something odd about the storm. The lightning flashed a bluish glow into the cottage and hung there, changing into a mist which evaporated. When it was over, the cottage was filled with daylight. No rain or sign of a storm."

Stanton said, "We have had a drought and no rain for a long time."

Christopher twirled a quill in his fingers, eyes on Leanne. "What was the precise date ye came to be in Dunbar Cottage?"

Leanne bit her lip. "I don't know."

Adela thought back to that day, and her face burned. "I remember the day Marcus found us in the cottage, and he said Stanton was up north buying horses." She refused to look at Marcus, remembering how he had seen her in her chemise, so she settled her gaze on Stanton. "Do you have those dates written down?"

"Aye," Stanton answered. "Marcus, how many days had I been gone when ye met these lovely lasses?" His eyes flickered to Kellie.

"Ye had been gone no more than two days I do believe."

"This narrows the date." Adela made a note on her paper, struggling with the use of a quill dipped in ink. At least it was legible. She froze as an idea struck her. "I'm sorry, but why didn't I think of it before? My planner will have the date we arrived. I'll check it."

"We have a beginning," Marcus stated as he reached for his quill. "Let us all put it upon the page."

Sounds of scratching on parchment filled the room like chickens searching the ground for food.

Christopher looked at Leanne, who averted her gaze. "Why did ye choose to come to England on holiday? Why Stanton Wake?"

"We are true Anglophiles," Adela said and noted the men's confusion. "An Anglophile is someone who admires England or English customs, history, and so on." Their faces lit with a measure of understanding. "We discovered there was to be a seventeenth-century festival held in the village, found the cottage to rent, bought our plane tickets, and rented a car."

The men's faces clouded again.

Kellie expelled an exasperated breath. "We're getting side-tracked. By the time we explain a plane and a car, we'll all be dust under someone's feet."

"Kellie is right," Leanne chimed in. "We all have English ancestors, so that played into our visit too." She crossed her arms. "We're forgetting something important though. No one has mentioned prayer. Don't we need to ask God for help? He is the one who placed us here for whatever reason, and if He wants us to go home, He'll surely reveal the way."

Adela nodded.

Christopher said, "I do not believe God wants to hear from me after all I have done." He pressed fingers to his forehead.

"'Tis Stanton who does attend church with regularity," Marcus chimed in. "Mayhap God will listen to him. My life, in truth, may not warrant an answer."

Stanton coughed, clearing his throat. "Far from the pious sort am I."

Marcus slapped him on the back and grinned. "'Twas not meant to embarrass ye."

Adela lifted her chin, her eyes meeting Marcus's. "What's there to be embarrassed about? Being a Godly man is something that should be the norm, not the exception."

His expression sobered, but he did not speak, and in his eyes, Adela saw the hint of turmoil and pain that lingered there so often.

She wondered once again what secrets Marcus held close, and what was it from his past which seemed to still have such a firm hold upon him?

CAROLE LEHR JOHNSON

Chapter Twenty-Three

The evening drew to a close, the pungent scent of musty late summer air surrounding Adela as she walked to the gate to meet Leanne and Kellie. When she arrived, only Leanne was there.

"Where's Kellie?" She sank onto the bench, relieving her weary feet. At least, she could sit for most of the evening in the library where they all went to go over more books and notes.

Her mind wavered between their group that met each night and came away with nothing of importance and the need to get Andy medical assistance. Christopher's face grew more haggard with each meeting, concern etched on his handsome features.

Though Andy had improved, Kellie said it wouldn't last. Adela's heart grieved for the child.

"Kellie ran to the stables to ask Stanton something about a horse." Leanne shrugged. "I'm not sure what's going on there, but she's grown attached to the hunky steward."

Adela bit back a laugh. "Let's just hope it's not a rebound relationship."

Leanne dropped onto the bench. "Yeah."

In a few minutes, Kellie bounded toward them. "Sorry, I'm late." Within her expression was something Adela couldn't quite place, a mix of trepidation and intrigue perhaps.

She and Leanne joined Kellie and headed toward the cottage to freshen up before their nightly meeting.

"We're not meeting tonight." Kellie quirked her brows. "Stanton said Marcus has gone to London on business but will return tomorrow night."

Adela stared at her. Marcus went to London? *Again.* Why hadn't he told her?

Leanne said, "So that's two nights we won't meet? We don't need to delay this. Andy needs help."

"I know. Stanton said it must be important business to take Marcus away. He was secretive about it, but I couldn't pry it out of him."

They walked home in silence, Adela's mind going over the reasons Marcus would leave now when they had agreed their task was of the utmost importance. When they arrived at the cottage, she pulled out her planner. It was the first week of September.

Something pricked her memory, something about the date, but she couldn't coax it forward. She exhaled and let it go.

After their evening meal, the day's toil hung on her until all she longed for was bed. She drifted to sleep quickly but woke in the middle of the night. The bright moon shone through the window, spilling ethereal bands of light across her bed and onto the floor. Her skin was clammy as she lay there, unable to recapture sleep. An uncomfortable restlessness settled over her. If only she could grasp what was just out of reach. Just as her eyes fluttered, she sat up in bed.

It was the first week in September—1666! The exact week of the Great Fire of London! Marcus was in grave danger.

Adela flew from her bed and began to dress, trying to keep from waking Leanne and Kellie. She tiptoed downstairs and shoved on her boots. She had to get to Stanton and tell him what she knew. They had to help Marcus.

Moonlight illuminated Adela's path as she hurried to the stables, the horizon was aglow with blazing orange reminding her of brilliant flames seeking something to devour. "Oh, God, please protect Marcus."

She hastened her steps toward the stable. When she stepped beyond the hedgerow, no lights greeted her from the structure. Her footsteps shuffled through the straw-laden floor as she made her way up the narrow stairs to Stanton's quarters. She fisted her hand and raised it to knock just as the door burst open.

Stanton halted inches from her, shock registering on his chiseled face.

"Mistress Adela." His eyes shone with concern. "What is wrong?"

She grabbed his forearm. "Stanton, we must help Marcus. It's not safe right now in London. He's in danger."

Stanton stepped onto the landing and closed the door behind him. His face clouded with confusion. "Why? What shall happen in London on this day?"

Adela gulped for air as panic seized her, her mind bringing forth the historical details.

"A great fire will destroy much of the city. It starts at a bakery on Pudding Lane. It will happen quickly. Most of the buildings are built of flammable materials. It's going to burn like a pile of straw."

Tears clouded her vision. "The fire's been burning for two days!"

Stanton gripped her arms to steady her. "Come. We shall go to my office. Ye need somethin' to fortify ye." He guided her downstairs. Once she sat, he fetched a glass of brandy and placed her hands around it. "Sip slow. 'Twill strengthen ye."

"No, I can't. I must keep a clear head if I'm to go to London and warn Marcus."

Stanton stood over her, his hands clasped behind his back. "Ye go to London? No."

Adela looked up at him. "Stanton, I have to help him."

He remained silent for a moment before responding. "I shall go. I know where he is goin'."

She slumped in the chair, relieved from his words. "Thank you, Stanton."

"I shall be ready to ride in a trice." He turned to leave and paused. "Please stay until I return."

The sound of heavy footsteps among the straw and up the stairs calmed Adela's pounding heart.

Marcus was blessed to have such a good friend in Stanton Yorke. If only he could get to Marcus in time.

CRÆD

Marcus rode hard, pushing Roman to his limits. He must needs reach London, find Gillian, and make her understand divorce was the only answer. Her infidelity was the grounds for his reasoning. He had not been unfaithful to her. There had not been another woman to tempt him thus—until Adela.

He would marry her.

Before she returned to her own time, he had to end his marriage to Gil. He would not be at liberty to propose to Adela until he could offer her everything. Stanton had been right. Though he talked not to God any longer, his conscience had nipped at his heels until his spirit struggled within at the thought of marrying a woman while still wed to another.

Divorce also did not sit well with him. He perceived God would rather that than lie to Adela and marry her without honor.

Deep in his soul, he would not be able to forgive himself nor look into her beautiful emerald eyes and feel honesty in his heart. He could not spend the rest of his life with her without being completely truthful.

His thoughts drifted as Roman thrust onward, London's silhouette ahead, the dipping sun to their backs. He prayed the information his hired man discovered was yet accurate that Gil lived with a man who owned a tavern near St. Paul's.

His gaze focused on the city in the distance. A thick, dark mist hung above, a golden glow as the backdrop. The closer he drew to the city, an acrid smell met him, and Roman slowed his pace, throwing his head back with a whinny.

Smoke.

Marcus patted the horse's neck. "Steady now, old boy." He slowed their pace and entered the city through Ludgate, St. Paul's rising high. He brought his arm to his face, covering his nose.

The further they plunged, light fled along the packed, dingy streets. Buildings rose above, crowding him in—a strong reminder of why he was glad to be out of London's oppressive closeness. He rarely came to areas of this ilk, preferring to ride Roman in one of the many green and vast parks in Westminster near his family's townhouse.

The closer he got to St. Paul's the stronger the stench of burning buildings. Horses, carts, and people streamed past, carrying meager possessions. Ahead, he saw the tavern for which he sought, flames licking the side of the building, yet engulfing it not.

With ease, he bolted from Roman, tied him to a nearby post out of harm's way, and burst through the door of the tavern.

A muscled man behind the bar shoved bottles into wooden crates with speed.

"Sir!" He shouted above the din of panic. "Where is Gil . . . Gillian DeGrey?"

The man's chin jerked up, sparse black hair whipping around his beefy neck as the wind gusted through the open door. "Aye. She is up there, useless wench! She is bedeviled with her spirits, laudanum, money, and men."

The sound of shattering glass broke his tirade. "Take her if ye must. 'Tis no longer my concern." He resumed his packing.

Marcus took the stairs two at a time, hesitating on the landing. Three doors faced him. When one door would not give, he slammed his shoulder into it, and the crack of splintered wood sounded over the shouts and shrieks of the panic below. The second door revealed a chamber full of smoke. His eyes watered. A moan carried through the cloud. A limp form lay sprawled on a narrow cot in the corner near the window. Faded curtains were aflame.

He rushed through the smoke and dropped to his knees by the bed. His wife's wide blue eyes stared at him. Coal-black hair tumbled over her shoulders, matted, and dirty.

"*M—Marcus?*" She lifted a lithe hand into the air above her. The nearly imperceptible lisp in her voice a murmur over the sound of flames engulfing the tavern walls.

"Aye, Gil, 'tis me. I have come to—" He would not continue the lie which lay upon his lips. *I have come to help ye.* "Let me aid ye, and then we shall speak of why I came."

Marcus slid his arms beneath Gil and lifted her to his chest. It was as if lifting a sack of feathers. He rushed for the door, seconds before flames engulfed the room, and barely escaped the burning tavern.

He looked down at Gil, taking in her gaunt cheeks, eyes encircled with black shadows caused by laudanum, the now shell of the woman he had married. Despite the hatred he had nursed in the years since her departure, he knew he must do all he could to save her.

She looked up at him, tears streaming down her smut-covered cheeks, her voice barely a whisper, "Marcus, sorry I

319

am. I want to say it before I die."

"No. Say not a thing. Ye shall live."

"No. 'Tis hell I merit for the pain I wrought." Her cough was deep and harsh. "A just reward."

Overwhelming grief and compassion gripped Marcus. Tears filled his eyes. "No, Gil, God can forgive all if ye seek Him."

A fleeting memory of Adela reading scripture to Kellie and Leanne came to mind—*The steps of a good man are ordered by the Lord, and He delights in His way.*

Had he been a good man? He thought not.

His head dropped to his chest. "Gil, ye are not the only one at fault for our marriage. Please forgive me for not loving ye with the depth of sacrifice Christ showeth His church."

"Marcus . . ." Her hand caressed his hair, then fell limp to her chest, breath coming in slow, strangled gasps. She looked up at him, the sorrow in her eyes as one haunted by death's coming.

CB&O

Adela walked back to the cottage, sluggish with fatigue and worry. Never had she felt so helpless.

When she closed her eyes, she saw Stanton racing into the horrors of the Great Fire of London. Although she knew few lost their lives, it still destroyed much of the city in only four days.

The seriousness in his eyes and demeanor before he left told her much. He had believed what she told him of the fire in London, which had strengthened her.

Above it all, while she waited to learn of Marcus's fate, she realized she was in love with Marcus DeGrey—for good or bad. She loved him.

Her mind was a muddle of emotions, every muscle aching from stress. She didn't know if he genuinely loved her. He'd kissed her, yes, and asked her to stay in this time with him, but did he truly love her? And why was Stanton so secretive of the reason Marcus had gone to London?

"Adela!" She glanced up, pulled from her thoughts with the shout.

Kellie's voice rang out again from the cottage gate, where she stood hands on hips and face blazing. "Where have you been? Leanne and I have been worried sick."

"Sorry. I had a disturbing dream which woke me early, and I had to tell Stanton. Marcus is in danger. He's headed straight into the Great Fire of London."

"So?" Kellie's voice held confusion.

Adela's mouth dropped. "So? Is that all you can say? Marcus could die there!" Moisture formed on her lashes. She couldn't bear the thought of losing him. God had sent her more than three hundred and fifty years into the past to meet him. She had to try and save him.

She stilled, a revelation coming to her. God *wanted* her to be with Marcus. Nothing had ever been so clear to her . . . *ever*. She wasn't here to *save* Marcus. God didn't need her help. She and Marcus were supposed to be together.

Her mind wanted to explode with the possibilities. If God had wanted them to be together, he could have had her born in this time—or had him born in her time. But . . . then they would have been different people entirely—formed by the era they each came into naturally.

"You don't look well." Kellie took her arm and led Adela to a chair at the table where Leanne ate breakfast.

Adela's head ached. She tried to explain the thoughts tangled in her mind of why, what if, and when, but she didn't know where to begin.

Kellie brought her a cup of tea and told Leanne where Adela had been.

Leanne asked, "Didn't you say only a handful of people died in the fire?"

Adela nodded. "Yes, but Marcus could be one of them."

Softly, Kellie said, "But he couldn't be. You saw his portrait at the manor, and the tour guide never mentioned he died in a fire."

Adela's eyes widened, her heart pounding. "True. She didn't, did she?" Also, she'd blacked out the date of his death in the guidebook, deliberately avoiding it.

Leanne smiled. "Now, that's better. You're grinning like a lovesick schoolgirl."

She shook her head, but the grin remained. "Leave it to the two of you to bring me around. Thank you." She stretched a hand to each of them and squeezed. "My sweet friends."

Kellie stood. "I hate to break up the party, but we have to get to work. The sun is up."

Leanne moaned and then released a painful sigh.

Kellie laughed. "We feel your pain, but if we keep busy, the day will pass quicker until we hear from Stanton and Marcus."

She pulled Leanne to her feet.

Adela smiled, though it was slight. She mustered whatever strength she had left. She had to do what Kellie said—keep busy—and leave Marcus in the hands of God.

CREASO

Marcus's throat burned like the fire surrounding him. Men screamed as they tossed water by the bucketful onto whatever was in reach without the flames consuming them.

He carried Gil to Roman. The horse skittered as Marcus attempted to mount him while still clutching her to his chest.

He laid her over his shoulder with care, freeing both his hands to hoist them onto Roman's back.

One arm encircled Gil as he settled her against his chest. He gripped the reins and spurred Roman away from the fire and smoke.

Shame barbed him with memories. Had he been a stronger, more godly man and not retaliated with slurs equal to her own, he may have been able to counteract her rebellious nature. She had constantly pestered him about one petty thing or another, baiting him with verbal outbursts.

Gil was a shrew. No denying it. A vacuous, conceited shrew of the first order. Remorse hung over him like the thinning smoke as they made their way west of the fire.

The fleeing crowds diminishing, he pushed Roman harder, and they made their way to his London home. When he slowed to enter the stables, Gil brought her head up and moaned, her words breathy. "Nanette. I wish to see her."

Two of Marcus's groomsmen stood in the stable yard.

Marcus tossed the reins to one. "Michael, hold him steady. Walter, take Lady Gillian. She is injured." He eased her into the groom's outstretched arms and then dismounted.

Another horse thundered into the yard. "Marcus!" Stanton bolted from his steed, tossing his reins to Michael. His face glistened with fatigue, his brow furrowed and smudged with a day's hard ride. He opened his mouth to speak then noticed Walter holding Gillian in his arms, her head lolling to one side.

Marcus took her from the young man, cradling her in his arms. "One of ye fetch a physician." With long strides, he stormed into the townhouse bellowing orders for hot water, clean bed clothes, and warm broth.

Stanton kept pace with him, but Marcus did not address him until he deposited Gil onto the bed. A maid attended her, and he left the room, Stanton at his heels.

Marcus's valet met them in the hall. "Lord DeGrey, we have prepared a bath for each of ye." He glanced at Stanton. "I will show ye to your room, sir."

Stanton shook his head and looked at Marcus.

"Stanton, wash the road away and meet me downstairs for a meal. Methinks we shall both need it. Then ye can tell me what the blazes ye are doing in London." He turned on his heel and left his valet and steward staring after him.

Marcus closed the door and leaned heavily against it, his head resting on the dark-stained oak. A lifetime of anguish, regret, and something more unidentifiable weakened him in body and spirit. He closed his eyes, and a nudge of hope flickered.

He visualized the family Bible Adela read in his library. Her whispered words suddenly became audible again. *For this my son was dead and is alive again; he was lost and is found.*

Was he the prodigal? Was God calling him? It seemed as if he had been running his entire life, but from what?

The truth.

God, please forgive me.

The words seemed to rise from deep within him—a cry, a plea, a reckoning. He sagged with relief. The burden he had carried far too long had been lifted from his shoulders. The tub caught his attention, steam rising, beckoning him to wash the grime from his body and perhaps from his soul as well.

He shed his clothes and eased into the soothing water, submerging his head until he could hold his breath no longer.

At last, he felt clean.

CAROLE LEHR JOHNSON

Chapter Twenty-Four

Marcus saw the worry reflected in Stanton's eyes as he held the horse's reins in one hand, the other braced against the saddle. "Marcus, do ye not see what a mistake it would be ta bring Gil ta the manor?"

Marcus averted his eyes. "'Tis her last wish to see Nan. Shall I not honor it? In truth, she is her child, and they have been apart much of Nan's life."

Stanton gave him a pained look bordering on mutiny.

Marcus sighed.

"I am aware this shall create new challenges. Yet, I must see to it. Gil may soon not be with us." He leaned his shoulder against the brick wall of the stable, crossed one booted foot over the other. "I mean to honor her final wish."

Stanton shrugged, and one side of his mouth quirked in defeat. He gripped the pommel of the saddle and hoisted himself onto the horse. His hands tightened on the reins. He nodded to Marcus. "Reckon on this, should she recover, ye have ta be her husband again." He prompted the horse to sprint from the stable yard.

Marcus blinked, awakening from a deep sleep, Stanton's words echoing in his mind . . . '*should she recover.*'

Guilt assaulted him. He did not wish for her to recover. Yet, what if she *did*?

God would hold him accountable to be her husband in every way. His own thoughts of the previous night returned. Had he been a more kind, understanding husband in the past they may have worked through the difficulties and reached some semblance of a cordial marriage.

Now, he would have to do that very thing should she return to health.

Nan's sweet face flashed before him. He must needs do it for Nan. Determined to make things right, he took long, hard strides to the townhouse. He ordered his coach prepared and Gil made ready for the journey to the manor. He had sent a missive with Stanton to Mrs. Brimberry to prepare a room for their guest—their *lady*—and to alert the local physician of their impending arrival.

Marcus secured the maid who attended Gil to accompany them. He would send her back to London once Gil was settled and a nurse summoned to take over her duties. Kellie came to mind. Would she agree to aid Gil? He would speak to Adela first.

Adela.

How would he ever be able to explain about Gil? His heart

broke on such a revelation—for the future he had envisioned for he and Adela was fading away before his eyes.

 GREG

Mrs. Brimberry rushed into the kitchen waving a piece of paper in front of her like a lady's fan. She halted and sought Adela's gaze, holding it firmly, eyes narrowing.

"Make haste!" she cried. "Lord DeGrey shall arrive this eve with Lady DeGrey who is ailing terribly, even unto death. Prepare broth and gruel and make haste for her ladyship's arrival."

Adela stiffened, the knife suspended in the air above the vegetables, the housekeeper's voice a dull, muddled roar in her ears.

Marcus had a wife.

A fear she had never known moored her securely to an unknown dock, one of uncertainty, pain, no way of escape. The tears came unbidden, silently coursing down their path, dripping onto the worktable.

An image filled her mind. A raven-haired woman who resembled Nan. The painting in the attic that was slashed.

Sudden realization dawned on Adela. Mrs. Brimberry had *wanted* her to see it. But why?

Mrs. Brimberry jutted out her chin and sent Adela a superior look. "We have but hours to prepare." She ranted about preparations while Mrs. Henshaw sent the kitchen maids scurrying about to carry out the housekeeper's orders.

Marcus married? She couldn't believe it.

Her surroundings blurred—the aroma of baking bread, the

329

bluebells in a vase on the windowsill, movement around her.

Adela's legs trembled. A stool bumped against the back of her knees, forcing her to sit.

Mrs. Henshaw hovered over her, a damp cloth in her hand. "Me dear."

The kind-hearted cook tenderly wiped a damp cloth over Adela's cheeks. "'Tis sorry I am ye found out thus. The only secret me boy has ever asked me ta keep."

She sat beside Adela, continuing her ministrations, glancing at the door from whence the housekeeper left. "The woman has a cruel streak in her. She be spiteful when she be jealous."

When Adela looked into the woman's eyes, she saw tears shining, the catalyst which brought on her sobs.

"Mrs. Hen—Henshaw." She dropped her head onto the woman's shoulder and wept bitterly.

The cook placed comforting arms around her and gently swayed as if she were a child. "Oh, me sweet. 'Tis painful I know."

A new burst of sobs mingled with a gut-wrenching moan. "Oh, why didn't someone tell me? *Why*?"

The faces of all the men who'd broken her heart paraded themselves across her mind's eye in the form of Marcus DeGrey. The unrealistic visage of *her* version of Mr. Darcy.

What a fool she'd been.

The cook patted Adela's shoulder. "'Twas another's story ta tell. I had no idea ye were so fond of the master. Ye kept it well hid."

She took the cloth and dabbed her face. "Mrs. Henshaw."

"Aye, me dear."

"Why has he been so nice to me? Why has he shown me so many kindnesses, if . . ." Adela cried into the fabric.

"Oh, me sweet. He be a man who has been lonely for a time. All can see how much he was drawn to ye." She heaved an exasperated sigh. "'Twill not do for me ta tell his story. He would have me head on that platter. But it be time he told ye the whole of it. And I shall be tellin' him so when he returns, that I shall!"

The woman gave Adela an affectionate smile. "Ye have become like a dawter to me. I would not have ye hurt so."

Adela rose on unsteady legs and gripped the woman in a reassuring embrace. "Thank you. I don't know how I would have coped in this time without you."

Mrs. Henshaw pulled away and shot her a curious glance. "Ye say the queerest things, though I love ye all the same." Her smile was sympathetic as she released her. "Now, ta take care of the tasks Mrs. Brimberry has put before us. We shall sort out the other when tha master arrives." She gave Adela an emphatic nod.

The next hours passed with the bustle of preparations for the arrival of the lord and lady. Several times Adela caught herself on a sob but tamped it down with a task to occupy her hands and mind.

The broth she prepared for Lady DeGrey nearly undid her altogether. Kellie came to the kitchen to collect scraps for the stable kittens. She met Adela's eyes and halted inside the door. "What's wrong?"

Mrs. Henshaw stepped between them and took Kellie's arm. "Come. Tha bits and pieces for tha kittens are here." She led Kellie into the small room beside the kitchen.

Adela heard whispering and closed her eyes, praying for peace. The day couldn't end quick enough. She bit her lip and concentrated on stirring the broth.

How would she ever get through the day?

When Kellie returned, she held a small bowl piled with table scraps, her eyes downcast. It was the same dejected look she'd worn when she discovered Tim's infidelity.

It broke Adela anew. There were no tears this time, only dry sobs, as she hung her head in shame.

Kellie's compassionate embrace brought her to the brink again. "Mrs. Henshaw, may I take Adela somewhere private for a few minutes?"

"Aye. Follow me."

Mrs. Henshaw led them down the hall to her rooms. Kellie kept a firm steadying hand on Adela's arm. She was surprised to see the cook had a pleasant, but tiny parlor adjacent to her bedroom.

The older woman chose a pillow, plumped it with a loud thwack, and settled it onto the back of a small stuffed chair.

"Sit ye here, me gurl."

Kellie eased Adela onto the seat and sat next to her.

Adela looked up. "Thank you, Mrs. Henshaw. You are a kind-hearted woman."

The woman patted Kellie's arm. "Ye jest sit here a bit and take care of your friend. She does need a comfortin'. I shall tell any askin' tha Adela be unwell, and ye are tendin' her."

Mrs. Henshaw handed Adela a delicately embroidered handkerchief. She thanked her and took the finely made cloth into her hand and fingered it as the woman left the room

Adela blew out a shaky breath and leaned against the soft upholstered seat. "Oh, Kellie," she stammered. "I have been so stupid."

"You aren't the one who should feel stupid. Marcus knew what he was doing." Kellie gritted her teeth. "He misled you."

Adela placed a trembling hand on Kellie's arm. "No. He never lied. He merely left out the details of his life." She wiped her eyes. "Now that I look back, he may have tried to tell me a time or two. When we went to Nunney Castle, we took a long walk together while on a picnic. Several times he acted nervous, began to say something, then shut down, or we were interrupted. One way or another, he never hinted at being married though."

Kellie stood and paced, hands on her hips. "Yeah, but he led you on. He kissed you for heaven's sake!"

Adela opened her mouth, but Kellie shushed her. "No! I know what you're gonna say. He was kind and generous to the three of us, but I saw the way he looked at you the first time we met him. Something stirred in him. Then, as they say at the horse races, 'And they're off!'" She drew in a loud breath. "There have been too many things pass between you. Only the Lord knows Leanne and I haven't seen or heard all of it."

Adela's eyes widened, her thoughts on the kiss outside the cottage. "What do you mean? You and Leanne have discussed Marcus and me?"

Kellie's stare provided the answer before she confirmed it. "Yes, we have. We're not stupid, Adela. You. Love. Him."

Adela's lips quivered, and she closed her eyes on the pain the truth Kellie's words brought.

Kellie returned to her seat and placed a reassuring hand on Adela's knee. "*And* he loves you."

Adela sighed deeply. What did it matter now?

Kellie sighed. "The way he looks at you, the way he treats you, says it all. There's something deeper to this story, and it seems like we're about to find out."

Adela released a wounded laugh.

"I'm serious," Kellie continued. "There's more to this story. It just occurred to me we know nothing about this wife of his. Nan supposes she's dead, and the staff is extremely careful not to talk about Nan's mother. What's up with that?"

Adela nodded, dozens of questions surfacing from Kellie's disclosure. "Yes. You're right. There may be a genuine reason Marcus kept this from me."

Hope sparked in her spirit. *What if?*

A knock sounded. Kellie answered the door to one of the kitchen maids with a pitcher, a clean towel, and a small glass pot.

"Mrs. Henshaw asked me to bring ye this, mistress." She entered the room and placed the offerings on the table by the window.

Adela thanked her as she slipped out the door.

Kellie inspected the items. "Looks like Mrs. Henshaw sent warm lavender water, a towel, and scented cream." She dipped a finger in the pot, brought it to Adela, and spread it on the back of her hand.

Adela sniffed. "It's rose-scented." Her eyebrows lifted. "Is she telling me to wash my face?"

"Appears so." Kellie waggled her brows. "Let's get to it. Marcus will be here soon, and we're going to get to the bottom of this sordid story. Once and for all."

Kellie was right. She needed to know the truth, but it was as if the air had been completely knocked out of her.

Adela sent up a prayer for strength and guidance as she would soon have to face the man who held her heart, though he belonged to another.

⋘⋙

The kitchen was abuzz when Adela returned. Kellie offered an encouraging smile and squeezed her hand before departing.

Mrs. Henshaw handed her a large spoon. "Here, ye go, dearie. Stir the broth for me. Taste it ta see if it be to your likin'." The woman turned to finish slicing bread. "Ye are lookin' a sight better."

Adela forced a smile. "Thanks to your lovely lavender water and rose cream. It did the trick."

A small grin tugged at the cook's lips. "Aye."

They shared a smile and attended their chores for some minutes before the cook asked Adela to fetch parsley from the herb garden for the broth.

Adela gave a final stir. "Would you like anything else while I'm there?" She took the basket from the hook by the door and glanced at the cook.

The woman tilted her head and bit her lip, deep in thought. "Aye. Fetch some Jacob's Ladder. 'Twill be good ta make tea for Lady DeGrey's ills." Her tone held remorse. "Sorry, I am, me dear. But we must press on. Fetch us some lavender and I shall brew a pot of our own tea." She winked, then whispered, "I have currant scones hid away for us."

Adela disappeared and trudged across the gardens. The sweet, pungent scent of herbs calmed her spirit. She knelt, clipped herbs, and placed them in the basket. On a whim, she trimmed the wayward plants which had outgrown their spaces. She would make two bouquets—one for the kitchen and one for their cottage. Their mingling scents would bring a fresh, uplifting quality to the air.

The rattle of a carriage tore into her peaceful world through the hedgerow separating the drive from the gardens. She rushed toward the kitchen when a familiar voice reached her.

The basket slipped to the ground, and she moved to the hedge against her will. Through the thick bush, she barely made out Marcus's tall, strong figure. With trembling hands, she parted the foliage and peered through to see Christopher dart from the manor's entrance.

Marcus leaned into the carriage, and someone from inside helped a woman out and into his waiting arms.

Adela's heart squeezed with regret. To see another woman held by him was torture. She blinked back tears and watched as Christopher took the woman from Marcus. He yielded her without hesitation.

After wiping at tears, she collected the basket. Rather than take the longer path through the gardens, she sprinted across the terrace. The wide doors leading to the back of the great hall stood open to let the air flow through. She glanced to see Christopher carrying a petite, ebony-haired woman, her body limp. He wore a bitter, detached expression as they walked in her direction toward the staircase in the great hall's back corner.

Christopher's eyes met hers, but he didn't miss a step. His brow creased, and he gave a subtle shake of his head. When he turned to take the stairs, Marcus appeared from behind.

Adela froze, unable to look away. He was close enough to read the pain etched on his face and the torment in those grey eyes.

His step faltered, and a young maid who strode in their wake stumbled behind him. She righted herself and offered Adela a nod and curtsy.

Marcus whispered something to the girl and motioned for her to follow Christopher upstairs. He took one step toward the doors, but Adela held her hand up to stop him. She shook her head, but he continued on his path, his countenance rigid.

Adela ran toward the kitchen, thrust the door open with force, and flung it shut. She tossed the basket on the worktable and in a shaky voice asked Mrs. Henshaw if she could go to her parlor for a few moments to compose herself.

The woman nodded. "'Twill 'be a good time for a calmin' cup of tea."

As Adela passed through the door into the hall, she heard the kitchen door creak open and the sound of booted footsteps on the stone floor. She ran down the hall and into Mrs. Henshaw's parlor, quickly closing the door behind her and reaching for the lock.

There wasn't one. She braced the door with her back.

When it started to move, she closed her eyes and said in a harsh whisper, "Please just go away."

"I shall not go away. Ye must hear me." Marcus's voice at once sounded resolute and broken. "Ye must listen, Adela."

She planted herself more firmly, but the door didn't move.

No other sound came except his voice, closer than before, low and laced with emotion. "I tried to tell ye." He paused. "The day we walked in the woods. *My* story . . ."

Knees trembling, sudden bone-heavy weariness found her.

He repeated, "I tried to tell ye."

The flat, tremulous tone of his voice frightened her. She was so confused. How could she ever forgive him?

I forgave him. I forgave you. The still small voice rang in her mind. So kindly spoken. So real.

The tears did not come, but she choked back a sob. *Oh, God, why did You bring me here?*

Heavy footsteps echoed along the corridor, drawing closer with each step.

Marcus cleared his throat. "Why are ye here?"

Christopher's normally mild-tempered voice held a hard edge. "*Brother.* Gil is asking for ye and Nan."

Adela listened to shuffling, but no one walked away. "Not until I speak with Adela."

"Methinks ye would be on the other side of the door should she desire to speak with ye." He exhaled. "Of a truth, she does not."

"Stay out of this, Christopher."

His brother grew quiet and neither spoke for some time. "Marcus, just tell the woman ye love her, and ye were going to London to seek divorce."

"Christopher." Marcus's voice held sharp reprimand.

Adela clutched her stomach. *He was going to divorce his wife for me?*

In this time such an act would surely ruin him within the aristocracy.

Christopher spoke at the door. "Adela, will ye please speak to my wayward brother before I thrash him? He is much older, so methinks I can take him with no issue at all."

"Christopher," Marcus ground out.

Adela cleared her throat twice before she could speak. "Marcus, why would you divorce your wife and ruin yourself? What has she done that would warrant such a thing?"

No answer was forthcoming until Christopher spoke for him. "Because Gillian is a man-chasing drunkard dependent upon laudanum."

Marcus growled. "*Enough.*"

"Unbeknownst to my slow-witted brother, Gil even attempted to entice me to her bed while he was away."

A hard slam sounded against the wall, the sconce rattling.

"Within a fortnight of their wedding."

Another slam.

"Brother, let us face the truth, I am much faster than your attempts to—" Christopher grunted as a blow hit him.

Adela jerked the door open. "Stop!" she shouted. "Both of you." She pointed a finger at Marcus first, then turned it on

Christopher. "Why did you say such horrid things about Marcus's—" She choked on the word. "—wife?"

Christopher rubbed his jaw. "Because they are truth. He shall never admit it." He straightened himself and jerked his cravat into place. "All he did was avoid her and the situation. I tried to talk sense into her and so did Stanton. She offered herself to us both." He spat out the last bit with disgust.

"We even sent the priest to her." His features softened, sadness now in his blue-grey eyes. "She would hear no one. The woman is sick in all manners. Stanton and I agreed to find whence she came, but before we began, she disappeared, leaving Nan behind."

Marcus stood aside, his mouth agape, gazing from her to Christopher.

Christopher fixed his brother with a stern look. "Marcus, the only way I could get ye to see was to be crude in manner. Adela has long been kept in the shadows. She does deserve the truth. Should Gil survive, ye must needs address this as soon as is expedient." He gave Adela a bow, glanced at Marcus one last time, and strode away, rubbing his jaw.

Adela watched Christopher walk down the hall, her insides in turmoil. She wanted to grab Marcus and soothe his hurt, but something in her fractured. She turned to face him.

This man, who had somehow eased his way into her heart, her very spirit, had misled her.

A sense of disappointment rose inside her, not only concerning him, but herself. She had let herself be deceived, by not only Marcus, but countless men over the years with their big words and vacant promises. It had left her empty, hollow, her self-worth shattered once again.

Enough was enough.

She refused to fall into the same trap again—seeking fulfillment, approval even, in a man rather than God. I am at fault for desiring companionship with a man instead of my heavenly Father.

Adela stepped toward Marcus, her jaw clenching, words dripping with hostility. "Marcus, I feel used and lied to. I don't even want to look at you. You led me to believe I meant something to you, and all the while you had a *wife!*"

She shoved his chest, and he stumbled into the wall. "Right now, all I feel is loathing. For you and all the men in my past who have deceived me into considering they were something they were NOT! I'm sick of it. No. More."

Adela turned away sharply, stomped into the parlor, and slammed the door before she fell to pieces.

CAROLE LEHR JOHNSON

Chapter Twenty-Five

Marcus stared at the door, his heart splintering. He could not ignore the depth of pain and hurt in her eyes, the lines around them deep with fatigue and agony.

And *he* was to blame.

Why could he not have kept away from her? The moment he'd seen her perched upon the chair with a broom over her head attempting to rid Dunbar Cottage of a small lizard, he had been captivated as if by the call of a siren.

Although he had not given God much thought since his troubles with Gil, he did believe and tried to follow God's laws. Now, he would do the right thing by everyone in his life. He had a wife he did not love, but God commanded he love her anyway. Somehow, he must make Adela understand it all, he truly wanted her to stay and marry him, yet it could not be.

He took a step toward the door. "Adela, please shut me out

no longer. I am sorry." He felt so weary. "Please allow me to explain and beg your forgiveness."

"Marcus," Adela said, her voice was nearly a whisper. "Our time is at an end."

He released a short half-chuckle. "*Time*. Such a wondrous word." He shook his head. "Adela, I shall leave not until I am allowed to explain." He drew in a ragged breath. "There is no excuse. 'Twas my heart I did follow. Of that I am guilty. Sorrowful, I am, and shame will follow me the remainder of my days."

He heard shuffling on the other side of the door, then her voice sounded. "Lord DeGrey . . ."

The door shook as something crashed against it, and he jumped.

Adela's voice rose in pitch and anger. "Right now, I want you to go away! Because of you, I will never trust another man as long as I live!"

Her words cut deeply as if someone had run him through the heart with a blade. He wrenched the door open with such force one of the hinges gave way and hung drunkenly.

She backed away, her face ashen.

He paused at the threshold. "I am sorry. I wished not to frighten ye." He ran a hand over his eyes. "I am but a desperate man."

Marcus took two steps toward her and gently caught her hand in his. Adela's gaze was on the floor, his on her face until she allowed him to lead her to sit. The distance she placed between them created a dark and cruel void inside him.

His explanation came out hurried. "I went to London to tell

Gil I would seek a divorce from her. Proof of her manner of living would award the detachment without delay. I was to return to ye, plead with ye to stay in this time and marry me." He held her gaze, attempting to see in her eyes what she desired.

Her mouth dropped. "You seriously wanted to marry me?" Her tone was filled with incredulity. "Why would you marry me? I am no one. You need an heiress, don't you?"

Marcus released a bitter laugh. "Oh, *my* Adela. I do so love ye. Whilst I may not be the wealthiest of men, I need no heiress to pull me from ruin. Ye amuse and enchant me more than I can say."

"I cannot understand why God brought me to this time." She clasped her hands tightly in her lap, peering at them. "He could've made you be born in my time—or made me be born in this time and brought us together."

Marcus sighed. "I know, but there is one thing I now possess ye may not. An understanding that God can do all things, and it is not for us to question why nor how. We are not His equal nor must He consult us in order to achieve anything."

She searched his eyes.

He pressed on. "'Tis hard for me to speak thus, but I shall. God spoke to me once I rescued Gil from the burning tavern. He has impressed upon me that I married her and to her I should stay thus. Her disregard for our marriage is of no concern. Forgive her, I *must*."

Adela shivered. He wrapped an arm around her, and she wilted into his side. The scent of her was nearly his ruination.

She smelled of lavender and roses. It was more than the physical, he felt connection on the deepest level. His love for her overwhelmed him. The love God had sent to him.

But how could it be? His wife lived.

He pulled her close for a moment and then released her. "Though pains me it does, I shall submit to God's will. Gil may, or may not, survive her illness and injuries. Should she survive, I must needs attempt a reconciliation." He brought Adela's hand to his lips and kissed it. "Please understand."

Her expression was stoic. "Thank you for your honesty and for submitting to God's will. I must return to my own time. I must face that this is not where I truly belong."

She closed her lovely jade eyes, silent tears sliding down her cheeks. When she spoke, her voice shook. "Marcus Jackson DeGrey, I will never forget you. You are the love of my life, and I will cherish the memory of you forever."

Adela touched his cheek, slid her fingers down his jaw, and brought her mouth to his. The kiss was tenderness, passion, and injury intertwined. She drew back as if burned. "I am sorry. I should not have done that." She rose, wiped her eyes, and rushed from the room, leaving him in a state of suffering he had never known.

She had been the love of his life, and now he had lost her forever.

γβα

Booted footsteps approached. Christopher DeGrey rounded the corner. Leanne waited next to the manor kitchen. She had witnessed the scene between Adela, Marcus, and Christopher.

Christopher halted in front of her, his eyes imploring her,

perhaps wondering what she had seen and heard. "Mistress Leanne, what brings ye to this side of the manor?"

Leanne reached to gently touch his darkened eye and shook her head. "Where I come from, this is called a shiner." She laughed. "And it's a doozy."

He winced at her touch. "Ye must teach me these odd words ye speak so freely."

"*Master* DeGrey, I might just do that." She linked her arm in his and tugged him toward the kitchen. "Let's get a remedy for your black eye, shall we? And *you* can tell me why you were so gallant in defending my sweet friend."

Her words brought a smile to Christopher's face. He bowed within the confined space and restriction of her grasp. "Aye, my lady, I shall be honored to accompany ye to the kitchen."

Leanne cocked a sideways look at him. "You know, when you smile like that, I can almost buy the *brother-of-the-lord-of-the-manor thing* you've got going for you."

His laughter echoed.

"We need to find Kellie and Stanton and arrange a meeting to continue our—" She lowered her voice. "—time travel research."

"Ye are correct." He pulled her to a stop outside the kitchen door. "Leanne, I do not think it timely to include Marcus and Adela. Let us take on this task without them for now." His eyes searched hers for understanding. "They are in much turmoil at present."

Leanne nodded. "You're right. They have enough to consider right now." She marveled at how he was so much more than she'd initially believed. He was thoughtful, kind, and so darned gorgeous. His smile made her knees go wobbly every time he looked at her, and when he had asked her to marry him, she had to admit she was a bit more than flattered.

Maybe Christopher wasn't so bad after all. Leanne sighed. She had to get a grip on her feelings.

The man was impossible, but, boy, could he kiss.

∞

Marcus held Nan's hand, gently squeezing it with affection. "Nan, sorry I am this has occurred. I've explained about your mother being alive and why it was best ye knew not." His hand twitched with nervous anticipation. "When ye are older, I shall explain further. Just know she does love ye but has been ill—in her mind. No fault of her own."

How does one explain to a child her mother has no morals? Perchance it was because of her upbringing and how she was treated. It pained him to hurt his daughter in such a manner.

She blinked wide, blue eyes, so innocent and vulnerable. "Papa. Why is Mama here?"

He dropped to his haunches and caressed her blonde curls. "The sickness in her head made her believe she wanted things in life which led her from us. But now she desires to see ye for she is most ill."

"Will she die now, Papa?"

Marcus inhaled deeply. "Only God knows the answer for 'tis in His timing that all should occur."

Time. The elusive word that kept Adela from him forever.

"Come. Let us go to her side. She longs to see ye." Marcus pulled Nan into his arms and rose, holding her tightly against his chest, emotion overcoming him. "Nan, I love ye more than life itself. Never doubt."

Tears did not come easily for him, but in this moment, his control was not his own. She flung her arms around his neck and squeezed as only a child could.

"I love ye too, Papa. When I say my prayers each eve, I thank Him for ye, for ye are all I have." She pulled back, her tiny hand against his cheek, and smiled. "And now I have Adela. I love her as well as ye, Papa."

Marcus was uncertain what to say. Adela had been a godsend to them both. "Aye, my dear. And she loves ye."

He strode from the room with his daughter clutching him, and they went to Gil. Nan lay her head on his shoulder, soft curls against his neck, the scent of lavender clinging to her.

Marcus tapped lightly on the door. A weak, trembling voice bid them enter. Gil lay propped on ivory pillows, her black hair spread around her shoulders. The contrast of dark against light made her appear paler than she had been upon their arrival.

Marcus drew in a breath, bringing to him the memory of his father's death.

The room reeked of stale air, of something unidentifiable, a lingering, nearly tangible presence. Something he recalled from the deaths of both his father and mother.

Marcus eased Nan to her feet, took her hand, and led her to her mother. Gil's ashen arm lay on the bed, outstretched to welcome her daughter. A daughter she had abandoned.

The old anger rose. Gillian Yvette DeGrey was an unnatural mother. Christopher's words returned to his mind—'a man-chasing drunkard dependent upon laudanum.'

But she was now dying.

Her face revealed it, and her words came in the voice of the perishing, laden with regret. Nan timidly took her hand and stood by the side of the bed but did not release her hold on Marcus's hand.

"Ye are so beautiful. Much like your father who is a fine-looking man." An uncontrollable cough seized Gil. The nurse ran to her side, bringing a cup of water and a cloth. When the coughing subsided, she slumped onto the pillows, exhausted.

Gil's aquamarine eyes peered at Marcus. "I have little time left." She struggled to remove a ring from her finger. It bore a stone the color of her eyes. "My—" She swallowed and looked away from him. "—I want Nan to have this."

Her attempt to remove it failed. "Marcus, will ye please keep the ring for Nan?" He bent and gripped her hand. It felt like ice in the river during winter. The ring slid easily from the skeletal finger.

Their eyes met, and he read a lifetime of regret in their depths. "I'll keep it safe for her." He tucked it inside his coat pocket. "Until she is of an age." After their interchange, Nan stared at her mother, barely blinking. She took a tentative step closer to the bed and lay a hand on her mother's.

"Mama," she said in a small, timid voice. "I know ye not, but I love ye, for God tells us to love everyone."

A single tear slipped from Gil's eye. "My dear, Nanette. Ye are like your grand-mère. She would have loved ye so much, my child." Her cough returned but did not abate as quickly as before.

Nan placed a kiss upon her mother's hand, and they left the room filled with imminent death.

CRSO

Adela ladled broth into a bowl. The scent of warm, yeasty bread filled the room. Her stomach growled, reminding her she'd not eaten since breakfast, and not much at that.

"Adela, ye must halt and eat. Afore ye know it, ye will be as thin as that ladle ye be usin'."

She shrugged. "All right, Mrs. Henshaw. If you insist. I suppose I can choke down some of this disgusting bread."

The old cook chortled. "Aye. Of a certainty ye have forced down a number of loaves since ye been here, 'specially loaded with butter or cream."

Adela laughed fully for the first time in a while. "You are such a dear. I will miss—" She was interrupted when a serving maid rushed into the room.

Mrs. Henshaw held out a tray. "Here, Narcissus. Take it ta Lady DeGrey."

"Aye, Mrs. Henshaw," the small brown-haired girl said with certainty, though her manner was nervous. "Likely 'twill not be long til she do depart this earth." The maid took the tray and scurried out.

Adela's heart sank. She and the cook shared a sad look. She didn't want anyone to die, especially a woman who'd lived a life of debauchery without God. "Mrs. Henshaw, do you mind if I go speak to Lord DeGrey. It is of some urgency."

The woman cocked her head and narrowed her eyes. "If ye think it be necessary. Aye."

351

"Thank you." She kissed the woman's cheek and hurried from the kitchen.

☙❧

Leanne, Kellie, Stanton, and Christopher surrounded the table in the library. Books were strewn across the mahogany surface, along with papers of drawings and scattered notes.

Kellie sighed and reached for a volume of astronomy which lay among their research material. They had been at it for hours, not to mention countless nights but were no closer to finding answers.

As she flipped through the book's pages, a single word caught her attention.

The voices of her companions faded into the background, her mind focusing on the word—*equinox*. She scanned the page, which told of different equinoxes and their significance.

"Uh, guys." She lifted her head to meet their questioning gazes. "I think I found something of interest." She told them according to the book she, Adela, and Leanne had arrived during the vernal equinox, a time of atmospheric changes and shifts, and another was coming soon—that very month.

Stanton stood and read over her shoulder, the scent of leather mixed with fresh hay mingled with the aroma of tea and biscuits. He nodded and met her eyes. "Ye have found something indeed."

The full force of the discovery—his confirmation of it, the finality of leaving this time, of leaving him—fell heavy on Kellie's shoulders.

He held her gaze, and she was pulled as if magnetic toward him. His nearness drew her. His features usually unreadable now crossed with the briefest hint of pain and perhaps disappointment. He did not want her to go either.

Yet, she had to go.

Kellie broke contact first, returning to the book and fighting to quell the ache within her at the thought of leaving Stanton. She did not belong here, she reminded herself.

Christopher cleared his throat. "So, ye are saying ye arrived in this time on the *vernal* equinox and mayhap return on the *autumnal* equinox?"

Kellie looked at him, but before she could speak, Stanton said, "It appears so."

Leanne heaved a sigh. "This may be just the miracle we've prayed for." She glanced at Kellie. "Good find." She returned to the stack of papers in front of her. "Now, we need to determine the exact date of the upcoming equinox and make an attempt as early as possible that day. Have everything set up as it was when we traveled here. If the first attempt doesn't work, we'll keep trying all day."

Kellie noticed Christopher's gaze lingering on Leanne as she busied herself sorting through the papers and books. His own search had stopped while he watched her.

Stanton sat again and rustled papers to her left. She couldn't look at him.

The breakthrough was exactly what they needed and had searched for all this time, so why did it come with the air of disappointment?

Stanton said, "There is a fortnight until the equinox."

Kellie heard the restrain in his voice as if reining in emotion. She didn't say anything, *couldn't* say anything.

Leanne nodded. "We need to tell Adela and Marcus."

Stanton shifted in his seat. "Aye. Yet what of Andrew? Will he make it 'til then?"

Kellie sensed Stanton's attention on her. Instead, she met Christopher's pain-filled gaze and sighed. "If we can keep the little monkey still, he should be fine. He cannot overexert himself. If we take turns keeping an eye on him, maybe—"

Her voice broke, compassion and sorrow mingling. Kellie chided herself. She was a medical professional, facing illness, pain, and death often, even with children.

But fatigue and uncertainty had taken its toll.

A strong hand rested over hers, gentle and comforting. She raised her head to look at Stanton, the tenderness and care in his gaze nearly unsettling her.

Kellie closed her eyes, drawing on every ounce of strength she had left to not fall into his arms and cry.

CB80

Adela smoothed her hair as she headed for the library in search of Marcus. She passed through the dining room and into the hall leading to the entry.

Footsteps echoed in the great hall as she rounded the corner. Marcus carried Nan, her head resting on his shoulder. The child's face was somber. Her father wore a similar look, but his mouth was a grim line. When he saw her, his face shifted to relief and came toward her.

"Please take Nan to her room. Sleep is best for her now. When she is resting, come to the library. We must speak." He eased the child into Adela's arms and left them.

Nan's thick, groggy voice whispered into her ear, "Adela?"

"Yes, sweetie?"

"Why must my mother die when she has just found me?"

Adela hugged her close as they traversed the stairs. How could she answer such a painful question?

God, please send me words to give this precious child.

Nan didn't make it to her room before she fell asleep. Adela said a prayer of thanksgiving, glad for a reprieve in answering the child.

Adela kissed Nan's forehead and informed the maid to keep an eye on her.

All the way to the library, Adela let the series of events since their arrival tumble around in her mind, confusion clouding her thoughts. What was God up to?

Adela entered the library in a fog, expecting to find Marcus staring out onto the east gardens, hands clasped behind his back, deep in thought. Instead, he stood over Kellie, Stanton, Leanne, and Christopher seated around the table looking at books, charts, and papers in deep conversation.

Their talk came to an abrupt stop when Adela entered the room.

Leanne leapt from her chair and ran to her, pulling her forward. "You have *got* to hear this." She pushed Adela into a chair and plopped into the one beside her. "We think we know how we got here and how to get back. Kellie discovered it."

Adela met Kellie's eyes and was surprised to see the emotion overtaking her, the threat of tears.

"Adela," Marcus said, interrupting her thoughts. She

looked at him, standing behind Stanton, his smile woeful. "I asked ye to meet me here but was surprised to find the library occupied with researchers who have made quite a discovery."

"Stanton, would you explain?" Kellie asked.

With a husky voice he explained about equinoxes and their plan and why it *should* work. "The three of ye and Andrew must be 'round the cottage table on that date."

Adela nodded. "So, we have two weeks."

Christopher asked, "Ye said it had to be the three of ye. How do ye know ye can take Andrew?"

Leanne spoke up. "I'm going to hold him on my lap. He's such a small boy, surely it couldn't make a difference." Her voice faltered in its attempt to cover her doubt.

Kellie agreed. "And if the first attempt doesn't work, we'll do as Leanne said, we'll keep trying different things all day."

Adela agreed, and they put away their materials.

Marcus asked Adela and Kellie if he might have a word with them in his study. They walked with him into the next room, and he motioned for them to sit at his desk, though he strode to the window and looked out over the garden.

He cleared his throat and with a croak in his voice said, "Methinks the favor I am about to ask of ye may not be to your liking, but I must needs ask."

Adela sent Kellie a questioning look, and she shrugged.

"The maid who escorted us from London must return." He turned to face them. "May I trespass upon your duties to care for Lady DeGrey?" He closed his eyes. "She shall not be long with us. The physician from London said as much. With her addiction to laudanum, and the severe burns and smoke inhalation she suffered in the fire, there is little hope."

"Lord DeGrey, I am so very sorry," Kellie said without reluctance. "Of course, we . . . There's no need for Adela's help. I'll take care of her myself."

Kellie opened her mouth to speak, but Adela shook her head. "No. I will help as well. Kellie, you cannot take care of her at all hours." He words sounded convincing, but her heart screamed *no!* This was Marcus's wife.

Marcus's eyes held astonishment and admiration.

Adela dropped her gaze. How could she look at this man she loved when he was still married?

He had kept her in the dark, no matter his reasons or excuses. She had been a fool. There was nothing for her here. She had to go to her time. And go she would.

The smell of Mrs. Henshaw's cooking wafted into the room. Kellie's stomach growled loudly, and they laughed. "Guess we've been too busy today to eat properly." She stood and curtsied. "Lord DeGrey, if I may be excused, I'll make my way to the kitchen."

It was nice to hear his laughter again. She'd miss the sound. She'd miss *him*.

She rose to leave with Kellie, but he drew near. "Please stay a moment." His hand came up as if to touch her face, then dropped it to his side. "Please?"

Adela nodded but did not retake her seat. She swung around in surprise at the sound of the door locking.

Marcus pocketed the key and looked satisfied, his gaze intently on her. She edged back until she rested against the desk. "I wish not to be interrupted. It seems we cannot have a conversation without someone barging in." He stopped a few feet from her, his expression solemn. "I have things I wish to say to ye, Adela. Things no other should be privy to."

Her eyes widened, fear gripping her.

"When ye care for my wife, will ye tell her of how she may be saved for all of eternity?"

Adela's stomach tumbled. "What?"

He rubbed a hand over his jaw. "Aye. She would never take it from me. Most likely she would toss my past into my face as if foul water. No. It must come from another. From someone she knows not. I have heard ye speak of your faith, and the things ye did speak to Leanne and Kellie when reading your Bible together."

His eyes were pleading. "'Tis her only hope. And she has little time left."

As I have little time left with you. Two weeks. A fortnight.

"All right." She nodded, but her voice was small, timid, mirroring how she felt.

He edged closer to her. "Thank ye . . . my dear."

How many times had their eyes met and held like that? She could not—*would not*—look at him.

"Do ye remember what ye did speak whilst we were in Mrs. Henshaw's parlor?"

Adela shivered with the memory.

"Are ye cold?"

His voice was too close. "No. I'm not cold. I'm afraid." She couldn't control the tremor in her voice.

He whispered, "As am I."

The declaration made her look at him, and it was her destruction.

His grey eyes showed the depth of feeling between them, the drawing they both felt to the other. "Ye are the love of *my* life, Adela Mary Jenks. Yet, I am married and cannot promise ye anything. 'Tis my fate to let ye go whilst she lives. But I would not have her go to an eternal doom. Thank ye for speaking with her. 'Tis between she and God what she makes of it."

He pulled in a deep breath and released it. The fragrance of mint filled the air around them.

Adela smiled, though it faltered. "You've been sampling Mrs. Henshaw's biscuits."

"Aye." His grin weakened her resolve. "Now I must needs tell ye one thing more."

Marcus slipped his hand behind her neck, his other arm came around her waist, and pulled her close. "This is for me to remember ye for the remainder of my days. For I shall never marry again."

"No, Marcus. You *are* married." She tried to push him away, but the feel of his embrace overcame her senses, and she stopped resisting.

He looked deeply into her eyes. "Aye, and well ye knew this when ye did give me a final kiss as a memory for yourself."

His lips were warm and soft for a time, then his kiss boldened with urgency. The grasping of a memory they would never have again.

Chapter Twenty-Six

Adela gripped the stair's railing, tears slipping down her cheeks, as she made her way to Lady DeGrey's room. She would have to avoid Marcus for two weeks. There was no way she could put herself through another goodbye.

Her heart wouldn't survive.

She hesitated outside the bedroom door, brushed away the tears, and drew in a fortifying breath.

Her light tap on the door was answered by Kellie. "Hey there. Come in. She's sleeping. I'll stay a while and show you the ropes before I go."

Adela nodded, unable to speak, and took a seat by the window, leaving the bedside chair for Kellie.

Kellie came to her and whispered, "What's wrong?"

Adela shook her head, willing the tears not to betray her again.

Kellie knelt and gently grasped Adela's arms. "What did he say after I left? I heard the door close."

Adela's focus went to her lap, face heating.

"I see," Kellie said, reading her like a book.

"He . . ." Adela covered her mouth in an attempt to halt a sob, fearful she'd wake Lady DeGrey.

Kellie cocked her head. "He what?"

"Ma . . . Marcus—" More sobs erupted. "—said I'm the love of his life." She sucked in a breath. "And he kissed me. I'm ashamed to say I could not pull away." She buried her face on Kellie's shoulder.

Kellie patted her back. "It'll be okay, Adela. Time will take care of it." She laughed mirthlessly. "Yeah. *Time*, right?"

A string of violent coughs broke through their mourning. They looked up to see Lady DeGrey rolled onto her side in a tight ball, her face flaming from the exertion.

Kellie rushed to her, retrieved a damp cloth from the basin by the bed, and began bathing her face and neck. She spoke calm, soothing words to her patient.

Adela dried her eyes as she watched the display of her friend's ministrations. She was a caring, kind-hearted nurse and friend. After a few moments, the coughing subsided, and Kellie coaxed the woman to drink a few sips of water. Now calm, the patient lay back on the pillows, black hair tangled and twisted on the linens. Her eyes met Adela's, questioning her presence.

Kellie returned to Adela and handed her an ornate silver hairbrush. "Take this, and I'll introduce you."

Adela nodded and whispered to Kellie. "There's something

else I need to tell you. A request from Marcus."

Kellie leaned closer.

"Marcus wants me to tell her of salvation through Jesus. He said she wouldn't listen to him but might to a stranger."

Kellie bobbed her head, a mischievous glint in her eyes. "Very noble of him, especially *after* he kissed your socks off."

Adela hung her head, then rose on stiff legs and followed Kellie to the bed. "Lady DeGrey, this is Mistress Adela. She will help care for you."

Adela curtsied, feeling foolish. She was, after all, the *other* woman. This tiny, frail, once beautiful woman was married to the love of her life. Marcus DeGrey. Lord of the manor. Member of the nobility of seventeenth-century England.

What was she thinking? She'd never fit in here. No matter what he, or she, thought. Furthermore, this fragile beauty would live and continue on as Lady DeGrey.

"Adela," she said weakly "Lovely name."

Still clutching the brush. Adela nodded her thanks.

Lady DeGrey narrowed her eyes. The woman might be gravely ill, but Adela saw a flicker of life spark within them as she studied her, perhaps sizing her up.

The lady's voice was stronger when she spoke this time. "Well, are ye going to *use* the brush, or do ye plan to kill me with it, so ye may lay claim to my husband?"

CB&D

Leanne and Christopher sat in Stanton's office watching a sleeping Andy, who lay on a small bed in the corner. A fire blazed, warming the room against the autumn chill.

363

The boy's narrow chest rose and fell with even breaths, his lips parted, a slight sigh escaping from time to time.

"He's a very sweet little boy," Leanne told Christopher.

Her comment was met with silence.

She peered at the boy's father, who slumped in the armchair next to her. The only thing separating them was a small table with cups of warm cider and a candle, its tapered flame casting shadows over Christopher's drawn features.

He didn't look at her when he finally spoke. "Aye, 'tis his mother in him." There was no animosity in his tone. He hung his head. "She deserved better than me."

Leanne was unsure what to say. She knew nothing of their relationship or circumstances.

"Ye must detest me for not being a good father to him."

"No, I don't," Leanne said quickly and with sincerity. "I have no right to judge you, Andy's mother, nor do I know your situations."

Christopher took a drink of cider. "No. I suppose ye do not." He cupped his drink with both hands and stared into the contents. "From first I beheld her I was besotted. She was beautiful. We understood nothing other than lust. 'Tis all there is to know. Mayhap she thought because Marcus was my brother, she could have a better life. But when we were together, it did not seem so. A kinder, gentler woman never had I met until . . ." He met her eyes with a slight smile. "Until I met ye."

Leanne straightened, her mouth dropping. "Christopher, you have got to be kidding?" She laughed. "I'm not a kind, gentle woman. Adela has, at times, called me a pistol. She meant it with fondness." Her mouth quirked. "And . . . I am no one. Your family is of the nobility."

"Nor was she." He shrugged. "Yet I loved her. And I do believe she loved me."

"I'm sorry she died. It's too bad she didn't live to marry you and be a proper mother to Andy. I'm sure you would have been happy together." She reached across the short distance and squeezed his shoulder.

Before she could pull away, he clasped her hand in his, bringing it to his lips.

The action sent a shiver up her arm, an unfortunate one of pleasure. She exhaled sharply. Why did this man rattle her? With all his charm and flattery, he was the exact sort of guy she stayed far away from.

In Christopher's eyes, she saw his intent as he drew her toward him, his focus on her lips. Heart pounding, she tried to pull her hand back but found herself frozen under his touch as he reached to caress her cheek. She made the mistake of looking at his lips then, a sense of longing overtaking her senses.

But she was saved when Stanton walked in. Christopher released her, his hand slipping from her face. She instantly missed its warmth and comfort.

CB&SO

Adela bolstered her courage before reaching Gil's door. The days and nights had passed until Adela found she could no longer call her Lady DeGrey. She'd belittled and railed at Adela with every breath.

Kellie greeted her with tired eyes and a slight stoop to her shoulders. She whispered, "Her royal highness is sleeping, but I do wonder if she's not playing possum sometimes."

Adela edged closer to Kellie's side while she kept her gaze on the patient. "I wouldn't put it past her. It's only been a few days, but it seems weeks since we began caring for her, and she does not appear to have improved at all."

"She's getting worse. Her coughs are deeper, and the rattling in her chest is alarming." Kellie prepared the warm drink she kept ready for when the hacking began. "I'll put this by the fire to keep warm until you need it. And you will."

"I hate to sound like a ghoul, but how long does she have?" Adela's heart grew more troubled at the thought of someone in Gil's condition still refusing to seek God.

"Hard to say. Could be hours or weeks. Surely no more."

Adela brightened. "I've just had an idea. Well, God must have *given* me the idea."

Kellie chortled. "Can't wait to hear this."

She nudged Kellie playfully in the side. "I'm going to sit by the bed and read the Bible to her. What's she going to do—get up and beat me?"

Kellie threw her head back and laughed. "You, my friend, have a wicked streak hidden away."

"Don't we all? Gotta do what it takes, right?"

"Right." Kellie retrieved her shawl and told Adela good night.

A shaky voice came from the bed. "What are the two of ye conspiring about? How best to poison me?" A few small coughs escaped, but Gil maintained control of them. "Why not take *la corde* and achieve it with haste?"

Adela took her small Bible from her pocket and sat in the chair by the bed. "I do not know what *la corde* means." She thumbed through the book searching for a scripture to read.

"It means *the noose*."

Adela brought her head up with a jerk. Exasperation descended upon her, patience thinning. "Gil . . ."

The woman's face twisted with annoyance. "Ye have no right to call me that. Ye are beneath me in every possible way. I am your better. Unfit to shine my fine leather boots!"

Her voice rose with strength Adela did not imagine her capable. She did not sound like a woman on her deathbed.

With agile hands, Gil snatched the crystal glass on the bedside table and threw it at Adela. It struck the side of her cheek before crashing to the floor.

The door hurtled open and banged against the wall. Marcus caught it on the rebound and stilled, his eyes firmly on Gil. "What in bedlam goes on here?"

Adela had never heard his voice so harsh, seen his eyes so hostile. He stood feet apart, hands on his hips glaring at his wife. "Ye black-hearted—"

Adela rose and stepped between him and the bed. She lay a gentle hand on his arm. "Marcus. Please leave. You are too angry."

He brought his eyes to hers, tempering his expression. "*Adela* . . ."

His fingers reached out to tenderly brush the deepening bruise on her cheek. Anger resurfaced and he turned to glare at Gil.

"Go on, Marcus. Kiss your *maîtresse*. I know all about ye

and this *Adela*." She spat Adela's name as if a curse.

Adela's gaze switched from Gil to Marcus, watching the black mood this woman brought to him. She tugged at his arm. "Go, Marcus. Please."

He shifted his eyes to Adela. "I shall go, but understand this, if I hear of her attempting any further harm upon ye—" He shook with rage. "—or voice more vile words in your direction, I shall return her to her paramour in London, and they may rot!"

Marcus spun and left the room, his heavy steps echoing down the corridor.

Adela bent to retrieve the broken crystal, nicking her finger on a thin splinter of glass. She dropped the fragments onto the table between them and sat. "Gil. I shall not call you Lady DeGrey because you do not deserve the title." She saw the ire rise in the woman's thin face. "I do not say this to hurt you but to state a fact. Marcus has become an honorable man. He has been an exemplary father to Nan, a kindly lord of all his tenants, and a friend to me. Believe what you will."

Gil's face twisted into a mask of disbelief and hatred.

"I have refused him and am going back to my ti—to my home soon. In a few days, I will leave this place. God has spoken to Marcus, and he has accepted the fact he must be a husband to you. He has promised God to try his best to care for you and be the husband you need. The husband he believes he was not in the past."

Adela's eyes moistened at the words Marcus had spoken. They had come from him with pain-laced shame, yet his eyes held love for her. She lowered her head, unable to continue.

Stillness flowed, making it harder for Adela to compose herself. A soft voice broke through her torment. "What ye tell me is my husband is giving ye up for *moi*?"

When Adela met her eyes, she saw no hatred nor loathing.

"Yes. God spoke to him of his duty to his wife. Vows were spoken. He wants to mend the past and live for the future." Adela almost choked on the word *future*. She rose, clutching her Bible to her chest. "Please excuse me for a moment."

Her footsteps resonated down the hall, along with the echo of a memory that could never be—of she and Marcus together.

Adela sank onto a couch under a window, overlooking the flower garden where she and Marcus had walked often, intent in conversation.

"Mistress? Are ye not well?" Patience stood over Adela, her face full of concern, red wisps of hair escaping from her linen cap.

Adela blinked back the tears. "I'm all right. Would you do me a favor? Please?"

"Aye, mistress. Anything."

She drew in an unstable breath. "Will you please go to Lady DeGrey's room and sit with her for a few minutes? I want to take a short rest. I'll relieve you soon."

The sympathetic girl nodded. "No bother. Ye deserve a respite from that woman, to be sure."

"Thank you."

Just as Patience turned away, footfalls thumped closer. Marcus was upon her in an instant. He sat beside her and leaned down to place a tender kiss on her injured cheek.

"Of a certainty. I believed her changed after the remorse she showed me when I did rescue her. Ye deserve no such treatment."

Adela brought her fingertips to rest on the spot where his kiss was still warm upon her skin. "Time is drawing near. I'll be gone soon. We should not see each another again. It makes it so much more difficult. You and Gil need time together."

He gently squeezed her hands. "No. I shall see ye every moment I am able whilst ye remain. I *need* to see ye. To impress your image upon my mind." His voice faltered. "And my heart."

Adela inhaled sharply and shifted the conversation before she could relent. "What is a *maîtresse*?"

Marcus's face reddened. "Why must ye know?"

"Because that's what Gil called me." She flinched. "Among other things."

His head dipped in shame. "She called ye my mistress."

"What? Why would she say that?" Adela swallowed. "She assumes you and I . . ."

His smile was sad. "Is it difficult to tell when two are in love? Most assuredly when they are in the same room?"

"When were we in the room together in her presence? I don't recall it."

Marcus tilted his head in concentration until his pensive expression turned to one of clarification. "When Christopher carried her to the chamber the day we arrived, I was following them. Ye were on the terrace. She must have seen us then."

Adela's mind trailed to that moment. Their eyes had met, and he made to come to her, but she stayed him and ran. Yes,

Gil could have witnessed it. She dipped her head. "Yes. I suppose so. She's very perceptive."

Adela didn't voice Gil had likely overheard she and Kellie's whispered conversation in her room as well.

"Suspicious most likely. Those who are guilty."

"Methinks thou protest too much?" Adela smiled grimly.

His eyes crinkled in amusement. "Aye. I do receive your meaning. I was always faithful to her but found she did not return the favor." He lifted her hands to his lips.

Adela's heart ached at his touch.

She forced back her emotions, trying not to think of their limited time, but the smile she offered was edged with sorrow.

⟨⟩

Adela straightened her shoulders and faced the door as if bound for the gallows and sought to appear brave. Kellie spoke through the partially opened door. "Are you sure you want to venture in here again?"

"I must. Besides, it's been a few days since she threw the glass."

Kellie gently touched the faint mark on Adela's cheek. "It's healing nicely."

"Well, yes." Adela chuckled. "What else could it do?" She eased into the room.

"No worries. HRH is sleeping again. She seems to sleep more and more. The coughing is getting worse. As expected. It's really strange how much of her strength remains." Kellie smirked. "But I've heard people who are possessed tend to have super-human strength."

"Kellie!" Adela admonished. "What a thing to say."

"Get over it. It's true. Don't you remember the man in chains in the New Testament? He was so strong he broke the chains binding him."

Adela had to admit it was true, but she believed the poor choices Gil had made in her life were catching up to her and taking a final toll on her health. "Either way, we must show compassion. Even if it's not easy."

"*Adela.*" The word came out on a moan.

She moved to stand by the bed and peer down at Gil, her face flushed and head bathed with sweat.

Kellie brought a basin of cool water and a cloth to mop her forehead.

"No." The woman gasped out the words. "Want Adela."

Kellie's mouth twitched in surprise, her brows lifting, but she handed the cloth to Adela.

Adela dipped the cloth in cool water, wrung it out, and with smooth strokes wiped her brow. "Yes, Gil."

"I am . . . fearful to die." She coughed. "What must I do?"

Adela looked at Kellie, who smiled. She grasped the Bible with trembling fingers and breathed a quick prayer for guidance as she opened it, verses flooding her mind.

"Gil, if you want peace and reassurance in your soul you will live for all eternity in God's presence, you must accept Jesus is who He said He is. The Son of God, died, buried, and resurrected. John 3:16 says, '*For God so loved the world, that he gave his only begotten Son, that whosoever believeth in Him should not perish, but have everlasting life.*'"

She gripped the frail woman's hand. "Gil, do you accept and believe this?"

The woman looked at Adela without loathing or malice. She nodded and squeezed Adela's hand, tears slipping from wide, aquamarine eyes, black lashes matted with moisture. "*Oui*. I now see."

Her gaze was distant, yet understanding lingered there. "Marcus," she murmured, tears still falling.

"Do you want to see him?" Adela asked.

She coughed dryly. "No. Ye."

Kellie gave her a sip of water, and Gil's brow furrowed, but her expression seemed sincere, her eyes on Adela. "Take him. He belongs to ye. I never truly held him. When we met, he was such *beau garçon*. I chose him to be the one."

Adela drew back. What did she mean?

"Now, he is yours, Adela. Be good to him as I was not." Her breath hitched, a cough racking her body. "And Nan. Love *ma petite fille*."

Her gaze moved to the ceiling, breath slowing. After a moment, she closed her eyes, and her hand went limp in Adela's. Kellie felt for her pulse and shook her head.

Gil was gone, but based on her countenance, it was into peace.

CR80

Marcus stood over his wife's bed. She lay with arms crossed over her chest, hands loosely clasped in repose. Her pale skin white against ebony hair in waves about her face. He couldn't weep. The pain was too deep. She never loved him. She had

373

only used him to obtain what she desired.

A name. A title. A father for her child.

He had suspected as much when they married, but his feelings for her had obsessed him. What he thought was love was nothing more than youthful lust. She had been a most beautiful and beguiling woman.

Kellie entered the room, hesitating in the doorway. "Lord DeGrey. The undertaker is here."

The term she used evaded him for a moment, then he acknowledged her presence and nodded, heaved a sad sigh, and left. He must seek out Adela.

His search of every room in the manor revealed no sign of her. Did she avoid him?

Gil was gone. They had no hindrance in their joining. Of a certainty she knew this. Did she not?

His soul ached. Time drew nigh for their departure. No impediment stood in their way. Why would she not see him?

Days passed, and he saw her not. When he went to the cottage either Kellie or Leanne stood sentinel at the door and told him she did not wish to see him.

Marcus wished to demand entry, break down the door, as was his right as lord of the manor, yet he could not bring himself to do it. He owed Adela much. He would honor her wishes. It didn't stop him from going each day to the cottage only to be turned away.

Two days remained until the equinox.

In deep frustration, he mounted Roman and rode the hills along the river. It drew him to the first time he had seen her from a distance. By the river he had watched three women bring forth water to carry to Dunbar Cottage. He and Roman stilled under the tree overlooking the fields and the cottage beyond. He closed his eyes and imagined their slight figures laughing as they struggled with the water.

Thunder crackled overhead, clouds gathering into a dark stain across the sky. He flicked the reins and urged Roman back to the manor, his pain overcoming him.

CR&SO

On the morning of the equinox, Adela awoke to the sound of thunder, though shafts of morning sunshine crossed her bed through the open window, crisp autumn air blowing through it. She dressed and closed the window before descending to the kitchen to prepare a meager breakfast. She breathed in the quiet and prayed for the strength the day would require.

It was time for goodbye.

Within minutes, Leanne bounded downstairs followed by Kellie. Excitement laced Leanne's voice. "This is the day. We *may* be going home. Hopefully." She grinned and attempted to run a hand through her tangled hair. "I'm so ready for a long hot bath, a hair appointment, and a massage."

Kellie shot her a look. "You need it. You've really let yourself go."

Leanne swatted Kellie's arm, a wounded expression on her face. "You're a lost cause."

Adela managed a smile, grateful they seemed to be their old selves again. The strain of many months had fallen away with the thought of returning home.

Leanne turned serious. "If we can go back and get Andy the medical attention he needs, then all of this will have been worth it. Don't you think?"

Kellie and Adela both nodded. They wanted Andy to be well. No arguments there.

After breakfast, Adela cleared the dishes, a knock sounding on the door moments later. She stilled as Leanne opened it to usher Marcus, Stanton, and Christopher, who held Andy in his arms, inside.

The child's complexion was bright, but his head lay heavy on his father's shoulder.

Marcus met Adela's gaze, his face resolute, all emotion masked. He strode to her side, but he remained silent, holding her gaze. Pain threatened, her throat constricting as tears welled, but she held fast to God's prompting she must return to her time. Whatever God's plan was, she would be steadfast.

Leanne cleared the table, leaving only the items they had arrived with on its surface. She motioned for Adela to sit, then Kellie. She took Andy into her arms and sat next to them.

"Okay. I suppose we simply wait," Leanne said, wrapping an arm around the boy.

Adela saw Kellie look at Stanton who stood a few feet from the table with Christopher and Marcus by his side. She refused to look at Marcus. She could not live in what *may* be, but what *should* be. She belonged in her time and he in his.

It was as simple as that—except she somehow had to convince her heart of it.

No one seemed to breath, all holding a collective breath waiting for the inevitable, the impossible to happen.

The minutes ticked by. Time hung in the air like the calm before a storm.

Yet, nothing happened. They waited. More than an hour passed.

Christopher stepped forward. "Something is amiss."

He, Marcus, and Stanton joined them at the table, and soon they were all locked in discussion as to what was wrong and what they should do.

Leanne gave Andy something to eat and put him to bed. She and Christopher remained at the table, ate, and spoke of him. Stanton and Kellie walked back to the manor while Adela feigned a headache and went to her room, leaving Marcus to go and make the funeral arrangements.

Adela couldn't rest. A walk was what she needed.

She would go to Mrs. Henshaw and say her farewell to the kindly cook, yet she couldn't tell her it was goodbye. She took the footpath to the manor, so she wouldn't run into Marcus coming back from the village.

Just as she was about to traverse the path by the hedgerow to the kitchen garden, she heard a man's shout from the manor entrance. *"Où est ma femme?"*

Adela retraced her steps and paused at the corner of the manor to watch a stout man with curly blonde hair pound on the door. Her boot crunched on the gravel drive, bringing his head around sharply. He glared at her, then his face softened, and he bowed. "Mistress, how may I obtain an audience with Lord DeGrey?"

"Has no one answered?"

"No, mistress." He stepped toward her and halted several feet away.

The manor door jerked open with a groan, and the footman

stepped out. When he saw Adela, he offered a look of apology. "Mistress, sir, I beg pardon." He bowed and gestured toward the door. "Please follow me, and I shall announce ye to Lord DeGrey."

The stranger smiled and bowed to Adela. "Good morrow, mistress."

She returned the smile and made her way to the kitchen. What was he seeking? She did not know French. By the time she reached the kitchen, Mrs. Henshaw scurried to prepare a tray for Lord DeGrey and his visitor. The cook twittered, complaining about the Franchies invading their domain.

Adela hid her amusement. The woman was a dear, and her kindly presence would be missed. Adela sat at the table and waited for the hubbub to subside. When a maid disappeared with the heavily laden tray, the cook slid into a chair and eased a fresh cup of hot tea and a slice of cake toward Adela.

Adela lifted a bite to her lips. "This cake has to be your best ever." She closed her eyes in rapture. When she opened them, Mrs. Henshaw stared at her curiously. "Yes, ma'am?"

Hesitantly, she said, "There be somethin' most strange goin' on 'round here."

Adela sipped her tea. "Really?"

"Aye. And I usually know most everthin'." She narrowed her eyes. "Master Marcus telt Mrs. Brimberry the three of ye are not to be doin' your usual chores for a bit." Her wrinkled lips puckered against the cup, sipping the steaming brew. "Whilst I understand ye and Kellie takin' care of the lady afore she died, I am not understandin' why Leanne is takin' care of Andrew."

Adela took another bite of cake and nodded.

"The boy always took care of hisself mostly. Though I know Stanton, Timothy, and Martin do look after him for the most."

Shouts echoed through the manor. Heavy booted footsteps rang out, and then Marcus's voice matched volume with the stranger.

Adela rushed from the kitchen to the entry where Marcus trailed the visitor heading for the staircase leading to the upper floors.

The man's voice was sharp. "I shall find my wife, Lord DeGrey. The tavern keeper told me ye did collect her from his *établissement*."

Marcus stiffened.

The man turned to face him, expression stern, demanding, then he saw Adela, and his eyes calmed. "Mistress. Mayhap ye can assist me. I was told my wife, Gillian Yvette LeFleur, was brought here more than a fortnight past." His gaze swung back to Marcus and held. "The tavern keeper said as much. It was then I traced her to the DeGrey townhouse. With *pièce de monnaie—*" He rubbed his thumb and forefinger together. "—I found her to be brought here, *malade*."

Adela looked to Marcus and back to the man. "I am sorry, sir. I do not speak French."

Marcus answered with a scowl, his countenance darker than the storm brewing outside, his hands fisted. "He says he bribed someone at my townhouse to tell him she had been brought here, ailing."

Mr. LeFleur nodded. "So, ye are in agreement she is here?"

The indecision Adela read in Marcus's face tightened her

insides with fear. She sensed her intervention could avoid a nasty exchange.

"Sir, I'm sorry to tell you, but she has died." How was she to explain? "She was in a burning building and suffered from breathing in smoke. It hurt her lungs beyond repair." Adela blew out a breath. "Lord DeGrey brought her here to help her, but it was too late."

Mr. LeFleur's gaze shifted from Adela to Marcus and back. "Ah. This *fumée*, along with the laudanum, this is what killed her?"

Adela stilled, her palms clammy. *He knew.*

"*Oui*, mistress. I fully am aware of my wife's *dépendance*. We quarreled over it incessantly." He looked at Marcus again.

Marcus unclenched his hands. "Sir. Let us return to the parlor where we may speak further."

Adela stepped back. When Marcus passed, his hand deliberately brushed her arm.

She returned to an empty kitchen, all vestiges of the last tea she would have with her friend gone, the kitchen once more spotless. She trudged back to the cottage to see all in attendance except Marcus. Was that to be their goodbye?

Chapter Twenty-Seven

Kellie's steps lagged as Stanton escorted her to the kitchen for food to take back to the cottage. Silence swelled between them.

His eyes pierced her with a wistful stare. "Come by the stables when ye have your *takeaway*." The pensive look faded into a humorous glint.

She laughed and told him she wouldn't be long. When she pushed the kitchen door open, Mrs. Henshaw looked up from her chore at the worktable.

"Kellie, how are ye? Are ye seekin' nourishment?"

"Yes, ma'am. Adela and I are quite famished after the many days of nursing Lady DeGrey. Adela has a terrible headache, and I believe your cooking will take care of her ailments."

"Ye do flatter me." The cook grinned. "Come along and take what ye will."

The old woman eased herself to a stool at the worktable and watched Kellie put food into a large basket. Her eyebrows rose at the quantity. "Tha three of ye must be near on starvin'."

Kellie sent her an apologetic look. "We are. It's also for Andy."

"Me ole bones are a hurtin' with the storm comin'. Always can rely on that for sure." She rubbed her hands together as if to warm them.

Kellie stopped at the edge of the table. *Storm?*

The final piece of the puzzle! The lightning before they were transported to the past. She finished shoving food into the basket, gave the cook a quick kiss on the cheek, and rushed to the door where she paused. "You're a genius, Mrs. Henshaw. I shall miss you terribly."

The woman tilted her head, but before she could voice her question, Kellie left, rushing to the stables, where she caught Stanton pitching hay into one of the stalls.

"Stanton! It's the storm that's coming. We have to be in the cottage when the storm arrives. Will you find Marcus and Christopher and meet me there?"

His face clouded with uncertainty. "Aye?" He positioned the pitchfork against the wall and left without a backward glance.

The basket bumped against Kellie's leg as she ran down the path to the cottage. She mumbled to herself in agitation until she reached the door, shoved it open with a crash, and met Leanne's startled gaze.

"Shhh! Andy is sleeping upstairs. I think the poor child is worsening." Papers fluttered to the table. "I've been working."

"I found the answer. The solution to our problem." Kellie dropped the basket on top of their research material and sank into the seat next to Leanne.

"A storm is coming soon." She slammed her hand down with a thwack. "Remember the lightning, Leanne. Maybe it has to come from this storm."

Leanne stared, brows pinched together in concentration. "Yes! You're right." She stood and paced the room.

The door creaked open, and Adela and Marcus arrived, wearing vacant expressions. Stanton and Christopher entered on their heels.

"Stanton told us what you remembered." Adela stared at Kellie. "You may be right."

The six adults stood watching one another in silence. A hush enveloped the cottage. The low rumble of thunder sounded in the distance. An expanse of cold air slipped through the door, sending shivers through Kellie.

"Now, we wait." Kellie pointed to the basket. "Let's eat. I'm starved." Her trembling hands moved to pick it up, but a strong, tan hand grasped the handle, overlapping hers. She looked into the flinty grey eyes boring into her—wild like the approaching storm.

"'Tis heavy." He eased it away from her and held it at his side. "Clear the table." The words were low, hoarse with emotion. "The storm is far away, comin' slow. There is time enough to eat."

Kellie and Leanne cleared the table, and Stanton returned the basket to it. They ate in silence.

A creak on the stairs brought all to face Andy on the bottom step, rubbing sleep from his eyes. Leanne was first to reach him. "Hello, sleepy head." She knelt before him and ruffled his shaggy hair. His blue eyes flitted to each adult.

Kellie's heart broke at his frailness. She went to him and took his pulse. It wasn't bad, but he needed medical attention soon.

"Come, Andy. I bet you're hungry."

He nodded, hair swishing. Leanne took him by the hand and pulled him onto her lap. He ate bread and watched his father.

Thunder cracked closer, and Adela jumped. Kellie placed a hand on her shoulder. She appeared more nervous than any of them. These past weeks had been harder on Adela than anyone. She'd had to contend with Marcus *and* Gil.

Kellie prayed that after they went home her friend would find peace.

രു

Adela took her food and drink to sit on the settle by the fire. Over the past weeks, with her appetite almost nonexistent, she'd lost weight. She had holed up in the cottage and kept her distance from Marcus.

He had to get on with his life. Be a good father to Nan and possibly marry a kind-hearted woman to be her stepmother. Unshed tears lingered as the little girl's image formed in her mind. The pretty blonde curls like . . . Something tightened within her. So, like Mr. LeFleur. Could he be her actual father?

The man had bellowed about Gillian being his wife, and Marcus had been gone for a time in Barbados. She didn't want to question Marcus. She was sure he now had his own doubts of Nan's parentage. But what was the point? They were minutes away from leaving this time, and she'd never see he or Nan again.

The settle shifted slightly. Adela closed her eyes against the agony of their situation.

"Shall we part without a word?" Marcus's whisper at her ear was laced with pain.

"Marcus, I don't wish to hurt you."

"Please stay." His voice quivered.

"How can I turn away from a child in need? If I do not go back, how can he? It has to be . . ." She gasped, the truth washing over her.

"What?" He rested a hand on her shoulder, panic on his face. "Are ye unwell?"

Adela stood. "Come." She walked to the table, found the antique passport, and opened it with care. She sensed all eyes on her.

Leanne shifted Andy in her arms. "What is it?"

Adela placed the passport on the table and pointed to the picture. "What do you see?"

They all leaned in, and Adela said, looking at Leanne and then Christopher, "It's a man, a woman, and a small boy."

"Yes." Leanne agreed and looked at Christopher.

His mouth tightened, and enlightenment crossed his face. He removed all but the chair Leanne occupied with his son and one more which he moved next to them. He sat, took Leanne's hand, and placed the other on Andy's head.

Adela took Kellie's hand and pulled her away from the

table to stand by Marcus and Stanton. God was telling her—*them*—what He had intended.

She smiled through her tears. "Leanne, I will leave my journal behind the fireplace for you to find when you reach *your* time."

Leanne nodded with a sob and clung to Christopher and Andy.

Thunder rolled, and a deafening crash shook the cottage as a flash of lightning threw a blueish glow into the room. It suspended like a mist. Darkness stole the light, and silence cloaked everything.

Total and complete peace enveloped them.

When light returned, the sound of rain on the roof met her ears, and a sweet clean essence penetrated the air around them. Leanne, Christopher, and Andy were gone.

Adela felt the warmth of Marcus's hand in hers, and he pulled her close to his side. When she turned, Stanton and Kellie were locked in a tender embrace. Adela huddled in Marcus's arms. They'd crossed the boundaries of the universe because God had taken them to their own place in time.

Epilogue

Twenty years later . . .
Boston, Massachusetts

The audience rose and clapped as the tall man with hair the color of honey, stepped onto the stage, his smile widening.

"Isn't he handsome?" Leanne whispered as she and Christopher took their seats.

"Yes, my dear. Takes after his father." The bright smile, so like the young man on the stage, never ceased to warm her even after two decades.

Christopher kissed her left hand, the diamond wedding band glinting in the auditorium's bright lights. She smiled, and they turned back to the stage.

"Ladies and gentlemen, Dr. Andrew DeGrey."

More applause roared through the massive space as the night's esteemed surgeon bowed.

Dr. DeGrey accepted his plaque from the association president and went to the microphone. "It is an honor to be here to accept this award. One I cannot help but feel I do not deserve. God graced me with the passion and ability to care for children, particularly those who share the same heart defect that almost claimed my life as a child. He, in his infinite grace, brought me the care I needed through a gifted surgeon and urged me to, in turn, extend it to others. It is not I but God alone who gets the glory for any accomplishment."

Andy smiled at his parents on the front row. "I am unable to truly fathom how He brought me to this point. Though I know His timing is perfect, even if out of our realm of understanding."

Leanne squeezed Christopher's hand, her thoughts trailing back through the years to that fateful day in the cottage when she had returned without Adela and Kellie. A day never went by without her thinking of them, of how their stories had played out through Adela's words in the journal.

Each night, Leanne read a few pages from the time-worn leather book and imagined Adela telling her about the day's events as if in conversation. She had rejoiced to learn both Adela and Marcus, and Kellie and Stanton, had long and happy marriages. Tears flowed freely as she leaned against Christopher and viewed their portraits in the museum alongside a grown-up Nan and the seven children born to Kellie and Stanton. The walls were lined with their legacies.

Leanne closed her eyes and pictured her friends at the manor as they had been hundreds of years before. Sometimes, she could almost smell the baking bread in Mrs. Henshaw's kitchen, feel the cool water of the river beside the cottage, or hear the sound of horses and carts along the village road. Their loss was keenly felt, though it was one she shared with both Christopher and Andy. She pictured Adela and Kellie surrounded by love and happiness throughout the years as she had been too. And she could hear Adela's voice reading the final words in her journal.

For God alone knows the number of our days, the hairs upon our heads, and where each of us has a place in time.

THE END

Acknowledgments

There is not enough room to thank all who have supported my writing journey, but without the prompting and guidance of God, I could not write.

The support of writing partners, Morgan Tarpley Smith and Tammy Kirby, is invaluable. Thanks to my beta readers—Jennifer, Margaret, Marguerite, Nancy, Sherlyn, Tammy, and Morgan. To my husband, Max, and my son, Daniel.

My heartfelt thanks to Christine Bianco of Ingleby Manor in North Yorkshire, England. Christine kindly allowed me to use photographs of her lovely manor for the front and back covers. My stay there was so memorable. My friend, Kellie Fox, discovered this extraordinary historic manor when she, along with Tammy Kirby and I, made a trip there in 2017.

Staying in this sixteenth-century home was a memory I'll never forget and hope to return to one day.

The beautiful English countryside surrounding the manor was idyllic.

If you ever consider a trip to the U.K., a stay there is a must. Christine was an amazing hostess. The Victoria sponge cake she left in our kitchen was delish! (inglebymanor.co.uk)

My cover designer, Victoria Davies, did an amazing job as usual (vcbookcovers.com). And thank you, Monica Bruenjes, for my wonderful map (artistmonica.com).

God bless,
Carole

Author's Note

I have long been taken with British history, since most of my ancestors came from the U.K. For some unknown reason, the seventeenth century holds my attention more than most. After tremendous research, the story of three women traveling more than three hundred years into the past, came to fruition as a time travel, historical story with God's purposes at the center.

Time travel is a total fantasy distraction for fans of the genre, me included, but I do believe God can do all things. He can bend time and knows all things before they happen. So why not have a little fun with the story? As long as God is at its core and teaches us to trust Him, I see no wrong in it.

Thanks to Barbara Henderson at The History Quill for her historical expertise in seventeenth century England.

My list of research sources is so long I am unable to include all of them. If you are interested in history, the interactive London map is a lot of fun. Give it a whirl.

Culpeper's Complete Herbal: Illustrated and Annotated Edition by Nicholas Culpeper and Steven Foster

Time Traveller's Guide to Restoration Britain (1660-1700) by Ian Mortimer

Voices from the World of Samuel Pepys by Jonathan Bastable

The Diary of Samuel Pepys - pepysdiary.com

Interactive 1633 London map - mapoflondon.uvic.ca/agas.htm

Enjoy *A Place in Time*?

Here's a preview of another novel
by Carole Lehr Johnson

Permelia Cottage

Chapter One

Louisiana, U.S.A.
March 2016

One decision can change everything. That was Susannah Wilkinson's thought as the cool breeze touched her face. The sweet fragrance of gardenias lingered on the wind as she spoke with the young mother of a fifteen-year-old girl. The girl's gaze shifted downward, forehead wrinkling. Her mother stood her ground, a forefinger pointed toward the clinic as she emphasized why her daughter needed an abortion.

"You don't have to make a decision right now," Susannah pleaded, staring into the mother's eyes. "Please take time to read over this literature before you decide." Her gaze returned to the teenager then to her mother. "Once you do this, there's no turning back. It's life-changing."

The mother shook her head, leaning away from Susannah. Her hazel eyes reflected uncertainty. "I don't . . . I . . . *we* think this is the time to do it—while she isn't very far along. You see what I mean?"

Susannah sent up a silent prayer for wisdom. The woman stared at her, head tilted.

"I realize . . . but a child is a child no matter how far along your daughter is." One lone tear fought for release, and she blinked to keep it at bay.

The woman raised her pale eyes to meet Susannah's. "May I ask you a question?"

Susannah cleared her throat. "Certainly."

The growing crowd near them pulled her attention for a moment. She refocused on the question.

"Why are you so concerned about abortion?"

A sharp pain shot through Susannah. She drew in a quick breath as she clenched her purse strap. "Because I had to make this decision once."

The mother's eyes widened, her lips parted in surprise as she brought a hand to her chest. She smoothed her daughter's dark hair. A trembling smile softened her lips. "Well, perhaps we should talk a little more."

Susannah moved closer and whispered, "May I pray with you?" The woman nodded. Susannah motioned to a bench several yards away, partially hidden behind a large oak tree.

Loud noise from the robust crowd reached them, but Susannah ignored it. Protesters shouted and blocked people from entering the clinic. They prayed, had a brief discussion and said their goodbyes.

Susannah walked the two blocks to her car to gather more material. She fumbled with her keys and almost dropped them on the pavement. When she clicked the lock, she swung the door open and slouched into the driver's seat. With a ragged breath, her hands trembled as she ran them through her hair and then massaged her temples as sirens wailed in the distance.

The trauma of seeing someone come close to an abortion twisted her insides and tugged at her heart. Eyes closing, she collected her thoughts before she left the security of her vehicle. She walked back to the clinic as police cars arrived, lights flashing. Several people lingered on the sidewalk, and a white-haired woman stood to the side with her hands pressed to her face while tears darkened her purple blouse. A rock hurled through the air and struck a streetlight overhead raining shattered glass over the woman.

Susannah thrust past a few bystanders and reached out as the woman stumbled. Thick white smoke engulfed the surrounding area. She grabbed her arm and led her from the noxious cloud.

Once they escaped, Susannah coughed. "Are you okay, ma'am?" Susannah held her arm, and she winced at her touch. People pushed past them and scattered in all directions. She led her to a nearby bench and gently brushed small pieces of glass from her hair.

The woman gasped for air and clung to Susannah for support.

"May I see your arm?" The woman nodded. Susannah

pushed up her sleeve and noted a large red spot, the precursor to a bruise. "I think you'll be sore for a few days, but you should be fine." She reassured her with a nod.

"Thank you, dearie." Her aged eyes squeezed shut. "Those people who were arrested tried to keep girls from going into the clinic. Can you imagine? It was loud, and the voices so angry. You'd think folks would realize it's easier to catch more flies with honey than vinegar?"

Had the circumstances been less dire, Susannah would've laughed at the analogy.

"Yes, ma'am, you're right. I guess when we're passionate about something we get carried away."

"Honey, I suppose that's true." She shook her head, tears gleaming on her wrinkled cheeks.

CB&ED

Yes, one decision can change everything.

Susannah Wilkinson rushed from the Timlee Clinic mêlée to the restaurant, certain she'd find Diann already there. Conversations hummed as she settled against the back of her chair and contemplated the events of the day.

As always, when stressful things happened, Susannah thought of her son—the one person she loved more than life itself.

Their estrangement tore at her heart. She felt her lips curve as she remembered the early years when he would run to her with open arms and happy laughter. She swiped a tear from her cheek as their last painful meeting absorbed the good memories.

The gift was cradled in her arms as she entered his room. "Ryan, I have a going away present for you." She held out the wrapped package tied with a blue ribbon. He snatched it from her and mumbled 'thanks,' before he tossed it into his suitcase.

She avoided his eyes. "Aren't you going to open it?"

Ryan released an impatient sigh, grabbed the package, and yanked the ribbon free. Slender fingers shook as he ripped the paper, releasing an object to slide across the tile floor, making no move to retrieve it. He thumbed through the leather-bound journal that bore his name in gold letters then he returned it to his bag.

Susannah stooped to rescue the discarded pocket cross. Creases formed in her palm as she gripped it with force. She held out her hand, palm up. Her voice broke. "Keep this is in your pocket and every time you see it, remember I'm praying for you."

Silence met her words. His stony countenance grieved her heart. Time lingered as Susannah bit her tongue to stop the tears.

His blue eyes sparked. "I don't need your religion!" He pivoted, shoulders rigid, and slung clothes onto the bed.

His hurtful words echoed in her mind. The coppery tang of blood was a reminder to release her injured tongue. She left the room on wooden legs, the cross clutched in her fist.

The door slammed, rattling the pictures against the wall. One fell with a crash. When the silver-framed family portrait shattered, she picked it up with gentle movements, staring at the happy little boy that sat on her lap.

Memories of that special day released the dam, and tears of regret flowed.

CR80

"Sue?" The quiet voice interrupted her thoughts.

Susannah's gaze shifted from the tablecloth to her best friend's face, her forehead creased.

Diann slid into the empty seat and touched Susannah's shoulder. "Are you okay?"

"Sorry, I'm fine. Just lost in thought." She forced the downturned corners of her mouth up.

Diann glanced at her friend's fisted hand. "What did you want to talk about?"

Susannah shrugged and twirled the stem of her water glass as she watched the lemon float in circles.

"Well, I have news. But let me tell you what happened at the clinic a while ago." She gave Diann a lengthy, informative narration of her encounter with the woman and her daughter, the crowd, and the elderly lady hit with the rock. She toyed with her glass, wiped the moisture from her palms onto her napkin, and repeated the process several times.

Diann drew in a deep breath and let it out in a huff. "What's wrong with you?"

Susannah tilted her chin. "Excuse me?"

"You've been rambling."

Susannah slumped in defeat. "There is something I want to tell you—something you may not like."

"So, spit it out. We've been friends far too long to play games."

402

She leaned forward. "You're right. I asked to meet for lunch so I could tell you my news." She reached for her water glass to repeat the ritual.

"If you start that routine again, I'll take your water away from you." Diann's guttural voice didn't match the grin she wore.

"Okay, okay." Susannah pushed her shoulders back and stared into Diann's curious eyes. "You've always encouraged me to move on, follow my dreams. Now, I am." Lifting the glass to her lips, she took a long sip, and blurted out, "I'm moving to England."

Diann's face paled. "What? I didn't mean *move*, Sue. Move on. Let the past go. Have you lost your mind?"

"This dream has been with me for so long. I believe it's the right thing to do. I've always wanted to live in an English cottage. Why not now?"

"What about your son? He'll be having children in a few years . . . perhaps. You'll want to be near your grandchildren, won't you? I wouldn't be able to handle not seeing my grandchildren for months on end." Diann's eyes glistened as she rummaged in her purse. Susannah retrieved a tissue from her own bag. Her hand shook as she accepted it. "Are you sure you're not using this to run away from your estrangement with Ryan?"

Susannah averted her gaze and scanned the Victorian Tea Room, their favorite place to meet. Wood-trimmed chairs upholstered in eggplant chintz, tables with linen cloths, brass candlesticks, and fresh flowers in crystal vases. A Victorian sofa in rich brocade sat by a faux fireplace in a corner. Here, time froze. They loved this room because of its British flavor.

Diann had to understand her dream.

"I suppose there may be truth in what you said about Ryan." She pressed her lips together, her gaze scanned the creamy yellow walls, windows adorned with lace curtains bordered in heavy brocade panels. "But, with the money Aaron left me, I'll be able to fly home anytime I choose. Besides, Ryan has his own life and doesn't need me around. He's self-sufficient with a successful career."

Diann crossed her arms. "Are you listening to yourself?" Tepid sarcasm laced her voice. She sniffled and reached for the tissue. "This is a big deal. You'll be over four thousand miles away."

"I realize that, but I have to do this. It's my dream. When Aaron abandoned us, I thought I'd never hear from him again. To think he had a life insurance policy—and left it to me. The guilt must have eaten at him." His face appeared in her mind's eye, the face she first fell in love with, not the face of the man who screamed at her to do something her convictions could never allow.

"Well, it should have. I don't understand what got into him." She exhaled with a huff. "So, what exact plans have you made? I mean, are you going right away?"

"That's part two of why I asked you to lunch today. I want to go soon and spend about a month to explore, research real estate, and sightsee. I'll do preliminary research online first, as a starting point, but I . . ."

The server appeared with their order and brought their conversation to a halt.

Between bites Diann stated matter-of-factly, "You don't

need my help to plan the details. You're the travel writer, and I've never been to Britain."

"This is the thing . . ." Susannah grasped the napkin on her lap. "I need you to go with me." Leaning back in her chair, she bit the inside of her cheek.

Diann's fork suspended inches from her lips. "I . . . I'm not sure what to say. This is a surprise."

"I hoped you'd say yes."

"Wayne may not agree," she said, though Susannah saw a glimmer of interest in her eyes. "I've never been away from him for that long. What about my kids and grandkids? An entire month without seeing them?" She rubbed the back of her neck with vigor.

"Stop right there, don't try to convince yourself it's a bad idea. You and I both know you'd love to go. I'm not asking you to leave tomorrow. We'll plan this out." She met Diann's anxious gaze and waited.

Diann folded and refolded her napkin. "Deep down I'm thrilled at an adventure like this, but . . ."

"Don't decide now. Go home and discuss it with Wayne. Tell me soon, so I can make other arrangements if you can't go."

She tapped her fingertips at the base of her throat. "You would take someone else?"

"Perhaps." Susannah smoothed the wrinkles out of the tablecloth.

Diann lifted her chin and pushed her shoulders back. "If you're taking someone, it's most certainly going to be me. I'll convince Wayne."

Susannah grinned and pulled a small package out of her bag and slid it across the table.

Diann's head tilted to one side, eyes narrowing. "What's this?"

"A thank you gift."

Diann raised an eyebrow. "You knew I'd say yes?"

"That flash of determination in your eyes just confirmed how well I know you."

When ripped away, the rose floral paper revealed a decorated box. Diann gently removed the lid to disclose a long gold chain with an ornate carved oval pendant with *Live like you mean it* engraved in the center.

CR8O

England
May 2016

Susannah believed springtime in England was one of the most peaceful places on earth.

The fresh, varied shades of green colored the English landscape as the small tour bus wound its way through the countryside. Each turn revealed rounded hills dotted with sheep, cows, horses, or fields laden with crops. The idyllic landscape captivated her. She possessed a sense of belonging.

Finances had prohibited extensive travel in the past, but her recent windfall had changed that. Was she mad? She was considering a move to rural England. Was this really a fact-finding mission, or maybe just to get it out of her system? She had prayed. All seemed to fall into place. It could be a wasted trip with nothing priced within her means. At least she'd have a vacation with her dearest friend if it didn't work out the way she envisioned.

The bus tires crunched on gravel as they stopped in the car park of a quaint little village called Neville. Susannah and Diann followed the group into a local pub. Marcy, their guide, stepped between them and linked arms. "Come on, dears, you sit with me."

"Thank you, Marcy. That's kind of you." Susannah glanced over her head at Diann's scowl that translated into her displeasure that her personal space was about to be invaded. She was aware of all of Diann's idiosyncrasies—and vice versa.

Marcy guided them to a corner table with the view of a courtyard edged in ornamental grass around the perimeter. Flower beds teemed with the first stages of vibrant, colorful blooms. A low stone wall enclosed the garden and added the perfect touch.

Susannah's steady gaze wandered over the profusion of color. Purple phlox encircled a granite birdbath. A perpetual stream of water spilled from a lion's head fountain into a stone dish. She could get used to this.

Marcy's perky voice broke through the fog. "Susannah, are you all right, dear?"

Diann responded. "Don't mind her. She tends to wool-gather when she's in her favorite place in the world."

Susannah jumped in. "Sorry. I was admiring the garden." She poked Diann in the ribs with her elbow. "And she's right. I daydream a bit."

"Well, the garden is lovely. Neville is my favorite stop on the tour." Marcy's smile broadened. "It's a marvelous place."

Susannah empathized with the admiration in Marcy's eyes. Neville's enchantment called to her almost spiritually.

After they all enjoyed a variety of scones, sandwiches, and two pots of tea, Susannah walked outside with the group and breathed in the fresh air as they followed the stone path to the car park. Susannah closed her eyes and inhaled the sharp smell of mown grass.

She took out her camera. "You two go on ahead. I want to take a few more pictures of the pub."

A split path led to the side of the brownstone building. She admired the thatched roof and leaded windows and took a few pictures. Beside the courtyard garden, an elderly gentleman leaned against the gate watching her. On impulse, she strolled over. "Good afternoon. It's a beautiful day, isn't it?"

He removed the pipe from his mouth, beamed and replied in a strong British accent, "That it is . . . that it is. How're you today?" He wasn't a tall man, lean and sturdily built.

"Fine, thank you." She scanned the garden's color. "It's so delightful."

"It's been my favorite spot in Neville since I was a lad."

"So, you've lived here a while?" Susannah admired his thick gray waves.

"Yes, ma'am. All my life. This pub—" He used his pipe to point at the building. "—was built many years before I was born, and I'm ninety-seven next week."

"You don't look it." Susannah took in his straight back.

"Thank you. Don't act it either." His blue eyes twinkled with mischief. "At least everyone around here says. I still tend my gardn' and the one here at the pub."

"You do a wonderful job. I admired it throughout our afternoon tea. Would it be all right if I took a few pictures inside the garden?"

"That'd be no problem at all." He held the gate open to allow her to step across the stone threshold.

"By the by, the name's Hodge." He tipped his hat.

"Nice to meet you. I'm Susannah." She snapped a close-up of the fountain and stood back to appreciate it.

"Caught your fancy?" He had stepped from the gate to stand beside her. "It's original."

"How old is this place?"

He straightened. "My family built it in 1702."

Susannah rose from photographing a cluster of white phlox, surprised. "It's yours?"

"Yes, tried to keep it as it was, except for modern plumbin'. The entire lot looks as it did over 300 years ago."

It touched Susannah to imagine the love and devotion of one family to keep a historic place like this for so long. She said as much.

Hodge's grey eyes sparkled with pride. "Most don't appreciate it, but I can tell you regard commitment. I may be a sentimental fool, but it seems your interest is more than a tour stop."

"That's perceptive of you. I love history especially Britain's. My family came from here, and they passed little of the information down. I have an aunt who traced our genealogy, and I value it, but I want to learn about my ancestors on a more personal level—by visiting where they lived." She held his gaze. "And how you must be proud of the devotion of your family to this place. You're a part of it, and I long to be a part of where my ancestors lived."

"I understand that." Hodge grew silent for a few moments. With a croak in his voice, he continued, "Susannah, you're a special lady. I'd love to share our history with you, but you must be gettin' on that bus." He pointed with his pipe. "May I have your address? I'll be glad to send you every spot of information on my place. And Neville."

On impulse, Susannah gave him a gentle hug. "Hodge, thank you . . . I mean that with sincerity. You're so kind." She pulled a business card from her purse and gave it to him. He glanced at it, and with gnarled fingers tucked it into the pocket of his tweed vest.

"You best be gettin' on that bus before it leaves."

Susannah started toward the bus and turned back. "Hodge, say cheese."

He gave her a broad grin and waved as she snapped the picture.

೫ഉ

A few days later, after the tour wound through other villages with their castles, cottages, pubs, and gardens, Susannah and Diann returned to Neville. They settled into the Horden Inn. Susannah perched on the edge of her bed and scanned a brochure about the village.

"It says Neville also has tea shops, two churches, and a castle."

"Oh, I can hear your brain-wheels turning." Diann placed her shirts in a dresser drawer. "The obsession must be fed." She raised her eyebrows in mock surprise.

Susannah tossed a pillow at her, then rummaged through her bag for the realtor listings. "I like this village. There were a couple of cottages I found here in my research. This place spoke far more than any of the others. And it is one of the villages where some of my ancestors lived."

"Hey, you may be related to Hodge." Diann winked.

"Could be. I need to ask him more about his family."

Diann sighed and paused her unpacking. "Why don't we go for a walk? It doesn't get dark till late, and I'm restless. We may see some cottages from your list."

"You're always restless—got more energy than your four-year-old grandson."

"Ha . . . I wish. Grab your purse, and let's take it outside, sister!"

The cool early evening air was invigorating. Susannah pulled her light jacket closed and inhaled a familiar scent that she couldn't place. "I'm not sure what that aroma is, but I like it."

"That's another thing—your nose is too sensitive. What's that all about?" Diann gave her friend a tight-lipped grin.

"Sense of smell can trigger memories powerfully. Maybe it's an ancestral pull to this place."

"I never thought of it that way, but I suppose it's true. If I smell biscuits baking, I always think of my grandmother. She made the most wonderful biscuits." Diann tilted her head back and closed her eyes. "I can almost see and smell them right now. Browned to perfection, fluffy circles of joy."

Susannah's delighted laugh brought Diann back from her past.

"Such a nice memory." She chuckled as they walked on in companionable silence.

As they strolled along the main street, Susannah studied the brochure. That internal tug toward Neville wrenched at her again. The market cross remained at the square's center as it had since the 13th century. At the end of the street, St. Gregory's Church beckoned, parts of it dating back to 1085. A defensive fortified tower, built in 1330, rose above the lower stone structure. Late afternoon sun glinted off the grey edifice that cast it in an amber-hue. It stood proud as it had once protected the village from marauding Scots, the eight ancient bells waited to warn citizens. Susannah could very nearly hear the past sounds of this history-filled village.

They stopped in front of the enclosed churchyard, its gravestones tilted sorrowfully, etchings worn away by time and weather.

"I don't want to walk in there right before dark," Diann's voice wavered.

"What? Are you serious? You're not afraid, are you?" Susannah teased.

"Of course not. I'm not fond of cemeteries at any time of day . . . or night." Diann drew a deep breath. "It's so sad to see all those lives gone, not knowing where they ended up." She shoved her hands deep into her pockets and stepped away from the cemetery.

Susannah drew her gaze from her friend, entranced by the antiquity of the stones. "I wonder if any of my ancestors are buried here? It's too bad that most of the engravings have worn off on the oldest stones." Her voice was solemn. She traced the top of the churchyard's closed gate with an outstretched finger. The yellow facade of the museum across the street darkened in evening shadow. "Hate that the museum is closed."

"Yes, sad." Diann gave her a gentle shove.

Susannah realized her friend's sense of morbidity. She picked up her pace, leaving Diann to follow.

"Hey, where are you off to? I thought we would explore." She added, "Except the cemetery, of course."

"We are." She held up a map. Susannah pointed to the street they were on. "If we go this way and turn right by the pharmacy, and down a short way and take another right, there's a cottage for sale. I couldn't tell much from the photos. But you never know . . ." Her voice trailed off as she studied the map.

Diann reached for the map, and Susannah released it. They stopped at the corner and spotted The Wynd posted on the building across the street. "We're on the right track," Diann gave a wave. "We turn here."

Susannah simpered. "Aye, aye, Captain."

After a short walk, they reached a paved one-lane road. A house's exterior wall curved to follow the turn. It was a medley of older grey stones at the base and newer red bricks stacked to the roof. A few feet further, a white gate led to an alley of sorts. The sign on the gate read— Beware of the Ferrets. Diann and Susannah glanced at one another and burst out laughing.

A sandstone wall topped with moss lined the left side of the road, and on the other side were trees. Beyond a deep curve, the cottage stood to their left. A white-washed gate hung loosely on its hinges.

"Hmm . . . it's seen better days." Diann stood with fists on her hips, lips pursed.

Susannah squeezed between the gate and wall and slipped on a moss-covered stone. She grasped Diann's shoulder for support.

"I'm not sure this is what you were looking for, Sue. It's dilapidated."

They gaped at the shabby thatched cottage. The panes stared, dark and lifeless. Plaster crumbled amidst dark green ivy that clawed its way to the roof. What was left of the garden held more weeds than flowers. A few struggling blooms peeked out like small bright insects climbing barren stalks.

Diann hung back for a moment and moved to the front window and peered through the dirt-encrusted glass. "The inside doesn't appear bad, but it could use a coat of paint. I wonder if the structure is solid."

"It doesn't matter." Susannah stood rooted to the spot and absorbed the derelict sight.

"Yes, I suppose you're right. It's too dilapidated to consider."

"I mean, it doesn't matter." Susannah pulled the realtor listing from her pocket, glanced at the cottage, and envisioned it as it could be. The tug inside her tightened, and joy swelled. "This is where I belong."

About the Author

Carole Lehr Johnson is a veteran travel consultant of more than 30 years and has served as head of genealogy at her local library.

Her love of tea and scones, castles and cottages, and all things British has led her to immerse her writing in the United Kingdom whether in the genre of historical or contemporary fiction.

Carole is the author of two inspirational novels set in England, *Permelia Cottage* and *A Place in Time*, and the novella collection, *Their Scottish Destiny*. She is a member of the American Christian Fiction Writers (ACFW) as well as the president of her local chapter. She and her husband live in Louisiana with their goofy cats.

For more information, visit
www.carolelehrjohnson.com

Sign up for Carole's newsletter on her website for updates on her next release, U.K. travel features, recipes, book recommendations, and more.

415

Made in the USA
Las Vegas, NV
13 July 2022